Fate and Fury

Book 6, The Grey Wolves Series

By Quinn Loftis

© 2013 Quinn Loftis Books LLC

All rights reserved. No part of this publication may be reproduced, distributed, or transmitted in any form or by any means, including photocopying, recording, or other electronic or mechanical methods, without the prior written permission of the publisher

This ebook is licensed for your personal enjoyment only. This ebook may not be re-sold or given away to other people. If you would like to share this book with another person, please purchase an additional copy for each recipient. If you're reading this book and did not purchase it, or it was not purchased for your use only, then please return it, and purchase your own copy. Thank you for respecting the hard work of this author.

Dedication

For Bo, my best friend and husband. I would not be able to do what I love without all the help and support you give me. Thank you so much for being the amazing man you are. For Travis, you are the most precious gift God has ever given me and the joy that you bring to my life is beyond measure. For the readers, thank you so very much for giving my books a chance, it is because of you that I am where I am today.

Acknowledgments

Thank you to the Wolf Pack, you ladies amaze me and not a day goes by that I don't thank God for your help and support. Specifically thank you to Candace, you have become an invaluable part of my writing process and all that goes into publishing a book. I am so glad that we are friends.

Thank you to the Hell Cats for your words of encouragement and listening to me complain.

Thank you to the Quinnssentials, you are an awesome street team and I am so thankful for all your support and help!

Thank you to all of my friends and family for reading my books, supporting me and cheering me on.

There are many more to thank, I could write a book alone on all the people who have been so amazing in this journey I have been on. I hope you know who you are and I hope I have told you many times before how dear you all are to me.

Prologue

"How long must we hope; hope for help, hope for redemption, hope for retribution, hope for evil to finally lose. Because to be honest I'm ready to knock hope to the curb and tell her to step aside while I kick some wicked witch behind. See, I can keep from cussing if I want to, so bite me bitches." ~ Jen

"I told you she would be beautiful," Decebel held their baby girl in his arms and stared down at her with more adoration than Jen had ever seen in anyone's eyes. He seemed even larger than usual, holding such a tiny person in his arms.

"Duh, she came from me, what else could she possibly be?" Jen snorted.

Decebel looked up from Cosmina and smiled at her. "She is half mine you know?"

Jen let a wicked smile cross her lips, "As far as you know."

Decebel let out a low growl. Jen knew he couldn't retaliate while he held their daughter. Jen pumped her fist in the air. "Oh, heck yeah! You are going to hold her all the time because you can't do jack when she is in your arms you big teddy bear."

Decebel stood slowly, looking every bit the predator he was. He walked over to the frilly, yellow bassinet that stood at the foot of their bed. It was hideous but Jacque and Sally had been so proud of it so Jen endured its presence, but rolled her eyes every time she looked at it. He laid Cosmina down in it gently and caressed her little cheek with a finger. Then his face lifted and his eyes, uh, make that *glowing* eyes, Jen added to herself, met hers. Jen made a huge tactical error when she saw the hungry look in her mate's face. She took a step back. Never, ever retreat from a predator, it simply makes them all the more excited to chase.

"Did it dawn on you Jennifer, that maybe I could just put her down?"

Jen tried to speak, but only a squeak emerged. She cleared her throat and tried again.

"Of course it dawned on me," she said, flippantly. "I was just counting on the fact that you never let her out of your sight." Jen cursed herself when she picked up her foot to take yet another step back. Decebel grinned and it was her turn to growl. She was not prey. She would not behave like prey. But, as she watched her mate crouch down in an attack stance she decided that maybe today she was prey, and prey ran like hell when someone wanted to eat them.

"Jennifer," Decebel purred. "Are you offering yourself up for lunch?" His gleaming smile that was all canines had her shivering.

She took another step back and felt the door knob in her back. *Victory* she thought. She knew that Decebel would not leave their little Cosmina alone to chase after her. Decebel must have seen the triumph in her eyes, because just as she turned the knob and jerked the door open, he lunged with a huge snarl. Jen took off like the hounds of hell were on her tail and really, what else could you compare Decebel too?

She heard her mate growl, and then in her mind she heard,*"Chicken."*

"Maybe," she responded. *"But, this chicken lives to fight another day."*

She heard Decebel laugh and felt the familiar butterflies of desire stir in her. *Damn wolf* she thought.

"You have to come to back to our room sometime Jennifer, you can't run forever."

Jen rolled her eyes, *"I'm not running. I'm…simply choosing to take a long detour."*

"Don't be too long. I need you." Jen heard something change in his voice, a sort of desperation that was totally out of character for him. It seemed to be channeling through their bond.

"Dec, you okay? Is Cosmina okay?"

"Cosmina?" he said her name slowly as if he'd forgotten it.

"Decebel talk to me."

"I'm trying. I keep telling you that I would save you if I could. I keep trying to get to you, but you just keep dying and screaming and then our baby is born and she's so little and not breathing. I'm trying baby, I don't want him to touch you again, but I can't get to you, I can't save you. NOT AGAIN, I CAN'T WATCH THIS AGAIN. JENNIFER!"

Jen's eyes flew open as she gasped for breath. She blinked several times and slowly sat up.

"A dream," she muttered, "It was a bloody dream."

But not that last part. Not Decebel calling for her. That had been real. She could feel him, feel the heat of the hell he was enduring caress her skin and scorch her soul. He had somehow contacted her in her sleep and part of her wanted to fall back asleep so she could go to him, tell him she was fine. Well not really fine, she was pissed, but otherwise unharmed. She wanted to reassure him that she was coming for him and she would shred the gates of the In-Between down to rubble to get to him. The other part wanted to kill something, anything. Her wolf was restless and constantly paced inside her. Mate, mate, mate was a mantra in her mind as her wolf pined for him. It was maddening, and yet comforting, because she wasn't alone in her pain and fear. But, her wolf was able to do something that Jen was not. Jen's wolf didn't have emotions messing with her brain. Her wolf was focused on two things; get their mate, protect their pup. She would do anything for those two things. There was no crying, fear, or anger. Only determination to reclaim what was theirs. *Our mate,* she heard her wolf in her mind *he is ours, and we will kill the one who took him.*

Damn straight, thought Jen, *we will kill her and then stick her head on a spear in the middle of the battle field for all to see what happens when you mess with the females of the Canis lupus.* Blood thirsty, much? Maybe a little!

Chapter 1

"A Warlock King, a Fae, and a human walk into a bar…no really, it's not the beginning to a great joke, or maybe it is, but we really did go into a bar. The question is, would we come back out?" ~ Lilly

Lilly walked behind the Fae named Cyn and the Warlock King, Cypher, AKA her mate, according to him, though the jury was still out on her end. She followed them into a seedy looking bar at the very edge of the forest in the Balkan Mountains, were the Warlock's lived. Perizada of the Fae, whoever that was, had sent Cyn to them. That's all they knew, because that's all Cyn had told them.

Cyn had appeared and stood in the forest knowing that it would alert Cypher to her presence and she had waited. When he finally appeared she'd stated simply, "Perizada of the Fae has sent me to you. I am Cyn, Guard of the Council." That was it. No elaboration, no hey I'm here to lend a hand, just: *here I am, deal with it.*

Cypher had narrowed his eyes at the Fae guard, but didn't question her. Lilly however hadn't been quite so trusting. Although, Lilly had thrown the Spanish inquisition at her, Cyn had simply ignored her.

Now here they were, walking into this bar, full of shady looking characters. According to Cypher, there was a guy here who knew a guy that might know another guy that could help.

"Do you really think this is a good idea?" Lilly whispered up to Cypher. "I mean seriously Cypher, a guy who knows a guy who knows a guy. Do you honestly believe it's going to be worth all the work to find the guy at the end of the rabbit hole?"

Cypher looked mildly amused at her questioning, which made her want to stomp on his foot. She didn't, but it took every bit of her restraint.

"We aren't in Kansas anymore Little One, you are going to see some things, hear some things and," he said, before she cut him off.

"If you finish that with *do some things* I might just slap you, Warlock King or not, and how the heck do you know a reference to The Wizard of Oz?" Lilly raised her brow as she looked at him, waiting for whatever possible explanation he could have for *that* one.

Cypher winked at her, which did strange things to her stomach that she didn't want to think about.

"As I was saying, things are different here and information is found in the most unlikely places because the people who have that information usually do not want to be found. And, I like human movies. I'm not a total recluse."

"That really isn't comforting or encouraging in any way you know. Not the recluse part, but the people who don't want to be found bit, that's a little unsettling."

Cypher shrugged at her annoyed look and turned back to the bar when the bar tender finally acknowledged them. They spoke in a tongue that Lilly didn't understand and she was pretty sure it wasn't any form of human language.

Even speaking the strange language, Cypher still sounded commanding and confident. It didn't dawn on him to think that someone might not jump up to do his bidding, but then again maybe no one had ever told him no. Lilly smiled to herself and thought: *there's a first time for everything. Oh, King of mine.*

Finally, after several more minutes of the back and forth between King and bar tender Cypher turned and walked out of the bar. Lilly started to say something, but then realized that Cypher had taken her hand and was tugging her behind him. She quickly caught her footing as she stumbled behind him and looked back, over her shoulder to see that Cyn was pulling up the rear. Once out in the cool night air, she pulled her hand from his and threw them up in the air in exasperation.

"So?" She asked. "That was it? That really seemed a little anticlimactic."

Cypher shook his head at her and motioned towards the forest. She followed him into the dark foliage and was quickly swallowed up by the trees.

After walking in silence for several minutes, Cypher stopped abruptly and turned around. Lilly expected him to answer her question, but instead he glared at Cyn.

"Why did Peri send you to me?"

Lilly rolled her eyes, *oh now he asks*.

Cyn looked around the forest causing Lilly to look as well.

"You may speak freely, I've taken care that no one will hear," Cypher told the Fae.

"She has heard that the witch has come to you with a proposition for your help. She also heard that you were in possession of a certain human."

Lilly's mouth dropped open and a sound of indignation slipped out. "In possession? Are you kidding me?"

Cypher held up his hand to stop her, but never took his eyes from Cyn's face.

"Lilly is my mate."

"So says the barbarian Warlock King," Lilly muttered.

Cypher looked at her from the corner of his eye, "I don't recall you complaining about the intimacy between us earlier and as I told you I have never shared such intimacy with another female."

"Could we please refrain from discussing our intimacy in front of others?"

The blush that stained Lilly's cheeks made Cypher smile and he reached out and gently brushed a finger across her face.

"You are such a breath of fresh air little one."

Lilly let out an unladylike snort as she crossed her arms across her chest gave him her best *I am not affected stare*, which was the biggest load of crap she had ever fed herself.

Cypher looked back at Cyn.

"As I was saying, Lilly is my mate and therefore not a prisoner if that is what Perizada is thinking. As for the witch," Cypher stepped back until his back was leaning against a large tree. Lilly could tell he was trying to pick his words carefully, indicating to her that he did not fully trust Cyn. "She did come to me and there was an offer presented. At this point, she believes that I am going to help her. I have to tread carefully, because I have sworn a blood oath to her."

The Fae took a step back and for the first time Lilly saw emotion cross her face.

Lilly turned to Cypher with a frown on her face. "You haven't mentioned a blood oath to me. What exactly does that mean?"

Cypher shook his head. "It's not important right now."

Lilly rolled her eyes at the warlock King. "You have got to be kidding me. You just told this Fairy,"

"Fae," Cyn interjected.

Lilly slid the Fae a sideways glance, "A technicality," she growled. She looked back at Cypher as she continued. "You just told her that you swore a blood oath and the stoic Cyn actually showed some human emotion, and it looked an awful lot like fear. So, forgive me if I kind of think it is freaking important."

A flirty smile turned up on Cypher's lips. "So you are worried about your mate?"

Lilly let out a frustrated huff, throwing her hands up in the air. "I told you that I care for you. I don't understand it, but there it is so yes I'm worried about you."

Cypher stared silently at Lilly for a few tense moments, and then finally relented.

"A blood oath is a contract that binds my word to the one asking for a deed. It prevents the one accepting the contract from backing out."

"So what happens if you do back out since you've done this blood oath thing?"

"The witch can put me or any of my race in the In-Between and she could possibly kill you. I'm not real sure on the whole *you* part because again I don't know the ramifications of you being my mate."

Lilly pinched the bridge of her nose as she felt a headache coming on. "And, you didn't think maybe I needed to know this?"

Cypher shrugged, "There isn't anything you can do about it so why worry about it?"

Lilly shook her head at the warlock King. She knew that nothing she could say would help it make sense to him. There were no words to tell him that she wanted to know these things so that she could help him endure these burdens. In the brief time she had known him, she'd seen how the responsibility of his race was wearing on him. It was a lot, even for one with shoulders as broad as his, to bear for so long. Wasn't that what a mate was for? Okay yes, she was still on the fence about the mate thing, but she knew that she cared about him and she didn't want to see him come to any harm. She would figure out the whole mate thing when the time came to make a decision.

"Fine, I won't worry about it." She finally told him.

Cypher raised a single brow at her, "That's it? You aren't going to growl and snarl at me?"

"I'm not a wolf you know," she purposely added a slight growl to her voice in hopes that it would bring about that devastating smile he had, that she loved so much. She wasn't disappointed.

Cyn made an impatient shuffle with her feet, reminding them of her presence.

Cypher looked back at the Fae. "I have no intention of helping the witch, but I may not have a choice. If it comes to opening the Veil or Lilly's life then I will have to open the Veil and hopefully get it closed before too many demons escape."

"Nope, not gonna happen." Lilly said, shaking her head, "you aren't going to sacrifice the safety of the world, or my daughter, for my life. My daughter is grown and married and I know she will be taken care of. I've had a great life, though not a very long one, but that's okay. I won't let you choose me over several other races."

Cypher barely acknowledged her when he responded. "Well, it's a good thing it isn't up to you then."

Cyn spoke before Lilly could respond. "Peri wants you to open the Veil."

Cypher pushed off from the tree and suddenly standing before them was the warlock King, in all his Kingly glory. He towered over the Fae guard, who looked rather small when compared to Cypher.

"What did you say?" Cypher's voice was low and threatening.

Cyn didn't blink, didn't step back, or cringe the way most smart people, who valued their lives, would have. She simply answered his question.

"She wants you to open the Veil."

Chapter 2

"I think of you. When darkness swirls around me like a turbulent storm, when the very breath I take seems to tax my soul, when despair is my constant shadow; I think of you. I hear your voice, I smell your scent, and I feel your skin upon my own. Your pain is my own, your fear my best friend, and even though all hope seems to have seeped from the world leaving only despair, still, I think of you." ~ Sally

Darkness enveloped her. She couldn't move her limbs even though she was telling herself to. What she could feel was pain, panic, fear, anger, hate, rage, and many more emotions that she knew did not belong to her. Jacque tried to think back to what her last memory had been. She had been walking through the forest and then she had walked into a pond. *Bloody hell* she thought, *I walked into a freaking pond?* She remembered thinking it was the best idea she had ever had and just knew that if she went into the water she would find peace. Well that plan was shot to hell. Fane was gone, he was hurting, and she couldn't reach him. Jacque could feel him, sense him through their bond, but she couldn't talk to him.

She couldn't open her eyes, couldn't talk, but she could breathe. That was a good thing right? She was trying to think about the positive, but the more she felt Fane's despair, the further away the positive slipped from her grasp.

Jacque could even hear her friends' voices. She had heard Jen's declaration to kick Mona's ass and had wanted to join in the howl, had felt her wolf perk up, but she was just as paralyzed as Jacque. She remembered Mona causing her body to betray her by using her voice to speak and that had flat out pissed her off and she had pushed with everything left inside her to get the witch out of her mind. It had used up all of her energy and for a while, she felt like she was drifting further from the living into the shadow world. But, she refused to drift off into the emptiness without a fight. Jacque would not go quietly, not as long as drew breath, not as long as her heart pumped blood through her frozen body.

She knew Mona had done something to her and she just kept hoping that Rachel, Peri, and Sally could figure out a way to fix it. Jacque needed to be able to help them, because she didn't know how much longer their mates could last in the hell Mona had sent them to endure. She didn't know how long before the state of their mates began to affect them, and if their mates died, then they were all dead.

~

Sally sat staring off into the dark forest. They had been walking for what seemed like weeks, though it had merely been days. It was dark even though night had not yet fallen. Clouds continually blocked the sun and winter seemed to be clinging to the land as the evil that Mona was weaving continued to take over more and more of their world. Sally wondered if others noticed if the humans, who knew nothing of the supernatural world, picked up on the evil that was bleeding into the world. Evil beyond what they had could have ever imagined.

Sally knew that Alina had explained to them that the bonds with their mates wouldn't work in the In-Between, but she felt Costin. She couldn't communicate with him, but she felt his emotions. It was exhausting and terrifying, but she wouldn't wish it away. Sally would rather feel something, anything, than nothing at all. She wondered if he could feel her, if he knew that she was seeking a way to get him back. Did he truly know what he meant to her, had she told him? Sally began to doubt herself, doubt the bond between them. She felt so inadequate to be his mate. Costin was so confident, so funny, full of life, and she felt so bland next to him. He so openly expressed his feelings for her, continually telling her how much he loved her, and she would shy away, like a child. Her head fell forward into her hands as she felt the weight of reality fall onto her like a cloak. It covered her in doubt, fear, and she felt despair like she had never known.

"Sally," she heard the gentle voice behind her and turned to see Alina standing there. Strong, secure, sure Alina. How could Sally even dream that she could be that kind of mate to Costin.

"Sally, stop this," Alina told her firmly.

"I can feel him Alina," Sally told her, her voice tight. "How can I feel him?"

Alina shook her head as she took a seat on the rock next to the healer.

"I don't know. I can feel Vasile as well and it shouldn't be possible. We shouldn't be able to sense them at all. The only thing I can come up with is that Mona is somehow allowing the contact, but it's one sided. I can't reach out to him."

Sally nodded, "I keep trying to tell him it's okay, but he's lost in some horrible terror. I've never felt anything like it."

Alina wrapped an arm around Sally and pulled her close.

"We have to fight the despair that is coming through the bond. Mona's goal must be to debilitate us with the emotions our mates are feeling. As much, I would like to know what Vasile is going through so that I could help him through it. I am afraid that if I knew I would be of no use to him."

Jen came into view as she walked around to stand in front of them.

"I talked with Decebel."

Their heads snapped up, and the other females were on their feet.

"What?" The question came from each of them.

"I was dreaming, but I know it was real. He was calling for me and he answered me when I spoke to him." Jen's voice shook with emotion.

"What did he say?" Crina asked cautiously, not really sure if she wanted to know.

Jen shook her head, letting out a shuddering breath. "He was broken. I've never heard, such fear and pain. Decebel said that he couldn't watch it again. He said he was trying to stop him from touching me."

"They are seeing their worst fears," Peri told them from where she leaned against a tree staring off into the forest. "You know what your males fear." She left the statement hanging.

Alina nodded. "The ultimate horror for our males would be for them to have to watch another male touch us, to see us in pain, and to watch us die horrible deaths."

Jen growled and her eyes narrowed, when she realized what they were saying. "Are you telling me that Decebel is watching me be raped?"

Alina nodded, while gasps echoed across the group.

"And, more than likely, he is probably watching you give birth with horrific out comes." Peri added.

Alina growled, "Not helping Perizada."

Peri shrugged, "Anger is motivation. The males of your race are intense. I don't think we will ever fully grasp just how much they feel for their mates. They will not last long with their sanity intact if they continue to have to watch their greatest fears and insecurities played out like a broken reel. Their wolves will soon take over and they will become feral."

Elle stepped forward, glaring at Peri. "Why don't you just tell us it's hopeless since you're passing out all the warm fuzzies. Damn Peri, these aren't just wolves to us anymore. That's my mate, being tortured. I don't know him all that well and yes, he scares the hell out of me, but you, telling me that he's going to lose his freaking mind and be lost to me is not helping."

"Shut the front door," Jen laughed. "Elle just put Peri fairy in her place."

"Not helping Jen," Sally murmured.

"Psht," Jen waved Sally off. "When have you ever known me to try to be helpful in situations where chicks are about to break out into a cat fight," she paused thoughtfully. "Well, in this case it would be a fairy fight, but you get my drift."

"Would you freaking grow up?" Sally snarled at her best friend, and everyone was taken aback by the uncharacteristic meanness in Sally's voice.

Jen's eyes narrowed as she glared at the healer. "Need I remind you that I am your Alpha? I could wipe the floor with your gypsy ass, not to mention I am pregnant and very temperamental. Do not push me Sally."

"ENOUGH!" Peri's voice shook the ground around them and their heads all snapped to look at the regal high Fae. Light shone around her. She met the eyes of each woman letting them see the power that rolled through her.

"If you want to crush each other before the battle even begins, then by all means have at it. Don't come crying to me when Desdemona turns your feral mates loose on this world only to have you join them by their sides, as you rip innocent lives apart."

The night was silent, as the females considered Peri's words.

"Just to be clear, would a bitch slap be considered crushing?" Sally smiled, innocently.

Jen rolled her eyes. "I liked you better when you were more likely to sing Lean On Me than Another One Bites the Dust."

Alina stood up and folded her arms across her chest as she watched Peri's Fae form receded.

"What are we doing Peri? How long are we going to wander around the forest?"

"I'm not wandering aimlessly, if that's what you're worried about. There is a method to my madness."

"Just as long as you are aware that you are bat crap mad," Jen muttered.

Peri ignored the jab and continued. "At this point there is only one who can help us and he is going to prove to be difficult to find."

"Who?" Alina asked.

"King Cypher." Peri's voice rang with a tone of dread at the name of the King.

"What exactly is he King of?" Sally asked.

"The Warlocks," Alina answered, before Peri could.

"Seriously?" Jen snorted. "Warlocks?"

"You all might want to sit down for what I have to tell you." Peri resumed her place against the tree, and waited for them all to take a seat. Sally and Jen sat down on a fallen limb, while Alina, Crina, Cynthia, and Elle all sat at various spots with their backs leaning against trees. Jacque lay, covered in warm blankets, and aside from her quiet breaths, she was as motionless as death, a few feet away.

"Yes Jen, Warlocks are real and Cypher is their King. He has been their King for a very, very long time. Like all of the supernaturals in the human realm, their magic is waning. He grows weaker by the year and his race is dwindling in numbers. He had yet to find a mate, until recently, and like any of us we are weaker without our mate."

"So, he's found one?" Sally asked.

Peri nodded, the look on her face was apprehensive.

"Why do I get the feeling we aren't going to like who this mate is?" Jen muttered.

"Cypher is not a bad person, but he is in a difficult place. He needs to protect the future of his race and so he made a deal with Desdemona. Cypher is the only being who knows how to open the Veil to the underworld. In exchange for him opening the Veil, Mona promised him a mate. She delivered Lilly Pierce to the King."

"WHAT!"

"BLOODY HELL!"

A chorus of disbelief rippled through the circle of woman, as they took in the information Peri had just shared.

"Is she okay?" Crina asked.

"She is fine," Alina was the one who answered. Their heads all whipped around to look at the Alpha.

"You knew?" Sally gasped. "You knew and didn't tell us?"

"Vasile advised me not to and you know when an Alpha advises, what he is really saying is don't or else."

"Vasile wouldn't have done anything to you," Elle stood up.

"No, but I set an example for other wolves. And, Vasile had his reasons for keeping the information to himself. Lilly is safe. Cypher has not hurt her."

"And, who's to say that he won't?" Cynthia asked.

"Cypher won't hurt her because he loves her and has chosen her as his mate." Peri looked at Jen, and then at Sally. "I have one of the guardian Fae with him and she has reported to me that he has no intention of helping Mona. Lilly has talked some sense in to him."

"You trust him?" Jen asked the Fae.

"I have known Cypher for a long time. He is a good man and only wants what is best for his people. He made a poor choice, but the Fates have given him a second chance with Lilly."

"Yes, and we should all trust the Fates," Jen growled.

"I need you all to know that he isn't holding Lilly against her will. She wants to be with him."

"He isn't green with horns or anything is he?" Sally's face scrunched up as she asked.

Peri laughed, "No, he is actually quite handsome."

Jen cocked her head to the side and frowned at Peri. "Wait, why is he going to be hard to find if you have one of your fairies with him?"

"Because he is very powerful, and even though he is weakening, he has the ability to shield himself. Although, my Fae is with him I have no way of knowing where they are, no way of flashing to them, nor can Cyn, the guardian, flash to me. It's really quite inconvenient." Peri added in a tone that said she felt very put out by the King.

The women fell silent as the day wore on and darkness of night began to fall. Alina and Crina hunted and brought back small game for them to eat, and then they each, one by one, lay down for the night. They had set up a schedule for someone to sit with Jacque and rotated throughout the night. Jen was first. Just when Jen was about to take up her vigil next to her friend, she felt a gentle hand on her shoulder. It was Cynthia.

"The doctor side in me is coming out, and I need to know how you are doing Jen."

Jen smiled hesitantly. She was excited about her and Decebel's baby, but it was also a source of pain. Jen sat and Cynthia sat across from her, legs folded in front of her, elbows leaned on her knees. She waited patiently for Jen to answer.

"I feel fine physically," her hand instinctively went to her abdomen. "I haven't even been sick, no pain, and no weird other female problems I'd rather not describe."

Cynthia laughed. "As long as there isn't anything weird, you don't have to describe it. How do your moods seem to you?"

"At times I feel a little out of control, like I can't decide if I'm okay or a mess, you know? Then other times I feel like everything is going to be fine. Dec will be back, he will fix this whole problem with the Fates, and we'll have a healthy baby girl." Jen looked down at the ground, absentmindedly tracing a design in the dirt. "Those are the thoughts I have to cling to." She met Cynthia's gaze and tried to smile, but it didn't reach her eyes. "I'll let you know if there's a problem, okay?"

Cynthia returned the smile. "Okay, but when you start getting farther along, we will have to start doing physical exams."

Jen shrugged. "I'm no stranger to taking off my clothes doc."

Cynthia chuckled as she stood and headed off to her make shift bed. Jen looked down at the dirt where she had been tracing with her finger and her eyes filled with tears, as she saw she had drawn the markings that covered Decebel's skin.

She turned away from the drawing to face Jacque and took her hand. Jen held it between her own, rubbing it, probably more for her comfort than for Jacque's. She looked at her red headed friend and her heart ached to see her in such a helpless state. Jen stared, pushing her will at Jacque as if that would be enough to make her open her eyes. If Fane were here, he would be going crazy; but he wasn't. None of their mates were, and for the first time she felt alone. She needed Decebel, no matter how much it bothered her to need him, she did. Jen needed his strength and his comfort. She needed his brooding presence so that she would have someone to be sarcastic with and she knew he would be able to take it. Jen needed to hear him tell her she would be okay and that their baby would be okay. She needed him to tell her when she needed to shut the hell up, because as her fear rose so did her sarcasm and irritability and she knew none of the others needed that nor deserved it.

"Damn you Desdemona for taking him from me," she muttered, into the cold, dark night. Her eyes narrowed and she looked out into the forest, wishing that the witch would come walking out in all her evil glory. Jen never though she was capable of being cruel, but she decided then and there that she would peel the flesh from Desdemona's writhing body while she still lived. Was she a little blood thirsty? Maybe, but then the witch had taken her mate, putting him in danger and causing him immeasurable suffering. For that alone, she had signed her death warrant, not to mention all the other atrocities she had already committed in her long, meaningless life.

"Jacque where are you?" Jen asked her friend. "I want you to know that I will take care of you, always Jac. And, I'm going to give you hell for lying there on your back while we do all the work." Jen snorted out laughter to herself as she thought of the remark Jacque would give to that comment.

Her heart sank as she continued to watch the steady breathing of Jacque, but no other signs of life could be found. Jen wanted to run. She wanted to shed the human skin and let her wolf run free, howling at the pain that she felt for the loss of everything. Jen missed her parents and she smiled to herself, thinking it was a feeling she had never thought she would ever feel. But, when she stood to lose something that she never imagined loosing, she admitted that she didn't want to lose them, no matter how tense their relationship had always been.

She continued to sit staring into the night, a lone sentry guarding her friends. Part of her was eager to go to sleep hoping to hear from her mate again, but another part of her dreaded hearing the desperation in his usually calm, secure voice. He needed her just as badly as she needed him and here she sat unable to do a damn thing for him. Jen growled in frustration and gradually all the ugliness of her reality set in and took root in her heart. She bowed her head and closed her eyes giving into the monster of defeat, if only for a little while, she would let herself be weak, let herself fall apart while there was no one to watch.

Chapter 3

"I pride myself on my ability to hate indiscriminately. Truly, I look at the world from a viewpoint of total equality when it comes to the depths of my abhorrence. If life were fair, I would be honored for my impartial treatment and lack of favoritism. But, life isn't fair. Life is cruel and dysfunctional. It kicks you in the ass and then laughs as you crash into others, taking them down with you as you fall. And, that is why I love to be alive. It means I get to watch all of you suckers go down and rest assured, I will wish equal amounts of pain and disfigurement on each of you. If I'm lucky; I will get to be the cause."
~ Desdemona

"Tell me why I should believe that you are willing to betray your race? Why should I trust a Fae?" Mona glared at the cloaked figure that stood across from her.

"Perizada has been a thorn in my side for too many centuries. I am done standing in her shadow. I am done taking orders from a god that cares only for wolves and has no respect for my people. She expects us to jump up, rescue her weak children, and it is time for someone to do something about it."

"And that someone is you?" Mona crossed her arms. "If you are so brave, then why won't you reveal yourself to me?"

The Fae laughed. "You honestly believe that I would show you all of my cards at once? I am no fool. Think about what I have told you and decide quickly. You are not my only option." And then the Fae was gone.

Mona closed her eyes and reached out with her will attempting to follow the path that the Fae had taken, but there was no trace left. From the moment the person had appeared in the cloaked guise, Mona had been subtly attempting to unmask her. But, this was one of great power, able to block her attempts. That in itself told her something very important. If one, so high up in the Fae council was seeking her out; there was no doubt dissention among the Fae. A weakness had been exposed and it was only a matter of time before that weakness brought everything crashing down.

Mona laughed out loud. "I don't even need to lift another finger to destroy my foe. They are going to do it for me with their lack of loyalty." If there was one thing Mona knew, it was even the strongest defense could fall if a tiny crack emerged.

~

Costin closed his eyes and reached for Sally, his Sally, not the imitation that sat before him, broken and afraid. He didn't know how long he and his pack mates had been in their own personal hell, but it was getting harder and harder to have moments of clarity like the brief glimpse that he was experiencing now. The only thing that had allowed him to gain this insight was remembering the first moment in which he had felt her. It had been like a drink of water in a dry, parched land and it had brought him a minuscule amount of relief. Then it was gone. With every moment that he was forced to endure the unrelenting torture of watching his mate die, be tortured, raped, ripped apart, and taken from him, he prayed for one second of his mate's real presence. He knew that he was fighting not only for his life, but for hers as well. It was a fight he refused to lose.

He pushed out with everything in him, reaching through the bond, thin though it was, to draw her to him. Costin held his breath as he waited for her to answer him. One beat, two beats, his heart pumped in his chest and then, she was there. His brown eyed gypsy and all the gentleness that she possessed.

"Sally mine," he whispered, through cracked lips.

"Costin?"

For a moment, he imagined that he could hear her calling out his name. He strained his ears, listening for the sound of her voice.

"Costin?"

There it was.

"I'm here Sally," he spoke even though he knew it was an impossibility that he was truly speaking to her. If this were all he could have, then he would take it and run as far as he could.

"How can I hear you?" She asked him.

"You're not real," Costin, answered.

"Are you?"

Costin heard the Sally before him, the one he knew to be false, scream. He squeezed his eyes closed and clenched his jaw as he tried to focus on his mate's, calm, un-tortured voice.

"I am real my love. Real, scared, and so empty without you." He sounded desperate even to his own ears, but to hell with his pride. He was scared and empty. It was futile to deny it.

"We're trying to figure out a way to get you all out and we're doing it as quickly as we can. I love you Costin. I love you and I need you to fight." Sally pled with her mate, though she knew that she might be asking the impossible.

Costin struggled to hold onto the connection between them, but it grew ever weaker. The tortured Sally lying before him, once again, began to take over his reality and his Sally. His whole, sweet Sally was slipping away.

"NO!" Costin shouted into the bleakness of the In-Between. His eyes opened and he stared at the horrific sight before him, telling himself over and over that it wasn't real. It wasn't enough to convince him. His wolf struggled to get free, to rescue their mate and Costin knew the battle raging inside him was becoming too much. He was losing and no matter how hard he fought, the will of his wolf was growing stronger and more insistent. Costin couldn't make the wolf understand that what they were seeing wasn't real. All that his wolf saw was their mate, broken, devastated and terrified sitting before them, reaching for them, begging them for help. He threw his head back and a soul piercing howl ripped from his chest, but there was no one to hear him.

~

Sally woke with a start. Her breathing was rapid and despite the cool morning air, her forehead was dotted with sweat. Once again, she had heard his voice, heard his desperation and once again, there wasn't a thing she could do about it.

It was several moments before she realized that it was quiet, too quiet and her vision cleared as she blinked away the painful dream.

"Good morning sleeping beauty," Cynthia smiled over at Sally. The cool early morning air caressed her face as she tried to sort out in her mind between reality and the dream. She remembered Costin's agony and it was beginning to become her own. She looked over at Peri who was helping to gather their packs so they could continue on.

"Peri, we must hurry. Wherever you are leading us, we must move more quickly." Sally's words were laced with desperation and resolve.

~

Peri led them at a brisk pace as Sally's words repeated ominously in her mind. She had told them she had a plan, and she meant it, but she couldn't tell them what it was. She had told them they needed the help of the Warlock King, and at that time, she had believed it, but now she had a different plan. Peri knew that Alina would not approve. Her need to protect the women she no doubt now considered pack, herself included, would be too great to allow Peri to put them in such peril. But it was the only way to bring back their mates. Everything worth anything came at a price. Peri knew that all too well. She pushed on, looking back behind her to see if everyone was keeping up. Her only worry, and that alone bothered her because she never worried, was that Alina would figure out that she had been leading them in a circle for days. She had led them through the Transylvania Alps and all the way to the Carpathian Mountains and they were actually very close to their destination, but she wasn't quite ready. She didn't yet have the bargaining chip that she needed and so she had to keep their presence unknown and keep Alina and the others from figuring out her ploy. She looked back once again, and caught Alina's eyes. *Uh oh*, Peri thought to herself as she saw the light bulb in Alina's mind beginning to flicker. Peri knew that she was going to have to create a diversion. One that would hopefully take Alina's mind off of whatever she thought she had figured out. Peri smiled to herself as she thought: *it's a damn good thing that I specialize in chaos.*

Peri began to whisper under her breath, calling on the elements, drawing power to her through the life in the forest. It was harder than it should have been, but she knew that this was because of the evil that Mona had unleashed. Dark clouds began to gather overhead and they were suddenly enveloped in the murky forest with no light to show their way.

"What the heck is going on?" Cynthia yelled over the wind that began to whip and whirl around them.

Peri continued to chant so low that she could not be heard as she began to bring down rain. Lightning crashed all around, and thunder shook the ground beneath them. They all stumbled as they tried to stay upright and though Jacque's magically floating cot didn't need a steadying hand, Peri grabbed onto it anyway.

Peri called on the lighting again and sent it crashing down so close to the group that it briefly lit up the woods around them. Each saw the fear written on the faces of their friends. Peri continued to crash lighting around them lighting their way as she yelled for them to follow her. She ran through the pelting rain and tried to feel bad for scaring them, but she knew it was for their own good. She ran until she found the large rocks that she had been looking for. There was a large overhang that they could crowd under and wait out the supposed natural storm.

They all took cover and turned to watch the lighting dance and the thunder boom. The ladies shivered from the cold rain and tried to huddle together for warmth. After an hour, Peri began to try to calm the storm. She immediately became worried. The storm no longer heeded her command. The thunder and lightning continued, unabated. The rain continued to pelt their makeshift shelter. *I swear if I think the word worry one more time I'm going to stab my own eye out with a spoon,* she thought to herself, as she began to hunt for the magic that was thwarting her—the magic that was now controlling *her* storm.

Chapter 4

"You don't realize the sacrifice you are willing to make until your child is in need of you. You don't realize that you are truly capable destroying the world around you, crushing anything that gets in your path, bringing your enemies to their knees until you learn that the one thing that your world revolves around is being ripped from you. God help the one who gets in my way. Is it possible that even God might not be able to protect them from my wrath?"
~ Dillon Jacobs

"I know it sounds crazy, Dillon, but it's true." Wadim implored Jacque's father, and the Alpha of the Denver pack. He had called the American Alpha at the request of Skender, who, in Vasile's and the other top wolves' absence was carrying much on his shoulders.

"You're telling me that the Great Luna contacted you?" Dillon asked, incredulously.

"Like I said, I know it sounds crazy. She's calling the packs."

"The packs?" Dillon's voice was tight with apprehension.

"As in all of them." Wadim confirmed. "She gave the Fae moonstone. You know what that means."

"She means to have the Fae call us with it," Dillon's words were not a question.

The line was silent as they each thought about the ramifications of what was about to happen. Dillon knew the situation must be dire if the packs were going to be together in one location. There had been such division among them for so long he wasn't sure how they would be together without dominance posturing and bloody fights. It was quite possibly going to be the biggest damn disaster in their history.

"Who else knows about this?" Dillon asked.

"Only the Fae, myself, and now you."

"Once the Fae use the magic of the moonstone none of us will be able to resist the call." Dillon knew he wasn't saying anything

Wadim didn't already know, he just felt the need to voice it, almost as if saying it out loud might help prepare him for the inevitable.

"There's something else," Wadim's voice dropped. "I haven't heard from Vasile or Decebel since they left."

"They went traipsing off, attempting to take on this witch on their own. What the hell did you expect to happen?" Dillon growled. "Contrary to what you all believe Vasile is not invincible."

Wadim returned the Alpha's growl. "He's handling a situation that should be all of our responsibility. You never should have left."

"He told us to leave!" Dillon snarled.

"You're an Alpha. You knew what he was taking on. You knew that this could affect more than just the Romanian Grey Wolves pack. It's your job to discern when you are needed, so don't preach to me about whether we hold Vasile in too high esteem."

"Are you giving me orders?" Dillon's voice was low and challenging.

"I'm only telling you what you refuse to acknowledge. This isn't a Romanian pack problem. This is an *all* packs problem. You are needed. All of us, are needed and the Alphas are going to have to step up and set an example for their pack mates."

"You aren't telling me anything I don't know Wadim," Dillon let out a frustrated breath. "I will begin to gather my most dominant wolves. Give me a couple days and we'll be on our way."

Though Wadim knew Dillon couldn't see him, he closed his eyes in relief.

"Wadim, do you know if Jacque is alright?" Dillon didn't mask the worry in his voice.

Wadim didn't answer right away. Finally, he breathed a resigned sigh.

"She was with the others, I have no idea what has become of them. So, to be honest, I don't have a clue. I'm sorry to have to tell you that."

"We'll be there soon." Dillon told him, without responding to Wadim's explanation, and then hung up without a goodbye.

Wadim looked at the phone after Dillon had hung up. He shook his head as he considered the Alpha's words. He had to agree, this could definitely be the biggest catastrophe known to their kind. So many dominants together, ready for battle. *Yeah*, he thought: *the world, as we know it, could be destroyed by Desdemona, or just maybe, by the wolves themselves.*

~

Cypher ran full speed, with a screaming Lilly, thrown over his shoulder, and Cyn on his heels. He dodged trees and low hanging limbs. He jumped over holes and stumps, his feet moving at an inhuman pace.

"YOU SAID THEY WOULD HELP!" Lilly bellowed over the sound of the wind whipping past her face.

"NOT NOW LILLY," Cypher yelled back.

Lilly rolled her eyes as she attempted to hold on to Cypher's waist as he ran. She couldn't believe they were in this position. Cypher had assured her that this *being* could help them understand the ramification of opening the veil now that Cypher had found his mate. Cypher had been all: *he can help; he knows what I will need to do*, he... blah, blah, blah. Instead, they had met a group of creatures out of Lilly's worst nightmares. Now the monsters...no, monsters wasn't the right word. Now, the *dragons* were streaking towards them, jaws agape, and ready to swallow them whole.

Lilly looked up when she heard the loudest screeching sound that had ever pierced her ears. Her eyes widened as she saw the shape of wings impossibly large and a long tail soaring through the air. A giant dragon took a nose dive at them.

"Uh CYPHER, COULD YOU PLEASE SHIFT INTO 5th GEAR NOW." Lilly's voice shook a little as she watched the dragon get closer and closer.

Just as Lilly was sure she was about to become the creature's noontime meal, Cyn turned and in a move worthy of a Hollywood movie, stretched her arms out as she flew back through the air. A bright light flew from her hands streaking towards the dragon. It hit the creature right between the eyes and it abruptly changed its course, lifting itself back up to the sky. Before Cyn hit the ground, she pulled her legs up to her chest and threw her body backwards, wheeling her legs around, and landing on her feet. She turned without missing a beat and continued running.

Lilly looked up at the Fae and gave her thumbs up. She swore she saw a small smile on her usually stoic face.

Cypher continued to run. After a mile there had been no sign of the beast and he finally slowed.

Lilly tapped him on the back. "Could you put me down, now so that I can chew you out properly?"

He stopped and placed her upright on her feet. She looked up into his handsome face as she crossed her arms across her chest. Her foot started tapping of its own accord as she tried to formulate the words she wanted to say.

"So, what the hell was that?" She growled.

"Well, to you it would probably be called a dragon, but it's actually called a drahiem."

"I wasn't talking about the freaky beast chasing us; however we will get to that in a minute. I was talking about you saying that we would get help from your brother, but instead we nearly became lunch."

Cypher's eyes narrowed. He turned from her and stared back in the direction they had just come. It had been a very long time since he had talked to his brother. Although, the last time had been quite tense, he hadn't expected such hostility.

"Maybe he didn't realize it was me," he said, weakly.

"Cypher look at me." Lilly uncrossed her arms and reached up to tighten her pony tail that had come loose in the race to get away from the drahiem. "Is there history between you and your brother that you haven't mentioned?"

"It's complicated," Cypher answered.

"Try me," Lilly said, dryly.

Cyn leaned back against a tree seemingly unaffected by the run or stunt that she had pulled. She watched Cypher with sharp eyes and waited for his explanation. If Cypher's brother really was their only chance, then whatever had come between them was going to have to be dealt with.

Cypher gazed off into the distance as he let the memories that he had buried come to the surface.

"It's been centuries since it happened and I really thought he was over it by now."

"It was a woman wasn't it," Lilly asked.

"Yes, but not like you are thinking. He was mated. She was one of the sweetest females I had ever known. She didn't deserve what happened and I couldn't save her. He blames me for her death and rightfully so." Cypher's usually confident tone dropped in defeat.

"I don't believe that. If you didn't save her then it couldn't have been a choice by you. It must have been the circumstances. All of you alpha males think that everything falls on your shoulders and you forget that you aren't perfect."

The side of his mouth lifted slightly as he watched the woman he now called mate defend him. If only she knew the "circumstances" as she called them. Would she think less of him? Would she refuse to trust him to protect her, to protect her daughter?

"There is rarely peace among the supernatural races."

"You don't say?" She snorted, sarcastically.

Cypher chuckled. "Is your daughter like you?"

Lilly smiled. "If you mean is she the coolest thing ever? Then no, she is even more amazing than me."

Cypher smiled. "I can't imagine that."

"Don't get off topic." She narrowed her eyes at him.

"When there is peace," he continued, "it is not long lasting and is tenuous at best. Something as simple as a perceived disrespectful word can break the truce. There had been peace for some time between my kind and the trolls that live in the mountains."

"Trolls?" Lilly's eyebrows rose.

"Surely you realize there are more supernaturals than just the ones you know about, little one."

Lilly shrugged. "Doesn't mean it's not still freakish."

"Thea, that was my brother's mate, was hell bent on uniting us and creating an alliance with the trolls. My brother warned her to stay out of the council business, but that only spurred her on. She sought out the leader of the trolls to try and speak with him, but it wasn't the leader she met in the mountain that day." Cypher paused and thought back to that day. He could still see Thea walking away from him after he had told her that as her King he forbid her to seek out the trolls. He had seen the defiance in her eyes and knew that she wouldn't listen. If only he had followed her, if only he had told his brother sooner. He was drawn from the memories by a warm hand on his arm. He looked down at Lilly, her eyes full of understanding. It gave him the courage to continue.

"She came to me, imploring me to see reason, those were her words. I told her that she was not to go, but something in her eyes told me she would defy me. I had met with the leader of the trolls and I knew that he wouldn't hurt her. He was actually an honorable male, but like any leader, he not only had loyal followers, but corrupt followers as well. I figured he would walk her back to their keep, all the while sporting a dubious smile, chuckling at her innocence. And, he would have, had it been him who had met her. But, when she went to the troll mountain, she was met by two of the trolls that spoke out against the peace between their races. They saw an opportunity to destroy that peace. She never had a chance. And, they succeeded in destroying the peace. The enmity between warlocks and trolls still exist to this day. I can't even describe the things they did to her. I should have followed her. It was my job, as her King to protect her, even if it was from herself."

Lilly shook her head. "It was your brother's job, and even then, she had free will. Regardless of the outcome and how horrible, Thea made that choice. I don't say that to be mean, but you cannot take responsibility for her choice."

Cypher couldn't believe that he didn't see condemnation in her eyes, but instead saw understanding and empathy. He didn't deserve it. Regardless of what Lilly said, she didn't understand the responsibility he had for his race. He had failed to protect that which was most precious to his brother and he had known she would go. When he and his brother had found her body, he had lost it. His torment and pain were so tangible that Cypher felt it in his soul. As soon as the shock wore off he had turned on Cypher. He could hear the words reverberating in his mind, a broken record of endless truths.

"You are our King; you knew what she would do! You should have come to me! You should have warned me. This is your doing; her blood is on your hands." His brother screamed at him. All Cypher had been able to do was bow his head in defeat. He fell to his knees in shame at the truth behind his brother's words. He allowed his brother to beat him until his closest guards saved him from his brother's wrath. He wanted to die, wanted his brother to kill him. It was what he deserved. The council locked his brother up until they felt he was no longer a threat. But, Cypher knew that if his brother were given the chance he would kill him. Time passed, years, decades, centuries, and still, there had been no word from him.

"Cypher."

He realized that Lilly had been saying his name while he was remembering that horrible day. His vision refocused on her and he smiled at the determination in her face.

"It's not your fault. Say it with me," she coaxed.

Cypher shook his head. "I'm sorry love, but this time it is."

Lilly could see that nothing she would say was going to change his mind. She knew when to back off. Now, was not the time, but the day would come when she would make him understand.

"So, what now?" she asked him.

Cypher looked over at Cyn. "Do you know how my brother could have gotten the drahiem in this realm?

Cyn frowned as she thought. "It's actually quite a surprise to me that he was able to get them to cross through a veil. They are very suspicious animals."

"Do you know anything about drahiem, like any weaknesses they might have?" Lilly asked.

The expression on Cyn's face did not look promising. "There are very few things that can kill one and they aren't the friendliest of beasts."

"You don't say?" Lilly laughed, sardonically. Cyn continued as if Lilly hadn't spoken.

"Your brother appears to have convinced them to serve him as guards. This is a mystery to me. Their skin is thicker than leather, nearly impenetrable. If that weren't enough it reflects light so that a glare that blinds their opponents. It is like water being hit just right by the sun, it can be blinding. Their eyes have a clear sheath that slides into place when they are in battle, their tails are lined with deadly spikes and their mouths excrete a poison when it pierces flesh that causes paralysis." Cyn explained, dryly as if she weren't describing a near indestructible foe.

Lilly thought for a moment, going over the description that Cyn had just given them. Her brow furrowed as she considered it.

"Wait," she said, stepping towards Cyn. "You said its skin is *near* impenetrable. That means that it isn't impossible, it can be done." Lilly's eyes filled with a small amount of hope.

"Is there some sort of weapon that can get through their thick skin?" Cypher asked.

Cyn looked grim.

"Why do I think this is going to be some other impossible task that could most likely get us killed?" Lilly asked, wryly.

Lilly nearly laughed when the corners of Cyn's mouth tipped up in an almost smile.

"There is one weapon that can kill them. It is an arrow made of a special metal that is only forged by…"

"The elves," Cypher interrupted, ominously.

Cyn nodded. "The elves," she agreed.

Lilly held up her hands as her eye brows rose. "Wait one second. *Elves?*" She shook her head and let out a frustrated breath. "I know now why my daughter and her friends are constantly using words like bloody hell, shut up, and mother of pearl."

Cypher tilted his head to the side as he watched his mate.

Lilly looked over at him at laughed at his confused face.

She waved him off. "Don't ask. Okay, so exactly how many supernatural species are there?"

Before Cypher could answer, they heard an all too familiar thundering sound above them. They each looked up just as one of the beasts they had been discussing flew overhead, its great wings beating the air around it.

Just when they thought they had not been noticed, the beast turned his head down and pierced them with its freaky eyes.

Cyn's usual composure cracked for a brief moment as her eyes met Lilly's.

"Did I mention that they have an excellent sense of smell?"

Lilly's eyes widened. "Um, no, you sure as hell didn't."

Cypher grabbed her and smoothly lifted her into his arms, this time cradling her against his chest.

She groaned. "Here we go again."

Cypher took off at a sprint, his speed increasing with every step. Lilly looked over his shoulder and saw that Cyn was right on his heels. Lilly looked up into the sky, attempting to block out the speed at which Cypher was moving, ignoring the trees blurring past them. She saw the huge draheim and cringed when a roar pierced the sky. *How on earth can the people within a 50 mile radius not hear and see the beast*, Lilly asked herself. When the beast made a nose dive for them she decided that it was a question that could wait for an answer, provided they lived through this.

~

Mona stood on the hill, looking out over the Carpathian Mountains. She felt the disturbance in the air. The magic causing her skin to tingle and she had answered its call. She didn't understand why Peri would conjure a storm, and she was sure it was Perizada based on the purity of the magic. Whatever it was Peri was up to, Mona had taken the wheel. She wouldn't keep it up for long because she had other matters to deal with, but she felt like it was a good way to let them know that she had not forgotten their little group, wandering lost in the woods. She was surprised to see them out of the Transylvania Alps, but oh, she had definitely not forgotten them and knew just who she would have the demons dispose of first.

She stroked Octavian's mane and felt his restlessness as he stomped his hooves on the withered grass.

"Ready for a run my old friend?" She asked the large, black steed.

Octavian replied with a snort. Mona continued to hold the storm with her mind as she climbed up onto the horse. She would make them suffer a little longer and before it was all said and done, she might just throw in for fun an ice storm.

She whispered a location to Octavian and with a smooth start he took off in a gallop. For such a large animal, his movements were graceful. Mona let her mind wander from the ride as she thought about her next move in the chess game she had created.

Octavian wasn't any normal steed. The journey to her destination, which should have taken days, lasted only the afternoon. She climbed down and left Octavian to graze on his own. She let out a breath and finally released the unyielding storm she had stolen from

Perizada's power. She let out a slow breath and shook off her slight weakness that the storm had caused.

The forest around her had grown quiet and her eyes narrowed when her skin tingled with the realization that she was being watched.

"Come out, come out, wherever you are," she sung into the air. She began to mutter a spell to reveal the unknown intruder when Ainsel the pixie king stepped from the shadows of the trees.

"What are you doing here Desdemona of the old coven?" His voice was tight with anger as he stared up at her.

Mona smiled at him as she took a seat on a rock across from him. She knew that it would make him more amiable if she didn't appear so imposing.

"I've come to tell you that I'm in need of your services once again."

The king laughed, and indignation filled his tone. "You think that I would help you, when you did not fulfill the first bargain we had? Are you mad?"

"Well, if you mean mad as in angry, then no. But, if you mean mad as in bat shit crazy, well frankly that's pretty much a given." Mona's eyes gleamed with wickedness.

The king regarded her, taking in her behavior. He wouldn't call it happy, for he could see that she could never be capable of true happiness. He decided that the closest conclusion that he could come up with was that she was giddy, like a child who had gotten into the cookie jar and not gotten caught.

Mona stared into the king's eyes as she began to chant.

I call on the magic that attempts to leave this place,
You will answer my call to give aid to this race.
You will gather at the veil and pull it wide,
You will not allow it to falter or to hide.

I call you, I gather you, to do my will,
I shape you and form you for the veil, be still.
No other can release you from my care,
It's only my desire you're allowed to bear.

Mona turned to the Pixie King, "Give me your hand."

Ainsel regarded her warily.

"Oh, for goodness sake man, I'm not going to cut it off. The spell requires your blood, a sacrifice, like any good spell."

He slowly lifted his hand to her and she snatched it. She reached into her cloak and pulled out a knife, and in one smooth motion ran it across is palm. Mona tipped his hand over and let the blood drip to the forest floor. The air around them grew thick with magic and Ainsel's eyes widened briefly at the ripple he saw appear as if a seam had been cut into the universe. He hated to give her the satisfaction of seeing his relief, but he couldn't help the wonder that he knew was painted on his face...

"There," she said, smugly. "I have opened your veil permanently. I have upheld my end of the deal."

The king wrestled inside with his anger, but also knew that if he did not help her she could destroy him and his race.

"What is it you need?" He finally asked.

She smiled triumphantly as she began to tell him. "The contact who is supposed to help me open the veil to the underworld has, so far, not delivered. I believe he might be planning to betray me. And, since you were so good at tracking down the dogs for me," she shrugged nonchalantly. "I figured you could handle this with no problem."

"Who is this contact?"

Again, Mona strived to look bored and indifferent as she picked inexistent lent from her clothes.

"Cypher," she had barely gotten the word out when the Pixie King choked.

She looked up to see his eyes were saucers and his breathing had become shallow.

"Y-y-you, want me to capture the warlock king?" He stuttered out.

Mona nodded as she stood. Ainsel took a step back as he looked up at her, his mind still reeling over the information she had just dropped on him like a ton of bricks. His shoulders felt heavy with the weight of her request.

"He will never expect you," she mounted her steed and looked down at the little king. "I don't know how long it will be until he shows himself to me, but you need to have him in your sights and be ready to take him down if I need you to."

Ainsel raised his hand to halt her. "How am I supposed to take the warlock king out exactly?"

Mona shrugged. "Be creative." And, before he could respond she was galloping off into the forest, the trees swallowing up her retreat leaving nothing behind, but the slight disturbance of the foliage she passed.

Ainsel stood there in shock, unable to process what had just happened. Desdemona had opened the veil to their world, a veil that was unstable and had been closing and opening on its own. He knew it was just a matter of time before it closed for good. Mona had sought out his help with the wolves and in return, she was to keep their veil open. Originally, she had not kept up her end of the deal and he figured that she never would. But now, she needed him again. He didn't trust her, not as far as he could throw her. He would carry out this task she had given him, and he would be watching over his shoulder for the inevitable knife that she would eventually plunge into his back.

~

Alston, highest member of the Fae council stood at the opening of the veil from their realm to the human. Nissa, Gwen, and Dain were with him. The Great Luna told them that Mona had blocked Peri from crossing, but not that *they* couldn't get through.

He held the moon stone in his hand and the weight of the responsibility that came with it settled over him like a heavy blanket. The packs had not been united in millennia. They were too volatile to bring together, and that was exactly what they were going to do. They were going to cross the veil into the human realm, and call every pack the Great Luna had created. It would be the largest gathering of super natural beings in their history.

"Alston," he heard his name spoken softly behind him from Gwen. He turned back to look at her.

"Shall we go?" She asked.

Alston let out a deep breath and as he stepped through the veil, his voice reverberated over each of them. "So be it."

They stepped out of the Veil into cold, crisp air and a canopy of tall, ancient trees towered over them. Night had fallen in the human realm and where there should have been stars in the sky, only dark clouds could be seen. The ground crunched beneath their feet from the light frost that had accumulated and the leaves of the plants shimmered like diamonds from the frozen droplets.

Walking slowly, further away from the Veil, they each turned to face one another in a circle. Alston pulled the moon stone from his pocket where he had slipped it when they'd crossed the Veil. He looked down at the small, seemingly insignificant rock, and shook his head. This stone was about to change the course of history.

He looked up to the faces of his kin, their eyes filled with determination, but shadowed by doubt. He leaned down, laid the stone on the ground in the middle of their circle, and then joined them again.

"We must wait for the moon to reveal itself from the clouds. The Great Luna indicated this night would be a full moon." His words seem to reverberate into the night and they each turned their faces up one by one.

The night grew silent and the air stilled. All of nature seemed to be holding its breath, waiting, and watching.

The four Fae watched the night sky as the clouds began to slowly part. Gradually, little by little, the moon began to shine through the opening. And, then it was there, full in all of its beauty. The clouds encircled it but it shone fully, as if it were looking down on them. Though no heat came from the moon, its light bathed them in a different kind of warmth and they knew it was from the Great Luna. The light from the moon hit the moon stone that lay on the ground and it began to glow, a soft white light at first, but quickly grew in brightness.

Alston was the first to speak as he began the ancient chant to call the Luna's children. It was a chant that had never been spoken out loud. And, one by one, they all joined in.

By the power of the moon,
It's light over all it looms,
By the radiance of the stone,

You are not your own.
We call you.

You who are strong,
You've wandered far too long,
You who lead the weak,
It is you your creator seeks.
We call you.

Your time is now, your purpose is here,
Division is gone, restoration is near,
Heed the call, baying into the night,
Make yourself ready for the fight.
We call you.
We call you.
We call you.
The Packs of the Great Luna,
WE CALL YOU.

The final words rang into the night as the four Fae lowered their hands and looked back up to the moon. The calm that had draped over the forest began to dissipate as the wind began to blow and the trees swayed in a timeless dance. Over the howl of the wind they heard her voice as clearly as if she were standing before them.

"Ready yourselves. It is done."

Nissa looked over to Alston and let out a shaky breath. "Why does that sound strangely ominous?"

It was Dain who answered. "Because, that is the only word that could possibly describe the joining of the packs."

Chapter 5

"I felt it in my soul as I stood in the cool evening air. She beckoned to me, urging me to hurry, telling me time was short. As I stared up at the moon, the moon that shouldn't be full on this night, I knew that every wolf looking up into the sky, anywhere in the world, would see a full moon. The Great Luna had sent out her call and we, her creation, were to answer it. For the pack." ~ Victor, Bulgaria Pack

"Is that what I think it is?" David, Beta of the Coldspring pack asked his Alpha as they stood on the porch of the pack headquarters.

Jeff didn't answer right away. He dwelt upon what the moon was saying to him. He didn't know how, but he knew that their creator was calling them? Finally, he looked over to his Beta. "Yes, it's the call of the moon. We're being summoned."

"What does that mean?" David asked. The Coldspring pack was a very young pack and didn't have the knowledge and history like the other packs did, especially since they had been operating under the radar when Lucas Steele had been their Alpha.

"I'm not sure exactly, but I know who does."

Jeff pulled out his phone and flipped through his contacts until he found the name he was looking for. *Vasile*. He dialed and waited for the line to connect.

It was only two rings before his call was answered.

"Hello?" A deep voice answered from the other end.

"This is Jeff Stone of the Coldspring pack and I'm calling to speak with Vasile."

There was a pause on the line, some scuffling, and then a new voice came on.

"This is Skender, I'm Vasile's fourth. Vasile is a little tied up at the moment. Is his regarding the call of the packs?" Skender asked.

Jeff let out a deep breath. "Yeah, about that, what exactly does it mean?"

"The moon stone is the way the Great Luna calls the wolves to her. We are being summoned to come."

"Come where?" Jeff asked.

"Close your eyes, Jeff Stone, of the Coldspring pack and focus." Skender's voice was deep and soft as he spoke to the Alpha.

Jeff closed his eyes and listened. He felt it deep in his soul and could hear her voice like a gentle whisper of wind against his flesh.

"Carpathian Mountains," Jeff muttered under his breath.

"Very good," Skender answered. "Your pack is young and you wouldn't have known what to do, but the others will know. If she is calling them to the Carpathian Mountains then they need permission to be in Vasile's territory, which means you will come to the pack mansion." Skender gave Jeff the information that he would need to get to the Romanian pack headquarters and then explained the rest of what it meant to be called.

"The moon stone isn't just a call to gather," Skender said. "It is a call to arms. There is a threat to her creation and she is rallying the troops, so to speak. Obviously, you can't bring your entire pack. There are twelve packs in various places around the world and to have them all together in one place, would be not be wise. So, you are to bring yourself and your top three. You may bring your mate as well, but the top three must leave their mates with your pack. This is not a vacation, Alpha." Skender's voice grew more serious. "There are things going on of which you are unaware, but you will be soon enough. Get on the first plane here. Do not waste time." There was a pause and then in a formal tone Skender spoke. "For the pack."

"For the pack," Jeff answered, automatically.

Jeff ended the call with Skender, and then looked over to his Beta and the other two at the top of his pack.

"We're going to Romania. Get packed. I'll explain on the way."

~

Denver, Colorado

Dillon stood next to his assistant Colin, along with his Beta, Lee, and his other top two wolves. Dalton, and Aidan. They were just about to board the plane when they felt it.

"Wadim said this would come," Dillon explained, softly.

Lee looked over to his Alpha; the line of his mouth was tight giving his face a severe appearance.

"We've never been called before Dillon, in fact, though we've learned about the moon stone in our history, it's never been used."

"Well, it's being used now," Aidan spoke up and though he was usually the most light hearted of Dillon's wolves, tonight, with the call of the moon and the information Dillon had shared, he was as focused and intense as his pack mates.

As their ticket numbers were called to board the plane, Dillon looked each of his wolves in their eyes, waiting as one by one they lowered them.

"Remember what I told you. We were created for such a time as this. The Great Luna needs us, our pack mates need us, the world needs us, and so we go."

They spoke as one, when they answered their Alpha.

"For the pack."

~

Vratsa Province, Bulgaria

Adrianna watched Victor pack quickly and efficiently. She felt the pull, the call of the moon stone, but Victor didn't want her to go, not after what had happened at The Gathering.

"Are you sure?" She asked for the hundredth time.

"Luna," Victor stopped his packing and walked over to his mate. "We are called and gathered as one pack for one reason."

"War," Adrianna answered. "Yes, I know that. I'm an Alpha Victor, you know I can fight."

"I don't doubt it for a second." He smiled at her and the adoration he felt for her showed in his eyes. "But, I'm taking Andrei, Sergey, and Pavel. Leaving the fourth in charge, and you are more dominant than he. I need you to stay and lead our pack. Keep them safe for us. That is what would help me the most." He took her hands in his and pulled them to his chest. "You are strong and I don't keep you here to protect you from harm. I keep you here to protect the pack."

Adrianna leaned forward and kissed her mate. Before she pulled back, she whispered against his lips. "For the pack."

~

Ramnicu-Valcea, Romania
Serbian Pack Mansion

Seraph answered his cell on the first ring.

"Seraph," his voice was clipped, as he answered.

"You are in charge of Decebel's pack as his fourth," Skender began speaking without introducing himself.

"Yes," Seraph answered though Skender hadn't been asking.

"You will need to come here. The others are on their way."

Seraph's words came out in a hushed voice. "All of them?"

"The call has been sent. Be here as soon as possible. Just you. Set up whoever is supposed to be in charge after you and let them know what is going on."

"For the pack." Seraph spoke without thinking, before ending the call.

~

"They're *all* coming." Wadim stood next to Skender, peering out into the crisp spring afternoon. Winter continued to hang on like a claw, refusing to relent to Spring, whose time had already come.

"They should begin arriving with in a few days," Skender answered.

"What the hell are we going to do if Vasile and the others aren't back by then?"

Skender looked over at the historian, and longtime friend. He chuckled briefly at the shirt Wadim wore, it said: *Save a garden, eat a rabbit.* Then the smile faded as his eyes met Wadim's.

"We fight." Skender's words reverberated in the quiet room. "And we have to assume they won't be. We must prepare for the worst."

"For the pack." Wadim answered.

Chapter 6

"I dreamed I was running. I was trying to find you. Searching. Every time I got near you, you were gone. I was growing so tired and my breathing was labored, but still I ran. I called out your name but you didn't look back. I started to fall, but you weren't there to catch me." ~ Jacque

"You must wake up." Jacque knew that voice. It was so familiar to her and yet foreign at the same time.

"Jacquelyn, you must wake up."

The voice was growing more insistent, pushing into her mind, trying to force its will on her. She wasn't ready to wake up. The world was in chaos, her mate was gone, and her friends were broken by their loss, why on earth would she want to wake up?

"Because they need you love, I need you."

"You need me?" She asked the voice.

It was a male voice and it sounded strange, like he was straining under a great weight.

"Who are you?" She finally asked.

"I am yours," he answered, through gritted teeth.

She tried to think. She'd heard those words before. Her mind was a whirl wind of images and words all jumbled up like a bowl of alphabet soup. Nothing made sense.

"Luna," the growl in his voice, brought the barrage of thoughts to a halt. "I am Fane, your mate. I have been captured. You are under a spell and you must fight it! I can feel you slipping away. I think that is the only reason that I am able to block this horrid place. My wolf and I can feel us losing you. You must not succumb. Fight Jacquelyn. Fight!"

"Mate? Fane?" Her voice sounded small in her mind. The words brought forth images now of only one. A tall, dark haired, powerful male with the bluest eyes she had ever seen. In her mind's eye, she could see adoration, when he looked at her, and felt the love when he kissed her. This was her mate, her Fane.

She reached for him again with her mind, but all she found was emptiness. A profound sense of loss slammed into her and she tried to cry out, but nothing would emerge from her useless vocal chords. *Fight*, he had said, *fight the spell*. Jacque didn't know how to fight the spell, didn't understand, so she started to think of anything real and tangible, things that she knew were true. She thought of her mother and how it had been so long since she had seen or even spoken to her. She thought of her two best friends and all the things they had endured together. She thought of her pack, her new family, and the acceptance she felt with them. Then she thought of Fane, her other half. He was her home. Without him, nothing else had meaning. She let the thoughts bring the emotions and she let the emotions flow throughout her body. She didn't know if it would work, but she wouldn't give up. She would fight, for herself, her friends, and for Fane.

~

It was dark when the storm finally stopped. Peri stepped out from under the overhang of rock and looked up into the now, clear sky. Mona had been in that storm. There was no doubt about it. Peri had lost control of the storm. No, the storm had been wrestled from her control. They were only alive for one reason. Mona wanted them alive for now. She looked back, as the other ladies began to climb out from their protected spot and saw that they all seemed all right. They were a little soggy, but alive and well. All but Jacque, who continued to lie still and quiet.

"Are you going to tell us why you've been leading us in circles for days?" Alina asked Peri, as she wrung out her hair, splattering water on her already soaked feet.

"So you noticed?" Peri's brow rose as she watched the Alpha female.

"I have a nose Peri. It wasn't hard to catch our scent as we kept coming back to the same places." Alina looked around at the others. "I'm just surprised no one else noticed."

"My mind has been a little preoccupied," Jen spoke up. The others grumbled Jen's sentiment as they staggered wearily to lean against the forest trees.

"Well it's about to get un-preoccupied," Peri motioned for them to follow. "Let's get a fire going and get dry and warm. I have crap to tell you and you aren't going to want to be all soggy for it."

"Does anyone ever want to be soggy while getting information?" Crina asked.

A collective groan rippled through them as Jen spoke.

"I can think of several scenarios where being soggy while obtaining vital information can be a very fun activity."

"You walked into that one," Cynthia told Crina.

Crina snorted out a sharp laugh. "I'm too tired to think about Jen and having to filter all of my statements right now."

They gathered around the fire that Peri had conjured up with her Fae mojo, as Jen referred to it, and slowly began to thaw and dry out. They ate Fae bread and sat quietly staring into the dancing flames of the fire. Sometime later, Peri began to speak.

"If my plan goes like I hope it will, then this time tomorrow we should have your males back in our care," she announced to the group. Heads flew up, eyes widened impossibly so, mouths hung open, and there was stunned silence before the bombardment of questions started at a quick-fire pace.

Peri held up her hands to silence them.

"I'm going to explain, good grief, keep your panties on." Peri waited until they had all stopped blurting out questions. Alina gave her a pointed look that said get on with it or I'll eat you for breakfast, so she got on with it.

"I'm taking us to the troll who guards the bridge to the In-Between. I have a bargaining chip for him."

"A troll?" Rachel asked, softly. "Last I remember trolls where not the most friendly of beings even on their best day."

Peri nodded. "That is true, but you forget healer, trolls are greedy. Shiny things easily sway them. The trick is in the wording. I can't just say we want to go in to the In-Between because then he will not let us out. I can't just say that we want to go in and out, because then he would not let us bring anyone back with us."

"Jen is practically Johnny Cochrane when it pertains to loop holes. Just run it by her and she can tell you if it's fool proof." Sally eyed Jen across the fire. Jen gave a slight smile to her friend, but that's all she could muster.

"So what happens if the troll goes for it?" Cynthia asked.

"The simple part is he opens the veil and we go through."

"What's the hard part," Elle asked, dryly.

"Making it out alive with the males."

"Oh, is that all?" Crina quipped.

"You guys are just one big bowl of rainbows and butterfly soup," Peri snapped.

"Okay wait," Jen raised her hand to Peri. "I just have to know, how the hell would you get rainbows and butterflies in a bowl. If you did, who the crap would want to suck down some butterfly guts?" She shrugged her shoulders. "And who is Johnny Cochrane?" She asked Sally.

Sally and Crina both tried to muffle their laughter at Jen's comments, but failed miserably.

"Go on and let it out," Peri told them as she crossed her arms. "If you try to hold those laughs in your mouth any longer their liable to come out your ass."

That comment broke the peace and they were all laughing. It was the kind of laugh that started in their toes and radiated up their bodies until they were writhing around like they had bees swarming inside. They laughed until tears flowed from their eyes and their stomachs throbbed with the effort from it. Peri stood there watching them, wondering how in the world any of them even dressed themselves in the morning.

"Are you finished?" She asked once the laughing had trickled down to a few random giggles.

"Wait," Jen cautioned, and looked around as if expecting something then looked back at Peri. "I think we're good."

"As I was saying, the In-Between is dangerous, not because things will attack you, but because your mind becomes your enemy." She began to walk slowly around the outer ring of their circle as she spoke. "We must get in quickly, and I don't care if you have to sing the sound track to *Greatest Love Songs of the Century* a hundred times to keep your mind focused, then do it. If you have to shout as loud as you can over and over that you are real and your mind is lying then by all means shout. But, you must not give in to the thoughts."

"If the guys can't even do that, how do you expect us to be able to?" Elle asked.

"The males have been sent there. We are going of our own will. There is a big difference. Because we aren't going there as a form of punishment, it will not affect us the same way. It will be a much weaker disruption in our minds, but it will still be there. It will dig in deep, rooting out your darkest fears, so you might as well face them now. I want you to close your eyes and picture what your worst nightmare might be. Make it real to yourself, breathe it in, feel it on your skin, bask in the heat of the fear it erupts in you. Once you have it in your mind, imagine yourself facing it and winning. Imagine standing up to that fear and telling it to...."

"Go suck it?" Jen added, helpfully.

"If that's the terminology that gets the job done, Jennifer, then by all means, tell it to suck it until hell freezes over. The point is to face the fears that are going to be thrown at you, face them, and defeat them because the greatest fears are the ones your mind creates. Those are the only fears that can truly have power over you. Don't let them."

They all sat in silence, their eyes closed and their minds twisting and turning, taking them on turbulent rides through the terror that lie deep inside each of them. Peri watched as their faces changed and morphed as they went through the process of dealing with their fear.

One by one, they opened their eyes. Sally squinted against the brightness of the flames from the fire. She felt as if a weight had been lifted from her shoulders. She had pictured her greatest fear, had stared it straight in the face, and she had not fallen before it. That was her triumph. It was still there, simmering in the dark, but she had faced it, and it had not broken her. She wouldn't let it. Not now, and not when they entered the In-Between.

Everyone finally settled down to get some sleep. Like every night, they took turns taking watch. Sally's eyes drifted closed and she hoped that she would speak with Costin again. She hoped that she could tell him that tomorrow she would hold him in her arms. But, it wasn't Costin she dreamed of. To her surprise, it was Jacque.

"Jacque?" Sally took a step towards her friend. They stood in the forest near a fire much like the one Sally had been sitting at before sleep.

"I'm fighting Sally. I'm fighting, but I need help." Jacques words were laced with desperation and she looked tired, as if she hadn't slept in weeks.

"What are you fighting Jacque?" Sally asked. "I've tried to help you but I can't get through."

"I'm pushing against the spell," responded Jacque. I'm thinking of everything I can to bring myself back to our world. Fane told me to fight, that you all needed me. Please Sally, help me."

Sally closed the space between them and wrapped Jacque in her arms. She couldn't believe how real the embrace felt. Maybe her mind was just that desperate to have her friend back. She felt tears gather in her eyes as Jacque squeezed her closer.

"I've been so alone," Jacque's words were muffled as she pressed her face into her friends shoulder.

"We've been with you this whole time," Sally tried to reassure her.

"I know. I can hear you, I just haven't been able to move or respond. It's like something has wrapped itself around my brain or something."

"I will get Rachel and we will see if we can help you, okay? We won't let you stay like this Jac, you need to know that."

Jacque pulled back from their embrace and collected herself. A slow smile stretched across her face.

"You had better get me awake. I hear that we're going in to rescue our men."

Sally nodded with a smile of her own.

"Jen hasn't started using military lingo just yet, but I figure it's coming."

Jacque gave Sally one last nod, as if to say: *let's do this*. And then, Sally felt the dream fading, slowly morphing into another dream... one that she would never forget.

Lying around the circle, one by one each woman slipped into her own dream. The Great Luna was blessing them, helping them bolster their wills. They each got to meet with their mates. Brief that it was, they were able to tell them to hold on, that they were coming for them very soon. Tears streaked down their faces as their fleeting moments of time with their men slipped away.

Morning came much too quickly and the chill crept into their bones, drawing them to consciousness. The females were solemn and even Jen was more subdued than ever. But, a sense of urgency, which seemed to grow with every second, danced at the edges of their nerves. They gathered their few belongings, ate some Fae bread, and every now, and then smiled encouragingly to one another.

It was Jen's singing that finally broke the silence as the words to *Leaving on a Jet Plane*–Jen style of course, rang out into the gradually lightening forest.

All our crap is packed, we're ready to go,
We're standing here moving too slow,
I hate to tell you all to get in gear.

But the dawn is breakin', it's early morn,
The troll is waiting, he's scratching his horn,
If you going any slower I will die

If you kiss me I'll kick your ass,
Shove you into the grass,
Let's just get the show on the road

'Cause we're leaving, coming or not,
Can't leave our men left to rot.
O'Crap, we need to go.

By the time Jen was finished with her rendition of the song, the urgency was still there, but instead of the solemnness as its company, now hope had taken root.

"I don't know how you do it," Peri said, shaking her head.

"It's simple," Jen told her. "You just pick a song and go with it. I believe my versions are always better than the originals."

"That's just because you use explicit words in yours and questionable content," Sally chuckled.

"That is definitely a bonus."

They were all finally packed and ready to go. They stood staring at each other, and steeling themselves for what was to come.

"I have another song for this moment, shall I share?" Jen asked.

A collective, "NO," rang out among them.

Jen held her hands up in surrender, muttering under her breath. "Good grief. Let a prego chick down gently."

The group had just begun walking when they heard a small whimper coming from the direction Jacque occupied. They all froze, waiting in rapt silence to hear it again. After a few moments, they heard what sounded like another whimper. Sally and Rachel were the first to reach Jacque's side, and they both instantly laid their hands on her. They closed their eyes and tried, like they had so many times before, to push through the shield that was keeping them out of Jacque's mind. But, there was no resistance this time. They slipped right in and what they saw amazed them. They saw a cage with a writhing, living darkness trapped inside. It was as if Jacque had pushed the evil from her mind and locked it up. Sally and Rachel called to her, drawing her back from the place where her wolf had taken her to protect her. Slowly, they felt her coming to consciousness until finally she opened her eyes.

Jacque looked up at eight pair of eyes staring, hopefully, down at her. She drew in a painful breath, her lungs stretching under the amount of air filling them. She blinked to clear her blurred vision and attempted to use her voice, which had lain dormant for so long.

"Hi," she croaked.

Silence.

Then the inevitability, that was Jen, broke in. "That's all you have for us, hi? Really Jac, we've been lugging your butt around for more than a week and all you can say is *hi*."

Jacque smiled up at her friend and her eyes sparkled. "I missed you too Jen."

Jen winked at her. "Well, you woke up just in time. We have a black ops assignment and you need to start pulling your weight."

"And, so the military lingo begins," Crina muttered.

Peri pushed around Jen so she could examine Jacque more closely. Rachel and Sally continued to try and expel the evil that was still inside Jacque's mind, although it was contained. They chanted in a language the others did not know and pushed with the magic drawn from the nature around them. Peri laid her hand on Sally's shoulder and shared her own magic with the healers and it was enough. Jacque's eyes closed and she let out a breath that seemed to have been frozen in her lungs. She felt the evil dissipate and the murkiness that had been filling her insides fade away.

She started to stand, but was stopped when Peri put a hand on her shoulder.

"Hold on there, wonder woman. Take a few minutes to get your bearings."

She handed Jacque some Fae bread and a bottle of water. Jacque looked at the bottle and grinned. "Where exactly did you get a bottle of Aquafina water?"

Peri shrugged. "I have my ways."

Jacque gulped the water, allowing it to wet her dry throat and cottony mouth. She could feel it following the path of her esophagus. It was cool and refreshing and helped her body rejoin the living. She took a bite of the Fae bread and remembered that it was supposed to give them energy that they would not otherwise possess on their own. Within minutes, she felt its effects. Finally, she stood, her legs a bit shaky, and her muscles stiff from disuse. She grinned as she watched all of her friends hold out their arms, waiting to catch her if she fell. The symbolism in that thought was profound and hit her like a herd of elephants. These women, her pack, and friends, had been there for her when she *had* fallen. They had caught her and eased her to the ground instead of letting her fall to her demise. They had cared for her, wept over her, talked with her even when they thought she couldn't hear. Yes, she thought as she looked at their eager faces, outstretched arms, that they would always catch her.

She waved them off. "I don't need eight mother hens cramping my style."

Reluctantly, they backed up and gave her some room to move. She took a couple hesitant steps forward and when she didn't fall over, took a few more. She stretched up on her toes, reaching her arms up in the air feeling her muscles resist against the motions. She felt good, better than good. She felt ready to get her mate back.

Peri saw the fire beginning to emerge in Jacque's eyes and knew what was coming. She held up her hand to stop the inevitable. "Let's give it a little while, let you get used to moving and being conscious again. You won't be any good to us if you just fall over while we're in that hell hole."

Jen stepped forward and held up her hand. "I'd like to point out that if she just fell over like a fainting goat, for one second I'd laugh. That's all."

"Thanks for the positive thoughts, Jen," Jacque said, dryly.

"I'm always there for you babe." Jen grinned.

Jacque's eyes met Peri's and there was a fire that lit them burning with unwavering determination. "We aren't going to wait any longer, Peri. They have been in that place for long enough. My mate is not going to rot in that terrible place, because I'm some pansy that can't pull it together after being asleep for a few days."

"When you put it like that you sound pretty awesome," Sally pointed out.

"Well, I *am* awesome, dammit," Jacque stomped her foot.

Jen threw her arms up in the air. "That's it, people, decision made. Jacque has stomped her foot. If she can cuss and stomp her foot at the same time, I say she's ready to barge through the gates of hell."

Peri looked over to Alina. "You okay with this?"

Alina looked her daughter in-law over. She saw nothing by a will of steel. "She's going with or without us."

Peri nodded. "That's what I was afraid of." With a huff, she waved for them to follow. "Well, hold on to your butts, it's about to get messy."

"Jurassic Park," Sally, Jen, and Jacque all yelled out at once at Peri's movie quote.

Peri looked back at them and shook her head. "I think your parents must have dropped you guys on your heads five times too many."

"My mom claims it was only three," Jen walked alongside her two best friends, finally feeling a little bit more like herself. "But, I swear it was four because I remember this one time…"

Jacque slapped her hand over Jen's mouth, and the others let out a collective sigh.

Crina smiled at Jacque. "It's good to have you back."

"You're telling me that no one has been censoring this beast?" She motioned towards Jen.

"She's quite dangerous these days. We all wanted to keep our clothes dry and our hair on our heads." Sally said in defense.

Jen growled low, her wolf getting agitated along with her. "I'm standing right here you know."

"Actually you're walking," Jacque dodged the hand that reached out to smack the back of her head and laughed along with the others.

They walked, nearly two miles before Peri finally stopped. She turned around and held a finger to her lips. Motioning for them to come closer, she quickly glanced back over her shoulder before beginning to speak. Her voice was so low that they had to lean forward to hear.

"The bridge is just beyond those bushes. The troll is there and has very good hearing and a very good sense of smell. We are down wind at the moment so we should be safe. I'm going to approach him first. You all just sit tight and try not to screw this up."

Elle raised a single brow at Peri and narrowed her eyes. "How about *you*, try not to screw this up." Peri quietly clucked her tongue as her fellow Fae. "Come now Elle, you mustn't hold a grudge about the past."

Elle's face relaxed as she shook her head. She had learned long ago that arguing with Perizada was a futile endeavor.

With a final warning finger like a mother to a child, Peri turned and disappeared from view to face the troll.

"How long do we give her before we make our move?" Crina asked.

"There's no need to worry," Elle said, dryly.

"Why not?" Sally asked.

"That troll has nothing on Peri. The only reason she's going about it this way is to keep the balance of magic right. Going around blasting everyone into oblivion just because you can does not mean that you should."

A thoughtful look came over Jen as she listened to the Fae. "When did you get so Yoda-ish on us?"

"I have no idea what that means, but if it means I freaking rock, then I'd say always."

Their attention went back to the bushes where Peri had gone through and they waited. The opening to where their mates were suffering was most likely less than fifty feet away. Sally looked around at the girls and could tell it was taking everything in them not to just take off at a run. She too felt the urgency, but she steeled herself to wait. Wait for the exact moment when Peri gave them the go ahead, wait for the moment when she would enter the In-Between and possibly lose herself to its evil influence, wait for the moment when she would see Costin for the first time in what felt like months, even though it had only been a couple of weeks. Waiting seemed to be the theme of her life at the moment and if she were honest, she would say that it was a theme that sucked eggs. She smiled to herself at her thoughts because for a moment she felt the inner-Jen and realized she hadn't had many of those moments lately. Sally liked to think that it was because she no longer needed inner-Jen, she was becoming exactly who she needed to be, exactly who they all needed her to be. It was time to let go of inner-Jen and embrace Sally, the gypsy healer, and mate to Costin. As she stood there, enduring the waiting, she absolutely loathed, and in that moment, she found the strength in herself that she had always turned to her inner-Jen for. It had been there all along. It had just taken trials, experiences, loss, anger, love, joy, and life to uncover it. And now, Sally, with her new found strength, was going to storm the gates of hell. *Okay, not all by myself,* she thought, *but it's a start.*

Chapter 7

"There is often a moment in life where you feel like you have run out of options. You think and think, trying to pull something from nowhere, but still no possibilities jump out and smack you in the face. It is in those moments that I would like to think that the best in me comes out. I shine in all my calm glory and levelheadedness and others bask in my controlled state. If that ever happens, I'll let you know... don't hold your breath." ~Lilly

Cypher, Lilly, and Cyn had been on the run from the draheim for nearly two days. They had taken cover in a cave after running through the freezing cold river to cover their scent. It had been nearly six hours since they had heard the beast fly over again, undoubtedly searching for its prey.

"You think we lost it," Lilly asked, Cypher?

His jaw was tense and the crinkles around his eyes deepened as worry, anger, and resolve all fought for a spot on his face. He had finally built them a fire and they were beginning to get dry and warm. As the cold dissipated from Lilly and her teeth no longer chattered, her mind began to work again.

Cypher looked over at her and his face relaxed a tiny bit. She smiled at him. He opened his arms to her and she went without thought. They were alive, uneaten, and that warranted a moment to process what had happened and what better way to do that than in the arms of a big, handsome, warlock? He pulled her close against his chest and she felt his warmth seeping into her. She relaxed and found relief in the knowledge that he would protect her. She could let herself just *be* for a few moments, completely trusting that he wouldn't let anything happen to her.

Finally, after several quiet moments spent rubbing her back and kissing her hair, he spoke.

"I have a responsibility to take care of the draheim. It can't be allowed to stay in this realm. It's too dangerous."

Lilly nodded. "I kind of figured that much. What do we do next?"

Cypher smiled. "I like it when you say *we*."

Lilly blushed and he ran a finger along her warm cheek. "I like it when I make you blush as well." Lilly didn't stop him when he leaned forward and kissed her. She didn't think about how awkward Cyn must feel having her and Cypher make out like two teenagers. All she could think about was how good the kiss was, how soft his lips were, and when they parted, how incredible he tasted. Her arms wrapped around his neck and he pulled her closer. The kiss lasted longer than Cypher had intended, but then he could never get enough of Lilly. He could kiss her every day, all day, and it still, wouldn't be enough. He would still crave her as he did now.

Lilly was breathless when they pulled apart and she knew that she was blushing furiously as the heat danced on her face. "You aren't supposed to be wooing me Casanova; you're supposed to be telling me the kick ass plan to take out the big, bad dragon."

"Sometimes a man just needs to kiss his woman, little one. And, right then there was nothing more that I needed than to feel your lips on mine."

His words made her heart beat faster and she felt the truth behind them clear to her toes. *Good grief Lilly, you're a grown woman, not some love sick teenager,* she told herself, but then added, *that means I get to do grown woman things right?* She smiled at the pun that she totally intended. Then she wanted to mentally slap herself for letting her mind even step a toe in that direction of thinking. Cypher must have noticed.

"What's going on in that beautiful head of yours?" He asked, with a wicked grin.

Lilly frowned. "Nothing you need to worry about. Now, what's the plan?"

Cypher's face changed in the blink of an eye from playful to utterly serious as if a light switched had been flicked inside his head. He knew the only way to kill the beast was with the arrow or sword forged by an elf. The problem? It had been a very, very, long time since he had seen an elf in the human realm.

"Before we were attacked, a second time I might add, you mentioned elves," Lilly prompted, then looked over at Cyn for confirmation. Cyn nodded.

Cypher let out a resigned sigh, stood up, and set Lilly back down in his spot. He thought better if he was standing and able to move. His brain just seemed to clear when he could move about freely.

"The elves are a very secretive race. They hold all of their knowledge close to their hearts, and for good reason. They may not be as powerful as the Fae, but they come close. They are also able to produce many things with their magic that no other race can. One such thing is the magical properties in the metal of their weapons. An elf blade, or arrow, or weapon of any metal for that matter, can kill anything."

Lilly's eyes widened. "Anything?"

Cypher nodded. "And some of us are very hard to kill."

"Which is why they hold their secrets close," Lilly's voice softened as she spoke her thoughts aloud. "If the wrong person, or supernatural, got their hands on the knowledge to make a weapon that could kill any and all of you, it could be disastrous."

Cyn finally spoke for the first time since they had stopped running. "It is imperative that Mona never gain this knowledge."

Lilly nodded and said in a wry tone. "That's sort of a given." She looked up at Cypher with raised eye brows.

"So how do we find the elves?"

"We don't," Cypher answered, ominously. "They find us."

"Well, that may not be entirely true," said Cyn. "I can find a veil to their land," she offered.

Cypher turned to look at the Fae. "How?"

Cyn shrugged nonchalantly. "I have a friend that is an elf."

"Can you contact this friend somehow?" Lilly asked.

Cyn shook her head. "Once we enter their realm we still could only find them if they wanted to be found."

Lilly stood and brushed the dirt off the rear of her pants, straitened her shirt and tightened her pony tail. "Alright then, we don't have time to sit around and watch the leaves blow."

Cypher looked over at his mate and his lips tilted up slightly. "Does anybody just sit and watch leaves blow?"

Lilly snorted. "People in little bitty towns in Texas will sit and watch paint dry as long as there is food to eat and company to eat it with, which really if you have company there is always food involved, oh and sweet tea. Never forget the sweet tea, that's like forgetting to put your pants on in the south."

Cyn frowned. "And you think we are strange?"

"No, I think you are strange—er, I never said, humans didn't have our fair share of strangeness."

Cypher took Lilly's hand in his and nodded for Cyn to lead the way. "I like your weirdness," Cypher whispered.

Lilly grinned up at him. "Are you trying to get brownie points?"

Cypher chuckled. "Little one, I don't need brownie points to get what I want from you."

Lilly's heart stopped in her chest at the insinuation in his voice. She didn't dare look up at him because then he would see the desire in her eyes, and know that he was indeed correct. The man was too yummy for his own good and the only thing he would need with brownies would be to, *STOP that thought right there Lilly Pierce* she admonished herself, then grinned because in spite of her age, and no matter what she said, she was completely smitten…and with a warlock King no less.

Cyn walked at a brisk pace through the Balkan Mountains. The closest veil into Othea, the realm of the elves, was deep in the Carpathian Mountains along the Frumoasa river.

She didn't have a clue as to how Thalion would react to them entering his realm, but at this point, there was too much going on to really worry about offending him. Although, she supposed you should always worry about offending people who made weapons that could kill anything. They were going to have to get some modern transportation if they wanted to get there quickly.

"We're going to have to go into Ruse to get something to drive," Cyn called over her shoulder.

"Wait," Lilly said, holding her hand up as she stopped. "You know how to drive?" She looked up at Cypher.

He rolled his eyes in exasperation. "Why, do you think we've been living in caves, grunting, and using animal bladders for water containers? We change with the times Lilly, we adapt. If we did not we would never make it in this world."

Lilly realized that she was making them feel like they weren't smart enough to learn new things and she felt like an ass. She looked at Cyn and then Cypher. "I'm sorry. I guess I thought that since you live in the mountains away from civilization that you couldn't possibly know about technology."

"We stay hidden, because it would become very suspicious to humans when they began to notice that we do not age."

"Good point," Lilly agreed. "Okay Cyn, lead on. Let's go get some wheels."

Cyn continued on at a more brisk pace.

Cypher didn't have any trouble keeping up, whereas Lilly was pumping her legs as quickly as she could without actually running.

"Why do you talk like that?" Cypher asked.

"Like what?" Lilly asked, her words sounding airy from her heavy breathing.

"Wheels?" Cypher's brow rose.

Lilly laughed and it too sounded winded. "I have a teenage daughter," she frowned, "well *had* a teenage daughter. It's hard, not to pick up on her lingo."

Cypher thought about that for a moment. "So she talks very differently from you then?"

"It's like a whole other language," Lilly told him, shaking her head. After that Lilly fell silent, not because she didn't have anything to say, but because she barely had enough air in her lungs to keep her feet moving, much less joke around with Cypher.

After what seemed like days of walking at a brutal pace, the trio walked out of the forest and onto a street in a place Lilly assumed must be Ruse. They jogged across an empty street, unnecessarily, as appeared that the road was used very seldom, and then passed behind a cluster of buildings. Cyn led them through an alley in between the buildings and when they stepped out of the alley Lilly's breath caught at the dichotomy spread before her. Directly in front of her lay, the quaintest village Lilly had ever seen. But, instead of horse drawn carriages, which would have appeared much more natural, there were a smattering of late model vehicles parked here and there along the sides of the street. The earth tone colored buildings were constructed very close together and sported high, pointed roofs. Most were adorned with inviting front porches containing flickering lanterns, which hung on the walls next to the doors. It appeared to be a very old town, and Lilly felt as if she had been thrown back in time. People meandered along the street, stopping to talk to one another or frequent one of the many adorable shops lining the street. Lilly soon realized that each of the shops served an important function; a butcher, a seamstress, a general store. *No Old Navy's here,* she thought.

Cypher took her hand and they turned left on the street and began walking. Lilly noticed Cyn peering into each vehicle they passed. They stopped in front of a brown sedan that was pulling up to the curb. Lilly watched as Cyn approached the car as the driver stepped out. Cyn began speaking animatedly to the man and though Lilly could not hear the words, she guessed that Cyn was attempting to talk the man into allowing them to borrow his car.

Lilly looked up at Cypher and saw that he wasn't watching Cyn, but the street around them. He scanned the area disguising his actions as if he was just admiring the buildings. He managed to keep from looking like he was searching for a crazy witch so evil that curling up next to a starved lion sounded more appealing than being in the same room with her.

She squeezed his hand to get his attention and he paused his pursuit. "What's Cyn telling that man?" Lilly nodded in the direction of the Fae in question.

Cypher's lips quirked. "She's just convincing the man of why it is such a good idea to let us borrow his car."

"Convincing?" Lilly's eyes narrowed.

"Cyn's just using a little Fae magic to influence the man. We will get his car back to him Lilly. We aren't thieves."

Lilly's brow rose. "So says the warlock king who made a deal with the devil."

Cypher glowered at her. "You know, I'm not going to help her?"

"Yes, I know," Lilly, told him as she squeezed his hand in reassurance.

Finally, Cyn looked back and waved them over.

Twenty minutes later they had put some miles between themselves and Ruse, and some poor man that was sitting at home thinking his car was getting repaired and would be returned as soon as it was in a safely operable condition.

Cypher drove in silence as he tried to contemplate the ramifications of what they were getting ready to do. He had never considered that he would one day have a human mate. And, now that he did, he was beginning to realize just how dangerous the match would be for her. He glanced at her from the corner of his eye as she sat in the passenger seat. Instead of eagerly watching the sights and sounds of a country she had never seen, her eyes were focused on the road ahead and he would bet his life that her mind was focused on the coming trial. Pride swelled in his chest as he thanked the Fates that they had given him such a strong mate, a mate who was willing to do what was necessary.

Lilly felt Cypher's eyes on her. She looked over at him and met his yellow eyed stare. Her breath caught briefly as she took in his inhuman beauty. She had to admit that if she was going to be married to someone, she could do much, much, much worse. She smiled at him and then went back to staring at the road ahead and trying not worry about Jacque, trusting that Fane and his pack would take care of her. She missed her daughter with an ache only a mother would understand. She knew if she wanted to see Jacque again, then they had to do the things necessary to keep the world, as they know it, safe. If they didn't succeed in stopping Desdemona, the repercussions would be devastating.

Lilly didn't know how long it had been since they had last stopped for a bathroom break, which under her current circumstances she did not want to discuss, when Cypher pulled over on the side of the road. He parked the car as far off the road as he could without driving into the forest. He climbed out of the car without ceremony and Lilly scrambled to join him. Cyn moved so quietly that Lilly hadn't noticed the Fae exiting the car. Cyn pointed up into the forest. "We are going to have to hike up there. We need to move quickly, but we must be wary as we get closer to their veil."

Cypher nodded and looked down at Lilly. "Are you ready?"

Lilly took a deep breath and let it out with puffed cheeks, the air blowing the wisps of hair around her face. "Cypher, sweetie, no one is ever ready for this kind of thing." She patted him on the back and walked passed him, following Cyn as she started off.

~

"What brings you to me Perizada, high Fae, friend of the pack, teacher to the healers?" The troll's voice was deep and gravely, as if he's spent a millennia smoking Pall Malls.

"Thurlok, bridge master, gate keeper," Peri gave the troll a slight nod; not because he deserved her respect, but because it never hurt to flatter the one you needed to bargain with. She stepped around so that he and the bushes, which the others hid behind, were in sight.

"I've come to make an exchange," said Peri with deliberate slowness. Trolls were not the smartest of creatures on a good day, and Thurlok had been stationed at the bridge for a very long time. She imagined his brain might be a bit sluggish from lack of use.

"A bargain?" He asked eagerly as his hands rubbed together and his eyes widened like a greedy child in a candy store. Peri nodded and he grew impatient. "Come now, female, what is it?"

Peri was purposefully peaking his interest, leveraging the troll's natural appetite to possess things of great power or value.

"First, I will tell you what it is that I want in exchange for what I will offer."

Thurlok motioned with his gnarled hand to get on with it.

"I, and eight companions, would like passage into and out of the In-Between. Upon our exit, we will be bringing back prisoners who were unjustly captured. Nine will go in and seventeen will come out. We will be unharmed as we enter; I fully understand you are powerless to protect us once we enter. Upon our exit, we will remain unharmed. You will not share the knowledge of us ever being here or of the identity of the individuals being rescued." Peri went over the request in her mind to ensure that she did not leave any loopholes that the troll might use to his advantage.

Thurlok's stared at Peri, his overlarge eyes growing even bigger. In his time as the guard of this waypoint, few beings ever requested to go in voluntarily and he certainly hadn't had anyone be rescued on his watch. He knew of the ones she spoke of, the males that Desdemona had cast into the In-Between. He also knew that if they got out somehow, she would be out for blood, and it would probably be his blood she would seek first.

"That is a very dangerous request," he responded calmly, trying not to show her just how curious he was. "What do you have that is of such great worth that I would give up the witch's prisoners?"

"Something one such as you could never imagine, ever even laying eyes on." She paused dramatically before she spoke. "A stone of the Fae," she finally said.

If Thurlok's eyes were wide before, now Peri was certain they were going to pop out of his head. She was right to say that he would only ever dream of laying eyes on the stones, very few ever did, no matter the length of their lives.

Peri watched the troll closely. His thoughts flickered on his face. She could tell he was examining the situation from every angle, trying his best to determine if she was trying to trick him somehow. Her plan hinged on his lack of knowledge of the stones; very few understood how they actually worked, or the purpose behind them. She waited patiently, not wanting to appear too eager and stir Thurlok's suspicion.

"Do you think he's going to hurt himself thinking that hard?" Jen whispered, as she and the other females watched from the cover of foliage.

"It's quite possible his head might explode," Sally answered.

"That would suck, seeing as how we need him to let us into that hell," Jacque added.

"Okay, can I just ask; is that what you thought a troll would look like?" Jen asked no one in particular as she watched Peri talk to the short male with dark skin, a tuft of white hair on his head and small pointed ears. His eyes were large and black, but his face was otherwise unremarkable. His nose was not large or small; his lips were neither plump nor thin. His body was bulky and he seemed to stand a little crooked. He wore brown pants with suspenders and no shirt. His chest was bare and his belly round and plump. He didn't wear any shoes and didn't seem bothered by the rough ground.

"What did you expect them to look like?" Crina asked.

Jen shrugged. "I don't know. More troll-ish maybe."

"Troll-ish?" Cynthia snorted, with her brow raised.

"Yeah, you know, less human," Sally agreed.

"You guys watch too many movies," Cynthia told them.

"You can only have so much sex you know," remarked Jen, nonchalantly.

Jacque looked over at Jen and wiped a hand across her forehead, "Whew, so glad you said that. I was beginning to think that being pregnant might have curbed your pension for mentioning sex at the most inappropriate times."

"I'm a little out of practice. Dec is my inspiration for inappropriate sexual comments. When we get him back I'm going to have to make sure to make up for lost time."

"Well, we eagerly await all the witty comments that you are storing in that wicked mind of yours," said Alina.

And, though Jen couldn't quite decide if the Alpha was being sarcastic or not, she added, "Never fear, I will not disappoint."

"Of that we have no doubt," Crina muttered with a sly smile.

As they continued to watch the stalled exchange between Peri and the troll, they all muttered a collective *about time* when the troll finally spoke up.

"You have a deal Perizada of the Fae." Thurlok made a motion with his hand and suddenly a dagger appeared. He held out his left hand and sliced open his palm. A thick line of bright red blood oozed from the cut as he held out the dagger to Peri. She took the dagger and, without hesitation, sliced her own palm. She held out her hand to his and he took it in a firm handshake. As their hands clasped, Peri spoke clearly into the quiet forest.

"Blood of yours, blood of mine,
The truths I speak now entwined.
All we've said shall come to be,
Or death to you and death to me.
The ties that bind can't be undone,
Not by many, not by one.
Fulfill this bargain from me to you,
Then it will be finished and finally through.

They both watched as the magic wrapped around their clutched hands, and then around them, digging deeply into their bodies. As suddenly as it had begun, it was over.

Peri stepped back and made a motion with her right hand. As if on cue, the other women emerged from the forest. Thurlok took a step back, but caught himself. Backing away from a predator only encouraged it to chase. The eight other females stood beside Peri and stared at him.

"Are you expecting me to do a trick or something?" He snapped at them.

"Now, now, Thurlok," Peri crooned. "Play nice. The she-wolves and healers won't hurt you."

Someone cleared their throat and Peri glanced over at Elle who was staring at her.

"What?" Peri asked, shaking her head, her voice rising in exasperation. "I can't guarantee what you will do. You pink haired fairies are always unpredictable."

Jen started to speak, but stopped when Sally stepped around Peri, directly in front of the troll.

Peri laid a hand on Sally's shoulder stopping her from speaking. She leaned forward and whispered into her ear.

"I know you are ready to get to your male, but it is never wise to offend the one who holds the cards."

Sally's shoulders stiffened, but she gave a curt nod to let Peri know she understood.

Peri motioned towards the bridge as she looked at Thurlok. "We've made our bargain troll. Open the veil."

Thurlok spoke in an unusual language as he drew symbols in the air. His eyes closed as his voice rose and the air around him swirled.

Sally and the others stood transfixed as they watched the veil to the In-Between appear. Suddenly where a bridge and trees had been there was a cavernous opening with stairs disappearing into the darkness beyond it.

"The veil will remain open for 2 hours." Thurlok told them.

Anger flashed in Peri's eyes as she realized she had missed a very important detail. Time.

"Is that going to be enough time?" Sally asked.

"Yes," Alina spoke from Sally's right.

"How do you know?"

"Because there is no other option."

"We're wasting time," Jen hollered as she headed towards the veil at a jog.

The stairs leading down into the In-Between were narrow and only allowed for them to be single file. Peri had moved Jen out of the way and taken point, and, as usual, Alina pulled up the rear. The stairs were clearly visible but Sally couldn't figure out what was emitting the light that illuminated them. The walls around them were made of gray stone and felt warm to her fingers as she pressed against it for balance. She followed behind Jacque and, like the others, her eyes constantly moved, watching for danger. Her skin tingled and she felt the magic inside of her welling up, like a charged battery waiting to be plugged into something. As they descended further down the stairs, the air began to grow thick and warm. Sally felt the hair on the back of her neck begin to stick to her as sweat began dampen her skin. She glanced back over her shoulder to Elle and saw that she too was sweating. Elle gave her a small smile and wiped her forehead with the back of her hand.

Finally, the stairs ended. One by one, they each took the final step, emerging into a wide hallway. They all stood restlessly shifting from one foot to the other. The need to move, to take some sort of action was palpable among them. Peri closed her eyes, her lips moved as she murmured. A few moments later, her eyes snapped open and she pointed to the right.

"That way," she said curtly and began walking. Peri felt the undeniable urgency to hurry, the knowledge of their limited amount of time, foreboding, in the back of her mind.

They hadn't been walking for longer than two minutes when Jen suddenly stopped. Her eyes were unfocused as she looked down the hallway and her breathing had become labored.

Cynthia stepped up beside her and laid a hand on her shoulder. "Jen," Cynthia spoke her name softly, trying not to startle her. "Are you alright?"

Jen's hand went to her abdomen as she gasped. Her blue eyes widened and a sob broke from her chest. "Tell me it's not real," she whispered.

Sally stood directly in front of Jen and placed her hands on either side of her face. She closed her eyes and reached into Jens mind. She felt the darkness before she saw it, a swirl of black evil surrounding Jen's mind. And, in the center of that darkness was Decebel. Sally's eyes opened and her head jerked back.

"It's Decebel's mind that she's seeing and his emotions that she is feeling," Sally told them.

"We must be getting close to them if the bond is beginning to open up without any help from the mates," said Peri. Again, she felt the sense of urgency. Behind that urgency was something just out of her grasp, something more than their ever shortening allotment of time. But, when she tried to pinpoint her fear, it would scurry away and all that was left was the part of her urging her forward. *Move fast Peri. Can't stop. Have to hurry*, her mind told her. Even as they stood looking at Jen, Peri knew they should be moving.

"Jen," Sally patted her friends face. "It's not real honey. It's what Decebel is seeing. Come on Jennifer, pull it together."

Jen squeezed her eyes closed, but then quickly opened them as the images burst forth even more strongly across the back of her eyelids. She nodded and patted Sally's hand that was still against her face. "I'm alright gypsy lady." She took several deep breaths attempting to push away the panic attack that was brimming up inside her.

"Ladies, you need to be on your guard. Your minds are your enemy in this place. Your mates are going to be broadcasting and you mustn't react to the things you might see or…" Peri's words were cut off by an ear piercing howl and it was joined by another, and another, and still more until the walls shook from the noise.

Without thought Sally took off at a dead run. She knew that howl, knew it like she knew her own voice. She felt the pain radiating in the sound, felt the hopelessness and the loss. Something inside her reached out for the wolf she claimed as hers. *"Costin,"* she called his name through the bond that had opened when the howl came. *"I'm here. I'm coming for you."* Another howl, another lash of pain that took Sally's breath away as she ran. She heard heavy breathing beside her and saw that Jacque and Jen were on either side of her running just as hard and with just as much determination in their eyes. There were footsteps and heavy breathing behind them and Sally knew that the other women were right on their heels. She had no clue where she was going, but she knew it was the right direction.

Jacque pushed her legs as hard as she could. The air brushed her face and the hot air brought no relief from the heat. Her lungs burned with the effort to take in more oxygen as her muscles cried out in need. She ignored the pain, and thought of only one thing, *get to Fane*. He was on the verge of losing control of his wolf. Peri had warned them that it could happen and Jacque knew if she didn't get to him very, very soon it would be too late.

"Jennifer," Jen heard the desperation in Decebel's voice, it was a sound that she never wanted to hear again, because she knew what he was seeing, and it nearly broke her. *"Decebel, hold on a little longer babe. We're almost there."* She could feel the confusion in his mind. He didn't know what to believe, or what the lie was? What was illusion and what was real? She pumped her arms faster and called on the speed of her wolf. He needed her; she had to get to him.

"STOP!" Perizada's voice reverberated off the walls. The hallway that had been filled with howls, heavy breathing, and stomping feet, was suddenly silent.

"Look at me," Peri's voice was a command and slowly, one by one, they turned to look at the Fae. Alina's eyes glowed dangerously at the one who would keep her from her mate and she took a menacing step forward.

"Do not do something you will regret Alpha," Peri's eyes met Alina's briefly, and then looked back at the group.

"What are your greatest fears right this moment?" She asked them.

"Can't we have this little discussion after we have the guys back?" Jen growled.

"NO!" Peri snarled back. "We will have it now. What is your greatest fear?"

"We aren't going to make it in time," Sally whispered as she met the Fae's eyes. "We're going to be too late. Their wolves are taking over."

Heads nodded as the others agreed with Sally.

"Exactly," Peri smiled at Sally as if she were her star pupil. "Now, what did I tell you about this place? It uses your biggest fear. You think that you hear your wolves howling for you and instead of stopping for a moment and thinking you take off like a bunch of yahoo's running to who knows where into who knows what."

"What are we supposed to do?" Alina growled, her eyes still glowed in anger.

"Use your bonds. Jen just proved that they are fully operational, so suck it up, and accept that what you are going to feel and see from your mates is going to be unpleasant, but it will tell you if what you are hearing is real. Your fears had you running towards a noise that was only in your mind and you would have continued to run, never going anywhere because your fear is that you won't make it in time."

Sally's hand slapped over her mouth as a gasp escaped and her eyes widened. The realization hit Jacque, Crina, Elle, and the others.

"We would have run forever," Crina muttered.

Peri nodded. "Until there were no more shoes left on your feet. Now, the worst part," Peri motioned to their right. "What do you see?"

This time the gasps rippled through all eight of them as they saw the steps, they had descended only a short time ago.

Chapter 8

"I felt arms surround me and wetness on my face. I looked up into brown eyes brimming with tears. Her lips were moving, but I couldn't hear anything. My wolf stirred, begging for release. He could save us from the anguish. But, the beautiful brown eyes stared into mine and the urgency in them had me holding off the phase. I narrowed my eyes trying to hear what she was saying, trying to understand why this *Sally was so different from the other, the one I couldn't save. I knew I couldn't endure one more moment of seeing my mate suffer, so I closed my eyes to the crying Sally and called on my wolf."* ~ Costin

"The stairs," said Alina shaking her head. "How is that possible, we were running, I felt my legs moving, the wind on my face," her speech grew more urgent with every word. "I know I was moving."

"We started walking when we got down here and you pointed in that direction Peri," Cynthia pointed out.

Peri nodded. "We thought we did. Our minds were telling us we were moving because our fear is to not make it in time. I couldn't figure it out at first, but I knew I needed to hurry. I didn't bother to examine why I all of the sudden knew we just had to go, without thinking about a plan or anything. It was this place, using my fear against me." She let out a deep breath and shook her head.

"The mind is a very powerful tool," she said, solemnly. "And, in this place it is your enemy."

"So if we can't trust our minds," Elle prompted.

"Trust your instincts," finished Peri.

"My mind is screaming at me to run," Sally said as she stared down the hallway she thought she had been running down, "in that direction," she pointed.

"Crina, use your nose," Peri told her. "What does that direction smell like?"

Crina closed her eyes and took a deep breath. She let her wolf out enough to use her senses, to break down the mixture of smells into individual scents.

"I smell," she paused, "nothing."

"Good, now what about that way?" Peri nodded.

This time all of the wolves took in deep breaths. Jen spoke first. "Decebel." She started to move, but Rachel grabbed her arm.

"Wait," Rachel said calmly. Jen looked at the healer and then at the others. She could see the realization on each of their faces. Their mates were close. Very close.

"Now," Peri said as she looked at them, her voice that of a teacher instructing her class, "follow what you know is a fact."

"Our mate's scents are that way," Jen announced. "Does everyone else agree? Because, I really don't want to run standing in place again thinking I'm getting somewhere like a dumb ass only to find out I'm in the exact same place I started."

Jacque nodded. "I hear you, and yes, our mates are that way."

Alina took the lead and they began walking briskly. Every so often Alina would stop and take a deep breath. The other wolves would follow suit while Elle and Sally tried hard to ignore the irritation building, because they needed to hurry, they weren't moving fast enough.

"Sally, stop." Jen's words wrapped around Sally like a steel band and held her in place. She hadn't even realized that she had turned and was walking away from the group. Her mouth dropped open and her eyes widened.

"I didn't realize," Sally began.

"You can't smell Costin. You don't have anything to go on, but what your mind is telling you," Peri explained. "You are going to have to trust your friends, your pack mates."

Sally nodded, but didn't say anything else.

"Peri, something is not right," Alina looked back at the Fae.

"What do you mean?" Peri asked.

Alina pointed and they all turned to see that, once again, the stairs were mere feet from them.

Jen threw her hands up in the air. "You have got to be kidding me!" She growled in frustration.

Peri's eyes narrowed as she stared at the stairs. Why weren't they getting anywhere? She had pointed out their fear. They were aware of it and not allowing it to dictate their actions, so why weren't they making any progress. Her head snapped over to Jacque.

"When you came down those stairs, what were your biggest worries?"

Jacque answered, without hesitation. "That we wouldn't find them in time."

Peri pointed at Rachel waiting for her to answer the same question.

"I'm afraid that two hours wouldn't be enough time to find them and get them out." Rachel told her.

Peri smacked herself on the forehead, as she realized her mistake.

"Finding them," she said, "not only are we afraid that we won't make it in time, we're afraid that we won't be able to find them."

"Bloody hell," Sally murmured.

"Our own fears have been keeping us right here?" Cynthia asked, with raised eyebrows.

"Picture your mates, ladies," Peri instructed as she walked over and stood on the bottom step so she was a tad taller than the rest. "Cynthia, make yourself useful, since you have no mate to picture, and sing."

Cynthia's eyes narrowed. "You want me to sing?"

"Did I stutter?" Peri snapped.

"Can I ask how singing will help?"

"It will keep them grounded on what's real. Give them an anchor so to speak."

Cynthia didn't say anything more, but thought for a brief moment and then started to sing.

I have seen what man can do,
When the evil lives inside of you.
Many are the weak,
And the strong are few.

Her voice carried as she sang, filling the room with a deep, rich music that reached into each of them.

Peri spoke over Cynthia's singing, but made a motion to Cynthia to keep singing. So she did.

"Picture your mates, think of how they smell, look, and sound. Focus on details no matter how small. What color are his eyes? What does his hair look like when the sun hits it and light touches the individual strands? What does his skin feel like under your fingers? What does your mate's scent smell like to you and how does it make you feel? Put all your energy into remembering them, every detail."

Sally let Peri's voice draw her in and she pictured Costin. His hazel eyes sparkling with mischief and his lips turned up in a playful smile. She pictured his dimple that always made her heart beat faster and heard the laughter that usually accompanied it. She pictured him standing before her with his hands on her hips, as they had been when he had been teaching her how to bartend. She pictured his lips moving towards hers and she remembered how he had smelled, how his scent had called to her. It called to her now. Her eyes had drifted closed as she thought about her mate, but when the scent of him hit her nose, they immediately snapped open.

Sally's eyes widened as she look around the room where she stood. She hadn't moved from where she was standing, but the room she was in now was dark and made of earth. All the other females were with her, but there were more than just them. Kneeling on the dirt floor mere feet from each other were their mates. All oblivious to one another, each locked in their own misery.

Her head turned to the right slowly and the breath was wrenched from her lungs when she saw Costin. He was leaning over and looked like he was stroking something, but there was nothing in front of him. Sally ran to him and knelt down next to him.

"Costin," she whispered his name, as she brushed the hair from his face. "Costin, sweetie, it's Sally." His head turned slowly and his eyes locked on hers. His eyes were wild and desperate. He looked back down to the spot where he had been staring and then back at her. He was trying to decide something. She placed her hand on his face and reached out to see what he was seeing. She bit her lip to keep from crying out as she saw her body lying before him; naked, broken, bloody. She jerked away from the image and met his eyes.

"I'm real Costin. *I'm* real." She took his hand and placed it on her chest so he could feel her heart beat. "Feel," she told him. "I'm your Sally, the real Sally. I'm whole, unharmed."

Costin was staring at the hand she had placed against her chest. His eyes narrowed in concentration, his jaw clenched, and his breathing became shallow. After several minutes, he leaned forward and laid his head where his hand had been. He listened to her heart and felt it's beating against his face. He turned his face so that his nose was against her and then he slid his face higher until his face was against the bare skin of her collar bone. He took a deep breath and let out a low growl. His wolf stirred and though the man didn't want to believe that this was his Sally, the wolf refused to let him turn away. *Mine,* his wolf snarled. Costin's arms wrapped around Sally and pulled her tightly to him. She gasped at the sudden movement, but then wrapped her arms around him and returned his embrace.

"Sally," he whispered, his voice was rough and she felt his words rumble in his chest.

"It's really me, Costin. I'm real. I know you don't know what to believe, but I'm real."

Costin pulled back and looked at her. He reached up, brushed away a tear from her cheek, and felt the wetness against his skin. Then he leaned forward and pressed his lips to hers. There was no hesitation from Sally. She returned his kiss wholeheartedly. She kissed him as though her life depended on it. Costin felt Sally's lips mold to his, and then part when his tongue pressed against them. Her taste hit him hard and he ended the kiss abruptly pulling back to look in her eyes.

"It's you?" he asked, almost afraid to hope.

"Yes." She smiled and it lit up the darkness that had been surrounding him for so long.

"Can you stand?" She asked him. "We need to get out of here. We only have a limited amount of time."

"How are we going to find the others," he asked her as he let her help him to his feet.

"They're right here," she pointed to the other males around them, now being attended to by their mates.

Costin's eyes widened as he saw how close he had been to Decebel, Adam, Fane, Vasile, Gavril, Sorin, and Drake. It had only been mere feet between them.

"They'd been right here all along?" He looked on as the other males began to stand to their feet and the same realization hit them.

Decebel's wolf was so close to taking over. He was fighting it, but he didn't think he could watch his mate scream for another second. He was on the verge of phasing when he felt a warm hand caress his neck.

"Dec," the voice was small, hesitant, not anything, like he was used to hearing from her. He looked up and his eyes met his mate's. She wasn't screaming or writhing in pain. She wasn't swollen with their baby, and she wasn't bleeding in childbirth. She was whole, healthy, and beautiful, standing before him. She knelt down in front of him and tilted her head to the side. A low growl rumbled up from his chest as he saw his bite mark on her neck. He reached for her and she willingly went into his arms. He closed his eyes and ran his nose along her jaw line and down behind her ear.

"Mine," he told her as he pulled her closer.

"Yes, I'm yours," she agreed.

Decebel waited, dreading the moment when she would be ripped from his arms and he would have to watch all over again as their baby died, or his mate was raped, or tortured by an unnamed foe. He held her tighter, praying that it would be over, that he wouldn't have to live through any of it any longer.

"Baby," Jen groaned, "kind of squeezing too tight."

Decebel loosened his hold a little and when she started to squirm, he let out a growl.

"Not yet," he snarled. "I'm not ready to lose you again. Please just one more minute, let me hold you, please Jennifer."

Jen stilled her movements as she heard the pain in his voice. She realized that he didn't know she was really here. He thought she was still just his imagination and that he was going to have to watch those horrible things she had seen in his mind.

"Decebel, it's really me." She put both her hands on his face and held him away so he had to look her in the eyes. "I'm real. I'm not going to be tortured or raped. I'm here to get you out of this hellhole."

He continued to stare at her and Jen could see that he was trying to decide what to believe. She could see that he wanted to have hope, to believe that it was her. But, he was so scared that it was an illusion, a cruel trick by Desdemona.

She leaned forward slowly so as not to startle him and pressed her lips to his. Jen meant for it to be a small kiss, just to reassure him, but it had been so long and he smelled so, so good. She ran her tongue along the seam of his lips and when he groaned she smiled victoriously as his lips parted and he deepened the kiss. Jen wrapped her arms around his neck and let him pull her against him. She didn't want to stop, didn't want to put even an inch of space between them, but they needed to hurry. She pulled back and looked at him. She patted his face and smiled. "You with me?"

"It's really you? You're really here?" Decebel asked, as he gripped her hair in one hand and pulled her closer to him with the other.

"Look around babe," Jen told him.

Decebel slowly turned his head and his eyes widened as he saw the others. He stood abruptly, still holding Jen in his arms. She was really here with him.

"Decebel, put me down," Jen told him as she patted his shoulder.

Decebel shook his head. "No. If I put you, down it might not be real and I'm not ready to face that. I can't lose you. I can't watch you hurt any longer."

"I'm real baby," she pulled his face to look at her. "I'm real and I'm not going anywhere."

He nodded. "Okay, if you're not going anywhere then there's no reason I can't hold you."

Jen rolled her eyes. "Fine, hold me. Wear yourself out lugging my fat pregnant butt around, see if I care."

"Glad we're on the same page," Decebel told her and pulled her tighter to him.

"You're really not going to put me down are you?" She asked him after several moments.

Decebel shook his head as he continued to watch the others pull themselves together, gradually realizing one by one that their mates had come. They had said they would, and now they were here, to take them back from the grips of hell.

"Fane, please look at me." Jacque pleaded with her mate. He was kneeling on the ground while low growls emitted from him. His body shook under her hands as she gently rubbed his back. His sweat soaked shirt stuck to him and Jacque tried to give him some relief by pulling the shirt away from his skin.

"Fane, dammit, I said look at me," Jacque snarled.

Fane's head rose slightly at the command in her voice and his lip showed sharp white fangs. His eyes glowed blue and Jacque saw that Fane's wolf was very close to the surface. Seizing the opportunity, she grabbed his face while it was upturned and held his stare.

"Fane, it's me, Jacquelyn."

Fane's eyes narrowed and he took a deep breath, leaning closer to her to catch her scent. Cotton candy and snow hit his senses and nearly knocked him over. He howled loudly and the others joined in with him.

"Mate," his voice was guttural as he spoke. He reached up and caressed her face longingly. When he ran a finger along her lips Jacque opened her mouth and nipped his finger playfully with her teeth. As he started to reach for her, a voice behind him had him jumping to his feet, shoving Jacque behind him as he snarled.

Peri stood with her hands in the air as she looked at Fane.

"Peace, Fane, I mean no harm," she told him, calmly.

Fane looked at her, and then for the first time noticed all the commotion going on around him. He backed up further, pushing Jacque back until her back hit the wall. His wolf was urging him to protect her, to keep anyone from coming near her and hurting her. His eyes shifted wildly from person to person, all of them a possible threat to what was his.

"His wolf is in control," a deep voice came from the left.

Fane's head whipped around to meet the eyes of his Alpha and father. He knew him, but that didn't matter. Down here, nothing could be trusted, his wolf reminded him. He lifted a lip in a snarl at Vasile.

"Fane," Vasile's voice rumbled and Fane felt the push in it. "We aren't going to hurt her. You need to get control of your wolf."

Fane felt a small hand on his back and then and arm slipped around his waist from behind.

"Fane, come back to me love." He heard Jacquelyn's voice in his mind and something in him broke.

He turned around crushed her to him.

"I thought I'd lost you," he told her. *"I thought I'd never hold you again."*

"I'm here," she told him, out loud. "I'm here and we have to go."

Fane pulled back and looked down at her. He caressed her cheek and leaned down, kissing her gently.

"Don't leave my side."

His glowing eyes told her what his soft voice didn't. Fane was still not fully in control.

He turned back to face everyone and held Jacque's hand tightly in his own. He met his father's gaze and exposed his throat to his Alpha quickly, before watching everyone with weary eyes.

Peri gave them all a few more minutes as the couples continued to stand and look at her. Cynthia had taken over getting Drake to his feet since he did not have a mate. Peri found it odd that they didn't embrace each other, or ask each other if they were all right. But, as she watched each of the males eyeing one another, she realized that they didn't trust each other. They didn't trust that this was real, that the women that they each held close were genuine. Their minds were trying to come to terms with the notion that the mates, solid and whole in their arms, were not going to be ripped from them and tortured

Though she knew that they needed more time to come to terms with reality, she couldn't give them time. They needed to get the hell out of dodge and they needed to do it yesterday.

"Okay all you lovely, people," Peri's voice rose so that everyone could hear her. "As much as I would like to give you all time to process this, you are going to have to put on your big girl panties and just trust that your mates are here to save your assess and go with it. We don't have time to do a twelve step program, so pull yourselves together long enough to get out of here."

"Man I missed you," Adam said from across the room with a sly smile, one arm wrapped around Crina as he smiled at Peri. The smile was real and the words as sarcastic as ever, but there was still something off in his eyes.

"Yes, yes, I know. You want to pledge your undying love for me, yada, yada," she said, dryly, "Let's get moving people. Cynthia, start singing again, please, and maybe make it a happier tune so that we don't all want to shoot ourselves." Peri headed towards the stairs. She motioned for Vasile and Alina to come over.

"Alpha," she bowed her head slightly to him. "It's good to see you. Now, if you would be so kind as to lead your people out of here. Keep your wits about you. Listen to Cynthia's voice and don't think about your worries. If you have to, take a note from Jen's book and think about sex."

"I heard that," Jen hollered. Peri ignored her.

Vasile took Alina's hand and began to lead her up the stairs. He cleared his mind of any worries or fears. He only thought of the rich sound coming from Cynthia and the feel of his mate's, hand in his.

Peri directed each of them up the stairs, telling them each over and over to think only of Cynthia's voice. Peri was the last to begin the climb up the stairs and she herself focused on the doctor's voice pushing away the fears that were attempting to flood her mind. She refused to give them even a fraction of her attention.

When she reached the top of the stairs she stopped when she saw that everyone was standing there staring at where the opening should be.

"What the hell, Peri," Jen snarled.

"Has it been over two hours already?" Elle asked.

Peri reached out her hand and placed it on the wall. She closed her eyes as she concentrated.

"That sniveling little weasel," she spat at the wall. "It hasn't been over two hours. Our friendly, neighborhood troll thinks to trap *me*, Perizada of the Fae."

Adam laughed as he shook his head. "They never learn." He said to no one in particular.

Peri's eyes narrowed as she stared at the place her hand had just been. She spoke in a low voice, a beautiful language that rolled off her tongue. Her eyes gleamed and she began to glow as magic pulsed from her body. Suddenly the wall burst open and Thurlok stumbled back on the other side. Vasile and Alina were the first to pass through, and then the others followed. Once they were all out, Peri stepped through the veil, and let it close behind her. She stood looking down at Thurlok.

"You thought to trick me?"

Thurlok pushed himself to his feet clumsily. "I knew you could get out, Peri," he told her nervously. "I had to close it in case someone came by. It would look awfully suspicious should someone come by and see the veil just sitting open."

Peri watched him as a hawk would watch a mouse. He fidgeted under her stare as he waited for her response.

"I will let you live only because the blood oath was not broken." Peri turned to look at Vasile and Alina. "We need to go, now."

She took off at a brisk jog and trusted the others to follow.

"What about the stone?" Thurlok yelled.

"Check your pocket you dimwit," Peri yelled back, but didn't turn to see if he listened to her.

Peri and Elle got a fire started as the others grabbed logs to sit on. The camp was quiet and somber. They had run late into the night and were all exhausted.

Cynthia walked over to Peri and pulled her to the side.

"Why does that seem like it was a little too easy?" Cynthia said, squinting her eyes.

Peri let out a breath and pinched the bridge of her nose. "Rescuing them from the In-Between was never my real worry," she admitted.

Cynthia waited for her to go on. Peri looked over her shoulder at the group as she spoke.

"That was the easy part; the hard part will be keeping the males from killing anyone."

Cynthia's eyes narrowed. Peri motioned for Cynthia to look and so she did.

Decebel sat with Jen in his lap, her head on his shoulder. She was talking to him softly while his eyes shifted from person to person, narrowing and glowing amber. His shoulders were tense and he looked poised to attack, even though his mate was in his arms.

Costin sat with his back against a tree and Sally in between his legs, with her back to his chest. He held her tight and Cynthia watched as every so often he would kiss her hair or gently brush his finger along her cheek. But his eyes never left those around him. He never looked down at her, but instead watched each person carefully. She looked at each male and saw as they held their mates the distrust in their eyes as they steadily watched one another.

Cynthia looked back at Peri who was watching her expectantly.

"Now you see?" She asked her.

Cynthia nodded. "We would never be able to stop a fight if it were to break out among them."

Peri shook her head. "Not with these dominants."

"What do we do?" Cynthia asked.

"We're going to have to first make them aware of their behavior. So, that they might think before they act on instinct."

"And second?" Cynthia prompted.

"Second," Peri breathed, "hope against hope that no one does anything stupid."

"Then we're done for," Cynthia told her.

"Pretty much," Peri agreed.

Chapter 9

"If, when you find out that out the largest number of werewolves to ever gather in history are coming to your town, your first thought is, *did I pee on everything I want to keep*, then you might be a werewolf… or you have an over active imagination and an unhealthy fixation on the Calvin and Hobbes stickers portraying Calvin peeing on, well, everything. Choose your poison." ~ Jen.

Skender stood in the library of the Romanian pack's mansion staring out onto the lawn. Rows of cars lined the drive as, one by one pack Alpha's, and their top wolves arrived. It had been three days since the call went out and already six of the eleven other packs had arrived. The Alpha's from Bulgaria, Hungary, Poland, Ireland, Spain and Italy, plus their top three, were each currently in residence at the mansion. Only half of who would be coming had arrived and already things were tense.

He ran a hand through his hair and let out a low growl as his frustration and agitation grew. He was fourth in his pack. Dominant? Yes, but not dominant enough to prevent a war between any would be enemy Alpha's. Where the hell was Vasile? It had been weeks since he and the others had set out and though he knew through pack bonds that Vasile was still alive, that was all he knew. Before three days ago, Skender had just thought that it was taking Vasile longer than he anticipated discovering Desdemona's plan. But, then the call had gone out and that was when Skender realized that something had happened to Vasile and the others. For the Great Luna to send out a call to all her wolves it had to be bad.

A knock on the door pulled him from his thoughts. "Enter," he answered the knock.

Wadim walked in and without regard to formality, threw himself onto the large sofa in the middle of the library. He tilted his head back and closed his eyes as he let out a frustrated groan.

"We are never going to survive this," he told Skender. "I mean, it's not a matter of if the world will be destroyed. It's a matter of *who* will destroy it and *when* it is destroyed; a hell bent, bat shit crazy witch, ooorr, a pack of Alpha werewolves in a pissing contest?"

"Please tell me that's a figure of speech, and that there aren't really pissing contests going on," Skender growled. "We just got new carpet."

Wadim laughed. "Unfortunately, no. There are no real pissing contests going on, however, Radim, Beta to the Poland pack did have the bright idea to share with Seraph what a shame he thought it was for him that he came from a pack where the Alpha betrayed his own kind."

Skender rubbed his face with his hands as he shook his head. "Is either one of them dead?"

"No, and no blood was shed either. The Poland Alpha, Artur, has a good head on his shoulders and put his Beta in his place quickly and publicly. That seemed to smooth any rising hackles."

"Have you heard from the Great Luna again?" Skender asked.

Wadim shook his head. "No, but I'm thinking it might not be a bad idea to see if we get in contact with the Fae council. If my records are correct, and they always are, then the Fae would have been the ones to send out the call."

"Do you think they are going to finally step out of their safe little bubble and help?" asked Skender.

"The Great Luna set the plan in motion to force them into helping when she made us compatible mates with them, so yeah, I think they are finally going to get off their butts."

Skender stood staring down at the pack historian as he thought about the idea of being mated to a Fae. It seemed a very strange idea to be mated to one not of their own race. But, then again, he had been waiting to find his mate for so long and the darkness was creeping deeper inside of him. If his mate were a Fae, then he'd take her in a heartbeat.

"So what's the plan, Skender?" Wadim raised his brow at him.

"I think the next step will be to meet with all the Alpha's once they arrive."

Just then, the doors to the library flew open and in strode Dillon Jacobs.

"What the hell is going on and why are we just now hearing about the demise of mankind?" His eyes were glowing and his power filled the room. Dillon was pissed and unless they could get him calmed down, there was a good possibility that heads were going to roll.

~

Skender stood at the front of the large gathering room and briefly met the eyes of each Alpha. The ten packs from other countries and cities had finally all arrived and with the Romanian pack and Serbian pack already present, that made twelve. All under one roof and they were antsy. The tension among the dominants was tangible and had a human been present, it would have choked them.

"I've been on this earth longer than I care to admit and never in that time have we received the call from the Great Luna. Why now?" Drayden, of the Canadian pack, asked.

Wadim took a step forward and began to explain all that had happened from the Gathering until now. He condensed it as much as possible, but made sure not to leave out any vital details. As his story continued on, with every word, the Alpha's grew more and more tense.

"Why are we just now hearing of this witch that poses such a threat to us all?" Angus, Alpha of the Ireland pack spoke up.

There was a rumble of agreement across the room and Wadim fought the urge to back up a step. Unless he wanted to be chased, he knew better than to back away from these predators.

"You all know Vasile." Skender stepped forward, taking the pressure off of the less dominant historian. "He cares more deeply for our race than we can imagine. He was trying to prevent a war, and trying to prevent us all from having to be brought together, considering what might happen between our packs. He was not attempting to keep you in the dark, because he wanted to leave you defenseless. If we hadn't allowed the dominance in us to drive wedges between us, it might not have come to this. If Desdemona had thought that she had to contend with our entire race and not just a single pack, she might not have pursued this ridiculous plan."

"Are you saying that this is our fault?" Angus growled, with glowing eyes.

Skender held up his hands plaintively and dropped his eyes.

"No, I'm not saying that at all. I'm saying this is a pack problem. It's all our faults. Whether we like it or not, we are all pack. We may come from different countries, we may speak different, languages and live different lives, but we are all from the same Maker, all of the same blood and that makes us pack. Pack stands together, fights together, and is bound together." The silence following Skender's words was soul piercing as the Alpha's heard, not just listened, but heard what he was saying. If they understood nothing else, they understood the importance of pack. Wolves were not lone creatures. They depended on one another and they needed one another.

Dillon stepped forward and waited for Skender to invite him to stand before the Alphas. Skender gave a slight nod and stepped to the side.

"We might as well put aside petty rivalry and territorial posturing," he told them. "We all know we are going to stay and fight no matter the consequences. I personally think that the first step would be learning to fight together, as one pack. We need to know how each of us fights, how we move, and what our individual pack strategies are so that we can be effective when we go to battle." Dillon watched and waited for a response from the pack.

Slowly faces morphed into looks of determination and nods were given.

Dillon clapped his hands together and rubbed them slowly. "Great," he turned back to look at Skender. "Where's a good place to do combat training?"

Skender let a slow smile spread across his face as he motioned for the Alpha's to follow him.

"We have a gym and outdoor grounds we use for our battle training."

Skender lead them into the large gym and turned to face the group.

"There is only one rule in this gym. Respect your opponent."

"I think it might be wise to add just one more rule," Victor spoke up. "Don't kill your opponent."

"Good call," Wadim said with a low chuckle. "It would be a damn shame if the last thing I ever documented for our race was that we were dumb enough to kill each other before the witch got a chance to."

~

Thurlok stared at the stone in his hand as a wicked smile crossed his face. He considered the power that he now held and thought how foolish Perizada was to give one such as him an object this powerful. He frowned at the thought. He knew Perizada, knew her to be an intelligent foe. It didn't make sense that she would barter such a treasure. And, just as he began to wonder what the catch could possibly be, his palm was suddenly empty. A snarl emitted from his chest as he glanced quickly around him. He knew that it was gone, but that didn't keep him from searching all around the bridge. After several minutes of looking, he finally stopped and closed his eyes. He had been tricked. He did not like being tricked and raged boiled up inside of him as he thought about what a fool he had been to trust the Fae.

"PERIZADA!" He yelled into the night. "You will be sorry," he promised the emptiness between panting breaths. He would not let her get away with her treachery. He, who had guarded the entrance to the In-Between for so long, would not allow the insult to go unanswered.

~

Peri felt Thurlok's rage through the blood bond. She hadn't known how long the stone would stay in his possession. The Fae stones had a mind of their own and tended to turn up where and when they were needed. She had not worried that he would be able to use the power from the stone, because she knew that he would not have it for very long. She also knew that his wrath would be swift and that he would respond rashly because of it. She would need to be on alert, though she knew that his power was nothing compared to her own.

Costin hadn't been able to stop touching Sally for even the briefest time since she had found him and he knew that it was probably driving her insane, but he was fighting his wolf every second to keep from grabbing her and fleeing to a safe place. He knew that no such place existed, but his wolf didn't care. He felt they were vulnerable with so many dominant wolves so close to his mate, his fragile, human mate. He knew that his emotions were running on overdrive with all the memories of what he had endured in the In-Between and he didn't know how long they would remain open wounds.

"Stop," Sally's soft voice penetrated his thoughts as she gently turned his face to look at her. "I'm not annoyed by your touch. I'm not irritated, nor do I feel smothered, so please quit entertaining those thoughts." She met his hazel eyes and saw the raw emotion swirling in their depths.

"Being here is driving me insane, Sally," he told her, honestly.

Sally nodded. "I know, but in case you hadn't noticed, it's driving the others crazy as well. Truly, you are more of a threat to each other than to us females. You all are so consumed with the thought of one of us being hurt that you don't realize that there really is no threat."

Costin pulled her onto his lap and kissed her neck. "There is no reasoning with me or my wolf, love, not right now."

Sally rubbed his back gently and let out a slow breath. "Okay," then repeated, softly, "okay."

The morning light began to penetrate through the trees as the wolves and the Fae began to stir. Jacque looked around and as she saw the gaunt and tired faces of the males, she knew that none of them had slept. They were on edge and distrustful of one another and it broke her heart. They may have made it out of the In-Between alive, but they had not emerged unscathed.

"Hey," she felt Fane's breath on her neck and fought the urge to climb into his arms, pushing away everything else but him. "You alright?"

She leaned back against his chest as his arms came around her. He pulled her tight against him and she felt his chest rumble with satisfaction at his mate's eagerness to be close to him.

"Yeah, I am just worried about all of you." She turned her face up to look at him and the slight glow in his blue eyes called to her wolf. She wanted to be alone with her mate, needed to feel his strength surround her and submerge herself in his scent.

"If you don't stop that line of thinking I'm going to drag you off into the forest and throw my gentlemanly ways to the curb," Fane growled in her ear.

Jacque shivered at his words and blushed as she saw his thoughts. She slapped his hands that rested on her stomach. "Behave."

"You first," he parried.

She turned in his arms and looked up into his handsome face. His skin was lined with worry and fatigue and still he was the most beautiful thing she had ever seen.

"I'm so glad you're okay," she whispered to him.

His eyes softened and he leaned down and pressed a gentle kiss to her lips.

"Because of you," he murmured them.

His hands began to slide down her back and just before they reached her butt, she pulled them back up. Her eyes widened in surprise. "Feeling bold?"

He growled at her. "Mine."

"Yes," she nodded, "but now is not the time."

Fane stepped back and grabbed her hand. He began to pull her towards the semi-privacy of the forest. "I can make it the time." His voice was low and laced with the desire she could feel radiating from him.

Jacque pulled against his hold and he stopped instinctively at her struggle. He looked back at her as his eye narrowed.

"Fane, you know I want you. You can feel it just as I can feel it coming from you, but we are in danger and need to get back to the mansion."

"Do you have any idea what I have been watching for the past weeks?" His words rang in her mind as he took slow, measured step towards her, stalking her.

"I can't begin to imagine what you have been through, and I know that you need to know I'm okay, that we're okay."

"YOU DON'T KNOW!"

Jacque flinched at the snarl in her mind and the rage behind his words. She knew he was hurting, knew he felt out of control and for that reason she let the disrespect he had just shown her pass. He loomed over her as his body trembled with pent up hurt, anger, desire, and love for the woman standing before him.

"I'm the only one who has the right to touch you. I'm the only one who has the privilege of protecting you. I'm the only one who should know you, and I know it wasn't real, I know it in here," he beat his hand on his chest over his heart. *"But in here,"* he tapped his head, *"in here I keep seeing someone else's hands on you. Sometimes forced, and sometimes invited."*

Jacque gasped as a hand flew to her mouth. She had never considered that he might fear her actually turning to another, cheating on him, allowing another near her. So he hadn't only watched someone force themselves on her, Fane had watched her invite another to her bed. Her stomach rolled with nausea as she saw his thoughts, saw what he had watched. She turned and ran for the forest barely making it before she began to wretch. The thought of someone else was horrendous; actually seeing herself in the arms of another was too much. She finally understood his need to claim her. In his mind, they needed to consummate their bond again.

Tears streamed down her face as she heaved. Sobs pushed themselves up through her throat and she collapsed to her knees. She shook with revulsion and tried to push the images away. The worst part was the faces of those she had willingly taken; the two men who had taken her, one who had scarred her body and her soul. Trent, the human male she had dated, but never allowed to touch her in such a way. And worst of all, males of her pack, men she considered brothers. Those faces made her vomit more and she fought to keep from passing out.

"Jacquelyn, look at me." Fane's voice came from a few feet behind her. He wasn't touching her, he wasn't comforting her, and she knew she must revolt him. That thought tore through her soul, ripped right through her and she gasped at the pain.

"Jacquelyn," he said, more insistently.

He wouldn't want her any more. Not after seeing that. How could he, even knowing it wasn't really her, how could he ever move past those images. He would leave her and she would be alone. He would turn to another for his comfort and she would be forced to watch, as he loved another.

"JACQUELYN," Fane took a step forward as he snarled. His eyes glowed bright blue and his body trembled.

Suddenly Costin and Decebel were standing between him and Jacque. Their bodies were tight with readiness, eager for battle. Fane snarled and felt himself beginning to change. His hands grew long claws and his muscles began to bulge and strain against his clothes. He felt the power of his Alpha roll over him and knew his father was preventing him from changing all the way.

"Back off, Fane," Decebel growled.

"Who are you to stand between me and mine?" Fane met Decebel's eyes without blinking, and held them.

Decebel took a menacing step forward and since Fane did not retreat, the two dominants were nearly touching.

"You need to cool off."

"Get. Out. Of. My. Way." His clipped words, betrayed the calm he was trying to portray and the shaking of his hands didn't help either.

"You're going to wind up hurting her and later, when you have cooled off, you will want to kill yourself for the indiscretion you committed against the one person who doesn't deserve it."

Fane's eyes snapped passed Decebel when he saw movement. He didn't hear the yell, nor did he feel the arms that attempted to hold him back when he lunged for Costin who was attempting to help his mate stand. All Fane saw were Costin's hands on his mate, Costin's skin touching hers and the memories came rushing back.

"Peri, is there anything you can do to keep the neurotic werewolves from killing each other?" Jen asked, dryly as she watched her mate attempt to pull a seething Fane off of Costin. Costin was holding his own, but she knew that he was holding back, because he cared for Fane. He knew that Fane wasn't in his right mind at the moment. Jen would like to say that she didn't think Fane would ever hurt Jacque, but she had never seen him look at her the way he had been and, truthfully, it scared her.

"Fane stop this," Vasile's words wrapped around his son and pulled Fane back from Costin. He pulled against his father's hold, but couldn't budge. He stared at Costin, challenging him, daring him to touch her again. He would kill him, Fane's wolf decided, he had touched Jacquelyn, he had been one of the males she had willingly accepted, real or not, and Costin would have to die.

Costin must have seen the determination settle in Fane's eyes as he took a step away from Jacque.

"Fane, I would never hurt your mate," Costin told him, firmly.

"You touched her," Fane's eyes narrowed, dangerously. "You took her in a way you had no right to. YOU KISSED HER, YOU BEAST,"

"ENOUGH!" Vasile roared, cutting off Fane's words.

Fane fell to his knees as Vasile's Alpha command, pushed him to submit. He pulled his head up and his eyes met Jacquelyn's. Tears streamed down her face and he could see the fear and knew she was on the verge of running.

"Don't," he told her urgently. "Don't leave me."

"You don't want me," she responded, and flinched at her own words.

"I will always want you."

She shook her head. She knew what she had felt inside him, the revulsion that filled him.

"Not at you," he answered her thoughts. "At everyone else love, but never you." He held his arms open to her. "Come to me."

Jacque fought the urge to rush to him. She feared his rejection and knew that she couldn't handle it if he pushed her away.

"Jacquelyn, come now."

"Here we go with the damn dog orders," muttered Jen as she folded her arms across her chest.

"Let me go," Fane told his father, never turning away from Jacquelyn. "I'm not going to hurt her," after a long pause, he added, "or anyone else."

"Why is that not reassuring to me?" Crina asked, Jen softly.

"Because his wolf's eyes still stare out from his too handsome, albeit quite deranged looking, face."

"Yeah, that could be it," Crina agreed.

Vasile gradually let his hold on his son lessen as he carefully watched to make sure that he wasn't going to attack. When Fane didn't move, he released him fully.

Fane took a step towards his mate and stopped to make sure she wasn't going to back away. When she stood her ground, he took another step and another, until he was standing right in front of her.

"Please leave us," he spoke softly, but knew everyone would hear him.

Decebel let out a low growl and was going to take a step towards Fane until Jen stepped in front of him.

"He won't hurt her."

Decebel stared at his mate a moment before he finally relented. He took Jen's hand as he turned to follow the others to give Fane and Jacque as much privacy as the forest would afford.

Once they were alone, Fane placed two fingers under Jacquelyn's chin and gently raised her face to look at him.

"How could you possibly think I wouldn't want you?"

Tears slid down her cheeks as she tried to speak. Her lips trembled and she tried to look away, but he held firmly to her chin.

"How could you after watching that? How could you ever want to touch me again?"

Fanes eyes closed briefly as he realized that she had thought his emotions were directed at her. He wasn't mad at her and she didn't revolt him. She was his. His precious mate and he knew that she hadn't really been touched or kissed or loved by another. He knew it, but still his wolf and he needed to connect with her emotionally as well as physically. He needed to reassure himself that she still wanted him, desired him, and no other.

Jacque stood on her tip toes and pressed her lips to his. She reached up, ran her fingers through his thick, black hair, and moaned when he wrapped his arms around her and pulled her closer. She opened her mind to his and poured her heart into their kiss. She thought about their wedding night, about the blood rites and then the time after. She reminded him of their first time together and all the times after, showing him the only way she could in that moment, how much she needed him, wanted him, and thirsted for him.

She was his, no doubt, but he was also *hers*.

"You are mine," she told him. *"There is no other for me. My heart, my body, and my desire is for you alone."*

Fane's body shuddered as Jacquelyn's words reverberated to his very soul. His wolf and he was hers. He felt the truth in those words and it eased something inside him just a little. His hands roamed her body as much as he dared in their semi-private environment and he didn't think he had ever wanted to be alone with his mate more than he did in that moment.

She pulled back from his kiss gasping for breath and he smiled slightly at her swollen lips.

"Soon," she panted.

"Not soon enough," he growled.

They stared at each other as they tried to get their breathing under control. The image of her looking at him in fear flashed in his mind and his heart ached.

"I'm sorry I scared you," he whispered.

Her arms were still wrapped around her neck and her hands gripped his neck tightly.

"I wasn't scared of you; I was scared that I'd lost you, because of what you have endured. I saw what you had visually endured and even now, I can't think of it or I'll be sick again. Fane," her voice wavered as she tried to keep it together, "the thought of any man's, hands besides yours, is revolting. I don't want those images in your mind. I don't want our bed tainted with that."

"I'm sorry. It's my fault that I saw it. It was my fear that created it and after I saw it once, it just grew inside me. More and more I feared that I wasn't enough for you, that you would realize that you deserved someone better."

Jacque silenced him with her lips as she kissed him deeply. When she pulled back, again she nipped his collar bone as punishment for his doubt.

"There is no one better for me. Not in this realm or any other."

Fane pressed his forehead to hers and breathed in her scent. Then his eyes found his bite mark from the blood rites ceremony and he growled. He kissed down her face to her neck. When he reached the mark, he kissed it gently and then gave into his wolf.

Jacque gasped as she felt Fane's teeth sink into her tender flesh and as quickly, as the pain had started it was gone. A rush of pleasure brought another gasp from her and then a deep, throaty moan. She gripped him tightly as she felt the pull of his mouth and she smiled as she heard him sigh in contentment. He liked the way she tasted, she heard his thoughts loud and clear, and it only made the experience that much more intense and intimate. Finally, he released her and licked her neck tenderly. He kissed the bite several times before he nipped her ear and growled. "Mine."

"I think you've established that wolf-man," she teased.

"Want to reciprocate?" He asked her as he tilted his head to the side giving her a clear view of his neck. He wanted her bite, wanted his scent running through her veins, but he knew that his Jacquelyn was a very private person. The only reason she had let him bite her was because she had felt his need. She had compromised, since they couldn't make love, she submitted to his bite instead.

"I want to, you know I do." Jacque pleaded for him to understand. She wasn't rejecting him.

"I know love, I know you do. It's not fair of me to ask it of you when I know how you feel about it."

"It's just so intimate. I feel I might as well be standing here naked." She laughed at her insecurity and reveled in the laugh that erupted from Fane.

"As much as that idea appeals to me, I wouldn't want others to see you so I can understand why you don't want others to see you bite me. It is intimate and under normal circumstances I would not have done that here."

"I know," she told him with a smile, "but I'm glad you did. It's calmed your wolf."

"Yes," he agreed. "He definitely feels more secure with you at the moment."

"Are you going to lose it again?"

Fane knew she was teasing, but the truth was he didn't know. It was a possibility and so he wouldn't lie to her.

"I don't know."

She kissed him gently before stepping back, but keeping hold of his hand.

"Okay, we will cross that bridge when we get there," she shrugged then as she turned to pull him towards the others, "or fall off."

"Thanks for the vote of confidence babe," he muttered.

Jacque laughed, "If worse comes to worse I'll just have to let you ravish me like a caveman."

Fane growled, "Don't tempt me."

The others were waiting for them just over a hill. The camp had been packed up and they were ready to be on the move again.

"Did you finally give in and just let him have his way with you, Red?" Jen asked, with a wicked grin.

Decebel, who had an arm wrapped around her, pulled her tighter and growled.

"Relax B. You'll get your roll in the hay soon."

Decebel leaned down and nipped her neck sharply. "You're writing checks, Jennifer."

"Yeah, yeah… that I can't cash. I get it, but maybe rough is what I'm aiming for Dec, ever think about that?" She rounded on him and raised a single eye brow in challenge.

"You really want to do this now?" He growled at her.

"Good grief," Peri groaned, as she rubbed her forehead. "The Great Luna, save us from horny, dominant werewolves, and the mates that are determined to push them over the edge they are precariously perched on."

Vasile stepped forward so that he stood where he could see the whole group. He let his power loose and watched as one by one the wolves dropped to their knees; all except Decebel and Gavril. Gavril willingly went to his knees of his own choice, but Decebel remained standing.

"I know you all are feeling a bit territorial with your mates. I understand that you feel the need to connect with them, to reestablish your claim and bond, but you are not pups to be ruled by your needs and desires. You will pull yourselves together, you will hold it together until we are safe, and you have a private room to lose it. Are we clear?"

Rumbles of agreement met his waiting stare and after several moments of Vasile's intense gaze, he pulled his power in and let them up.

Some of the tension that had been growing between the males abated, though not completely.

"Okay, let me catch you up to speed," Peri began speaking. "The Great Luna had the Fae council send out the call to the packs. She is not asking politely for you all to unite, she is demanding it. They should already be gathering and hopefully by the time we make it back to the mansion they will be there and in one piece."

Vasile rubbed his brow as worry seeped into him. "Skender is in charge right now, and though he is dominant, he is no match for an Alpha, let alone eleven of them."

"Skender is diplomatic, Vasile," Decebel assured him. "He can keep the peace. Not to mention, Dillon Jacobs will be there. He is levelheaded and smart, and should be able to curb any violence."

Vasile let out a deep breath and though he knew Decebel's words to be true, he also knew that Alpha's didn't mix, no matter how levelheaded or diplomatic they might be.

"We need to move quickly," Peri continued. "Mona is going to learn of your escape soon enough and she will not let it go unanswered. She knows that we are in these mountains and she will use anything she can to take us out.

"Well, let's quit wasting time here trying to kill each other and get a move on." Elle surprised them all with her sudden candor.

Sorin smiled at his mate. "Feeling feisty?"

She returned his smiled innocently and kissed his cheek. "I'm as eager as the rest to get back."

Sorin's eyebrows rose in surprise and his response in her ear was anything but innocent.

Peri shook her head as she turned to lead them. "I'm highly disappointed Elle, what happened to your prudish behavior?"

Elle laughed. "It took a back seat when I was given a mate so hot that he could cook bacon on his abs."

Jen reached over for a high five from Elle as she grinned. "Good one fairy."

Elle nodded. "I know, right?"

Peri picked up the pace hoping to make them keep their talking to a minimum as they traveled. The males were on edge and it wasn't going to take much to cause another fight like the one that had just erupted.

"Are you alright?" Sally asked Costin for the hundredth time since Fane had attacked him. She felt his warm breath on her neck as he kept stride next to her.

"I'm fine Sally mine, quit worrying about me." He winked at her and she smiled because it still gave her flutters and made her want to throw herself into his arms.

"Feel free to," he told her as he saw the thoughts in her mind.

Sally rolled her eyes at him, but took comfort in his returned playfulness. He wasn't any less possessive or protective, but his demeanor had almost returned to normal.

"Dec," Jen spoke tentatively to her mate. He was angry, she didn't really think it was at her, but she knew she hadn't helped.

"Jennifer," he responded, not unkindly.

"We good?"

"I will be better once I can look you over thoroughly, and once Cynthia examines you and lets me know our little girl is alright."

"I'm fine babe, promise." She tried to reassure him, but she knew he was telling the truth; he wouldn't be all right until he had looked her over himself.

"I love you, Jennifer," his voice suddenly sounded urgent in her mind.

"I love you to. I'm glad your back."

"You missed my bossy, brooding, possessive ways?" He teased.

"Wouldn't have you any other way, babe."

"I'll remember you said that," he warned with a smile, knowing she would get the reference.

She laughed out loud, as they jogged through the quiet forest.

"Tombstone." She confirmed with a smile at him and the slight upturn of his lips sent a thrill through her. He was safe, he was with her and now she could focus on saving the world, saving their baby, and anything else that needed saving.

"Feeling ambitious?" Decebel asked with a smirk.

She smiled wickedly at him, "Oh babe, you have no idea."

Chapter 10

"For centuries we have managed to stay out of the affairs of humans and other supernatural races. I do not feel that it is in our best interest to get involved in the tribulations of others. Unfortunately, what I feel does not matter to those outside of my own race. I should have known it was only a matter of time before trouble should show up at our door. However, I could have never imagined that the trouble would include not one race or two, but all of the supernaturals save ours. Just goes to show that my imagination is very bland.
~ Thalion, Prince of the Elves

"Are you sure this is what you want to do?" Lilly asked as they stood before a clearing in the vast forest.

Cypher was staring intently into the clearing and Lilly knew he must be seeing something she was not.

Cyn made a motion with her hand and suddenly there was ripple in the air. Out of nowhere, a seam appeared and, like a curtain, the space in front of them parted and she could see through it to the other side. It did not match the forest around them and for that reason she knew that she was looking into the realm of the elves.

Cypher looked down at her and the answer was evident in his eyes.

"Okay, okay," she groaned, "we don't really have a choice do we?"

"We cannot walk away from a dangerous situation hoping that someone else will step forward and deal with it. We might not be the first ones to discover the draheim in the human realm, but we are the only ones willing to fix it."

"For someone who was willing to make a deal with the devil, you sure are turning out to be noble and selfless." Lilly told him with a wink.

"I am not so noble as to give up the woman who was kidnapped to be my mate." Though the words came out softly, Lilly felt the possessiveness behind them and tried to deny the warm feeling it gave her. She was wanted. After being discarded so many years ago, someone wanted her and she didn't know how to respond.

Cyn's throat clearing drew their attention back to the open Veil. "Ready?" She asked them.

In response, Cypher walked towards the Veil without hesitation and stepped through it. Cyn motioned for Lilly to go next, and then followed closely behind.

Lilly's mouth dropped open as she turned in slow circle.

"Have we just walked into a Disney movie?" She asked, in awe of the scenery around her.

The sky above her was the most beautiful shade of blue she had ever seen. The sun shown down on a grassy meadow and the blades blew in the wind rhythmically. The trees around them were tall and strong with large leaves that were a bright vivid green. Birds fluttered from tree to tree, chirping happily. Lilly felt as if at any moment a beautiful big eyed, tiny waisted princess would emerge, spinning out of the trees singing some ridiculous song about nature, or love, or needing to get away from her wicked mother.

"Technology has not polluted their realm the way it has in the human realm," Cyn explained.

Lilly made an "*oh*" expression with her mouth as she continued to take in the realm before her.

"Do we find them or do they find us?" Cypher asked the Fae.

"We will go deeper into the realm, but they will definitely find us before we even know that they are upon us."

"Excellent," Lilly groaned, "because you know I didn't want this little adventure in our story to be easy or anything. I mean seriously, where would the crazy excitement in that be?"

Cyn's brow furrowed at her and Lilly laughed. "Sarcasm Cyn, it's a coping mechanism I learned from my daughter and her best friends."

Cypher took Lilly's hand in his and smiled at Cyn. "Just nod your head like you understand and it might make her stop."

A slight smile crept up on Cyn's lips and that made Lilly smile even wider.

"Let's go," Cypher said, as he tugged on Lilly's hand. "Stay alert," he added.

"Have I mentioned that I'm so hungry that I might consider gnawing one of my arms off?" Lilly asked in between breaths as she kept up with Cypher's long strides.

"Only twenty three times," Cyn answered, not sarcastically, just stating a fact.

"What's the quota for mentioning hunger before food is finally the answer given, instead of a dry retort?"

Cypher chuckled at his mate. He loved her quirky sense of humor, and her ability to handle stress so well. He even loved when she complained, like now, because it meant he got to hear her beautiful voice.

"I haven't exactly set one," Cyn answered. "But, when I do, you'll be the first to know."

Lilly's mouth dropped open as she eyed Cyn. "Were you just being sarcastic? Oh... my gosh you were... you just totally tossed sarcasm at me like a pro."

Cyn shrugged. "I'm learning to cope with you."

That comment brought a cough from Cypher as he tried to stifle his laughter.

Lilly's eyes narrowed but the sparkle in them made it clear that she wasn't really irritated. "I'll let that one slide because I figure you need the practice."

An hour later they finally stopped and Cyn reached in the pack that she carried on her back and pulled out a loaf of something that looked a lot like bread. She tore off two pieces and handed one each to Cypher and Lilly.

Lilly glared at the bread and then looked up at Cyn. "Please tell me this is just an appetizer."

"It's more than it appears to be," said Cyn.

As they ate their bread in silence, Lilly began to realize that Cyn was right; there was more to this bread. She felt full despite the small amount she had eaten and she felt her body being infused with energy. She was just about to remark on this when suddenly Cypher was on his feet from one breath to the next. His eyes narrowed as he stared into the trees and his head tilted to the side, listening. Cyn had stood as well and was looking in the opposite direction as Cypher. Lilly started to stand but stopped when Cypher looked at her and put a finger to his lips. She moved more slowly as she rose, trying not to make a sound.

Cypher narrowed his eyes as he searched for the elves he knew were watching them. He'd felt their eyes on them for several minutes now. He also knew they had been following them for quite some time. He didn't feel like they were in danger, but he preferred to be able to see his potential adversary, and not have wonder if they were indeed planning to attack. He looked over at Cyn and saw that though she too was alert and looking into the forest, her stance was relaxed, indicating that she did not feel a threat either.

"You would find out our purpose for being here a lot quicker if you revealed yourselves." Cypher's voice carried though he didn't yell.

Silence met his words as they waited to see if the observers would reveal themselves. Several moments passed. Finally, a tall form stepped around one of the large trees. He strode forward until he was in the center of the clearing and the light of day revealed his appearance. He was tall with long lean muscles. His hair was blonde and straight, hanging down his back. There was a single braid in front and some sort of adornment woven into it. He took a step closer revealing sea green eyes, high cheek bones, thin lips drawn tight in a straight line and a strong jaw. His ears were slightly pointed at the tips but not any larger than a human's. His clothing looked as if he had walked straight out of Lord of the Rings, complete with a bow slung across his back. He didn't say anything right away he just stared. His eyes landed on each of them, evaluating the level of threat.

"I am Thalion, of the Elves. What brings a human, a Warlock King, and a Fae Guardian into our realm?"

"We went to a bar first, but that joke didn't seem to pan out, so now we're going for a human, a warlock and a fae walk through a Veil. Doesn't quite have the same ring, but we're hoping the outcome is better than at the bar." Lilly knew she was rambling and she had tried to tell herself to shut up, but for some reason her mouth just kept moving. Cypher glared at her and she mouthed *"Sorry"* to him.

Cypher shook his head letting out a deliberate breath then looked back to Thalion.

"It seems you know who I am," Cypher told him.

Thalion nodded once.

"We have come seeking your aid. A draheim has made its way into the human realm, whether by accident or on purpose, we do not know. What we do know is that you make the only weapon capable of killing it."

Thalion's eyes narrowed. "Why do you think it needs to be killed? Why not return the creature to his own land?"

"Whatever he once was he is no longer. All that is left in him is a raging beast. He tried to kill us, and from what I could see in his eyes there was no intelligence left in him. He has been trained to murder. More than likely, anything good in him has been beaten out of him." Cypher answered.

Thalion seem to think about this for a moment. He looked over at Cyn. "What do you say Guardian?"

"I think it is very important to weigh the consequences before any life is taken. We all serve a purpose in this life and we must be careful not to throw off the balance lest we invite evil to fill the void. With that in mind, the only thing that can come from this beast's continued existence is harm. More than likely, if we were able to get him back to his realm, his own kind would kill him. We have enough danger in the human realm as it is. We do not need another one."

Thalion stared a few moments longer at Cyn before a slight smile curved his lips, only adding to his beauty.

"How have you been, Cyn?" He asked, and the formal elf that had been standing before them was suddenly relaxed and staring at Cyn with obvious endearment.

Cyn blushed slightly and Lilly's eyes widened at the scene before her. *Bloody hell,* she thought. *The elf has the hots for the fae. I so, did not see that one coming.*

"I'll be better once there is no longer a witch trying to destroy the werewolves and unleash a horde of demons into the human realm," she answered, honestly.

Thalion's eyes hardened and he took a step towards her. "What is this that you speak of?"

"We threw the balance off many years ago and now we are reaping the consequences of our actions." Cyn dropped her eyes from Thalion's as she continued to speak. "Desdemona, the last of the witches, has become very powerful. That power has only made her greedy for more. She discovered that gypsy healers have returned to the packs. She wants them. She has already attempted to kill the Romanian Alpha in an attempt to get to them. She was unsuccessful, but she will not be swayed."

Thalion took another step towards Cyn and another until he stood less than a foot away.

"Why are you just now coming to me with this?" The look in his eyes burned with rage, but even stronger than that was the obvious care he felt towards Cyn.

Lilly took slow steps, not wanting to disturb the exchange between the elf and fae. She reached Cypher and looked up at him. "Are you seeing what I'm seeing?" She whispered.

A small smile crept onto his face as he leaned down and placed his mouth next to her ear.

"I do believe Thalion has set his sights on our little fae." Lilly shivered as his warm breath caressed her neck and she turned her head back to the couple in question in an effort to shake off Cypher's effect on her.

"I know that you do not mingle in the human realm, nor burden yourselves with the problems of others," she answered and her voice wasn't accusatory. She was simply stating a fact, as she often did.

Thalion's eyes narrowed even more. His jaw clenched as he tried to keep control of his emotions. Only Cyn affected him this way. It had been so long since he had laid eyes on her, and still the hold that she had on him was undeniable.

"You truly believe, I would not help if you asked?" Thalion's question dripped with challenge.

Cyn shrugged. "Why would you?"

Thalion held her eyes as he reached up and ran his fingers down her jaw to her neck. Cyn couldn't hide her reaction to him as the speed of her breathing increased. Thalion chuckled as a smirk flashed across his face and then was gone. He dropped his hand and turned to face Lilly and Cypher.

To their surprise, Thalion found a stump to sit on. "Tell me."

"We don't have much time," Cypher told him.

Thalion nodded. "I understand, but I need to know details before I lead my army into the human realm."

Cyn gasped and Lilly's head swung around to look at the Fae. It was the first major emotion she had seen from her.

"You're going to help?" She whispered. "Why?"

Thalion's sea green eyes met hers. He didn't bother to hide the emotions swirling behind them.

"Because it's you." Cyn stared at Thalion. She didn't have a reply to his candid answer and for once, she wished that she had Lilly's quick wit and smart retorts.

She continued to watch him as she began the tale of all that had taken place in the human realm. She started with what had happened to the Romanian and Serbian packs.

Thalion sat silently, watching her intently as she spoke. As soon as she had finished, Cypher smoothly transitioned into his part in the story. Lilly had taken a spot on the ground in front of a tree. She leaned back against it, her legs stretched out in front of her, her head leaned back, and her eyes closed as she listened to the rumble of Cypher's deep voice. The cadence of it seemed to match her breathing and she felt herself beginning to doze off, and when his voice suddenly stopped, her eyes popped open. She blinked a couple of times to clear her vision and then looked at Thalion. He sat with a furrowed brow staring at the ground as if the answers would suddenly be written in the dirt.

"Thalion." Cyn's voice held a hint of apprehension as she watched him struggle with the information they had shared.

Thalion finally looked up and met Cyn's eyes. "I will have the necessary weapons made and my army will join with you to fight." His jaw tensed. "I have been foolish to ignore the happenings in the mortal realm."

Cyn smiled. "Well, you aren't the only ones. It took a moon goddess to get my race to act."

"What do you mean it took a moon goddess?" Thalion asked, with narrowed eyes.

"The Great Luna has caused matings between the wolves and Fae. She also gave the command to the Fae council to call the packs together," Cyn explained.

Cypher took a step forward. "You haven't mentioned this."

"I was waiting for the right moment."

"When you say 'the packs,'" Thalion interrupted. "Do you mean *all of them*?"

"If by *all of them* you mean *all of them*, then yes." Cyn nodded.

Lilly shook her head at Cyn's sarcasm. "I've created a monster," she grumbled.

Thalion continued to meet Cyn's gaze as he thought of the implications of her words. "For the Great Luna to be involved,"

"It's bad," Cyn agreed.

"Um, I have to agree that this all stinks to high heaven, but can I ask something," Lilly spoke up. "I know you said that you are Thalion and we know you are an elf, obviously, but can you just clarify exactly how you are able to bring an army to help us?"

A ghost of a smile crept across his lips. "Of course, I am not just any run of the mill elf. I am Thalion, Prince of the Elves."

Lilly's eyes widened. "Prince," she murmured, and then looked over at Cyn. "You didn't mention that your contact was royalty."

Cyn shrugged. "You didn't ask."

Thalion stood and the others did as well. "I need one night to get everything together," he told them. "I'm going to ask that you pass back to your realm and wait for me there." Then he walked over to Cyn and took her hand. "Excuse us for a second please," he said to Cypher and Lilly as he pulled Cyn several feet away.

Cyn looked up at Thalion in surprise. He frowned at her.

"Don't look surprised, Cyn. You've known for a long time."

She dropped her eyes, not wanting him to see the truth behind them, but he wouldn't let her hide that easily. He tilted her chin up with a finger until her eyes met his.

"Why have you stayed away for so long?"

"Why have you?" She countered.

"You know that it is hard for me to leave. I don't have someone in place to take over while I'm gone like the wolves do. I don't have a council watching over my people like the Fae do. It is me and me alone that the burden falls to."

Cyn nodded. "I know."

Thalion's eyes narrowed. "And?"

"And what? We both have responsibilities that we can't just walk away from. I am a guardian, you are a prince, and those are the facts. We do not have the luxury of following our hearts."

A small smile appeared on the prince's face. "So, your heart leads you to me?"

"You know it does," she whispered, shyly.

Before she could anticipate his next move, his lips were suddenly pressed to hers. It was a firm, quick kiss—it was a promise.

"I'll see you very soon." He gave her one last meaningful stare, and if looks could wrap arms around a person and possess them, then she would be locked in his.

Cyn walked back over to Lilly and Cypher in a daze.

"You didn't see that coming did you?" Lilly asked.

Cyn shook her head, still unable to put any words together.

"Yeah well, there's a lot of that going around so welcome to the club."

~

"SHE DID WHAT!" Desdemona yelled and the walls of the small building shook. The windows rattled and threatened to shatter as a wave of her power whipped through the air. Mona stared in the direction of the voice, though she could not see the owner. Once again, the Fae traitor had come to her, offering her information, because she hated one of her own.

"They are no longer in the In-Between," the Fae reiterated.

"Yes, I kind of figured that's what you meant when you said that Peri *rescued* them," Mona spat at the cloaked figure. She still could not determine the identity of the Fae and it was really beginning to tick her off.

"Don't take your incompetence out on me," the Fae snapped back.

Mona froze. Very few beings would dare to talk to her that way and live to tell about it. She turned slowly to face the figure. Her hands itched to work their magic and the darkness swirled inside her pulsing, pushing to be released.

"I told you that I could help you Desdemona. I also told you that you were not my only option. I bring you this information to show you that I am telling you the truth when I say I want Perizada stripped of her power, kneeling before me knowing that her death is upon her."

Mona couldn't help the shriek of laughter that bolted out of her. "Damn, I thought I was blood thirsty, but I'm beginning to think that some of you so called good guys are even nastier than little 'ole me."

The cloaked figure stepped forward and the darkness around it slowly faded as the hood fell away. Mona laughed as she saw who stood before her.

"You have got to be kidding me," she clapped her hands with glee. "This is just too much. Does Perizada have any idea that you, Lorelle, are so hard up for her demise?" Mona watched as a small flash of emotion passed over the high Fae's face and was gone just as quickly as it appeared.

"I feel the element of surprise is much more satisfying when plotting the demise of one's sibling, don't you?" Lorelle's eyes filled with a hatred that Mona fully understood, though she didn't know one of the Fae was capable of such loathing.

"Thurlok is still at the bridge, though he is cowering under it in hopes that you will not find out what he has done."

Mona turned and glared out of the window into the poor, tiny village tucked away in the mountains, untouched by progress or time. She had been surprised when Lorelle had asked her to meet in such a place, because it was not a setting that most Fae would choose to spend time, owing to their disdain for anything quaint and opulence free. Had she any semblance of caring she might have thought the village charming, but as it were she could care less if it burned to the ground.

Mona turned back to Lorelle, "You have tracked them?"

"Yes, she keeps us informed of their progress. She believes that we all have truly seen the error of our ways and are fully on board with the Great Luna's plans."

Mona's skin crawled at the mention of the deity who created her foe.

"Where are they?" She snapped.

"They are making their way back to the Romanian stronghold. They are moving quickly through the forest and it seems that Peri is able to influence the plants and animals to aid them. They are drawn to the light she and the healers represent." Lorelle explained.

Mona's eyes narrowed as the she bared her teeth. "Well, we will just have to remedy that, won't we?"

Though Lorelle had allowed her selfish desires and quest for her own power to twist her intentions into something evil, she still shuttered under the feral violence that surrounded Desdemona. It enveloped her completely, leaving no space for compassion, sympathy, or regret. Even now, something in Lorelle still opposed the idea of hurting her sister. But, she could see that Mona would gladly tear the wolves, limb from limb, reveling in their screams of agony, and then casually eat a meal afterwards without a second thought to the lives she'd just destroyed.

If she were honest with herself, she would admit that she didn't want her hate of Peri to twist her that far, but somehow honesty just wasn't her strong suit.

Chapter 11

"I watch her sleeping. I can't tear my eyes from her for even a second, for if I do I will see her battered, broken body. She's so worried about me. I try to put on the smile she needs, but I know she sees through me. My desperation to touch her, taste her, and smell her are complete giveaways to what is really going on inside of me. I can feel it from the other males, even Vasile. The effects of the In-Between run much deeper than we could have ever imagined. Though we are free from the physical prison, I fear that it could still be what destroys us." ~ Costin

Sally stood breathless from the brisk pace that Peri insisted they keep. They had been pushing through the forest for two days and still the males teetered on the edge of violence. The once unified wolves that had trusted each other were leery and edgy around one another. Their eyes darted, constantly waiting for the danger they seemed so sure would come. The males wouldn't let their mates more than a foot from their sides, Costin included. Sally would have laughed at their ridiculous possessiveness, but the fear in their eyes crushed any humor.

Costin walked up to her. He was not out of breath she noticed, irritably. His hand reached up and brushed away hair that had escaped from her pony tail while they were running. His touch was tentative and gentle and she hated that he, who had once been so confident and bold in his pursuit of her, was now hesitant to touch *her*—his mate.

"Not for the reasons you think," he told her as he held her eyes.
"Then why?"

She could feel his need to protect her and, though she appreciated it, in that moment it enraged her. She knew that she was his and he felt an unwavering, all powerful need to protect her, but he was hers too, dammit. How could she protect him, even from himself, if he didn't let her in?

"You feel the tension, especially because you are a healer. The darkness that we all have kept at bay, the control we have kept on our wolves, is all but gone. We are fighting what we have always feared would destroy us."

"Why? I thought your true mates balanced that darkness. I thought we helped you keep control. I know you all have been through hell. I know you have this insane need to protect us, but you have us back. The physical touch is there and the mental bond is strong. Why are you not in control?" Sally's voice broke the silence. She was desperate for an answer, and hopefully one that she could fix. Costin, being so distant and yet possessive beyond reason, was beginning to scare her. The others turned to watch them and Costin tensed at all the attention. His head bowed as he broke eye contact with her and Sally felt shame running off of him like a turbulent rain storm, hell bent on wearing away his resolve as rain from the storm would wear away earth and rock.

"They won't let us be what they need." Rachel's voice broke the pin dropping silence. Sally's head snapped around to the other healer.

"What do you mean?" Sally asked.

Gavril stepped up beside his mate and placed a hand on her face gently pulling her to look at him.

"Don't." His voice was a growl though she didn't seemed threatened by him.

Rachel shook her head at him. "This has to be said! One of you, or all of you, is going to end up killing each other. I won't let your own pride and misplaced good intentions destroy us. We can't go marching into a mansion full of Alphas and dominant wolves with you all so edgy. You have your friends, your closest confidants, men you trust with your lives and you are willing to die for and even with *them* you can't control your possessiveness. When one of those males gets too close to your mate, how on earth do you think you will be able to keep from ripping his throat out?"

Jen's hand flew to her mouth as she stifled as gasp. "Bloody hell," she whispered through her hand. She hadn't considered the other packs. She had been hoping that with each day, the males would begin to relax and trust one another again. She might as well have been hoping for world peace and all that other crap that the

Miss America chicks were always spouting. The tension between the males was not lessening; it might even be getting worse. Decebel was possessive on a good day, but now that she was pregnant and he had just endured the very worst depths of hell. She didn't even know if *possessive* was an adequate term for what he would be once they got back to the mansion.

"So you're saying they are doing this to themselves?" Jacque asked, before Jen could and she nodded at her best friend for taking the words out of her shocked mouth.

Rachel met the eyes of each male briefly before she finally nodded.

"I did something that I would not normally do because I don't like to invade someone's privacy, not even my mates, but I'm worried."

Gavril stiffened next to his mate and his eyes narrowed as he looked down at her.

"What did you do Rachel?" His voice was not unkind, but brokered no argument that she was to answer him.

"I searched inside of you." Rachel hurried on before Gavril could respond. "We have been mated for centuries Gavril, centuries! We have been through much together, and in all that time, you have never drawn away from me. But now, you have. You only touch me when it gets unbearable for you not to. You only use the bond when absolutely necessary. You constantly keep your body between mine and anyone else's. You are treating me more like a possession than the other half of your soul!" Rachel's voice had risen to a near yell as she released the pain that had been building over the distance her mate had put between them. "I'm the light to your darkness, or have you forgotten that little detail of our mating? I was created for YOU! Do you get that? When you are hurting, I'm the one who can comfort you. When you are joyous, I am the one who can truly understand that joy. When you are raging and the wolf fights to take control, I am the one who can calm him. ME! The darkness that was consuming you when we met was breached and conquered by my light. Your need to protect me, your need to bear this pain on your own is destroying my light. The In-Between gave the darkness a place to seep through back inside of you and instead of welcoming our bond as you once did you nurture the darkness. You caress IT as a lover INSTEAD OF ME!" Rachel was gasping for breath when she finished and the air seemed to spark around her as her temper flared.

Sally's chest was tight as she mirrored the pain and anger that surged from Rachel's words. She had not been able to put into words what she had been feeling, but Rachel had tied it up in a rage induced bow. She looked over at Jen and Jacque and could see the realization snapping into place in their minds. Even Elle, Crina, and Alina looked stricken by the truth in the healers' words.

"The worst part," Rachel tried to hold back the sob that pushed out with the words, "the worst part is that you know what you're doing, yet you don't stop it."

Alina stepped forward as the anger in Rachel, which had been so much more prominent than her pain, began to subside and the hurt began to take over. Alina's face was stoic and the distance between her and Vasile shadowed the usual compassion that shined in her eyes. She took a deep breath before she spoke and the voice that came out was one of an Alpha.

"I have been trying to figure out what it is that has been causing the distrust and suffocating grasp of our males. Hearing what Rachel has seen inside of her mates mind, inside of his soul, I know that she speaks the truth. My wolf echoes loudly the truth of her words. But, my wolf and I are not in agreement on how we should feel about this revelation." Alina's eyes narrowed as she honed in on Vasile. "Had you not been aware of what was going on inside of you, had you not knowingly been keeping me from you, I could have understood. I could have empathized." Her voice never wavered as her words filled the hush that had fallen over the forest; a hush that none of them seemed to notice. "As it is, you have decided for me what I can handle and what I cannot. You made the decision to keep a part of you from me. So, I am making a decision for you," she paused as she watched Vasile's fear morph into anger as he already saw what she was going to say. She said it out loud anyway. "You have denied me what I so desperately need and so I will deny you. Eye for and eye, yes? I don't do this to be mean, childish, or vindictive; I do this because it is time for desperate measures. I have no idea how to tear down the wall you have so diligently and fervently built between us. So, I will no longer use human ways to reason with you. I'm going back to the nature that comes so naturally to us—to the nature of the wolf. The wolf doesn't understand emotions as much as actions and the here and now. I'm giving your wolf something he can understand. Your touch is uninvited."

A collective gasp from the females and low snarls from the males filled the stagnant air. To a human, it would seem unimportant and possibly even silly, but to a Canis lupus, touch was vital. Touch between mates was as life giving as the air that filled their lungs. The need to touch and be touched, whether for comfort, encouragement, or desire, was at the core of the wolf's heart.

Vasile took a step towards her, but Alina held up her hand to halt him and took a step back.

"I am yours, Vasile, as Rachel has told her mate. I am the other half of your soul and when you are ready to give me the respect I deserve as such, I will give you back your rights to me. I never want you to have to deal with your darkness on your own. I want to help you get through the horror you experienced, but I will not beg. Not even for *you*." Alina turned and walked across the path, far from her mate. Vasile stared as he tried to see through the red haze that had begun to blur his vision. She was denying him. HIM! He stood utterly dumbfounded and unable to move because of it.

Peri watched in part horror and part awe as the Alpha female put her foot down. She was doing the right thing. The males were too far gone, they hadn't made it in time, and if they continued on this path, their wolves would take over. Words would no longer penetrate the darkness to the man's mind; the only thing that might work would be to take action that the wolf would understand. Though Peri wasn't a wolf, she had learned something about them as she had been around them for more centuries than she could count. She had come to realize that the man was protective, possessive, and utterly devoted to his true mate, and the wolf was even more so. What Alina was doing would result in one of two things, the males pulling their heads out of their asses and allowing their females to be what they were meant to be or the darkness would consume them and they would all die. *That would suck,* she thought. She stood a little straighter as she watched what was unfolding before her and her mouth dropped open. She began to gather her power knowing that it was a big possibility that she was going to have to use it.

Sally was the first to move after the shock of Alina's words had frozen them all. She looked at Costin and searched for any indication that he would deny Rachel or Alina's words. She saw and felt his shame at hurting her, but she also felt his resolve that it was the only way to protect her. That was enough for her to make her decision, though it nearly made her knees buckle as she turned and walked away from him. Her heart threatened to beat through her chest as it pounded inside her. Despite the cold air, her hands were sweating and she felt sweat trickle down her back. She swallowed against the pain of her choice, but knew deep inside of her that it was the only option. The thought of not touching Costin, of not feeling his touch, took her breath away and as she reached Alina's side the Alpha wrapped an arm around her to help steel her composure.

"Sally," Costin growled. *"Come back."*

She could hear the anger and pain in his words and she nearly ran back to him. She didn't want him to hurt but she wanted her mate back more than she worried about the temporary pain that the separation would cause.

"No," she answered defiantly, not even giving him the intimacy of their bond. His eyes narrowed as he caught the subtle defiance in refusing him access to her mind. "Your touch is uninvited," she told him with eyes full of unshed tears. Sally finally looked away, not down, as she would not show submission, but away because watching him shake with rage was too much.

Jen was next to move. She didn't say anything as she walked away from her mate, not until he reached out and snagged her arm.

Jen rounded on him and the fury pulsing from her gave her the strength to pull her arm away.

"I would repeat everything Alina just said," she snarled, "but it's just too damn much. So, I'll just say the parts I do remember. You know that you're hurting me, and frankly, that makes me want to stab you with a spoon, and still you just continue on your path to self-destruction, uncaring of how it's affecting me. You know that I am what you need to get through all this crap and yet, you deny me that privilege, and you deny me of my right to meet YOUR NEEDS! As a self-declared nympho this is the most painful thing to willingly endure," she took a deep breath and let it out just as Decebel whispered, "Don't." She ignored him. "Your touch is..."

"Don't do this, Jennifer," Decebel interrupted and though his words were controlled and quiet, it was scarier than if he had been screaming like a crazed maniac.

Jen let out a low growl as she started again. "Your touch..."

Again, he interrupted, louder this time. "DO. NOT."

Jen threw her arms up in the air in exasperation. "Bloody hell, would you shut up! I am not doing this Dec, you are. This is all you babe, so suck it up and deal." Jen knew there must be some formal reason that Alina had been so formal with her words, and so she squared her shoulders and looked into his narrowed, glowing eyes- and spoke quickly. "Yourtouchisuninvited." The words ran together as she tried to get them out before he could cut her off again. Decebel took a step back as if he had been slapped. Jen's eyes widened slightly at the action and slowly walked backwards keeping her eyes on his shocked face.

Decebel's face suddenly was wiped clean of emotion, his stone mask in place. His jaw tensed as he spoke. "I warned you from the beginning Jennifer. You are mine. I will not let you go. I will not allow even you to keep yourself from me." His eyes narrowed, dangerously. "I consider your actions a direct challenge to me. I will only say this one more time. Don't do this." When she didn't move, or speak, Decebel shook his head in resignation. "So be it," he growled, softly.

Fane hadn't realized that Jacquelyn had left his side while everyone's attention was riveted on Jen and Decebel. When Jen finally arrived at Alina's other side, he turned back only to realize Jacquelyn was half way across the path that was quickly becoming a dividing line. He lunged forward to grab her, but was stopped by an invisible wall. His head jerked over to the only one he knew powerful enough to conjure such a thing. Peri stood looking innocently at him, but he saw the twinkle in her eyes.

He tried to reach Jacque's mind, but she was blocking him rather effectively and he was sure it had something to do with what Rachel had revealed about them. The males *were* keeping their mates out. It was instinctive to protect them, to not want them to be tainted by their darkness.

"Jacquelyn," his voice was barely above a whisper as he clenched his jaw. She turned to look at him and she saw the tears gathering in her green eyes. He had caused that and he had pushed her to take this desperate measure as his mother had said.

Jacque swallowed hard before she finally spoke. "Your touch is uninvited." Sally and Jen wrapped Jacque in their arms comforting her, but knowing that it would not give her what she truly needed. Only Fane could do that.

Something in Fane snapped as his wolf realized that their mate was mere feet from them and yet he could not get to her. He pounded his fist on the invisible barrier as his claws emerged and his eyes glowed bright blue. He watched the girls holding her, and he snarled jealously. It was his right to touch her; she was his.

"You are mine," Fane growled.

Jacque pulled away from her best friends and looked at Fane. "Yes, I am, and I'm not leaving you." She turned and met the eyes of the other males. "None of us is trying to leave any of you."

Decebel snarled loudly, finally losing his resolve. "You each took one of us as your mate. You bound yourselves by blood to your mate. You joined your body and made yourselves one with your mate. You are no longer your own." He was shaking with rage and power swirled around him. "It is not your right to choose separation from your mate FOR ANY AMOUNT OF TIME!"

Surprise flashed across their faces when it wasn't Decebel's mate who responded.

"But it is your right to keep yourselves from us?" Crina's voice was steady, though as she looked over at Adam the hurt flashed in her eyes.

A snarl worthy of a wolf erupted from Adam as he pulled Crina to him.

He whispered feverishly in her ear. "We are too new at this to be making impetuous decisions. We are still learning how this bond works between us Crina; don't walk away now."

Crina stared at his handsome face; saw the desperation in his eyes to keep her at his side. His words were true, but she knew that he had been holding himself back from her as well. Whatever he had seen in the In-Between was creating a void between them. She turned to Rachel then, needing to know what was inside.

"Will you?" Crina asked, knowing that Rachel would understand what she was asking.

Rachel nodded and walked over to them. She reached up, placed her hand on Adam's chest, and closed her eyes. She could see their bond and it had been getting stronger, but then she saw the black haze in Adam's mind. She saw the wall he had put up between the bond and the darkness. Then the bond weakened because of it. Somehow, Rachel knew that if Adam would let her in, would fully bond with her, then they would have the same abilities as the other mated pairs. She opened her eyes and pulled her hand back as she looked up into Adam's face. Rachel could see the pleading in his eyes, begging for her not to expose his actions. She shook her head. Rachel would not enable him to keep his mate from what was her right.

Rachel turned back to Crina. "He tries to protect you, but the barrier he has put on your bond is keeping it from growing and developing. I believe you will be able to reach each other's minds. I believe that you will develop markings that will identify you as mates, but only if you allow the bond to grow. It appears exactly as the bond between wolves, but it withers under Adam's refusal to open it."

Adam's arm dropped from Crina as he watched the tears stream down her face. She stepped away from him and took a steadying breath. "Your touch is uninvited." Her voice wavered, but her rigid shoulders and upturned chin expressed what her voice could not. She turned and nearly made it past Peri's barrier, but Adam was as fast as a wolf. He grabbed her and spun her around, and then took her face in his hands he kissed her. Their lips barely touched when Adam jumped back as pain ripped through him. His eyes were filled with confusion as he looked at his mate.

"What was that?" He asked, as his hands fisted at his sides aching with the need to touch her.

"Your touch is uninvited," she repeated.

Adam closed his eyes as realization struck him. "That's why the words are so formal. They are binding aren't they, some part of the Canis lupus magic?" She nodded as she continued to back up.

He turned to Peri. "What undoes this?"

Peri *asked* him as she shook her head. "Now, now, Adam, I can't play favorites with you just because you are Fae."

Adam growled at her, and then looked back at his mate. She was so close and yet it felt like an ocean separated them.

Rachel left Gavril's side without a backward glance. Her shoulders were pulled back and her jaw tilted defiantly. Gavril made no move to stop her, nor did he speak.

Elle stood next to Sorin, staring at the females who had made their choice and she saw the pain it was costing them. She also knew that what Rachel had said was true. As the time from their rescue, passed Sorin had touched her less and less. He hadn't used their bond unless absolutely necessary. They'd had no time alone together, no time to talk about their mating. She hadn't even told him about her markings yet. All of this swirled in her mind and she found that she was hurt that he had kept her at arm's length. She had watched the male Canis lupus struggle with their darkness, knew what it could do to them. And still he wasn't allowing her in. She turned to look at Sorin and saw the moment he realized what she was choosing. Elle moved fast, knowing that he would never let her go if he got his hands on her. Sorin lunged and ran into the same barrier Fane had. He stared at her in disbelief, as her face betrayed no emotions, not until she spoke. "Your touch is uninvited." Her voice was so small, he barely heard her, but he felt it. To his very soul, he felt it.

Peri looked over at Cynthia and raised a single eyebrow. "Would you like to pick a team?"

Cynthia shook her head at Peri's ability to be so calm as they stood amongst enraged wolves with death in their eyes.

"I think it best that I be where Jen is," Cynthia said as she made her way to the women.

Peri watched as the males stood, rigid, and motionless, staring at their mates. She knew that if she lowered the barrier they would no doubt attempt to drag them back kicking and screaming. Although, judging by the gleam in Alina's eyes, she had a feeling that she would go willingly, only to then kick Vasile in his baby making parts.

"Remove the barrier, Perizada," Vasile ordered, his eyes never moved from his mate.

"Sorry, Alpha. Can't do that."

"Can't or won't," Decebel snarled.

"Tomato, *tomato*," Peri retorted.

Decebel bared his teeth at her, and then turned back to Jen.

"You would keep our daughter from me?"

Jen rolled her eyes. "Don't use the daddy card, B. She is toasty warm in this amazing body. If this party is still rolling by the time I go into labor it will be your own stupid fault."

"I may not be able to touch her, but I can touch you."

"Not anymore," Jen parried.

"I can hear her heart beat Jennifer."

His words stopped her retort and her eyes held his. Jen fought her every instinct to run to him, to have him wrap her in his arms and keep her safe.

"Make your choice B. Let me be what you need me to be."

Decebel closed his eyes and Jen imagined that he was counting to ten…or one hundred. It usually took longer for him to cool off when he was mad at her.

"You females do not know what you are asking. There is a reason we are trying to protect you. Sometimes you have to choose the lesser of two evils and we have made the choice that we feel is best for you. We never consulted each other on how to deal with this situation so for me to see that we all made the same decision, to not let the horror we watched touch you, tells me that it must be the right decision."

Peri started clapping slowly as she walked over to the females and turned to face the guys.

"Well said, Decebel. However I can't decide if that's the most caring thing I've ever heard from you or the dumbest." Her eyes lost her twinkling playfulness as she confronted them. "You see, when I hear you say that the majority making the same choice must mean it's the right one, what I really hear is, hi I'm Decebel and I'm a total dumb ass."

Jen growled at the Fae. She didn't like others insulting her mate. Only she was allowed that privilege.

"Pipe down, prego chick," Peri quipped. "Decebel you cannot believe that crap. If your logic is correct then we should all condone underage drinking, minors getting it on like rabbits, and thinking that reality TV shows are good forms of entertainment. By your logic, Alpha, when your daughter is seventeen and boy crazy it will be okay for her bear her lady bits because the *majority* of her friends are doing it."

Decebel took a menacing step towards her, his amber eyes glowing dangerously.

"Uh, Peri, not really helping," Jen snapped.

Peri watched the seething Alpha as he glared at her. She could see that her words had hit a nerve and that's what she had intended to do.

"Okay, as much fun as this has been, we need to be on our way." She looked one last time at the males. "Just a suggestion from one bad ass to another, it would not be smart for you to touch your women. So don't even try it."

Chapter 12

"Sometimes changed circumstances make a decision, even a decision that seemed liked such a good idea at the time, suddenly look really, really dumb. Now the question at that moment becomes, do you fess up and say hey, maybe I shouldn't have done that? Or do you stick to your guns, even if swallowing your pride might end up saving your backside? You would think there was an easy cut and dry answer to that question—not if you're mated to pigheaded werewolves." ~ Jacque

Mona stood over the scrying bowl as she sought out the exact location of her escaped prey. She had considered just letting them be for now, knowing they would be coming for her at some point, no matter how foolish that decision was. Then her pride had stepped up and she realized that if she didn't exact some sort of revenge, she would appear weak. She closed her eyes as she pushed out her will, allowing the magic of the scrying to show her where they were. Her lips pulled up into an evil smirk when she finally located them.

"There you are, little wolfies," she murmured, as she watched them in her mind's eye.

She watched as the females stood across from their mates with Peri in front of them, appearing to confront them. Maybe the escape was not necessarily a bad thing if it was causing strife between mates.

"Now, what to do with you," she said, as she tapped her blood red lips with her finger. She had allowed the males to be tormented, to watch horrendous things, things that hadn't been real. Now, what would it do to them if they really did see something happen to their mates?

"Hmm, this has potential." Her power had continued to grow and natural laws that once bound her were no longer obstacles to the dark magic she wielded. Mona reached into the forest, seeking out the dark creatures that lurked in the shadows. She drew energy from them, pulling it inside of her in order to shape it to her will. She weaved a spell as her mind and body felt drunk on the rush of power.

"Earth, water, wind, and fire,
Hear me now, feel my desire.
I call on your forces and your ancient power,
Rumble, blow, burn, and shower.
Let no female leave unharmed,
All males desperate and alarmed.
Every step will pulse with pain,
Every cry will be for his name,
Let fire come between each one,
Until they, fall and I have won.

Her eyes flashed open as she felt the power leave her body, the spell riding on the wind. It would grow in power as it sought out its quarry. Owing to the size and power of the spell, it would take some time before it reached her prey.

Mona let out a deeply, satisfying breath and wiped her hands on her clothes. "Well, I've threatened a pixie, plotted with a traitorous Fae, and will soon hear the screams of the wolves. If that isn't freaking awesome, I don't know what is."

"Who are you speaking to?"

The deep voice made Mona jump as she whirled around, ready to defend herself. A heart stopping shot of fear ripped through her as she stared, wide eyed at the one before her.

"How did you get in here?" She asked, after she had pushed the fear away and reminded herself of whom she was. But, that didn't change the reality of the individual who was standing before her. *This is bad*, she thought to herself, *very, very bad*.

~

Sally's eyes watered as she desperately tried to focus on anything but the pain, which had become a constant companion as she fought her need to be with Costin. He was behind her with all the other males and she could feel his eyes on her, burning a hole in the back of her head. She could feel him willing her to turn around, to come back to him. And she wanted to so very badly.

"How're you holding up?" Jen asked, matching Sally's pace as they continued trekking through the mountains.

Sally gritted her teeth and composed herself before she spoke. "I'm dealing," she finally answered.

"Do you think we're doing the right thing?"

Sally's brow wrinkled as she looked at Jen in surprise. "You're having doubts?"

Jen shrugged. "We're not the only ones hurting. Dec is in more pain now, than when I died."

"How?"

"I think because I'm rejecting what was determined for us before we were ever created. I belong by his side and I'm choosing to deny him that."

Sally frowned. "Not to sound childish or anything but they denied us first. There are consequences to every action Jen, and their action to keep their mates out has brought on this consequence. It's up to them to fix it."

Jen grinned at her and Sally saw the gleam in her eyes.

"You did that on purpose didn't you?"

Jen gave a little nod of her head. "I could tell you were really struggling and so I thought maybe you needed reminding of why we are doing this. Decebel is relentless, pushing on my mind, and I honestly don't think he is using his full power because I'm pregnant."

"Are you hurting?" Sally asked.

Jen's mouth tensed just before she spoke. "Badly." Then as only Jen could do, she pushed away the pain and sought out a way to ease the tension. "So I was examining my mate's oh so encouraging words from earlier. He said that we had given ourselves to them in every way, basically. Because of that fact, then we no longer can make our own choices. I found a loop hole."

Sally laughed as she shook her head. "Okay, I'll bite. What's the loop hole?"

"You," Jen grinned. "I thought about Crina and Elle, and they may very well fit into that category as well. However, I don't really know their business like I know yours."

"What?"

"Sally, my little wall-flower, you haven't given your body, as B so eloquently put it, to your mate. You've completed the Blood Rites, but that is only one of the ingredients in the mixed drink that is bonding."

"So," Sally drew the word out, waiting for Jen to elaborate.

"Oh good grief woman, I'm saying that according to Dec's jacked up idea of independent thinking, you my dearest, are still allowed such a liberty."

Sally laughed and though the pain didn't leave, for that brief moment in time, it wasn't consuming her.

She heard a growl and a powerful push as Costin shoved his way into her mind.

"It will be remedied as soon as this ridiculous tantrum of yours is over."

Sally's mouth dropped open and she couldn't believe he had just said that to her. She whipped around to look at him, and refused to give him the intimacy he was trying to force by using their bond.

"Are you seriously talking about making love to me while calling me childish in the same sentence?" Sally watched in satisfaction as Costin's eyes began to glow. She had struck a nerve and maybe it shouldn't have, but, damn, it felt good.

"Sally," he started, but Sally cut him off.

"I'm not real experienced in this aspect of a relationship, but I'm pretty sure calling your mate childish is NOT the way to go about getting some."

Jen coughed on a laugh and watched as not only Costin's face contorted in anger, but all of the males. She just couldn't resist this one.

"And by getting *some* she means tail," she paused and just in case their hazed over brains didn't register it she said it again a little slower. "Getting—some—tail. You know, because we're wolves?" Jen looked around and when she noticed Crina grinning she smiled, "I knew someone appreciated my sense of humor.""

The look on Decebel's face told her that if he could touch her in that moment he probably would have throttled her. She smiled to herself as she enjoyed the rage she brought out in him. Rage meant emotion, passion, and need. Maybe if she pushed just a little more he would finally let her in.

"Sally this is…" Costin took a step towards her but she was done listening. She turned on her heel and continued at a pace slightly faster than before.

Two long, and extremely frustrating days later…

Night had fallen more quickly Peri noticed and the hairs on the back of her neck rose. They'd finally stopped to make camp, though she hadn't wanted to, because they were within a day, day and half tops, from the Romanian mansion. She had considered several times calling and just having one of those blasted males come get them, but she knew that would be a blood bath waiting to happen. So, because of the possessive, stubborn, albeit almost broken, werewolves, they got the wonderful experience of nearly running through the Carpathian Mountains. She watched as the males prepared the camp, gathering wood for a fire, and laying out pallets, all the while darting glances at their mates.

Jacque tried to keep her eyes from Fane, but since she had laid eyes on him from her window, her gaze had been for him and him alone. At one point, as she was empting her pack, she swore she felt his hot breath on the back of her neck and she had to bite her lip to hold back a moan. When she had turned to look at him, he had been on the other side of the fire, with an all too knowing smirk on his face. She had narrowed her eyes at him and, being the mature woman that she was, shot him the bird. She realized her mistake when he was suddenly in front of her, still not able to touch her, but that didn't mean he didn't affect her.

"Is that an offer, Luna? All you have to do is ask. Ask me baby." His voice was a purr that made her shiver clear down to her toes. She hadn't realized that she had been leaning towards him until Jen's voice broke through the lust induced fog.

"Walk away from the sex on a stick Jacque," Jen's voice carried authority brought on by her Alpha status and it was almost enough to make Jacque obey—almost.

When she didn't move she watched a triumphant smirk tug at his full, bitable lips.

"JACQUE!" Jen snarled. "I know it's tough sweetie, believe me, I know how badly you want his hands on you, and his lips and his tongue and…"

"Jen!" Sally smacked her friend's shoulder.

"What?"

"Get to the point." Sally rolled her eyes.

"Right, Jacque," she started again, "as I said very truthfully, I know it's hard." Jen paused as she bit her lip. "Do you have any idea what I could do with that statement?" Jen groaned throwing her arms in the air.

"Jen, focus honey," Sally tried a little more softly.

Jen nodded. "I'm good, I got this. Jacque, if you give in now, for the next hundred years every time you tell him no he's going to be pulling up your skirt."

That got Jacque's attention. She pulled her eyes from Fane's smoldering gaze and turned to look at Jen. The other girls around her were covering mouths attempting to keep laughter at bay.

"Did you just say…?"

Jen nodded. "Yes, yes I did. If he knows that rocking your world, well technically it would be your bed," Jen tapped her cheek with a finger, "or the couch, or the kitchen table…"

"JENNIFER!" Decebel's voice, bossy, dark, and sexy, brought chills to her skin.

"Right, focus," she told herself. "If he knows that he has a sexual hold over you he will wield it fiercely. Oh damn," Jen exclaimed, with a slap to her thigh. "There's another one, can somebody please write this stuff down?"

Jacque took a step back from Fane, and then another and another. Jen let out a sigh of relief. "Finally, if I had to discuss sex as a weapon in any more detail to you I was going to have to give in and go rape my mate."

A ripple of laughter flowed through the females and even the males cracked smiles at Jen's words.

While Jen had been distracted, Decebel had moved silently behind her. He leaned as close to her ear as the magic would allow. He blew gently on it, knowing it was one of the things that drove her wild. He watched her shoulders tense. A slow smile formed and a feral gleam glowed in his eyes as he spoke. "You can't rape the willing, baby." Her moan was so low that he doubted anyone but him had heard it, and that was a good thing. He didn't like her making those sounds with other males around, but it did stroke his ego to know that he, and he alone, could affect her this way.

Jen heard the low chuckle behind her and she fought through the desire as she whipped around to glare at her mate, only, he wasn't there. Her eyes were pulled to where he stood, calmly leaning against a tree, arms folded across his chest, eyes glowing. He raised a single eyebrow at her and ran his tongue across his bottom lip. Jen cursed under her breath as she turned her back on him and stomped over to where Alina was sitting.

Decebel watched across the dancing flames of the fire as his mate turned away from him. His wolf snarled and he bristled at the blatant rebuff. He calmed himself with the knowledge that he had affected her. She may be able to push him away now, but it wouldn't last. He was going to have to play dirty with his female. He grinned to himself at the pun that he knew she would appreciate. Once she was back in his arms, he would share it with her. He felt a bone deep ache at the thought of her in his arms, sharing laughs, whispering in her ear, enjoying her warmth, and her light. His wolf was becoming more and more insistent that they do whatever it was their mate needed to get her back where she belonged. He wanted to share everything with her, needed that closeness. Decebel closed his eyes as he felt the darkness inside him, invading his mind, fighting for his control. He knew what he needed, knew that if he didn't take it, then the darkness that had nearly crushed him before Jennifer, and would consume him.

"I've noticed that you and Vasile haven't interacted since the whole keep your grubby paws off me scene," Jen said as she absently scribbled in the dirt, fighting the pull of her mate bond.

Alina glanced over at Vasile. He stared at her intently, and his eyes had rarely left her since she had denied him.

"We have been together a long, long time," Alina told her as she continued to meet her mates' eyes. "And have learned other ways to deal with disagreements."

"Is he angry?"

Alina chuckled quietly and turned back to Jen. "Vasile loses control when he is furious and that is when others think they should fear him." She shook her head. "But, it's when his wolf is contained and he is controlled that we should be frightened."

Jen glanced around Alina to see Vasile, her eyes dropped instantly and she looked back at Alina with a raised brow. "So what you're saying is he's biding his time. Like a hunter, he's waiting for the perfect moment to strike."

Alina nodded. "Yes, and Vasile is a very, very patient hunter."

The air was thick with anger, hurt, desire and need as it grew later into the night. Costin sat with his back against a tree so that Sally was in his direct line of sight. She was so tired, so emotionally and physically drained. It was driving Costin crazy that she wouldn't lay down and rest. He settled slightly after she finally fell asleep. He watched the steady rise and fall of her chest as she breathed and matched his breathing to hers. He wouldn't last much longer like this. His mate bond was not complete, they had only completed the Blood Rites, and his ability to keep the darkness at bay was not as strong as the mated males. He didn't know how Drake was doing it, although he noticed that Peri kept a very close eye on him. He focused his attention on Sally again and gave into the urge to look into her mind while she slept. Her shields would not be strong and he would be able to slip in easily. He couldn't touch her while she was awake, couldn't hold her, or kiss her. But, while she slept, he could enter her mind and there, all bets were off.

Sally felt him as he used their bond to ease into her thoughts. She knew subconsciously that he was doing it because she was asleep and her shields were down. She should try at least to keep him out, but when his arms came around her waist from behind, her resolve came crashing down. His hands slipped under her shirt to her stomach and he growled at the skin on skin contact. Sally's head fell back on his chest and Costin leaned his face down to her neck, kissing her softly and then nipping the mark he had left on her.

"This isn't real," she whispered, breathlessly as Costin's hands ran across her rib cage down her sides to her hips and back up again.

"Are you sure?" He asked her coyly.

Sally shuttered as his warm breath caressed her cool skin.

"I'm dreaming and you're using our bond to do this."

"What am I doing Sally mine?" Costin's lips moved against her ear as he spoke and when he tugged on her ear with his teeth she nearly crumbled to the ground.

"Costin," she whispered desperately as her breathing grew unsteady and her heart raced. Costin was relentless and continued his assault on her senses, touching, tasting, and scenting her.

"What am I doing Sally?" He whispered again. Sally's only response was a sultry moan.

"Sally!"

Sally heard her name and it wasn't Costin's voice calling to her. She felt consciousness pulling at her and she didn't want to go. She didn't want to leave Costin's arms, or lips for that matter.

"Sally!" the voice was more insistent this time. Sally tried to push it away with her hand, or at least she thought she did.

"Stop that," the voice growled. "Wake up."

Sally's eyes fluttered open and she saw Jen, Jacque, Crina, and Elle leaning over her.

"What?" She asked groggily. "What's wrong?"

"Well, where would you like us to start, with the heavy breathing, the sensual moans or the near orgasmic way you called out your mate's name?"

Sally felt the blood rushing to her face as she remembered what she had been dreaming about.

"I didn't know you had it in you Sal. I mean seriously, it was completely shameless."

Sally groaned as she covered her burning face.

"It's okay Sally. It isn't your fault that your mate took advantage of you while you were sleeping," Jacque piped in.

Sally's head came up at Jacque's words and she leaned around the girls. Her eyes found him immediately. The flames from the fire reflected in his eyes and danced around the hazel iris. With a wicked gleam and slight grin he mouthed, "Your move."

Sally threw herself back on her pallet while the girls still watched. She closed her eyes canceling out their curious stares as she muttered, "Check mate."

Chapter 13

"How did we get here? I've asked myself that question many times over the past several days. It's so easy to get caught up in the chaos of our wants, desires, and forgets that there are consequences to each of our choices. I sit with my best warriors realizing the path that we are on and have no idea how to jump off. I ask myself again, how did we get here? I know the answer, but I am not ready to face my own selfishness."
~ Ainsel, King of the Pixies

Ainsel stood staring through the trees towards the last known location of the veil to the underworld. The location Mona had showed him. He had agreed to help Mona stop the Warlock King from going back on his word, and the longer he stood there staring, the more foolish he realized his agreement had been.

Dae, the captain of his warriors, asked, "Are you well my king?"

"I am as well as can be expected in times such as these, Dae." Ainsel's face was grim, his lips drawn tight under the tension.

"You are only doing what is necessary to care for your own."

Ainsel looked at Dae. He was not only a warrior, but also a friend. "At what price? Are the lives of others worth less than ours? At some point we have to ask ourselves if doing what is necessary, is right, and if it is not then is it truly necessary?"

~

"You really weren't expecting him to help were you?" Lilly ask Cyn as they stood in the human realm, just beyond the Veil to the Elves.

"The Elves are a secretive race and do not give their loyalties lightly. They have never before entered into the affairs of the other supernaturals,"

"That is not a true statement," Thalion interrupted Cyn as he crossed through the Veil. Following closely behind him, more male elves emerged, all as tall and muscular as the one before. There were twenty elves standing behind Thalion when the parade finally ended.

Cyn watched Thalion calmly, though inside she was feeling emotions that she had buried, and for good reason.

She dropped his gaze and turned back to Lilly. "To answer your question simply, no I did not expect him to leave his realm to assist us."

"As interesting and no doubt romantic as I'm sure the story is, we need to be moving," Cypher interrupted as he took Lilly's hand and pulled her back to his side.

Thalion nodded his agreement, and then motioned for one of the elves behind him to step forward. The elf held out a beautiful bow with intricate designs carved into the wood. He also pulled a leather quiver of arrows from his shoulder and handed them to Cyn.

"As you know, we have our own magic. The arrows will continue to appear as they are needed."

"There isn't any way you could make that happen with chocolate is there?" Lilly asked, only half joking.

Thalion's head tilted as he looked at Lilly, and she felt like a bug on a microscope under his scrutiny.

"Okay, apparently the definition of supernatural is *one without a sense of humor*," she muttered.

Another of the elves stepped forward and gave Cypher a bow as well and a quiver of arrows.

"We will need to move quickly to track the beast. We had to use a vehicle to get here from where we encountered him," Cypher explained.

"We won't need to travel all that way again," Thalion informed him. "We can bring the beast to us, especially if he knows your scent already."

"How?" Lilly asked.

"I imagine Cyn explained that their sense of smell is beyond what you could comprehend, and once they start a hunt, they never abandon it. If he smells any of your blood, he will come."

"She decided to explain that part when the giant lizard started chasing us for the second time." Lilly's eyes narrowed at Cyn, who gave her customary shrug.

"I take it you are going to want some blood?" Cypher asked Thalion.

"That would be best. Draheim never stop hunting their prey once they have targeted it. As long as he thinks you are in his territory, he will come for you."

Lilly let out an exasperated laugh. "This just keeps getting better and better."

Cypher pulled a sheathed dagger from his thigh and cut a slash across his palm. He rubbed it on several trees and plants in a large circle. Once he was satisfied that it was enough, went over to Lilly and eyed her grimly. "This won't be pleasant, but it's necessary."

"Necessary rarely equals pleasant. Let's just get it over with." She held her hand out to him and he sliced the blade across her palm as quickly as possible. She winced and gritted her teeth against the pain. She chose different trees to place her blood in the opposite direction of Cypher so that they could cover more ground. Cyn followed behind Lilly also placing her blood on different trees and plants.

"So, what now?" Lilly asked.

Thalion leaned back against a tree, with his eyes steady on the sky. "Now, we wait."

Two hours and twenty games of tick tack toe later, Lilly's head tilted back to the sky at the unmistakable whoosh of giant wings on the wind. She rose to her feet and, like the others, waited for the beast to come into sight. Despite the danger they knew was flying above them, none of them could deny the magnificence of the draheim.

It made two large swooping circles, drifting lower with each one. Its head was pointed down as its large, snake like eyes searched for its prey. On the third swoop, it seemed to pause in midair, its great wings flapping, holding itself in place. The beast's eyes narrowed as he stared straight at where they were standing.

"How is it that there aren't humans freaking out all over the place over a great big dragon being in the sky?" Lilly asked as they continued to watch the hovering beast.

"The draheim are magical creatures. They can only be seen by those who believe there is such a thing," Thalion explained.

"Thalion, I noticed a small clearing about two miles east of here. I think it would be wise to lead the draheim there before we take it out." Cypher's eyes never left the sky as he spoke.

"Agreed." It was the last word said before the draheim took a nose dive straight for them.

Cypher grabbed Lilly and threw her over his shoulder in one fluid motion as he took off.

"Here we go again," Lilly yelped and grabbed onto his waist to steady herself.

The elves and Cyn were running alongside Cypher, having no trouble keeping up with the warlock.

The loud swooshing of wings caused Lilly's head to snap up. Her pulse raced as she looked into the eyes of one very ticked off dragon.

"If you don't mind, could you go a little faster please?" She tried to yell as she bounced against Cypher's back.

"WHAT?" She heard him yell back.

"FASTER! RUN FASTER!" She screamed.

She felt Cypher pick up his speed and still the draheim seemed to be gaining on them.

Lilly swatted her arms at the hulking beast. "Shew, shew, go on, nothing tasty here to eat."

Well, that didn't work nearly as well as it does on the neighbor's cat, Lilly thought. Her only consolation was that the creature had to stay just above the tree line. Its monstrous body wouldn't fit in between the trees. Suddenly a ferocious roar filled the air.

"MOVE!" Thalion yelled. The group began weaving in and out and around trees. Like a synchronized team, they moved with such fluidity that an onlooker would have thought them performing a well-rehearsed routine.

"WHY ARE WE WEAVING?" Lilly hollered. The answer came without anyone speaking. A blaze of heat hit Lilly's face as she watched the dragon rear its head back and blast fire from its mouth.

"Are you freaking kidding?" She yelled, this time to no one in particular. "It's not enough that it's a huge, flying, nearly impossible to kill dragon. No, it just had to have the added bonus of breathing fire!"

"Well, it is a dragon after all," Cypher, grunted. Lilly felt herself being lifted from over Cypher's shoulder as he put her on her feet and she saw that they had reached the clearing. Cypher pushed her back into the cover of the trees and pointed at her.

"Stay."

She crossed her arms across her chest as she glared at him. "I'm going to let that one slide since there is a gigantic freaking, fire breathing dragon flying behind you. Cypher swung around to see the beast diving into the clearing.

Cyn and the elves had all raised their bows as they stood as a united front against the draheim. Before any of them could get a shot off, the dragon roared more fire at them. They dove in different directions barely avoiding the blaze. Cyn was motioning with her hands and her mouth was moving as she faced the now burning trees and foliage. Lilly watched in awe as a light shot forth from Cyn's hands. The light wrapped around the fire, enclosing it in a shimmering cocoon. Immediately, the fire began to shrink until it was gone. The dragon's head whipped around to Cyn and Lilly almost laughed at the comical expression on its face. She was sure that the beast would have yelled, *"And who the hell are you?"* if it had the ability to speak. The draheim landed and the ground shook under its great weight. The elves had spanned out and were re-notching their bows. But, before they could loose the arrows, the dragon turned abruptly, using his long powerful tail to knock them off their feet.

Lilly covered her mouth as she gasped. "Ouch, that has got to hurt."

Cypher avoided the tail and finally fired an arrow. Lilly held her breath as she watched the arrow sore up, up and hit the dragon, only to fall uselessly to the ground.

Cypher looked at the arrow he had shot, that now lay on the ground. Before he had time to digest this information, he heard Lilly's voice as she yelled, "Incoming!" He turned just in time to see the destructive tail headed his way. He lunged upward with his powerful legs and tucked into a roll as he cleared the tail and landed on the ground, rolling up as the motion carried him. He ran over to where Thalion stood aiming his bow at the neck of the draheim.

"I shot him and the arrow bounced off," Cypher told the elf.

"You have to aim for its neck. It's the only place where the protective scales can be penetrated."

Cypher growled. "You didn't think to tell me that before we were dodging his fire and tail?"

Thalion shrugged. "You're a warlock; you should know these things." He let the arrow loose and it flew with exact precision to the weakest scales of the neck. The arrow looked so small and insignificant when it pierced the tough skin, but the shudder that ran through the beast revealed the power behind the weapon. It roared in anger, stomping its feet, causing the elves to dodge left and right. Cyn narrowly missed being squished like a bug as she rolled under the dragon. The arrows began to fly in rapid succession as they took advantage of the distraction caused by Thalion's shot. Fire flew from the beast's great mouth and its body swayed with every arrow that pierced its neck. Cyn managed to run out from under its belly and began sending out more light that was magical to put out the flames before they could spread into the surrounding forest.

As more arrows penetrated the draheim's neck, it began to stumble, roaring, and thrashing wildly. Blood began to spurt from the wounds, showering down upon warlock, elf, and Fae alike. Lilly watched the beast weaken and part of her ached at the thought of the life leaving another living being. She unconsciously stepped out of the cover of the forest, wishing there was some way that they could spare the dragon, but knew it wasn't possible. The draheim didn't belong in this world, and, according to Cyn, it had been twisted into something evil. Evil could not be spared. It would spread like the fire that spewed from the jaws of the animal and burn down everything in its path. She hadn't realized how far she had ventured from the trees until suddenly, a pair of glowing snake-like eyes had zeroed in on her. Lilly stopped in her tracks as the breath in her lungs became difficult to expel. She watched helplessly as, in an obvious last ditch effort, the huge draheim lunged for her, expelling flames from its mouth. Lilly's blood was pounding in her head, muffling her hearing. She heard, no felt, the beast's roar cascade over her. It fell before flames could engulf her and its jaws could snap onto her body. The monster hit the ground with a heavy blow, shaking the earth. The draheim let loose one more ear piercing roar, which joined with the wicked flames, before it came to rumbling halt a few feet in front of Lilly. Lilly's eyes widened as she watched the flames rolling towards her. In her mind, she was yelling at herself to move her damn feet, but she just stood there. She closed her eyes as she felt the heat of the flames on her face, her hair blowing back from the force. She was sure that she would be fried to a crisp at any moment. All she could think was that she hoped that Jacque was all right, and that she would live a long, happy life. She waited, frozen in place.

After a few moments, when nothing happened, she finally opened her eyes. She could see Cypher running for her. The other elves surrounded the great beast, ensuring that it was no longer a threat. Lilly noticed that the beast still drew breath. She saw the flames flickering out, being held in midair just a few inches from her face. Protecting her from the flames was a bright shield of light. Lilly's face broke into a huge smile as she turned her head to see Cyn aiming her hand at her. She gave Cyn a slight nod of thanks just as strong, massive arms wrapped around her, pulling her up until her feet no longer touched the ground. She pulled her arms out from the hold and wrapped them around Cypher's neck.

He buried his face in her neck, breathing deep, feeling her pulse against his lips. *Alive,* he thought, *she's alive.*

"Why didn't you run?" He growled as he pulled his face back to look at her. Lilly's breath caught as she saw the emotions swirling in his yellow eyes. "I was yelling at you to run Lilly. Why didn't you run?"

Lilly kissed him. He didn't need her words, he need reassurance that she was there, with him, in his arms. Cypher held onto her as if his life depended on it. He breathed her in and drank her down with everything he had. All hell was breaking loose around them, but in that moment, there was just her and just him. Lilly finally pulled back and pressed her forehead to his as she tried to regain control of her ragged breathing.

"I'm glad you're alive too," she grinned at him.

Cypher closed his eyes as the images of what could have happened flipped through his mind like a gruesome horror movie.

"Hey," Lilly's voice broke through his chaotic thoughts. "I'm here. I know I should have run and I was telling my chicken legs to get after it, but they wouldn't move. I just stood there like I was eager to be barbequed."

Cypher's lips lifted slightly, as he stared into her eyes. "So you're okay?" He asked her gently, as his brow rose in concern.

She nodded. "I'm good. How is everyone else?" She asked, looking over his shoulder.

Cypher set her back on her feet and took her hand as he headed over to where Thalion and Cyn were standing. They all looked at the great creature lying before them, its breathing shallow.

"Is there anything we can do to keep it from suffering?" Lilly asked.

Cyn stepped forward and placed a hand against its huge head. The glowing eyes focused on her and Cyn could sense the peace that the animal was searching for. It didn't like its existence any longer, didn't want to be what it was.

"Shh," she told him, gently, "it's over now. You can rest." She sent a pulse of magic into him and with a final breath, he stilled.

Lilly felt a tingling on her face. She looked down at her blood soaked clothes, caked in bright red splatters that had fallen from the dragon. Her mouth dropped open as all traces of the beast's life force vanished from her and her companion's clothes, evaporating with a twinkle.

~

"Still haven't heard from Vasile?" Dillon asked Skender after a long day of training with the other wolves. Aside from a few fights between young wolves, over who was more dominant, things had been progressing smoothly. There was a sense of urgency and determination that kept everyone in the group focused. The Alphas had been sure to keep the wolves busy, rigorously training them daily, to near exhaustion.

"No," Skender's voice was tense and Dillon could tell that the wolf was very worried.

"I would like to say that no news is good news," Dillon said, lightly.

Skender continued to stare out of the window, into the trees beyond the mansion. Something was coming, he could feel it, and it was making his wolf restless.

Dillon moved to stand next to him and brushed his shoulder against his. To a human it would have been insignificant, but to the wolf in Skender, it was reassurance from an Alpha. That simple brush let him know that Dillon had his back. Skender let out a slow breath.

"This is not my place," he told Dillon.

"Why? Because you aren't an Alpha or Beta?" Dillon held his hands out wide. "You are in the exact position that you are supposed to be in and you are doing exactly what you are supposed to be doing in this moment, and you're doing a damn good job I might add."

Skender turned to look at the American Alpha that he had grown to respect over the past couple of days, working with, fighting with, and learning to trust in battle. "You are a good Alpha, Dillon of Colorado."

Dillon laughed. "Go tell my wolves that."

"They know or they would not follow you, no matter how dominant you were."

Dillon gave Skender a slight bow of his head. "Thank you for that. Your Alpha will be proud to know how you have held things together, Skender. And, he will be back. Vasile is nearly impossible to kill."

Skender laughed then. "He's too stubborn to die."

"His purpose in this life isn't over," said Dillon, growing serious.

Skender's head tilted with a slight frown slipping onto his handsome face. "How do you know?"

"Because, I have to believe that someone who loves his people so fervently and would protect them against all odds can't possibly be taken from us when we need him most."

Chapter 14

"My skin crawled as my wolf perked up. I knew something wasn't right. She was too far ahead of me for me to reach her and even if I had, I couldn't have touched her. So I had to watch what had only been an illusion created by mind, now real before me." ~ Vasile

"We're only a few hours walk from the mansion," Peri told Alina as they continued to keep the brisk pace that they had maintained.

"Are you trying to make a point or do you just feel the need to point out our current position in an effort to create small talk?" Alina raised a single eyebrow at the Fae.

"Alina," Peri said in a mock sigh, "where is the sweet, compassionate Alpha female we all know, and love?"

Alina snorted. "She got locked in a closet when it became vividly apparent that our males would need to recover from their trial before they can kick the witch's butt. And, in order for them to do that they all need a good swift kick to the ba—,"

"Language," Vasile growled, from several feet behind his mate.

Alina held her hand up in the air and much to everyone's utter surprise, gave her mate the finger.

"Did she, did, I mean seriously, she…" Jen sputtered, as she looked back and forth between Alina and a growling Vasile.

"Yes, yes she did." Jacque laughed.

"It's official, Alina. You're my hero," Jen shot a fist in the air with a loud "Whoop!"

After several minutes of the girls chattering back and forth about Alina's retaliation, the group became quiet. They walked in silence. Soon, the only sounds were their breathing and the crunching of the ground beneath them. The air had grown still without so much as the rustling of leaves and the bird's song that had filled the darkening sky had become silent. The silence was broken by an earth-shattering scream, and then another and another.

"ALINA!" The sound of Vasile's voice rose above the screams of the females as they, one by one, collapsed.

Peri turned as she watched the last one fall. It was so fast, between one breath and the next, and all six of the mated females were writhing on the ground. She closed her eyes and felt the energy around her. Dark magic was clearly at work.

Costin was behind Vasile when he heard the screams. He didn't have to see Sally to know that something was happening to his mate. He felt his own heart skip a beat and nearly stop when he saw her small form hit the ground. It was happening again, only this time it was real. She was screaming, tears flowing down her cheeks as she wrapped her arms around her midsection. He ran for her, not worrying about where his feet landed. All he could see was her; her brown hair spilled carelessly across the ground, her tan skin taking on a green tint even as her lips were turning blue. He fell to his knees before her and reached for her. When his hands touched her, he felt a pulse of electricity rip through him and throw him back. He cried out. A chorus of cries rang through the air as the other males tried to touch their writhing mates. He looked over to Vasile and saw that the Alpha looked as helpless as he felt.

"PERI, FIX THIS!" Vasile growled.

"Don't you think I'm trying, dammit," the Fae yelled back. Her lips moved quickly and the stones of the Fae had appeared in her hands.

Peri reached for the magic of her people, the magic in the stones, and she tried to fight against the darkness that was weaving a spell around the females. It was a twisted web that kept getting tighter and tighter. When she realized she could not break it she decided to focus on trying to break the pack magic that kept the males from being able to touch their mates.

"Peri, what is going on?" She heard Adam's voice next to her, but didn't open her eyes.

"Desdemona, she's done something to the females, I can't fix it."

"Yet?" Adam asked, desperately.

"I don't know, Adam. I'm trying to figure out a way to allow you males to touch your females. If I don't I'm afraid that I just might be facing my death in the freaky glowing eyes of an Alpha."

She didn't open her eyes, but she knew that Adam was no longer standing beside her. Peri squeezed her eyes tighter and sought out every ounce of magic inside her ancient being. It wasn't enough.

Why won't you help them? Peri reached out to the Great Luna. *They're your children, why are you letting them suffer?*

She didn't expect an answer, but she got one.

Evil exists in their world and because of that they will face many trials. Pain will be their friend all too often, but it is how they handle those trials and what they do with the pain that will determine who they will become. I love them too much to cripple them by removing this thorn. Allowing them to endure struggles is not because of a lack of love. It is because I love them that I allow them to struggle so they might gain the strength to do what is necessary. The wolves have free will and they can choose to depend on me as their creator. They can choose to ask me for help or they cannot.

Peri frowned. *And, what about the times you don't help? What about the times your answer is no?*

Peri felt warmth envelope her as the creator of the wolves spoke to her. *Does a parent ever say no to her children? Does a parent ever mean harm for her children? I may not help them by preventing the pain, but the pain is necessary and I will always help them bear it. I will always be with them, holding them, reminding them that they are precious to me. My answer will not always be what they want, and they may not understand it at the time, but I will always have their best interest in my heart. They are mine, nothing can take them from me, but as they live in the world, they will endure the evil in it.*

So,. what am I to do to help them? Peri asked.

Be there, Perizada. Be there with them and give them strength when they have none. Offer them peace when they feel none and remind them that I have not forsaken them.

Peri watched as the females she had grown to love lay in pain, their tears drenched the earth and the males that loved them so fiercely sat helpless next to them, unable to touch, unable to help.

Jen couldn't remember the last time she had felt such pain. Maybe when she had been burned in the car fire, or maybe when Decebel had been taken from her, or maybe never. She could hear his voice as he called to her. Why wouldn't he touch her? Why didn't he pick her up and take the pain away? Then, through the pulsing pain that shot through every limb, she remembered that she had made it so that he couldn't. *Well,* she thought, *that's what I get for trying to prove a point.*

"Jennifer?" She heard his voice in her mind and for a brief moment in time, it was like a balm to her aching form.

"If you mention even for a second that I'm the reason you can't touch me I swear I'll skin you and put your pelt in our child's room."

"I love you too baby," he growled at her.

"Why is this happening Dec?" Jen's usually strong voice was laced with uncertainty and fear.

"I don't know love, but I'm going to fix it."

"Hurry," was the last word she got out before all hell broke loose.

Jacque screamed. She tried not to, but the hulking form coming at her was too much. Logan leered at her. It couldn't be him; he was dead. Wasn't he? But he was here, standing over her, smiling at her in a way that made her stomach crawl.

"Get away from me." She tried to sound stronger, but the pain that was stabbing her stomach kept her from breathing and her words came out as a whimper. "You're dead, I know you're dead. You shouldn't be here."

"Oh sweet heart, I'm here and I've come for what should have been mine." Logan's voice was just as she remembered it and she felt like oil had been poured on her skin, dirty, and sticky. She rolled over and vomited, just as his hand gripped her ankle, pulling her towards him.

"NO! STOP! PLEASE STOP, DON'T DO THIS," She screamed at the tops of her lungs, but he didn't stop. Her mind reached for a memory, something that she knew was real. They had been walking through the forest, she, the other females, and the males. They had been on their way to the mansion. How did she get here with Logan? How was he here touching her, oh god, he was touching her. She began to shake and her body felt cold, like it would never be warm again. She felt her clothes rip and a new scream erupted from her lungs. She opened her eyes, hell bent on killing Logan all over again. Only it wasn't Logan standing over her, it was Lucas. *What the hell?* She must be going crazy. That was the only solution; she had to be losing her mind. She kicked, screamed, and clawed at him. In her mind, her nails were raking his face, drawing blood that was raining down on her.

Fane watched as his mate screamed, clawing at an invisible foe. She was hysterical and through the screaming, he recognized two names, Logan and Lucas. She kept saying over and over "don't do this" and it was when he saw the desperation and fear in her open, unseeing eyes that he knew what was happening in her mind. It was the same thing that had happened in his mind, only now she truly thought it was happening to her. Once again, he sat helpless before his mate. His hands shook as he reached for her, knowing that he wouldn't be able to touch her. He watched as tears streamed down her cheeks and blood trickled from her lips as she bit them against the screams she was fighting.

"Jacquelyn," he whispered gently into her mind trying to be a calming presence even as he felt the chaos that was raging through her.

"Fane! Please help me please!"

"It's not real love; he's not real. Please come back to me. I'm here beside you and no one is touching you." Fane flinched when he saw in her mind what she was seeing. When he saw Lucas reach for her he howled, feeling a rage unlike any he'd ever felt before.

Maybe it was the gypsy blood in Sally, but she knew that what she was seeing wasn't real. Knew that she was actually experiencing what Costin had watched all that time that he had spent in the In-Between. Even with that knowledge, it didn't make it easier and it didn't make it go away. She closed her eyes against the hands that weren't Costin's on her body. She bit her tongue against the scream that threatened to spill out when she felt a knife pierce her skin. She fought every instinct inside to keep from calling out to her mate, but she wasn't that strong. Costin made her strong, Costin made her the Sally she needed to be and without him she felt alone and broken. She felt Costin trying to push into her mind, but she didn't want him there. She didn't want him to know what she was feeling, what she was experiencing. But, in the end, her fear and need of him won out.

"Sally mine," his soft voice filled her mind and she whimpered.

"Please, Costin, please don't stay. You don't need to see this." She tried to keep the images from him, but knew she had failed when she felt his anger and desperation.

Costin understood now why one by one the males were howling. He felt his own wolf tearing through him, raging for blood and bone.

Peri stood, helpless, with Cynthia and Drake next to her. They stared at the mated pairs and watched as rage and despair took over.

"We have to do something," Cynthia growled.

"You don't think I've been trying?" Peri snapped. "I don't know what else to do. You're a damn wolf; help me figure out how to fix the magic that keeps them apart."

Cynthia thought about it, trying to remember something, anything from their history that might aid them. She couldn't think of anything that would help, but she knew someone who would know.

"Do you have a cell phone?" She asked Peri, who gave her an *"are you freaking kidding me"* look.

"I need to call someone."

"What, you're using your *phone a friend* option at this point in the game?" Peri walked over to where Jen lay, ignored the snarling Decebel, and reached into her pack. She pulled out the cell phone that had been dead for days.

She pushed power into it, and then handed it to Cynthia.

"Hope you know that this is your only life line left. Asking the audience isn't an option and fifty, fifty just might get us killed by some pissed off mates," she told the doctor.

"You are just a bowl full of cherries," Cynthia snatched the phone away and started dialing.

"No my dear doctor friend, you are confused with someone who wants to blow smoke up your furry butt. What I am is a bowl full of *wake the hell up and smell the roses.*"

~

Wadim snatched the phone up when he recognized the American number.

"Hello," he asked, breathlessly.

"Wadim, it's Cynthia."

"You're alive?" He asked as he flung himself back on the couch letting out a deep sigh of relief. Skender and Dillon who had been talking with him about their next move, both moved closer to him.

"Well, for the moment the answer to that question is yes. However, it is liable to change at any moment."

"Why? Where are you? Where's the pack? What's going on? Where is Decebel?" Wadim had jumped to his feet at her declaration. He paced back and forth while the other two wolves in the room watched him with nerve wracking intensity.

"Okay, you are going to have to shut up and listen," Cynthia growled through the phone.

Wadim took a deep breath and gathered his composure. "Okay, I'm good."

"We're in the forest on the way to the mansion," she said.

"We'll send vehicles for you," Wadim interrupted just as Dillon made to leave the room.

"WAIT!" Cynthia yelled. The males froze.

Dillon, having taken all the waiting he could handle snatched the phone from Wadim.

"What the hell is going on Cynthia?" He growled.

"If you males would just chill out for two seconds and put away your need to control every damn thing around you I could tell you."

A pause. "I'm listening," Dillon responded, in a much calmer tone.

"It wouldn't be wise to send any males near these females right now." Dillon heard a scream in the background and felt his wolf rise up inside of him.

"Desdemona is working her bitchery and the females have a spell on them. The males can't touch them,"

"Why can't the males touch their mates?" Dillon snapped.

"Once again, keep your trap shut until I am finished."

Dillon bristled at the order, but ignored it when he heard Fane yell Jacque's name. It took everything in him not to crush the phone in his hand.

"It's a long story, but basically the females uninvited the touch of their mates. I can't get into the whys just now. At the moment, the males are watching their mates endure terrible visions, happening only in their heads. And, the males can't touch them to help! Peri has

147

tried to break the spell and tried to force the pack magic to break, but it's not working. We need to know how to restore the male's ability to touch their mates so we can move the females. Peri thinks that we can break Desdemona's spell by transporting the girls somewhere farther away. Sometimes this type of magic has a limited range. It's a shot in the dark, but at the moment I think we'd take just about any suggestion if it would fix this."

Dillon stared at the floor as his brain tried to process what Cynthia had just told him. He knew that Skender and Wadim had heard everything and he could tell from the looks on their faces that they were working it all out in their head, searching for any solution possible.

"HELLO!" Cynthia yelled. "Look, the world is falling apart as I know it and I don't have time for you to go into all freaky Alpha mode, so please help me."

Wadim moved slowly as he took the phone from Dillon.

"Cynthia," Wadim's voice was steady and he felt less panicked, as he discovered that he had a purpose and could be of help. "The males were in their human forms when the woman put the binding on them?"

"Yes."

"Okay, okay," Wadim, said again. "The males need to change. The wolf is not bound by the human female's desire. The mate bond from wolf to wolf is different than the human bond. I don't have time to explain it."

"What about Sally? She isn't a wolf."

Wadim thought about it for a moment, but then shook his head. "It should still work. Costin's wolf sees Sally as his equal, as his she-wolf regardless."

"Okay so if they shift they should be able to touch them?"

"I think so."

Cynthia growled. "You think so or you know so?"

"Crap Cynthia, it's not a freaking exact science. I'm going on what I've learned over the centuries of documenting our race, so truly, anything is possible, but what other choice do they have right now? By the sounds of it, they are on the verge of killing anything or anyone. Get those males to change and get them and their mates home." Wadim was breathing heavily when he finished and his heart was pounding in his chest. This is what it was to be pack. When one in the pack hurt, they all hurt. When one in the pack was in danger, they all felt the urgency to save them.

"Okay," Cynthia finally answered. "You need to have their rooms ready. The males are going to want their mates in their territory, surrounded by only their scents. No other males, unless you want a blood bath. Wadim, Vasile is not in control. You need to prepare the others for that."

The phone went dead. Wadim pulled it from his ear and looked down at it. He looked up at Dillon and Skender. "Did you get all that?"

Skender nodded.

"She didn't give us a time frame for how long till they get here," Dillon said as he looked out of the window to the forest. "We need to start preparing for their arrival now. It would devastate Vasile if he killed one of his own."

Wadim shook his head as he let out a humorless laugh. "I swear, I didn't think things could get any worse. After everything that has happened, you would think that I'd be smart enough to realize that, more than likely, things are going to always get worse—much, much worse."

"The important thing is that we stand united. Desdemona's first goal in any battle with us will be to separate us, either physically or by creating division among us. That must always be in the back of our minds. It has never been as imperative as it is now to put aside our pride, our dominance, and our need to control. If we fight as one she cannot win; she is no match for all of us." Dillon's words gave Skender and Wadim the encouragement and renewed determination to put aside their fears and do what they could, what was within their power to do.

Dillon waited as the other two males left the office. He closed his eyes and reached for his mate. He needed to feel the comfort and strength that came from being mated to one who is your perfect match. He felt the return of her love, felt her spirit spurring him on to be the man she knew him to be. That's what a mate was. She was the one who reminded him, in his darkest hour that there was still light in the world. As long as those who stand for good, fight evil, then there was always hope and hope was all they needed in order to stand firm.

~

"Where did the ginormous dragon go?" Lilly pointed to the clearing where the beast had fallen, the clearing that was now empty.

Thalion shrugged as if a giant dragon hadn't just disappeared. "He was not of this realm, so in death he would not stay here. He was returned to his realm where he will be laid to his eternal rest."

Cypher, Lilly, Cyn, and Thalion stood just on the edge of the forest while the other elves gathered the arrows so that no humans or other supernaturals would find them.

"Where do we go from here?" Thalion asked Cypher.

Cypher paused and looked at Lilly. She saw the question in his eyes and was touched that he was looking to her for advice.

"Might as well tell him, he's going to find out," she told him.

Cypher gave a resolute nod and looked back at Thalion.

"I made a bargain with Desdemona. At the time, I thought it was my only option. I needed a mate and I needed magic for my people. The magic in the human realm is growing thin since the Fae have confined themselves to their own realm. The divisions among the supernaturals were killing us slowly. Mona asked me for a favor, one that only the King of the Warlocks could perform."

Thalion's eyes grew wide and Lilly thought it probably wasn't a look that crossed his face very often.

"The underworld? She wants you to open the veil to the underworld." Thalion ran a hand across his face and for a brief moment, he looked much older than his young face portrayed.

Cypher nodded.

"What has changed?" Thalion asked.

Cypher's eyes fell on Lilly and softened when she smiled at him.

"Ahh," Thalion drew out. "So Lilly is the mate?"

"*My* mate," Cypher emphasized.

"Tell him the really good part, your majesty." Lilly's voice was dry and dripped with obvious irritation.

Cypher growled. "There is a slight problem. I made a blood oath with the witch."

Cyn was shaking her head. Even though she had heard the news already, it was apparent that she felt it just as stupid as the first time she heard.

"You made a blood oath with a witch?"

"That is what I said," Cypher barked.

"Why?"

"I was desperate. It's no excuse, but it is the truth."

"The truth sucks," Lilly, said with a sigh.

"Now, that I'm mated, I am unsure of how the spell will work, or how it might affect Lilly. It is also very important that I know how to quickly close the veil once it's opened. I was hoping my brother would shed some light on the situation, but it seems that he is still a tad cross with me about our past." Cypher explained.

"A tad cross?" Lilly asked, incredulously. "He released a giant dragon on us. I'd hate to see what he'd do if he was really angry." Lilly pursued her lips and stared at Cypher.

"Not helpful, little one."

"Not trying to be, big one."

Thalion held up a hand to stop the bickering of the two mates.

"The warlocks are *not* the only ones with the knowledge necessary to open the veil to the underworld."

"Why does that not surprise me?" Cypher glanced at Cyn.

"You didn't ask," she defended.

"Haven't you people ever heard of information that is 'need to know,'" Lilly asked? "Cyn, sweetie, that is information that is need to know, and should have been offered up without being asked."

Cyn nodded towards Thalion. "Hey, the prince of the elves knows how to open the veil to the underworld."

Lilly snorted. "Thanks for that Cyn."

"I'm just here to help," she responded.

"You are getting way too good at sarcasm. I think I liked you better when you just stood and stared at everyone."

"Do you know how it will affect Lilly?" Cypher, asked the prince.

"I can find out," Thalion told him. "We will have to visit our library back in the Elvin realm. We keep documentation there on all the supernatural races."

Cypher's brow rose. "You have records concerning the history of other supernaturals?" His tone of voice questioned whether it was wise of Thalion to have divulged this information.

Thalion didn't appear bothered by the king's question. "It would be both foolish and prideful to think that the actions of others would not affect us, even in the smallest of ways. The safety and well-being of my kind is my greatest priority, as I'm sure you understand. It would behoove any leader to pay close attention to the doings of others, especially those that might be a threat to his race. Such diligence is prudent in order to be a successful leader."

"So what I hear you saying is that we are going to be doing some more hiking?" Lilly asked, grumpily.

Thalion smiled. "Yes Lilly, mate of Cypher, we will be doing the unthinkable and using these appendages we call legs."

"Ha, ha, you are so clever," she told him, dryly.

"Come," Thalion motioned. "It's not all that far."

"I want to believe you, I really do," Lilly muttered, as Cypher took her hand.

~

Mona's uninvited guest had finally taken leave. After several minutes of collecting herself, she turned her attention away from the danger that had taken its leave, to the grief that was music to her ears and nutrients to her body. "If I were the dancing kind, which I'm not, I swear I would do a jig right now." Mona stroked Octavian's mane as she felt her magic pulsing across the distance finally having found its prey. She could taste the agony of the females and the rage of the males feeding her wickedness and urging her on. The chaos was a welcome distraction from the frustration caused by the continuing failure of the warlock king. She had to admit that there had been much that had not gone as planned and there were new situations she'd had to adjust to, but that was the way of war and she was no stranger to adapting to new complications.

She would give Cypher a few more days, simply because she was in a good mood; torturing people tended to do that for her. But, if she had not heard back from him by the end of three days, then he would endure her wrath. *Actually, his mate will bear my wrath*, she thought as she opened a small box and lovingly stroked the strands of hair tucked safely inside.

Chapter 15

"I've never known such fear, such utter despair. Not even in death did my misery meet such depths, for at least, in death, she was at peace. I thought I could keep her safe, or save her from any foe, but how can I save her from her own mind? She, who holds my heart in the palm of her hand and my child in her womb. She, who is so strong, so loyal, lies before me sobbing and broken. How can I ever make it right? How can I ever redeem such a time from her soul? If I could not prevent this, how will I prevent the death of our baby girl?"
~ Decebel

"So we have to get the wolves to phase?" Peri asked Cynthia though she had heard the whole conversation. Peri thought about it for a moment as she looked at the pairs in front of her. Her eyes landed on Adam and Crina. "What about Adam? He isn't a wolf and I don't imagine we will be able to get Crina to phase."

"You are throwing too many problems at me Peri. Let's just get the wolves to phase. We'll deal with Adam as soon as the others are in their fur." Cynthia took several breaths to calm hear heart rate and get her fear under control. Agitated wolves fed off of fear and she was not about to become prey for six dominant males.

Peri let go of her magic and revealed her high Fae form as light enveloped her and she appeared taller than before. She radiated light, peace, and goodness.

"Hear me great wolves, children of the Great Luna, I'm here to help. Remember our history, remember who I am; Perizada of the Fae, friend of the wolves, teacher of the healers. Hear the truth in my words as I tell you how you can help your mates."

One by one the males turned, taking up defensive positions in front of their vulnerable mates. Peri could see the feral rage that boiled just under the surface of each male. It might not be as hard as she thought seeing as how they were on the verge of allowing their wolves to take over any way.

"Vasile, who am I?" Peri asked the Alpha.

Vasile's eyes glowed a radiant blue and his body shook with the need to fight, to kill something. He narrowed his eyes as he stared at the Fae. He knew that he should trust her, that he had trusted her many times before, but his mate was totally defenseless, unable to protect herself in any way. Trust was not a male's first instinct when his mate was in danger.

"Vasile," she said his name again, firmer, and with more authority this time.

"You are Perizada," Vasile finally answered, "friend of the wolves, friend of my mate."

"Yes," Peri agreed with loyalty that rang true in her voice. "You need to phase, Vasile. Your wolf will be able to touch your mate. Your wolf will be able to carry her to safety. I will be your voice. I will be your guard. Trust me, as you have so many times over the centuries, trust me."

Peri waited and just when she thought she hadn't reached him, suddenly Vasile phased, his clothes shredding as he shed him human skin and took his wolf form. He turned abruptly and nudged his mate carefully with his muzzle, when there was no shock of pain he laid down and buried his face against her neck. Tears streamed down Alina's face as her mind raged against her with lies. Instinctively, she reached for Vasile's fur. She clutched it and pulled herself over and onto his back. She wrapped her arms around his great neck and wept into his pelt.

As soon as the other males realized that Vasile's wolf was able to touch Alina, they all began to phase until, where each man had been, now stood, great, snarling wolves.

"Well, now I feel so much better," Peri said sarcastically, as she began to drop her High Fae form. "Snarling wolves are so much more reassuring than raging males."

"Well, at least in this form they are useful," Cynthia, pointed out.

"True enough."

They watched as, one by one, the wolves coaxed their females onto their backs. Peri noticed that coaxing the cooperation of the females took some dominant commanding from the males.

Adam stood up but did not leave Crina's side. "Peri, what about my mate? How am I to carry her?" Anger radiated from the male Fae, and beneath the anger, anguish threatened to take over.

Making a split second decision, Peri glanced at Cynthia. "Cynthia will phase and carry Crina." Adam would hate the idea of another caring for his mate, but better a female than another male.

Adam glared at Cynthia, a silent challenge to take great care of his mate or there would be hell to pay. Cynthia gave a slight nod just before she phased. Adam paced next to her as Peri helped Crina crawl on to Cynthia's back and he stayed as close to the wolf as he could without touching his mate.

Peri turned to Drake. "You should phase, but stay at the back. I wouldn't put it past any of these males, who are bordering on psychotic at the moment I might add, to attempt to take you out in a misguided attempt to keep their female safe." Drake nodded and turned to walk back, far away from the group.

Peri took a roundabout way to get to Vasile so that she would be in his line of sight. She didn't want him to think she was sneaking up on him. For one brief moment she really wanted to hit a wolf, any wolf would do, upside its head, because of all the precautions she was having to take to keep from becoming wolf kibble. It was highly annoying.

"Lead the way Alpha. And, if you don't mind, be quick about it and try not to kill anyone."

Vasile lifted his lips in a wolf like smile.

Peri lifted a single brow. "Okay, don't ever do that again."

She waved out a hand, encouraging him to take the lead.

Vasile let out a loud howl that cut through the silence that had taken over with the witches curse. He took off in a burst of speed only capable by one of his race. The howls from the other males began echoing across the landscape as, one by one, they followed after Vasile. Peri ran parallel to the pack, watching for any danger they might not notice in their single-minded journey to get their mates to safety.

Decebel ran with an urgency that he had never felt before. He pushed his legs to a speed that he never knew he was capable of, all the while keeping his gait as smooth as possible, dodging fallen limbs and holes in the ground that might cause him to stumble and loose his precious cargo. The more distance that they put between themselves and the location where their mates had fallen, the clearer the air felt. His fur rippled as the wind blew through it and his eyes watered. His ears were erect, constantly twitching, listening for any sound that did not belong. His wolf felt desperate to get their mate to their territory, to get out from the open space where any attack was possible. He pushed and pushed never taking his eyes from the path in front of him, all the while remaining aware of the wolves that ran with him and the Fae that stayed just outside of the pack. He was desperate to feel his mate, to open their bond. But he was too afraid that she would become hysterical and let go of him, so he resisted, going against his very nature.

Costin took a small amount of peace at the weight he felt on his back, knowing that he was taking her to safety. It wasn't much, but it would have to be enough or he was going to lose his mind and his wolf was going to go feral. He didn't reach into her mind, but he wrapped his love around her so that she would feel his warmth. He didn't want her to think she was alone in her suffering, that he had abandoned her. He stretched out his stride, racing across the forest floor, more worried about speed rather than stealth. He tried to occupy his mind with ways in which to help her once the spell was broken, and it *would* be broken. He himself had struggled with the things he had witnessed in the In-Between. Those images had eaten away at him like a disease and threatened to create a chasm between him and Sally that he didn't know if he could repair. Now, his own battle with the memories paled in comparison to what Sally would go through once the curtain of lies was separated and reality was once again restored. For the brief time he had been in her mind, he had felt her disgust and embarrassment. He had seen in her mind how dirty and defiled she felt, and it was ripping him to pieces. Something that, though wasn't real, felt like it was taking the innocence she so fiercely protected; an innocence for which he had been beyond grateful for. He knew that Sally wouldn't be able to look past the curse and see that she was still whole, physically and mentally. Whatever it took, he would move heaven and hell to bring healing to the brokenness that the witch's evil had caused.

The pack ran as one, unified in the common goal of protecting the most precious thing in their lives. Fane's heart beat with the every step and he breathed evenly with control. A control that he didn't really feel he had. He knew that his wolf was keeping the man from coming apart. The wolf did not think with emotions, but with logic and instinct. It knew several things that needed to be dealt with. The man couldn't touch his mate, the witch cursed her, and in the current situation, she was in danger. Those things he could fix. He couldn't fix the damaged bond between them that the man had caused; he couldn't heal her battered emotions so he did not worry about those things. Fane let the wolf do the thinking for the time being because the wolf knew what needed to be repaired first. He felt her hands tighten in his fur and heard a small whimper escape her lungs. Like a whip being smacked across his flank, the sound spurred him to move faster.

For a brief time, it appeared that the rest of their journey back to the Romanian pack mansion would be much easier than their journey had been thus far. Peri attempted to be positive, hopeful that they would have smooth sailing back to the mansion. Just then, a bolt of lightning struck the ground very near them.

"Oh come on!" Peri yelled into the forest.

Thunder boomed across the dark sky and the ground shook. The wolves' steps stayed true. None of them stumbled or fell, even when the sky opened and the rain flowed down in sheets. Visibility became nearly nonexistent and the pack was forced to slow their speed.

"Is this all you have? No originality, Mona. Storms must be your specialty!" Peri was yelling. Though the rain drowned her voice out, Peri knew the witch could hear her. As if in response to Peri's challenge, the temperature dropped, changing the rain to skin slicing sleet. The wolves stopped, fearing the skin of their mates would be ripped from their bodies if they continued running. The wolves laid the women down, covering them with their bodies. They eyed each other warily as they sheltered their mates from the icy onslaught.

The sleet stopped abruptly and the wolves heard a loud whoosh. Despite the freshly wet ground and foliage, flames roared across the ground. The fire circled all around them, flames so high that they could not see past them. The wolves positioned themselves in a circle facing towards the fire so that every angle was covered. Their teeth were bared and low growls rumbled through out them. Peri paced around the wolves trying to think, to draw up a memory of what she knew of dark magic. An idea formed, just out of her grasp. When she opened her eyes and saw that the fire was closing in. The wolves were becoming more and more agitated. Peri squeezed her eyes shut and concentrated as hard as she could. Finally, it hit her; dark magic could not control elements unless the element was already present. Mona could create the rain because the clouds held water. She could create lightning because of the static electricity in the clouds. She could adjust the temperature because she could control the wind that was already present.

Peri smiled to herself. In order for her to be able to conjure fire, Mona would have to have a flame to begin with and last time that Peri checked, snow didn't burn. Therefore, the flames before them were merely an illusion, and a good one at that.

Peri whipped around to face Vasile. "It's not real," she told him. "The fire, it won't hurt us because it isn't real."

Peri knew that the instinct of the wolf to avoid fire would keep them from running through it, unless Peri could prove it. She turned and ran towards the flames, and as the heat from them grew hotter, she thought for one heartbeat that she might be wrong, but then she was through the fire without so much as a singed hair. She turned and ran back through and much to her surprise, saw Vasile leading the others towards her. Their need to get their mates to safety must have been overriding their fear of the flames. Vasile stopped around eight feet from the flames. He watched them dance and flicker for a brief moment before taking a running lunge. He passed through the fire and, like Peri, emerged safely on the other side. In less than a minute, all of the others had passed through the fire as well. Without another pause they were off and running through the storm once again.

The storm raged on, and still the wolves ran.

~

Skender saw them first. He was standing in the field where the packs had been training. Something had drawn him out, a restless energy in the air that crackled around him. He knew that Dillon had followed him out but had stayed back, a silent shadow.

"Dillon," Skender didn't raise his voice, he knew the Alpha would hear him, "are you seeing this?"

Dillon stepped up beside Skender and looked in the direction that Skender motioned to with the nod of his head. Up on a hill across the field, he saw the wolves slowly step from the cover of the trees, their mates clinging to their backs. Dillon and Skender watched from where they stood, but made no movement to come any closer. They saw Peri step out as well, standing closest to the large, black wolf that Skender recognized as Vasile. Dillon scanned the line of wolves using his enhanced eyesight until he finally spotted her prone form on Fane's wolf. Dillon started to walk forward, heedless of the danger, his need as a father overriding his commonsense. Skender grabbed his arm before he made it more than a few steps.

"Not yet," he said, simply.

Dillon nodded and stepped back, but his eyes stayed on his daughter and the wolf that carried her.

Peri appeared to be talking to Vasile and his response was a snarl. Peri threw her hands up in a manner that told them she was clearly irritated. She started towards them, leaving the wolves standing on the hill. Dillon growled irritably. It was taking the Fae forever to walk to them, knowing that she could have run or flashed to them.

Peri finally reached Skender and Dillon. When she noticed Dillon's posture and demeanor, it took everything in her not to slap the look right off his face.

"I'm going to say this one time, Dillon Jacobs, Alpha of the Colorado pack. I have had it with possessive, overprotective, controlling wolves. If you growl, snarl, bare your teeth, or snap at me I will personally make sure that every time you are in your wolf skin you have the uncontrollable urge to hump any leg that comes your way. Are we clear?"

Dillon gave a curt nod and waited for the Fae to continue.

"We have a very precarious situation. The wolves you see up on the hill aren't quite sane at the moment. We have been through quite a lot as we ran for our lives through the forest and they are tired, wet, cold, and carrying mates who are still enduring their own personal hell on top of being cold, tired, and wet. It is imperative," Peri paused meeting their eyes, imploring them to understand just how serious the situation was, "that there be no other wolves in their presence or line of sight. It's going to be bad enough that there are going to be scents of unknown males all over the frickin' place. Let's not give the pissed off wolves any excuse to make an example out of someone."

"We arranged everything as soon as we got off the phone with Cynthia. The other packs have been moved to the far side of the mansion, opposite all of the pack rooms. I can go back now and make sure all is clear," Skender told her.

"Dillon you must go with Skender."

Dillon started to argue, but Peri cut him off. "This is not the Vasile that you know. He will not care that you are an Alpha, or that you are Jacque's father. Give them time to sort out the situation and once it's safe you can see Jacque."

Dillon did not look happy about it, but he refrained from growling.

Chapter 16

"We all have our dark secrets. The things we keep hidden in the shadows of the closet that we keep eight different types of locks on. We feel certain that if anyone knew those secrets then there would be no way we could be worthy of their love. We would be outcast. So, we hold tight to those secrets, letting them eat us like a disease, slowly devouring our self-confidence and sense of worth. The saddest part to all of this is that there is a simple cure for this disease; trust. Trust the ones you hold dearest to your heart to love you no matter what, for it is by that love that you are redeemable." ~ Cynthia

Peri waited until the two males were out of sight before she turned back to the pack. She motioned, and slowly Vasile started towards her and the others fell in step behind him. They moved slowly, cautiously, their eyes darting around and their ears twitching. Peri felt like they were walking a tight rope and at any moment one of them was going to fall off, but instead of plummeting to their death they would cause someone else's.

Peri glanced over at Adam once they had finally reached her. "How are you holding up, Adam?" The question held none of the usual snarkiness that was common from Peri, but showed true concern for her brethren.

Adam looked tired and tense. She could see that his fingers twitched with the need to reach out and touch Crina and it was killing him that he couldn't.

"I'm dealing," he finally told her.

"Good enough," Peri nodded. She turned around and faced the pack mansion and, with a nod of finality, took a step forward. "Let's do this," she said and motioned for the others to follow.

When they reached the door Peri let out a deep breath and found that her hand was shaking. She snorted to herself. *The unflappable Peri shaking in her boots*, she thought. Without further hesitation, she pressed the latch on the door handle and pushed it open. She stepped inside and said a silent prayer. The mansion looked like a ghost town. The foyer was empty, as were the stairs, and the railing above that looked over the living area. She walked further in so that the wolves and Adam could come inside.

Vasile walked slowly into the mansion and it angered him that he was afraid to step into his own home. Not afraid for his life, but for the lives of others. Somewhere inside of him, he knew that things weren't as dangerous as he thought it to be, but his wolf urged him to get away from the others. If they were alone with their mates, then they could relax, and think about the other imminent problems. They wouldn't be worried about keeping others away from their mates. He sniffed around, his lips curled back at the unfamiliar scents, but then he caught the scent of his mate and knew that it was because this was a hallway that Alina walked daily. He followed it, not bothering to check to see if the Fae was following him so that she could open the door. Vasile reached their room and finally turned to see if he had been followed. Much to his relief, Peri was right behind him. She reached passed him to the door, turned the knob and pushed the door open. Vasile trotted inside and then pushed the door closed with his hind leg.

"You're welcome," Peri snapped. She turned and looked down the hall, watching as each mated pair stood in front of their rooms. Even Decibel, Jen, Costin, and Sally still had rooms in the mansion. She walked down the hall, one by one opening the doors. All except for Adam and Crina's, he was able to handle that one on his own. Peri stood in the now empty hall, and for a single breath, she felt lost. She didn't know what she should do, what her next move was to be. She knew that she couldn't break Mona's curse on her own. But, the curse would have to be broken if the women were ever to invite the touch of their mates. That left only one choice, and though she knew Vasile would likely not like it, he would just have to get over it if he wanted his mate healed.

Cynthia quickly phased back into her human form as she stood in Crina's closet. They were close enough to the same size that she was able to borrow some clothes. She knew that she needed to move fast to get each of the women in dry clothes and warmed up. It was likely going to be an unpleasant experience as she dealt with the snarling mates, but then such was the life as a Canis lupus—never a dull moment. And, apparently never a moment when one's life wasn't in danger. She grabbed some loose yoga type pants and a t-shirt and made her way out of the closet to see Adam sitting in a chair next to the bed where Crina lay. The pain she saw on his face was heartbreaking. Cynthia could see that the Great Luna had not spared the bond between Fae and wolf; it was every bit as strong as between two wolves. She moved cautiously towards the bed, deciding it was best to treat Adam as she would a dominant mated wolf. He was just as deadly as the males of her race and very possessive.

"Adam," she said softly. "I need to get her into dry clothes."

Adam looked over at her. His eyes had the remnants of shed tears.

"I know you don't want her to be touched, but it's for her safety." Cynthia continued to take slow steps towards the bed, bracing herself for an attack that could come at any moment. She felt encouraged when she made it to the bed safely, though Adams eyes never left her. She talked to Crina as she touched her, reassuring her that she wasn't going to hurt her. It was a struggle as Crina fought her and Adam threatened her, but after nearly thirty minutes she finally had the she wolf in dry clothes. Cynthia made her way to the door only glancing back at the mated pair once. Adam was whispering to Crina and she had rolled towards the sound of his voice. It was a heart breaking sight.

Cynthia made her next stop Jen and Decebel's room. She needed to see how Jen was doing and make sure there were no problems with their baby. She knocked on the door and heard a low growl. Decebel had apparently decided to stay in his wolf form, probably because it allowed him contact with his mate. She pushed the door open very slowly. "Decebel, it's Cynthia," she told him, unnecessarily, since he would recognize her scent. No lights had been turned on in the room, which wasn't a concern for Cynthia because she could see just fine. However, it did make her feel better when facing an unstable wolf to have any and all shadows revealed by the light. So she flipped the switch and squinted briefly while her eyes adjusted. She saw that Decebel was curled up on the bed next to Jen who had her fists entangled tightly in his fur. Cynthia had decided that the best way to deal with Decebel was to be matter of fact. Leave no room for argument with him.

Cynthia made her way to the closet as she spoke. "She needs dry clothes on and since you aren't able to do that, I will help you. I also need to check on her and the baby."

Cynthia moved efficiently, gathering dry clothes for Jen. When she came out of the closet, she stopped short, face to face with a large wolf. He growled at her and stepped around her to the closet. She realized that he was going to phase, presumably, so they could communicate. Cynthia waited until he emerged, dressed. She was not about to approach his mate without him in the room. When Decebel walked around her, fully clothed, she followed him to the bed.

"Be very careful," he told her, with a suppressed growl.

She slowly undressed Jen and Decebel was thoughtful enough to get towels for Cynthia to dry her off before putting the dry clothes on. Jen groaned with every motion and cringed when Cynthia touched her.

"I'm so sorry, Jen. I'm not trying to hurt you," Cynthia told her, gently. She raised Jen's shirt and pressed her ear to her stomach. This was yet another advantage to wolf hearing. She didn't require any special equipment to hear the heartbeat of the baby. She listened closely as she closed her eyes and tuned everything else out. Then she heard it, the steady, fast little heartbeat. She smiled gently and felt a tear slip down her cheek, for there was no sweeter sound than a healthy heartbeat of a baby safe in the womb.

"The baby is alright?" Decebel asked, stiffly.

"Yes, her heartbeat is strong. I will need to get an ultrasound very soon."

Cynthia looked up at Decebel and saw that his glowing, amber eyes were on Jen. Cynthia decided then that the only way she would ever take a mate is if he looked at her the way Decebel was looking at his mate. She left quietly, not wanting to disturb them any longer.

Cynthia made her way from room to room until all of the females were in dry clothes. All of the males had phased back into their human form and growled at her freely, though she didn't take offense. Vasile was actually the worst and that surprised her, because he was never out of control; it was never a good thing for a wolf of his power to be out of control.

"Where is Perizada," Vasile snarled.

Cynthia tried to keep the fear down so that Vasile did not see her as easy prey. She kept her eyes on the floor and her tone very neutral.

"I don't know Alpha. She left just after all of the mated pairs retired to their rooms."

Vasile paced the room restlessly, never getting more than a couple feet away from the bed where Alina lay.

"She picked a fine time to leave," he snapped.

"Alpha, if I might say, I don't imagine Peri would ever abandon those in her care. Perhaps she is trying to figure out a way to break the curse on the females," Cynthia explained.

Vasile didn't acknowledge that Cynthia had spoken.

"How are the others doing? How is my son?"

"They are coping. It was a very smart idea to keep the other wolves far away."

Vasile turned back to his mate when she made an especially painful noise. Cynthia winced and wished for the hundredth time that she could do something more to help.

"Thank you Cynthia for your help; I know this isn't easy for you. Please let me know the minute Peri is back."

And just like that, she was dismissed.

~

Peri stood before the council in the great meeting hall. The walls were tall, and white polished stone. The ceilings were so high that it was hard to know if there really was a ceiling at all. The floor beneath her feet gleamed under the soft glow of the Fae lights that floated throughout the room. She felt a strong sense of déjá vu as she stared at the other members of the council. It didn't seem that long ago that she had stood before them, petitioning for their help. Once again, just like on that occasion, they were feeding her a load of crap.

"We have told you, Perizada, that we have played our part. We did what the Great Luna asked of us. We called the packs." Alston's tone was dry and bored, and it made Peri want to slap him.

"Do you honestly believe that is all she intended for you to do? All hell is about to be loosened upon their world and you think that all you are required to do is use a rock to call on the wolves?" Peri's voice rose with every word.

"Don't you think you are being a little dramatic?" Lorelle asked.

Peri's eyes snapped over to her and they narrowed. "*You* would know of dramatics wouldn't you Lorelle?"

"Come now, Peri, let's not let family feuds cause any more problems. Since you seem to think the sky is falling it would be wise not to add to your predicament." Alston brushed his long hair back from his face and stood from his seat. "I think this meeting is over. We have told you what we have done, the part we have played. Now Peri, since you have always been the ambassador to the wolves, it's your job to take it from here."

Peri's mouth dropped open at the audacity of the highest member of their council. She was hoping that at any moment the Great Luna would drop a bolt of lightning on his head.

"Okay listen up ass hat," Peri's voice boomed throughout the meeting hall. "I realize that you may not believe this, but your crap stinks too, just like the rest of us. You aren't any better than the next person in line, human or supernatural. Pretty soon, all of the races will need each other's support—even the Fae.

"I'm telling you now, if you keep this up, all of you are going to end up standing alone covered in ashes, bruised faces, singed air, bloodshot eyes, looking from left to right saying, *"what happened, where'd my eyebrows go?"* And, you know what my answer is going to be? They went down the toilet *bitch*, along with the rest of the world. So how about for just a tiny blink in your completely undeserving long lives, you think about someone other than yourselves and step up to help? Can you try that for me?"

The six council members stood with their mouths agape, staring at Peri as if she'd grown a third arm. Finally, Lorelle cleared her throat and schooled her face. "And if we don't?"

Peri smirked at the one and only sister she had. "Then I will save Mona the trouble of having to fry your butts. I'll take you out myself."

Alston snorted. "Be realistic, Peri. You don't have the power to challenge us. Not unless you possessed all of the Fae stones."

Peri pulled both hands from the pockets in her robes and held them out, fists clenched and palms upward, to the Fae arrayed before her. She slowly unclenched her fists, revealing the five Fae stones, two in her left hand, and three in her right. The Fae stones, which only appeared in times of greatest need, lay ominously in her outstretched hands.

"How do you like me now bee-otch?" She grinned, wickedly.

"What do you need from us?" Dain finally spoke up.

"Why, Dain, thank you, it's so nice of you to ask," Peri's voice dripped, with false congeniality. "I have this small, teeny, tiny problem. You see the nasty old witch has put a spell on the mates of the wolves, well seven of them to be exact. They are experiencing the very same torments that their mates experienced while trapped in the In-Between." Peri didn't bother to tell them that their mates couldn't touch them. There were just some things that were need-to-know, and these Fae didn't need to know. "I can't break the spell by myself and the two healers are also under the spell so I cannot ask for their help. That leaves me with you bundle of joy."

"We will come with you," Dain nodded, "we will help these wolves who obviously mean so much to you."

Peri rolled her eyes. "I'm glad that you all have decided to come to your senses. But, I do hope that you are acting for the right reasons. And, don't expect someone to bow down at your feet and kiss your toes for saving the day. Saving the world is the most thankless job ever. If you don't believe me, then go ask the humans who do it daily." The Fae continued to goggle at her. Peri clapped her hands together and rubbed them as if they were cold and she was trying to get them warm again. "Enough with all of that, let's get down to business."

~

Costin lay next to Sally on his bed. He was as close to her as he could get without touching her and yet it felt like they were worlds apart. Her eyes would flutter open occasionally and the lost look that glazed over them nearly broke him. His Sally was shutting down. She was escaping into herself to get away from what she was going through, even though it wasn't really happening. She didn't have a wolf to turn to for strength and help; she only had the deep recesses of her mind to run to. She was trying to get as far away from the bad things as she could, but it also took her far away from Costin. He continued to try to speak to her using their bond, but she had effectively severed it. The only thing that he knew to do at that point was to talk to her, to share with her, his heart, his love, his longings.

"Sally mine, I know you are in there. I know that you are protecting yourself, and I'm glad for that. I miss you. I miss your skin, your hair, the way you smell when I touch you. Did you know that you smell different when I touch you? I don't know if Jacque or Jen ever explained that to you, but as your mate, you respond differently to me. There's a desire that isn't there with anyone else and that causes you to give off a different scent. It's the most alluring scent in the entire world. But, because I can't touch you, it's gone. I miss the way you blush when I flirt with you and how soft your lips are when I kiss you. You know what's crazy? Not too long ago, I didn't have any of those things and I was still able to live. Sure, it wasn't a great existence, but I was alive. Now, that I have you, I can't live without those things, Sally. Not just because of the Blood Rites, but because I couldn't go on without you being in this world. So you see, when this is all over, you have to come back to me. Whatever it takes, my sweet love, I will do it. I will take away every nightmare, every soul haunting memory, and replace it with my love. Do you hear me Sally?"

Costin's voice filled with the unshed tears that he had been fighting and he unconsciously reached out to touch his mate only to withdraw his hand quickly. "You have to be okay," he whispered. "You have to, because I am not okay without you." He let his mind drift back to the quiet moments that he had been given with her, his brown eyed girl, so many soft laughs, and sweet smiles. He thought about the night that he had held her in his arms as she slept. It was the first time she had ever slept in a bed with a male, and it was the best night of his life. He had been awake for hours after she fell asleep. He had listened to her heartbeat and the rhythm of her breathing. It had all been music to his ears.

He smiled when he remembered the night he had taught her how to bartend. She was so easy to be around and he knew that he constantly had a ridiculous grin plastered on his face because of her, but he didn't care. As long as his Sally was happy, healthy, and safe, he didn't care about anything else. Yet, here she lay next to him, and she was none of those things. How many times could a man fail the woman he loved, before it became too much? He didn't know the answer to that question, but he did know that if there was anything that he couldn't handle in this world, it was watching his mate suffer, and not being able to do a damn thing about it.

"I will make it right, Sally mine," he whispered, into the room, his quiet voice mixing with the sound of her occasional whimpers. "I will make it right, and kill the one who made it wrong."

~

Decebel paced the room like a caged animal. His breathing was rapid and he was holding back his wolf by a thin thread. His eyes continually darted back to the woman on their bed and with every glance his heart broke all over again. He knew that the other males were feeling exactly the same, only he had one thing they didn't, a child. A child made in love with the woman who completed his soul. There was nothing more that he wanted in this world than to hold his baby girl in one arm and his female in the other and he swore by everything he could think of that he would do that very thing.

"Think, Decebel, think," he muttered to himself, for the thousandth time. His brain was a fog of rage and worry. His heart felt as if hundreds of needles were puncturing it, stabbing over and over with every desperate sound from his mate. Every thought was out of his grasp, every breath was a struggle and he was beginning to wonder if he and Jennifer would ever have a happy ending. They had been through so much since they had met and he just felt it was a matter of time before they didn't make it out as they had so many times already. He turned abruptly when he heard his name.

"Dec," Jen whispered. He was at her side in the blink of an eye.

"I'm here baby," he told her, gently. He looked at her gold locks and longed to sink his fingers deep into the strands, like he had so many times before. He needed to see the spark in her blue eyes and hear the sharp slash of her tongue when she snapped her sarcastic remarks at him. Some might be hurt or annoyed by it, but he knew that was how his Jennifer showed her love. If she ignored you, then that was when you should be hurt. He watched as her lips tensed and her eyes squeezed shut. He knew when her body shuddered that she was in pain, or at least she thought she was. Decebel knew first hand just how powerful the mind was and how it could make the body feel.

"Jennifer," he murmured as close to her as he dared. "Come back to me baby. Hear my voice. Know that what you feel isn't real. We are real, and *I* am real. Remember us, remember our love, and remember my touch and no one else's. I know it's hard. I know what you see and feel seems so real, but it isn't." Decebel fought to keep the growl out of his voice, but it was so hard because he was beyond frustrated at being so helpless. "This must have been how you felt when I lost my memory," he told her, "to know that the one person you would do absolutely anything for, is the one person that you can't do *anything* for. Sometimes life truly sucks," he chuckled, "that sounds like something you would say."

Decebel knelt on the floor beside the bed and laid his head down. He breathed in her scent and tried to keep from losing his control, which was about as likely as Mona becoming a nun.

~

Jacque was still, too still for Fane's peace of mind, but he supposed that it was better than the uncontrollable shaking and screaming. He knew that she was experiencing the things he had seen while in the in-between. He didn't think it was ever possible to be as scared for her as he was when she had been taken by Lucas, but at that moment in time, he had passed scared a few hours back. He thought briefly about going to check on his mother, but he couldn't bring himself to leave his mate. He knew what Jacquelyn would want him to do, but she wasn't able to boss him around. He was going to do exactly what he needed to do, and that was be as close to her as the stupid binding words would let him.

As he stared at her, he considered something that he hadn't really thought of. Since meeting Jacque, he couldn't really remember a time when he was truly mad at her, but he was now. He was so mad that she would keep his touch from her, that she would take away that comfort for him. Fane knew that his desire to touch Jacque so often might eventually make her uneasy, so he had explained the deep meaning of touch between wolves. It hurt deeply that she knew what touch meant and was still willing to take it away from him. He didn't want to be angry, but sometimes that was a much easier emotion to process than fear or pain. So, he latched onto that anger, clinging to it like a life raft to keep from drowning in the turbulent sea of his anguish.

"Why would you do this Jacquelyn? I know you were angry at me for not being more open, but can you see now what I was trying to protect you from? Can you see now that I didn't want you tainted with images of such brutality and hurt?" Fane closed his eyes briefly as he tried to calm himself. He knelt down close to her ear. "This is not acceptable my love. Never again, do you hear me? Never again, will I allow such foolishness. I told you that I would protect you, even if it was from yourself. You need me, you need my touch right now, and because of your rash, emotional decision, I can do nothing but sit here, useless and frustrated. I'm angry with you love." For some reason he needed her to know that, not because he wanted to hurt her, but because he needed her to understand just how much he loved her and needed her. "Don't you see? Haven't I shown you since the day I took you as my bride just how much I need your touch? How many nights have I simply reached for you, for no other reason than to feel your skin on mine? How many times have you found comfort in my arms, skin on skin?" Fane wanted to snarl, wanted to throw something or hit something. He had so many emotions inside him and no way to get them out.

He fell to his knees and threw back his head, letting out a mournful, angry howl. It welled up from the darkest place in his soul and crashed its way through his lungs and out of his throat. He knew his eyes were glowing and his canines had lengthened. His wolf was as angry with their mate as he was and wanted to hunt something and tear it apart. Soon he would feel the blood of a witch, warm in his mouth as he tore her flesh from her bones. She would answer for this crime against his mate. She would answer for all the evil that she had brought on their race and her death would not be quick and certainly wouldn't be painless.

~

The howls shook the mansion as one by one the wolves joined in the somber cry. The packs that had been moved to the furthest side of the mansion from Vasile and Alina and the other mated pairs were restless as they heard the utter hopelessness in their brother's call. They stood outside on the grounds, some phasing to their wolf form, others staying in their human flesh, but all of them answered his call.

Drayden, the Alpha of the Canadian pack, walked over to where Dillon stood, a silent sentry watching over the wolves.

"What would cause a man to sound like that?" He asked Dillon.

Dillon's eyes didn't leave the field where the packs roamed as he spoke. "That is the sound of a man who has reached the end of his rope. His sanity is hanging on by a thread and his wolf is ready to tear apart the first piece of fresh meat stupid enough to walk in his path. That is the sound of a male whose mate needs him, and yet he is unable to be what she needs."

"Is there anything we can do to help?" Drayden asked.

"Pray," Dillon, said somberly. "Pray that we are victorious, and that the mates of these males are restored, because the wrath of a witch is no match for the wrath of even one male Canis lupus whose mate is beyond any hope."

Wadim and Skender walked silently through the mansion, both restless because of the state of their Alpha, and both needing to do something.

"Should we go see if he needs anything?" Wadim asked.

Skender would like to say that he knew the answer to that question, but he was truly at a loss. He didn't know how Vasile would respond to them, even though they were pack and he was Vasile's fourth. But, like Wadim, he felt like they should do something, anything.

"Where are you two headed off to?"

Skender and Wadim whipped around at the sound of the feminine voice, both in battle stance. They were definitely on edge if they couldn't even distinguish the voice of one they both knew so well.

"Peri," Skender nodded as he stood up straight. Wadim followed suit.

Peri walked towards them and, from the shadows behind her, six other forms stepped forward.

"Who have you brought into our territory Perizada?" Skender asked with sudden formality.

"Pipe down Skender," she told him with a flick of her wrist. "These are the other members of the Fae council. They have come to help me break the curse on the females."

Wadim's eyes widened with hope. "Can you really do it?"

Peri looked offended. "Do you poop in the woods?"

Wadim laughed. "On occasion."

"Then on occasion we can break curses."

Someone cleared their throat behind her and Peri rolled her eyes.

"Skender, Wadim allow me to introduce you," she turned and pointed to each Fae as she called their names. "That is Disir, Gwen, Lorelle, Nissa, Dain, and lastly the highest among us, Alston."

Skender and Wadim didn't know if they should bow, or what, so the both just gave short, sharp nods.

"Now, if we all feel our egos have been sufficiently stroked, could we please go and fix these females so that we don't have a bunch of feral males killing everything that dares to breathe in their direction?"

Skender turned to lead Peri towards Vasile's room. They hadn't taken two steps when suddenly growling, snarling, and yelling came from the direction where Skender had left the other packs.

Peri rolled her eyes with a huff. "Well, don't just stand there, let's go stop them before they all kill each other and leave us in a worse state than we are now, which honestly would be hard to do considering I thought hell was as bad as it got."

They started running towards the far south door that would open into the field. Skender crashed through the door first and stopped so quickly that the others crashed into him. They all stood staring at the chaos in front of them, frozen at the site.

"What the hell," someone yelled from their right. Skender turned to see Dillon in his human form holding off another wolf that had phased. "Don't just stand there, do something," he yelled.

Skender and Wadim ran into the fray, separating fighting wolves, throwing bodies far from each other. Skender was able to make some submit, others he had to fight in order to get them to back off. With every fight he broke up, another ensued. The wolves were out of control Fane's howl had stirred the darkness in them and the combined presence of so much dominance was only stoking the fire.

Victor ran full speed towards his second, Andrei, who was in hand to hand combat with Tyler, the Springfield Alpha from America. Victor knew his second couldn't win against the Alpha if he decided to do more than make him submit. He crashed into the pair and grabbed Andrei by the back of the neck. His second turned on him with a deep snarl.

"Peace Andrei," Victor growled and pulled on his Alpha power. Andrei fought the command for several seconds before he finally submitted. Victor turned back to Tyler who was still in a battle stance.

"We don't need to do this, we are all on the same side," Victor told him.

Tyler's eyes were wild and Victor could see just how young this wolf was, especially for an Alpha.

"I am not giving you a command, I am simply asking you to tell your wolf to step aside. You are not in any danger here."

Tyler stood up fully and his shoulders relaxed. He looked around at the battle going on around them and with a smirk looked back at Victor. "You were saying?"

Victor chuckled. "Well, you aren't supposed to be in any danger, at least not from our race. Let's get as many of them under control as we can before they do any permanent damage."

~

Vasile felt wave after wave of power flowing through the air. He knew that power; it was Alpha power, lots of Alphas. He stood from where he had been kneeling by his mate's side. He paced, as his wolf grew even more restless. If there was that much power being released it meant one thing, the packs were fighting. He couldn't have that, not now, not here. His mate was helpless and the last thing he needed was a bunch of feral wolves running around like crazed idiots. He grabbed the cell phone from his bedside table and dialed Cynthia's number.

"Alpha," she answered on the first ring.

"Please come to my room." He hung up without ceremony.

Less than three minutes later, Cynthia knocked at the door. Vasile swung it open, trying not to rip it off its hinges.

"Please watch her. Keep her safe. If anything happens to her I will kill you."

"Yes Alpha," Cynthia told him as she bared her neck to him. He stormed out of the room and the walls shook when he slammed the door shut behind him.

Cynthia stared at the closed door and knew that the wolves that had begun to fight, were in over their heads. They had never felt the full force of Vasile's power. She smiled to herself as she thought about how much she wished she could be out there when he had them all on their knees.

With every step Vasile took, his anger grew. He continued to feel the power that shouldn't be present and his wolf raged at those who would dare come into his territory and act in such a manner. He was their host, and it was his hospitality they were trampling on by acting like animals.

He reached the door and pushed it open stepping out into the mess. He felt his wolf pushing, wanting, and needing to join the fight, to make someone's blood flow. Vasile reined him in. He needed order, not more anarchy. He pulled power from his pack and watched as all of his wolves engaged in the fight dropped to their knees. He pushed that power out as he roared. "THIS ENDS NOW!" Vasile's eyes glowed and he felt the claws on his hands grow, his skin tingled with the need to phase, but he held it together. He continued to force his will on all those who dared to disobey. He forced those who had phased into their wolves to regain their human form. His eyes traveled over the large group, meeting eyes as, one by one, they fell. In less than a minute, men kneeled where wolves had just raged. The sudden silence fell over the field like a blanket smothering fire.

"Who do you think you are to come into my home and spit in my face with such a display?" Vasile words were controlled, and those who knew him knew that that was a bad sign.

"Angus, Artur, Victor, Dragomir, Jeff" he called out the Alpha's names with an authority they could not ignore. "Ciro, Gustavo, Drayden, Tyler, and Dillon stand."

Each Alpha stood and walked forward, weaving around the other kneeling wolves.

"The rest of you are to go to the rooms that you have been given. I will let your Alphas decide your punishment. Be glad that it is not me meting it out. My wolves, your behavior is inexcusable. You will be dealt with. You have pulled me away from the side of my mate, which frankly pisses me off."

There was a snort of laughter towards the back of the kneeling group. As he recognized the sound of one of his wolves, Ciro, the Alpha of the Italy pack, tensed.

"Is there something funny?" Vasile asked as he stepped around the Alphas who stood in front of him.

"No disrespect Alpha, but your more concerned with staying in the bed your mate warms for you, instead of taking care of your pack?" A chorus of coughs, growls, and snarls flowed over the group and before the sound could die down Vasile had moved more quickly than the wolves could track. He had the offending wolf by the throat on his back. His face was less than an inch from the wolf's and Vasile fought harder than he ever had for his control.

"What is your name?" Vasile asked.

"Rico," the wolf gasped from the hold Vasile had on his neck.

"Rico," Vasile repeated slowly, "you forget your place. It will be my pleasure to remind you." Vasile jumped back and ripped his shirt off. "Get up!" He spat.

"Vasile, please do not do this," Ciro asked, cautiously.

Vasile's eyes narrowed as he turned to look at the Alpha. "My allotment for mercy has been exceeded today. I am sorry, Ciro. But, I will not let an offense such as this go. I will not kill him."

"That is all I ask," Ciro nodded resolutely, accepting that he would not change Vasile's mind.

Vasile looked back at Rico who had finally gotten to his feet.

"I don't want to fight you," he told Vasile.

"I didn't ask what you wanted and you are not high enough in any pack to tell me what you want. You will learn your place. We are facing an evil like the world has never known. I cannot afford to have disobedient wolves under my command, nor can your Alphas. You made your choice when you spoke disrespectfully of me and my mate."

Vasile lunged and phased in midair. Rico jumped back just in time to keep from being tackled by the huge black wolf. Rico phased and bared his teeth at the Alpha. Vasile was much larger than the other wolf, though Rico didn't seem the least intimidated. That was his first mistake.

Vasile circled the smaller wolf. His lips pulled back from his teeth and his body shook with the effort to hold himself back. He was waiting; he knew that the younger wolf would grow impatient and make a hasty decision. He didn't have to wait long. Rico threw his body into Vasile, his shoulder caught Vasile in the throat temporarily cutting off the Alpha's air. Vasile laughed to himself. If this pup thought that air is what kept him alive, then he knew not of what it was to be mated. The only thing that gave him life was the woman lying beyond his reach in their bed. Next to her, air was optional. He spun around out of the shoulder that had been pressed into him and grabbed Rico's back leg. He crushed his jaws together and heard the snap in the bone. A collective groan vibrated in the background, but Vasile shut it out. He quickly let go of the leg and jumped back. He circled again, then lunged forward, quickly biting hard into the young pup's flank. He tasted blood in his mouth and his wolf wanted to howl for the victory of first blood. Over and over, Vasile lunged, bit, and jumped back. Rico never got close to Vasile after that first lunge. Once Vasile saw that there wasn't an inch of Rico's fur that wasn't coated in blood, he lunged a final time and grabbed the other wolfs throat. He pulled his head back and Rico's body went up and over Vasile's head as he slammed him on the ground. A loud grunt rushed out of the wolf's lungs. Vasile tightened his hold on the pup's throat and growled. He waited. Finally the wolf closed his eyes and stretched his head back fully exposing his neck. Vasile released Rico and snarled a final time. He stepped off of him and phased back into his human form. He stood, oblivious to his nakedness, and howled. The wolves all joined in and when he stopped, so did they.

"I will have order. Anyone who feels the need to exert their dominance please let me know, and I will remind you why that is not a good idea. This had better not happen again." He walked back over to the Alphas, effectively dismissing the other wolves.

"I'm not going to ask how you let this happen because I understand that controlling dominant wolves in this setting is difficult at best. What I am going to ask is what are you going to do to prevent it from happening again? We can't afford to be at odds with each other. If Desdemona figures out a way to divide us, she will exploit it. Don't give her that ammunition; she has enough without our help."

"Alpha," Vasile heard from behind him. He turned to see Peri standing there with the other members of the Fae council.

"Have you been standing there the whole time?" He asked her. She nodded nonchalantly.

"And, you didn't think to help?" A low growl slipped through with his words.

Peri stepped forward, not the least bit intimidated. Or at least if she was she didn't let it show.

"Excuse me, but I was trying to focus so that I could save your mate, as well as the others, from the spell that has been put on them. So no, I didn't consider helping. Not to mention, it's quite a show watching healthy young men phase back and forth. You know, there's that whole naked thing going on." Peri, looked at him pointedly.

Vasile rolled his eyes. "So glad to know that you were so concerned that you felt the need to watch the fight instead of trying to stop it."

"I pick my battles, Vasile. And, far be it from me to stop fine men from getting naked. If it ever comes to that, just shoot me."

"I may just shoot you now and get it over with," Vasile grumbled. "You say you can take the spell off of Alina?"

"I believe we can," she motioned to the other Fae.

"Let's go," he turned to go but stopped and looked over his shoulders at the Alphas. "Deal with your crap, or I will." Then turned and walked away.

Peri looked back at the Alphas and grinned. A few of them were naked from their phase. She raised her eyebrows suggestively. "If any of you need help dealing, by all means, let me know," she told them with a laugh as she watched a few of them blush. She followed Vasile and left the blushing wolves. She had work to do, but that much needed breather had helped clear her head of all the worry that had been cluttering it up.

"So how do we break the spell?" Vasile called back.

"Not a clue," she volleyed.

Chapter 17

"I really thought that eighteen years ago, when I found out that the man that I loved was a werewolf, that I had exceeded the level of weirdness that my life could ever handle. I was wrong, so, so wrong." ~Lilly

"Okay, I will admit it Thalion," Lilly smiled as they entered a room holding more books than she had ever seen. There were shelves overflowing with bound volumes and table after table stacked full of them. Even the floor of the large room in which she stood boasted piles of more books. "You were right. It didn't take long."

"I tried to tell you."

"Yes, well, my track record with supernaturals is a little rough, so forgive me if my first thought was to think that you were full of crap."

"I'm going to try and not be offended by that," Cyn told her.

Lilly smiled at the Fae as she walked around the room, looking at the shelves of books and papers stacked haphazardly in every corner. From the outside, the building looked like a home from a fairytale. The inside, however, resembled a huge study, containing scattered tables and several different seating areas containing plush couches. A huge fireplace stood on the north wall, boasting a crackling fire that cast a warm glow throughout the room.

"Why does the outside of this place look like a regular house?" Lilly asked.

"Keeps anyone who doesn't belong here, out." Thalion explained. "Not that we have many visitors, but it's always better to be safe. There's a lot of information contained in these tomes, most of which, many other races would not want to be public knowledge."

"In other words," Cypher cut in, "if they found out this place even existed they would burn it to the ground."

"Huh," Lilly nodded, "alright then."

"What are we looking for?" Cyn asked.

Thalion walked slowly around the room, his eyes roaming over the books. "It's a brown, leather book. The only distinguishing mark on it is the word *Nushtonia.*"

Lilly looked over at Thalion. The word was not English and frankly not any language she had ever heard. "What language is that and what does it mean?"

"It's the language of the underworld," Cypher answered.

"They have their own language?" Lilly's brow wrinkled as she looked at Cypher doubtfully.

"Yes, and it is wise not to use it," Cyn shot Thalion a warning look.

"They have no power here," he told her.

"Word travels faster and farther than you know. You have spent far too much time separated, cut off from everything going on."

"Haven't we already been over this?" Thalion asked.

"Maybe, but that doesn't mean you don't need to hear it again."

Lilly held her hand out for a high five from Cyn, who simply looked at it. Lilly rolled her eyes, picked up Cyn's hand, and slapped it against hers.

"So what does this *n* word mean?" Lilly, asked again.

Cyn let out a slow breath before finally answering. "It's hard to translate into the human tongue, but basically it means *open this and the world as you know it, is over.*"

"All that from one little word?" Lilly asked.

Cyn shrugged. "I said it was hard to translate."

"So if the word on the outside is demon language, than is it safe to say that this book was written by demons?" Lilly asked.

"That is correct," Thalion, told her as he continued to scan the vast library.

"How did you come across a book scribed by the demons?" Cypher asked.

"That is an interesting story," Thalion said evasively, "and perhaps should be told at a better time."

"When exactly would be a better time, considering we need to do the exact opposite of what the title tells us not to?" Lilly asked, dryly.

Thalion looked over his shoulder at her. "Fair enough. Make yourself useful and help look for the book while I tell you the tale."

Lilly, Cyn, and Cypher began going through shelves and stacks of books as Thalion began the story.

"A very long time ago…"

"How long exactly?" Lilly asked

Thalion's lips tightened, as he narrowed his eyes at Lilly. "If you want me to tell the story you are going to have to listen, and if you are talking, you cannot be listening."

Lilly held her hands up. "Proceed," she muttered.

"It was so long ago that the Warlock King was not even a thought in the wind," Thalion continued. "The human world was very young and the disobedient children of God had just fallen, creating the underworld. Your God because of their desire to be like God forsook them. They craved and desired, the one thing that they should have never wanted, and that was to be as great as their creator. During this time of peace, the supernaturals traveled freely between the realms. We all knew of the fallen, the angels that had become demons, and knew that they were never to be released from the hell in which they had been cast. Their evil was beyond anything that we had ever known. The leader of them, Lucifer, had declared war on the human children of God and desired more than anything to take their souls, to drag them to the hell he and his were stuck in for all eternity. All of the supernatural races were warned by an angel of God to never allow the demons from the underworld to escape their own realm. The veil was sealed by the angel and hidden from all.

Unfortunately, evil always seems to find more evil. All evil things are drawn to each other, seeking out those who would help them in their cause. Though the veil to the underworld was hidden, the evil beyond it was great and as more and more lost souls were cast there after their death, and so the evil grew. It began to permeate the air around the Veil such that other beings could detect it. There was no one who knew how to open it, but that didn't stop them from trying.

As the sons of men began to allow evil into their hearts, and as they began to stray farther from their God, they began seeking out other ways to fill that void inside them. They began to worship other beings, or objects. They sought out meaning for their lives in ways that caused darkness to creep into their hearts. God desired men to have free will and he would not force their loyalty to him. Sin was corrupting the world and Lucifer was allowed some control in the human realm. That sin gave Lucifer just the opening he needed to whisper lies into the ears of those who would listen. He pointed them in the direction divinity and sorcery where they learned how to contact the dead. They thought that they were contacting loved ones who had passed on, but in reality they were drawing the demon spirits to them and giving them power, so much power that the demons began to be able to manipulate the actions of men and women still living.

Once again, an angel of God came to the leaders of the supernatural races. He asked that we keep a close eye on the evil gathering in the world. The veil to the underworld was no longer a secret to all men. They began seeking it out under the direction of the demons that had seeped into their hearts. Surprisingly however it was not a human that became the tool used to make it possible to open the Veil.

One male continually sought out any interaction from the malevolent beings. Over time the demons relentless bombardment of his thoughts led to actions that they themselves directed through him, and one day he found himself at the Veil. The demons continued their assault on his mind and he became so attuned to their wickedness that he clearly heard, the directions on how to open the Veil. He followed their instructions to write the ritual in a book, so that when the appointed time came, the book would be read, and the ritual performed. I happened upon the male when he was attempting to read a language that he didn't even know, though he had written it. I took the book and tried to destroy it, but nothing I tried was successful, so I hid it in our vast library. It has been here, untouched ever since."

The room was quiet once Thalion's voice no longer filled the space. The group continued to look for the book and it was awhile before someone finally said something.

"That does not explain how the Kings of my people have known how to open the Veil," Cypher pointed out.

Thalion did not respond, but paused in his searching.

"Thalion," Cypher prompted.

Finally, Thalion turned and looked at the King.

"The male that found the Veil, the one who wrote the book, he was the Warlock King."

Cypher's eyes widened and he froze where he stood. He felt like he couldn't get enough air in his lungs and what air he did get in was thick and difficult to exhale.

"That still doesn't explain how the others have known," Lilly said, as she walked over to Cypher's side. She took his hand and rubbed it gently, a silent reassurance that she was with him.

"Cypher understands how they all have known," Thalion said, as he continued to stare at him.

Cypher nodded. "When the King dies the next in line is given his memories, all of them."

"How?" Lilly asked, as she tilted her head back so she could fully see his face.

"Blood," Cypher told her. "All things come from blood; life, memories, healing, and even evil."

"I hate to break up this moment of painful revelation," Cyn quipped as she walked over to Thalion, "but I found it." She handed him the very book they had been looking for.

Thalion felt a chill run through him as he held it. Cypher's eyes landed on the book and he felt an unexplainable need to take it, to protect it.

"Cypher?" He heard his name being called, but it sounded like it was coming from far away.

"What's he doing?"

"He's drawn to the book because of the knowledge that it holds." Thalion's words snapped Cypher out of the trance he had been in.

"Evil is drawn to evil," he repeated what the elf had said while telling the story. "Is that why? Is the darkness in me trying to connect with the evil in that book?" Cypher's voice was thick with contempt and his heart tightened painfully in his chest as he was once again reminded that he had made poor choices so many times, and some very recently.

"No," Lilly said firmly as she planted herself directly in front of him. He looked down at her and he was able to breathe a little easier as he saw the determination in her eyes.

"You are not evil. Have you made bad choices? Most definitely, but we all have. We have all, at one time or another, done things that were, for lack of a better term, sinful. It's how we handle the aftermath that determines who we really are and what path we are on."

Cypher raised his hand so that he could cup Lilly's cheek. He touched her gently, as if she were precious and fragile. His eyes softened as he leaned down and pressed a gentle kiss to her lips.

"You make me better; you push out the evil," he whispered against her lips.

"Then kick the idea that you are evil to the curb," she snapped. "My heart could never fall for someone evil, so that settles it."

"You've fallen for me?" Cypher suddenly forgot about the book, his evil and everything around him, his attention was for Lilly alone.

"Like that's news to you," she answered.

"I hoped, but I did not know little one. What it means to me to hear you say it is beyond words for me."

Lilly let him pull her into his broad chest and, for a few breaths, they took comfort in the love that was growing between them.

Half an hour later, they crossed back into the human realm. Thalion had called on his warriors again and so a Fae, human, and Warlock King stood, surrounded by the elves.

"So what do we do now?" Cyn asked.

"It is time for me to meet with the witch." Cypher pulled his shoulders back and steeled himself for the coming confrontation. "But, before that, I need to call on my own warriors to meet us at the Veil; along with the wolves, and" he glanced at Cyn, "I'm assuming the Fae?"

Cyn shrugged. "It's never wise to count on the Council, they are too selfish, and if they determine it is a risk that they don't feel worth bearing, then they will not come."

"Must be nice to think that you pee gold," Lilly said, as she crossed her arms across her chest.

"Do I even want to know what that means?" Thalion asked.

"You'll figure it out," Lilly assured.

"We could move a lot quicker, Cypher, if you would let me flash," Cyn told him.

Cypher didn't look convinced.

"Why won't he let you flash?" Thalion asked.

"Because she is not the only one I'm keeping from flashing to us," Cypher explained.

Thalion nodded. "Right, you've been making sure others can't locate you."

"Exactly," he agreed.

"That was all fine when we didn't have the information we needed. We have it now," Cyn pointed to Thalion who was the caretaker of the book until such a time that Cypher would need it.

"Let me flash to your people, I will tell them to meet us and then you guys can begin your journey to meet Mona."

Cypher thought about it and finally realized the wisdom in her plan.

"Okay, take this," Cypher removed a necklace he had tucked under his shirt. "Show it to Gerick, he is the leader of my warriors. He will know that I have sent you if you show him this talisman."

Cyn took the necklace and put it over her head. "Okay, see you guys soon."

"Cyn," Thalion stepped towards her. "Be safe."

Cyn nodded and gave him a small smile. "If I don't see you again..."

"I'll see you on the other side," Thalion finished for her.

Then she was gone.

Cypher had Lilly climb onto his back, and then with Thalion and the warrior elves, they took off. They moved so quickly that they barely disturbed the forest around them.

"Where exactly are we going?" Thalion yelled to Cypher.

"I'm going to have her meet us thirty miles from the home of Vasile, Alpha to the Romanian wolves."

"Then you plan to see the wolves?"

Cypher nodded. "I decided that it would be wiser to combine our forces and devise a plan. We all have a common enemy here."

They ran in silence the rest of the way. Finally, when Cypher could feel the magic of the wolves pulsing on the air, he stopped. He wasn't sure that they were exactly thirty miles from the mansion but he figured if he was feeling the pack magic this strongly he didn't need to get any closer. He didn't put Lilly down right away, but instead looked around the forest. The air felt off, it was thick with magic.

"The packs have gathered," he told Thalion.

"I can feel it too," Thalion agreed.

"Feel what exactly?" Lilly asked, as she wiggled to make Cypher put her down.

"Magic, strong magic," Cypher explained.

"What does it feel like?" She asked.

"Like something crawling across your skin." Cypher, turned to Thalion, "I think it would be wise if she did not know you were here."

Thalion agreed. "Let us take care of your mate while you meet with the witch."

Cypher hated to let her out of his sight, but he also didn't want her to grab Desdemona's attention.

"Okay," he relented.

He grabbed Lilly around the waist, pulled her to him, and kissed her fervently. He wrapped his hand in her hair and pulled her head back, demanding that she open her mouth. She complied eagerly as her arms slipped around his neck and she pulled him closer. Cypher slowed the kiss down and then kissed her nose, her cheeks, and forehead. He nipped her ear and kissed down her neck to her collar bone, and then finally back up to her lips. When he pulled back to look at her, he chuckled at the dazed expression on her face.

"Stay safe," he commanded.

"Is there more where that came from?"

"Most definitely," he told her.

"Then no worries, I don't plan on dying until I see my daughter, and then indulge, a little more, in a certain Warlock King."

He smirked. "Just a little?"

"Let's not get technical on the depth of the indulging okay?"

She turned to follow Thalion and Cypher slapped her butt.

Lilly laughed, as the forest, with a slew of warriors at her back, swallowed her up.

Cypher waited until he could no longer hear the retreating Elves before he called out the witch's name. "Desdemona," Cypher called and he focused all his attention on his voice traveling on the wind, seeking out his target. He had no idea how far away she was, so he knew he might be in for a bit of a wait. He began to walk around the forest keeping to a small area. His mind wandered back to the revelation that Thalion had shared. He couldn't believe that one of his own kind had been touched by evil so deeply. A king had been possessed and controlled. That King brought evil into their race and it had been passed down from King to King. How long had it taken for the memories to fade enough that the kings no longer remembered why they had the knowledge to open the veil to the underworld? At some point in history, they had simply accepted the knowledge without questioning. They had accepted evil into their midst and never wondered about its origin. He wondered then, if they had accepted it, would there be a way to reject it? Were they redeemable despite holding on to something of this magnitude for so long?

Cypher didn't realize how long he had been pacing and thinking until he realized the light was beginning to fade from the forest and night made its appearance. He backed up to lean against a tree and listened to the sounds of the forest. Humans never bothered to listen to the sounds around them and didn't realize that they could learn so much without ever seeing anything. Suddenly a hush fell over the forest and Cypher knew she was approaching.

"You rang," Desdemona's voice carried.

He waited until he could see her before he responded. Once again, she was mounted on her black steed and the evil that poured off of the witch equally poured off her horse. She dismounted and walked slowly towards him.

"I did," he finally answered.

"You are ready to uphold your end of the bargain?"

"I will be."

Her eyes narrowed, dangerously. "What do you mean, you will be?"

"I've requested my warriors come to protect my mate. You have to know that I will not leave her to fend for herself against the demons you are unleashing."

"Technically you are unleashing, but then who's getting technical?" Mona laughed.

"I need two days," Cypher told her.

"Your warriors will be here in two days' time?"

"Yes."

"And, they are only here to protect your woman?"

"Yes."

"Would you take a blood oath on it?" Mona watched the King carefully, looking for any sign of weakness.

"No, I've shed the only blood I ever will for you. It is enough to take my word."

Cypher waited for her response. His eyes never left hers. He would not allow her to think she was more dominant than he. Though they were not wolves, there was still a struggle for power, because in any race, weakness made you prey, and prey was eaten for dinner.

"Fine, you have two days. But, then you will…"

"You don't need to remind me of my obligation witch. I will be there," Cypher barked at her.

She stared daggers at him as she mounted her horse and flew by him, nearly knocking him over; another power play. The move did not trouble Cypher because her time was coming and the power she flaunted so stridently now, would soon be stripped from her, along with her dignity, her pride, and then her life.

~

"I think the best way to go about this, since it's our first time, is to do Alina alone." Peri stood in Vasile's room, with the six other Fae council members gathered around her.

Vasile stood between the bed where his mate lay and the others in the room.

Peri had asked for Cynthia to be present just in case Vasile lost his cool.

"And what exactly do you expect me to do?" Cynthia had asked Peri.

"Help," she told her.

"How? Have you ever seen an enraged wolf? There is nothing that I could do to stop him."

"I know," Peri patted Cynthia, "but you being in the way would give me time to get away."

That hadn't gone over very well with the doctor, but for some reason she had come anyway.

"What exactly are you going to do?" Vasile asked.

"We are going to use the stones and try a cleansing spell. It's a spell meant to clean out the spirit, to push out any darkness that has gotten in, but I don't know if it will work to break a spell."

"There's only one way to find out." Peri took a step towards the bed and when Vasile did not move she gave him a pointed look. Finally, after lifting his lip in a snarl, he stepped aside so that she and the others could get closer to his Alpha female.

Peri took the stones of the Fae and laid them around Alina in a circle on the bed. The Fae gathered in a circle around the bed as well and clasped hands. Peri sat down next to Alina and laid her hands on the female's head. She closed her eyes and she began to chant.

"Alina, Alpha, precious to your mate,
Hear my voice, this is not to be your fate.
The darkness binding, twisting inside
Seeking shadowed places in an attempt to hide.
I call you now from the evil you came,
You are not strong; you have no power I can't tame.
Alina, mother, precious to your pack,
You fight this evil so we can bring you back.
There is a light in you that is alive in your heart,
No curse or spell can ever touch that part.

I am Perizada. I call on the power of my race,
You are finished; you will leave without a trace.
I will pull you from this body wrap you up tight,
Then cast you far from this place with all my might.

Alina! Hear my voice I command it of you,
Open your eyes to everything that's true,
Fight the horror fight the fear and lies.
Fight and you will win as darkness dies.

Open your eyes Alina. Open your eyes

Open your eyes."

Peri's voice filled with anger as she watched the spell wrapping itself around Alina's mind. The Alpha was tired and worn out. Her mind was weak and no longer able to pick fact from lie.

"OPEN YOUR DAMN EYES ALINA! YOU WILL NOT LET HER WIN!"

The stones around the she-wolf began to glow so bright they were nearly blinding and still Peri persisted. She yelled as tears streaked her face. This woman she had grown to love, considered a friend, and respected so much, was letting the evil win and that was not acceptable to Peri.

Vasile walked over behind Peri and placed his hand on the Fae's shoulder. He pulled power into him, wolf magic, and pushed it into Peri along with his thoughts.

"You come back to me Alina; we are not done in this life. Don't you dare give up!"

He waited for something, anything to tell him she had heard him.

Her eyes fluttered open and, after several blinks, her vision began to clear. Peri shuddered as she felt the spell leaving Alina's body. She pulled it into her grasp and walked over to Alston. He wrapped his hands around hers and spoke so low that no one could here. When he dropped his hands, Peri opened hers and let out a sigh of relief. It had worked.

"Vasile," Alina's voice was weak as she turned to look at him. Tears flooded her eyes and she reached for him. He hesitated and she misunderstood, thinking that he didn't want to touch her.

"Don't," he told her sternly. "You know better than to think such falsehoods. I have always wanted you and will always want you."

"Then why are you there," she pointed to where he stood, "and not here?"

"Do you not remember?" He asked.

Alina closed her eyes to think.

"Don't, please," Vasile leaned towards her. "Please, don't close your eyes."

Alina looked at him and saw in his mind what she had done.

The pain on her face made Vasile's arms ache to hold her and he shook with the effort to keep from gathering her in his arms.

"Please," she whispered to his mind. *"I am yours."*

"You will allow me to have what is mine?"

"Please," was all she could get out.

The pack magic was broken as soon as Alina had confessed her need for him. Vasile climbed into their bed and pulled her into his arms. He didn't take his eyes off her when he growled at the Fae in the room. "Leave us."

Peri and Cynthia went from room to room telling the males that she and Cynthia would need to bring all their mates to Cynthia's room. It was neutral territory and should help the males feel less threatened. Once they had moved all of them, with mostly no problems, Peri explained what had happened with Alina.

"So, she is fine now?" Decebel asked, eagerly.

"Yes, she is curse free and Vasile has his arms around her now. It was rated PG when we left, but I imagine they have moved on to more interesting acts. The point is they can touch again." Peri clapped her hands together and then rubbed them. "So, we ready to do this? It may take a little more effort and I will need to touch each female at some point. Also, Vasile pushed his magic through me to Alina and that seemed to be the catalyst for her."

"What are we waiting for?" Fane snarled.

Peri rolled her eyes. "I swear I'm going to have a nice wolf pelt rug one of these days," she grumbled as she and Alston placed the stones around the females lying on the floor.

Peri started on the right side, Rachel being the first female. She laid her hands on her head and she pushed into her mind, just as she had with Alina. She chanted as she pulled on the curse. She felt Gavril's hand on her shoulder as he helped draw Rachel from the dark place the curse had dragged her to.

One by one, Peri touched each mate. She made sure to call them by name and allowed each male to reach out to their females through her. Once again, the stones glowed as power began to fill the room. The Fae council chanted out loud this time as they watched Peri begin to weaken, straining with the effort to remove the spell. She was nearly ready to collapse when Dain stepped out of the circle towards Peri, who was by Sally's side. Costin looked up to see the male Fae coming towards his mate and he lunged. His teeth were bared and his eyes glowed as he reached for the man he thought meant harm to his mate. He stopped in mid jump when he heard her voice.

"Costin," Sally's voice reached into him and drew the man back. She was calling for him. His mate was calling for *him*. He was by her side an instant later and nearly touched her before he remembered that he couldn't.

"Sally I need to hold you, please invite me."

Sally blinked, as she tried to focus on what he was saying. Her mind was a jumbled mess and she kept trying to push away thoughts that would only lead to tears.

"I need you Costin," The words were barely thought and Costin had scooped her up and left, without a backward glance, heading straight for his room.

He laid her on his bed and sat beside her. He stroked her cheek and his heart broke when she pulled away from him.

"Sally, look at me," Costin tried to keep the growl from his voice; he didn't want to scare her any more that she already was.

She slowly turned her face towards him, but she wouldn't meet his eyes.

"Don't be submissive to me," he told her as he gently tilted her chin up, ignoring her flinch. "You're my mate, my equal, and you will always meet my eyes."

She stared up into his hazel eyes. He was so handsome it nearly hurt to look at him. She ached for his touch but she feared it as well.

"Why?" He asked her.

"I'm not clean, I'm not…"

"You're mine," He interrupted and then continued out loud. "You are mine and I am yours."

"They t-t-t," Sally erupted into tears as she tried to explain to Costin. She needed him to know because he wouldn't want her anymore. At this moment, she was so broken that she knew that if he left now she would just curl up and die. But if he stayed because he didn't understand then she wasn't really his anymore, and that would hurt even more.

"Costin, I was a virgin," she finally got out.

"You still are love," he told her gently. *"I would remember if we had indulged in something that is bound to be amazing."*

Sally shook her head, frustrated that he didn't understand.

"No, it wasn't you. Someone else did it, Costin, and I couldn't stop him. I tried, I promise."

"I know baby, but that wasn't real. It didn't really happen."

She continued as if she hadn't heard him. *"That's not the worst part, oh god, that's not the worst."* Tears flooded her eyes and sobs broke through her chest. She reached for him, though she knew she had no right to. Not any more.

"I…" She tried to tell him but she couldn't. Shame washed over her and so she showed him instead. She buried her face in his neck and played the images for him of the things she had endured, the things she had done. Her body shook and she bit her bottom lip to keep from crying out.

Costin wrapped his arms around Sally and pulled her onto his lap. He saw the things in Sally's mind that she believed had happened. Costin wouldn't lie and say that it didn't make him angry, but not for the reason Sally thought. It made Costin angry, because it took something that was to be special and beautiful for her and cheapened it; stole it from her, making her think that she had cheated on him. Costin had endured the same images in the In-Between and he had prayed that he would be able to keep those images from her, to keep her safe. Yet, here she sat utterly devastated.

He didn't know what to do. She wouldn't believe his words. He could see the ferocious determination to push him away because she thought she no longer deserved him, that she wasn't worthy of *him*. It was ridiculous; if anyone wasn't worthy, it was him. Sally was his precious and amazing Sally, with a heart of gold and a gentle spirit.

"I love you," he told her and she shook harder, but he wasn't going to stop, not until she understood with absolute certainty that he was not leaving her.

"I love you Sally. I love you and I'm not leaving." He pulled back so that he could wipe the tears from her cheeks. She fought him, but he was stronger. He held her shoulders still and looked at her.

"I'm going to kiss you now; do not fight me."

Sally tried to shake her head, but Costin wrapped his hand around the nape of her neck and held her still. She refused to open her mouth and Costin nipped her lips in admonishment.

"Open your mouth, Sally." His voice was a deep, husky whisper in her mind, it made her shutter, and for a moment, she forgot her pain and fear. She opened her mouth and when their tongues met, she moaned. And, just like that, the sound brought an image to her that made her want to vomit. She tried to pull away, but Costin refused to let her go. He continued to kiss her and Sally gasped when she saw the images in his mind.

Costin decided the only way to fight Sally's mind was to give her something else to think about.

"Let me replace those images Sally mine. Those were false things, lies that never happened. No one has touched you intimitley. No other has kissed you as I do and nobody has taken what is so precious to us both. They are lies that were put in your head by a spell. When we are married I will replace those with something real." He didn't wait for a response. He continued to kiss her as he laid her back on the bed. He blanketed her with his body, putting just enough weight on her to make her think about him. Costin moved from her lips across her jaw line. She tilted her head back, giving him access to her throat and he took advantage of it. He kissed her, nipped her gently with his teeth. He made his way across her neck until his lips hovered over his mark.

"I'm going to bite you, I don't want you to be alarmed," he told her softly. She nodded slowly as she drowned in the feel of his body, the touch of his hands and the caress of his lips. Costin wrapped his hand around her neck so that she wouldn't jump and make him accidentally tear into her soft flesh. He tilted her head back and sunk his teeth deep into her neck. Her blood filled his mouth and he felt his wolf howl in victory. They had their mate back; she was in their arms where she belonged. Costin's other hand slipped under the back of her shirt meeting flesh with flesh and his wolf took comfort in the touch. He pulled his teeth back, licked the wound. He felt the rightness in the act and felt his heart flood with love for the woman before him.

"Sally," he groaned her name as he kissed down her collar bone, and then pulled back to look at her. As he stared into her eyes, he shared with her his desire, his passion, and need for her. He knew she wanted to wait until they were married to mate, and he would honor her wishes. He hoped once they were married and mated that every time he touched her, she wouldn't have the memory of what the curse had shown to her popping up. So, he vowed that once she was his wife was going to make sure that a mere touch from him would flood her mind with the desire that he alone could unleash on her.

"Do you see how much I love you, how much I want you?" Costin asked her, gently.

She nodded against his chest. Costin rolled onto his side and pulled her with him. He wrapped his arm around her, keeping his hand up under the back of her shirt. His fingers traced the markings he knew traveled the length of her spine, marking's that matched his exactly. He kissed her hair and pulled her tighter against him when she shivered.

"Costin?"

"Yes?"

"I love you." Sally clung to his shirt as she pressed her face against him and breathed his scent in. Breath after breath she began to calm, and she relaxed against him.

"I love you, Sally mine and I will love you more tomorrow." Costin gently pried one of her hands from his shirt. She whimpered and tried to hold on.

"Shh, Sally," Costin crooned to her, as he took the now free hand and slipped it under his shirt so that her hand was on his skin. Sally let out a sigh, as her hand slid up his stomach to his chest. Her fingers moved slowly against his skin and she didn't realize how much she'd craved the simple touch of his warm flesh.

As Sally relaxed against him and her touch soothed him and his wolf he was finally able to process all that had happened. He had come so very close to losing her, maybe not physically, but mentally and emotionally, she was fragile and if he wasn't careful he could hurt her even worse than she had already suffered.

He felt her breathing slow and realized she had fallen asleep. He buried his face in her hair as tears he had fought for so long slipped from his hazel eyes. He was holding her so tightly he feared he might hurt her, and still it wasn't close enough. It was then, when she was unaware, that Costin fell apart.

~

"Decebel," Cynthia's voice came through the door.

Jen struggled to sit up, but he gently pushed her back down.

"Hey, just cause I said you could touch me again does not mean you get to push me around," Jen snapped at him.

"Yes, it does," he told her as he walked towards the door. He pulled it open to see a very tired Cynthia Steele standing before him.

"I know you guys want to be alone, but I really need to check on Jen and the baby."

Decebel opened the door wider and stepped aside so that she could walk through. She walked over to the bed where Jen lay.

"How you feeling?" Cynthia asked, with a sympathetic smile.

Jen shrugged. "Well if you would like me to be honest, I feel like someone who has been beaten, taken against her will, given herself to the wrong man, lost her baby, screamed at the man she loved, and cried for things that hadn't really happened."

"Jennifer," Decebel growled from the other side of the bed.

"Basically, I feel like crap doc," Jen finished, without acknowledging her mate. He sat down on the bed next to her and took her hand. He brought it to his lips and kissed it gently.

Jen refused to look at him, she knew that if she did she would lose it and she wasn't ready to lose it just yet.

"I need to listen to the baby for a minute and check your vitals okay?" Cynthia asked.

Jen nodded.

Cynthia pulled Jen's shirt up to expose her abdomen and saw that she was beginning to show.

"When did this happen?" She asked.

Jen looked down at her stomach and saw the small hump.

"It wasn't like that a week ago," Jen told her.

Cynthia gently probed her stomach and then laid her head against it. She closed her eyes and listened for the fast flutter that would indicate that the baby was doing well. It didn't take long before she heard it. She smiled as she listened. It was a strong heartbeat, a healthy heartbeat. Cynthia clenched her eyes tight as she thought about the fate of the little being with the strong heartbeat, a fate she didn't deserve.

She lifted her head and smiled at Decebel and Jen. "She's doing good. I'm going to do some research on the gestation of wolves, it's been a long time since I've been around a pregnant Canis lupus, but I'm pretty sure the gestation is not the same as a human."

Jen nodded as she pulled her shirt down.

"The Fates said they would take her in nine months' time," Jen pointed out.

Cynthia thought about it. She wondered if the Fates were jerking Jen's chain. Surely, they wouldn't allow her to have the child and watch her grow only to then die, in such a short time.

"With the Fates, anything is possible. I'll look into it. It may just be that the baby will be bigger than a regular human child."

Jen frowned. "That would not be cool."

Cynthia got out the blood pressure cuff and stethoscope and checked Jen's heartbeat and blood pressure, both of which were normal.

"Now, this might be uncomfortable," she looked up at Decebel. "You might want to step out."

Decebel's eyes began to glow. "I'm not leaving her."

"Dec, babe, calm down," Jen told him, as she squeezed his hand.

"I need to do a pelvic exam Jen," Cynthia told her.

"Doc, I know you must know about the birds and the bees, but in case you need a refresher, Dec had to have seen all this in order for me to end up in this particular situation."

Cynthia chuckled. "Some wives aren't comfortable having a pelvic exam done in front of their spouses."

"Mate," Decebel snarled.

Jen rolled her eyes. "He's a tad touchy right now."

Cynthia leaned over to help Jen remove the sweatpants that she had put on her before the curse had been broken, but Decebel gently pushed her hands away.

"I've got it," he told her.

"What is your problem?" Jen asked, as he helped her remove the pants. He quickly covered her with a sheet and gently rubbed her stomach.

"Leave it alone, Jennifer," Decebel said, not unkindly.

Cynthia did the exam as quickly and efficiently as possible, keeping it all very clinical. Decebel stared at Jen's face the entire time and twice leaned down to gently kiss her.

"Okay," Cynthia said, as she pulled off the medical gloves that she had donned and threw them in the trashcan next to the bed. "Everything looks good."

Jen snorted. "Seriously, nothing in that area ever looks *good*."

Cynthia laughed, a genuine sound and a much needed release. "Okay, I can agree with that, I guess I should say everything is as it should be."

Jen nodded. "Better choice of words."

Cynthia packed up her stuff and turned to go. Just before she opened the door, she turned back and looked at Jen, avoiding Decebel's gaze. "Just in case you were wondering, it is alright for you to be intimate."

Jen grinned. "Are you telling me I can get it on like Donkey Kong?"

Cynthia let out a chuckle. "Hmmm, maybe not like Donkey Kong. Why don't you stick to Curious George just to be on the safe side?" With that, she opened the door and closed it quietly behind her.

The smile faded from Jen's face as soon as Cynthia was gone. She couldn't look at her mate. The thin thread by which she had been hanging was about to snap and she knew that he had been through enough already. She bit her lip in attempt to hold herself together and turned her head away from him.

"Jennifer," Decebel reached over and gently pulled her chin, so that she was looking directly at him.

"Baby, talk to me."

"How did you survive so long?" She asked.

"What do you mean?"

"I mean in the In-Between," he flinched, as she spoke of the hell he had been in. "How did you survive watching all of those things for so long?"

"I just kept telling myself that it wasn't real." He stretched out beside her and propped up his head on one elbow.

"I tried to tell myself that. I tried Dec, but it felt…" Jen closed her mouth against the bile that she felt rising.

"Shh, baby, it wasn't real, none of that happened." Decebel rested his hand on the small swell of her stomach. "This is real," he told her as he gently rubbed her, "my touch, our love, our baby, all of this is real."

Jen was nodding, though the tears had begun to fall. Decebel reached over and pulled her into his arms. "I've got you baby. I'm not letting go."

Decebel struggled to keep his rage contained as he felt the strongest woman he had ever met, fall apart in his arms. He didn't try to get her to talk. He didn't ask her how he could help, he just held her, and if that was all she ever wanted from him ever again, it would be enough.

"Not for me it wouldn't," Jen told, him through their bond. *"Make me forget Dec."*

Decebel pulled back so that he could look into her blue eyes.

"It's too soon Jennifer, give yourself time." He gently brushed her hair from her face and kissed her forehead.

"Have I ever let you get away with telling me what I needed?" She didn't wait for an answer. "I'm telling you that I need you. I keep seeing and feeling those faces, those hands," Jen let out a choked sob as she stared up into his amber eyes. "Don't make me beg."

Decebel sucked in a breath as he saw the fear in her eyes. Fear that he would reject her, fear that he would be disgusted by her, fear that he would no longer want her.

Decebel growled at her as he leaned down. His lips caressed her face gently until they hovered just above hers. "You never have to beg. I'm yours and I will always give you what you need. What do you need baby?" His lips brushed against hers as he spoke. "Tell me what you need Jennifer and it's yours."

Jen trembled as she felt his hand slip under her shirt. He stroked her abdomen and then trailed his fingers up the side of her body tracing her markings.

"You," she breathed out, softly.

He pulled back to take his shirt off and grinned at her when her eyes widened.

"Does that mean I still do it for you?"

Jen smiled through the tears as she nodded. Decebel helped her remove her shirt and then pulled her body tight against his. He kissed her deeply and growled when she ran her fingers through his thick, dark hair.

"I love you Jennifer," he told her over and over as his hands roamed and his lips followed. *"You are mine. Every inch of you, every strand of hair, every soft moan, every beat of your heart, belongs to me."*

Jen's heart swelled with love as she listened to his words and then felt the truth behind them with every kiss and touch.

"Baby, open your eyes."

Jen opened them to see him hovering over her. He kissed her cheeks, her nose, and across her jaw before kissing her softly on the lips.

"Keep your eyes open," he whispered. "I want you to see who is with you, and who is touching you, who is loving you."

"Okay," she told him, softly. And she did. And, they were still open long into the night when he lay beside her watching his fingers as they traveled up and down the markings that ran from her hip to under her arm.

"Are you okay?" Jen asked him.

He looked up from his hand to meet her eyes. "As long as you're with me, I'm okay. Are you? Did I hurt you?" He laid his hand across her abdomen as he asked.

Jen shook her head. "You didn't hurt me." She placed her hand over his, loving the warmth she felt from his skin. Her eyes felt heavy though she tried to hold them open.

Decebel chuckled. "You can close them now, beautiful."

Jen growled at him.

"Don't go starting something you can't finish," he teased.

Jen felt something inside her loosen at his teasing. It was right. They had grieved, they had held each other, made love, and now they just needed to be together, doing what they did best.

"Crap, for a minute there with all the tender loving and what not, I forgot that I was mated to a perv." Her eyes sparkled with laughter.

"Oh, we can't have you forgetting something so important." He grabbed at her playfully. "Come here and let me remind you."

Laughter filled their room, where once tears had been, as Jen let Decebel heal her heart over and over. Bit by bit he reminded her who he was, and who she was to him.

~

Fane closed their door and turned the lock. After finally getting her to invite his touch, he helped Jacque undress and into the shower as silent tears slid from her eyes. He had tried to get her to lie down, but she kept insisting that she needed to get clean, that she felt dirty. So, he helped her shower and then dried her off and carried her to their bed. He climbed in next her, pulled the covers up over them, and enveloped her in his arms.

Jacque wrapped her body around Fane's, seeking the heat from his body, needing to feel all of his skin against all of hers. She didn't realize that she had been whimpering until Fane started speaking to her softly. He smoothly transitioned from English to Romanian and back again, as he attempted to soothe her.

"Luna," he pulled her face up to look at him. "Tell me what to do. Please, I don't know what to do."

Jacque stared into his glowing blue eyes as she felt the beat of his heart against her chest. He wiped the tears gently from her cheeks and kissed her slowly. When he pulled back, he saw that her eyes were glowing as well. "Sing to me," she whispered.

He brushed the red curls from her face as he stared into her eyes and began to sing the song he had shared with her on the night before his battle with Lucas, and night that now seemed so very long ago. His eyes softened when she ran her fingers across his lips as he sung.

As his rich, deep voice reached into the broken parts of her soul, Jacque grabbed onto his words like a lifeline. She ran her hands across his shoulders and chest, following the touch with her kiss. Fane's words trembled slightly as she pushed him on his back and laid her body over his. She laid her head on his chest and tried to melt into his touch as he ran the tips of his fingers from her shoulders to the backs of her thighs. She took comfort in the touch that she knew so well. She pushed away her pain and fear and latched onto the feeling of hands that knew her better than she knew herself and a man who loved her more than any other ever could.

The room was quiet when the song ended. Fane continued to caress her skin wherever he could reach and kissed her hair as he breathed in her scent.

"Fane,"

"Yes love."

"We'll get through this," Jacque made it a statement, needing to hear herself say the words out loud.

"Together," he agreed.

He rolled her over quickly yet smoothly until she lay beneath him. He stared down into her eyes, as his fingers brushed gently against her jaw. He leaned down, kissed her, and groaned when she yielded to him instantly. Jacque opened her mouth and welcomed the deep kiss as his tongue explored her. She pulled back and smiled at the surprised look on his face.

"You told me touch was healing to wolves, that it brought comfort and security," she told him.

He nodded.

"I need healing, comfort, and security Fane," she whispered, against his skin as she kissed his neck, shoulders, and chest in between each word. She pushed his hands, showing him through their bond where she wanted them to be. Fane's chest rumbled as he felt her need and was surprised when he realized it was every bit as great as his own.

"You need me, my touch, my kiss, my love," he hovered over her, looking down at her face and body.

There was a time when Jacque would have blushed under his gaze, but not now, not when Fane had shown her just how completely a male loved his female in their world.

"I do," she agreed.

"Good," Fane growled, as he lowered his body to hers.

No more words were needed as they clung to one another. Fane met her every need and Jacque took greedily from him, knowing that it pleased him to provide for her in any way, whether it be physical or emotional. She let go completely, knowing that he would always provide for her, always protect her and always love her.

"Always," she heard his whisper in her mind and felt the certainty of it in his touch as he made love to her.

Chapter 18

"Okay people, so we've reached the part in the story that is considered the calm before the storm. Everyone is getting in their "I love yous" and "goodbyes" and blah, blah, blahs because they know that all hell is about to break lose. It's all very touching, but honestly, it's time to put on our big girl panties, and I do mean that literally, and batten down the hatches because hurricane Mona is heading our way people. So get your butts out of your mate's beds, yours truly included, and bring the rain." ~ Jen

Lilly, Cypher, Thalion, and his warriors gathered around the fire. The night was chilly and the knowledge of what was to come only made the cold harder to endure. Cypher and the elf warriors had been able to kill some rabbits for dinner. Though it wasn't the most filling meal, it was enough. When they were done eating, Cypher pulled Lilly over into his lap where he sat leaning against a tree. She snuggled into his chest and tried not to worry about her daughter, or Mona, or Cypher, or anything else she had no control over.

"What's she like?" Cypher asked.

Lilly tilted her head up to look at him. She smiled warmly. "She's the best person I know."

Lilly knew he was asking about Jacque and it warmed her heart that he wanted to know about the most important person in her life.

"She is full of life. She's got a smart mouth on her; she's stubborn, beautiful, and loves with her whole heart."

"Sounds like someone I know," Cypher told her, as he kissed her forehead.

"We're alike in a lot of ways," Lilly agreed. "But, she's better than I am and I'm glad for that. No parent wants their child to inherit their faults or make their mistakes."

"What mistakes have you made Lilly? What deep secrets does your heart hold?"

Lilly considered whether she should tell him about Dillon, about how Jacque came to be a part of this world.

"Haven't you wondered how it is that Jacque is mated to a werewolf?" She asked him.

He nodded. "Yes, I've wondered, but I figured you would tell me when you were ready." He paused. "Are you ready?"

She shrugged. "It's not like we have anything better to do."

Cypher tightened his hold on her and kissed her neck, "I love hearing your voice, but I'm sure I can find something to do that I would love just as equally as listening to you."

Lilly laughed. "I'm sure you could."

"Sooo," he prompted.

"I fell in love when I was young. He was handsome, fun, and not human. Within days of meeting him, my heart was his. For as long as I can remember, I've always possessed what I considered to be some sort of sixth sense. It doesn't always happen, but sometimes I just feel like I know something about a person and that was how I felt about Dillon. I knew something was very different about him. When I confronted him about it, he told me what he was. At first, I was a little freaked, but then I saw that he was still the man I loved. What I was not prepared for was when he told me that I was not his true mate."

"How were you together if you weren't his mate?" Cypher asked, gruffly.

"He loved me. He told me that there was a possibility that one day he would meet his true mate and if he did, he would have no choice but to go, that his soul would cry out for her. At the time, I didn't care; I just wanted to be with him. Time went on, things were good, and then the impossible happened. I got pregnant. Canis lupuses have a very hard time conceiving with each other, to conceive with a human was unheard of. As soon as I found out, I rushed home to tell him. I walked in, ready to share the good news, only to find a note with my name on it and all traces of Dillon were gone."

Cypher stroked her hair as he felt the heart that, though mended now, remembered a time when it had broken.

"I never tried to find him. He didn't know he had a daughter until this year. Jacque didn't know anything about her father or what he was until Fane came to Coldspring and claimed her as his mate."

"So, you have seen Dillon recently?" Cypher asked, and Lilly could tell he wasn't happy about it.

"Yes."

"Do you still love him?"

"Not the way that you think. I love him, because he gave me Jacque."

Cypher tried not to be jealous, but the idea of his mate with another man was not sitting well with him, even if it had happened so many years ago.

Lilly felt Cypher's arms tense up. She looked up into his face and saw anger and possessiveness in his eyes.

"Talk to me Cypher," she said to him, gently.

"I don't want to share your heart," he told her, honestly.

"You will always have to share my heart. Jacque holds a big chunk of it."

Cypher shook his head. "That's not what I meant. I expect to share with her and I'm happy to do so, but I hate that he held it at one time." Cypher closed his eyes and tried to sort through his emotions before he continued. "I don't want to sound like a petulant child, but I want you to be all mine."

"I am all yours, Cypher, or at least that's the direction we are headed, but you have a past as well. If I remember correctly on a certain night when you held me in bed I asked you if you had been with a woman and you said yes."

"None that I have loved, none that have ever had any hold on me," Cypher argued.

"They had to have held something sweetie, for you to be in their bed." Lilly snorted at her own joke, but noticed that Cypher didn't find the humor in it.

"That was a good one; you have to at least give me a little credit."

He growled. "It was crude."

"Yes, well so was the act of you sleeping with women solely for gratification, but then it happened right?" She shot back.

"Are you jealous little one?" He asked with a gleam in his eyes.

"No," she answered, in a clipped tone.

Cypher pulled her against his chest and put his mouth directly next to her ear. "Since the moment I laid eyes on you I have forgotten any other woman who has crossed my path."

"And your bed?" Lilly asked.

"In my mind, there is only you, Lilly. All I see is your face all I want is you. You are right we both have a past. I will try not to let your past make me into a jealous fool."

"So, when you meet Dillon, you will be nice?" She asked, cautiously.

"Why would I meet Dillon?" He asked.

"Because he is Jacque's father and if you are my…" She stumbled for words because she still wasn't sure what to call him.

"Your mate, Lilly, I'm your mate."

"Okay chill out. Geeze, if you are my mate, then you are bound, at some point, to meet him," she paused before she added, "and if they called the packs, he is probably going to be at the Romanian mansion."

Cypher's breath froze in his lungs. He hadn't expected to have to meet his mate's former lover in a matter of hours.

"Cypher?" Lilly turned to look at him. "You okay?"

He took her face in his hands and kissed her gently at first, but then his lips pressed harder and he pulled her tighter. After several minutes, they were both breathing heavily. Lilly blushed as she thought about the others sitting nearby. It felt like any time Cypher's lips met hers she forgot about everything else.

"You are mine," he told her firmly.

"Cypher, Dillon has a mate. He isn't going to try to take me."

"I need to know that I am not competing with a memory Lilly. I need to know that your heart is yours to give and not in the hands of a man who gave you up."

Lilly smiled up at him as she ran a finger across his lips.

"You have nothing to worry about, Warlock King. I got my heart back a long time ago and for the first time I'm ready to give it to someone who wants to keep it."

Cypher pressed his forehead to hers. "Forever?"

"That's all I'm asking for," Lilly smiled. "But, I swear if we do this, and then some time down the line some chick comes out of the woodwork claiming to be your woman, I will castrate you. I just need you to know that upfront."

Cypher cringed. "Then lucky for me there is no woman lurking in my past, or waiting in my future."

"Good answer," Lilly kissed him quickly on the lips, and then snuggled into him.

"Sleep little one," Cypher's chest rumbled with his words. "Tomorrow is going to be interesting."

Cyn crept up slowly on the sleeping group. The warlock warriors at her back moved just as silently as she, which surprised her because of their size. She paused when she felt a hand on her arm. She looked over to see Gerick, Cypher's head warrior, put his finger to his lips. He motioned for the others to surround the sleeping group and Cyn smiled when she saw the mischief in the warrior's eyes.

"How is it that I have come across so fair a maiden in the woods all alone?" Cyn closed her eyes as she admonished herself. She hadn't bothered to check if the forms that appeared to be sleeping were really all people.

Thalion wrapped an arm around her and pulled her against his chest.

"I'm glad you made it back safely," he whispered against her neck.

For just a moment, Cyn relaxed into his hold. For just a moment, she let herself think of what it would be like to be his, but just as quickly, she let it go. She pulled away from him and turned to face him.

"I should have known that someone would be keeping watch." She had made a rookie mistake and it irked her that Thalion had witnessed it.

"You were just eager to get back to me," he teased.

"It's not long until daylight," she told him, ignoring his jesting. "Have you all come up with a plan?"

"We're going to the Romanian mansion," he said, nonchalantly.

Cyn rolled her eyes. "They are on the verge of war with a witch, have twelve packs gathered under one roof and you think you can just march up and ask to break bread with them?"

Thalion thought about it for several minutes. He hadn't dealt with the wolves much, and the few occasions that he had were a long time ago.

"What should we do?" He asked.

"I'll go first."

"No," Thalion shook his head.

Cyn shrugged. "Too late." Then she was gone.

Thalion growled in frustration. "Females," he muttered.

Cypher had heard the sound of his warriors approach, though he kept the pretense of being asleep. His arms were wrapped securely around Lilly, who, to his amusement, was snoring loudly. He waited until finally Gerick stepped in close enough. He moved swiftly grabbing the warrior's ankle and tossing him back. Gerick landed on the ground with a loud thud and a gasp as the wind was knocked out of him.

Cypher smiled at his general. "Gerick," he nodded.

"My King," Gerick coughed as he climbed to his feet. Gerick made a motion with his hand. Silently, Cypher's warriors stepped forward from the trees.

"Nice work," Thalion said, as he walked back into the circle. He made a series of clicking noises and suddenly the sky was raining elves as they fell from the tree tops.

Cypher looked up at the Elf Prince, who shrugged. "You never know who might be lurking in the woods."

Cypher laughed. "True enough."

The morning light began to break through the heavy covering of the trees and Lilly finally began to stir. She yawned and blinked a few times. Her eyes widened as she saw eyes, lots of them, staring at her.

"Cypher?" She sat up and pushed away from his chest.

"Lilly, these are my warriors," he motioned to the large men staring at her.

"Why are they staring at me?" She asked, as she tried to smile and look friendly.

"They're curious about you. I've just told them that you are my mate and human."

"Hi," Lilly said, weakly as she waved.

A few gave her smiles. Others continued to stare at her as if she were a bug they were trying to visually dissect.

"You ready to stand up?" Cypher asked her, drawing her attention away from the others. She looked up at him and nodded.

"Definitely, I seriously need to p..." She stopped in mid-sentence as she considered her company. Cypher laughed. "Do you need some privacy?"

"That would be good," she told him. She walked off into the trees, promising not to go too far and making Cypher promise not to follow, though she could tell that he didn't like her going off alone.

When Lilly returned she saw that Thalion and Cypher were deep in conversation. She wasn't really sure what to do with herself so she leaned against a tree and tried not to stare at the warlock warriors, while at the same time trying to take in as much as she could by nonchalantly casting glances in their direction.

"You're a good fit."

Lilly jumped at the deep voice that had come from right beside her. She turned and had to look up to see a tall, wide man, with short dark hair, big green eyes, and a sweet smile.

"I'm Gerick," he told her. "I'm Cypher's general."

Lilly nodded. "It's nice to meet you Gerick. Um, what did you mean, I'm a good fit?"

"For him," he nodded towards Cypher. "You bring him balance."

"How can you tell," Lilly asked, as her forehead wrinkled in question.

"There is a peace about him that I have not seen since he was very, very young."

Lilly watched Cypher talk to Thalion and she thought about how he had looked when she first met him. He was still incredibly handsome, but she had to agree that some of the stress that had been on his face then, was no longer present. Even with everything they had been through and would undoubtedly be going through soon, Cypher did seem oddly relaxed. His eyes came up and met hers and he smiled at her. She smiled back and she agreed with Gerick, she and Cypher, for whatever messed up reason, were a good fit.

~

"Peri."

Peri jumped at the voice behind her. She pressed her hand to her heart as she turned and met Cyn's stare.

"Are you trying to kill me? Crap, give me a warning or something next time."

A single eyebrow rose on Cyn's face. "I asked you to show me where you were."

"Yes, but you didn't say you were coming now," Peri snapped. She stood in the field where only a day ago, a massacre between the packs was at its beginning. Vasile had once again proven why he was the strongest of their race. When other Alphas had tried to get their wolves under control and failed, Vasile's power alone brought them to their knees.

"What are you doing out here?" Cyn asked.

Peri glanced back at the field that she had been staring at before the other fae had arrived. "It's a long story," Peri answered.

"Isn't it always," Cyn retorted as she walked over to stand next to her mentor and longtime friend.

Cyn waited quietly, knowing that sometimes Peri just needed a captive audience for her to start a tale.

"Okay, so the damn wolves can't keep themselves out of trouble," she began and Cyn grinned to herself as Peri told her, in only a way that Peri could, the events that had taken place. Cyn listened quietly and when Peri was finished relaying her story, she decided that she would take her battle with the Draheim over the wolves and their mates any day.

"So, that's my mess," Peri told her, as she folded her arms across her chest. "How goes it with the Warlock King and the human?"

Cyn smiled. "Well, they're not near as bad as your wolves,"

Peri snorted. "For some reason I believe you."

"I told you that I had a surprise for you," Cyn reminded her.

"Yes, and you know how I hate surprises, so please tell me that Lilly isn't somehow knocked up, or that Cypher hasn't been surreptitiously plotting with Mona all along because she's having his secret love child."

Cyn rolled her eyes. "What's with all the baby talk?"

"Jen's pregnant, the Fates want her kid, and Decebel just might kill anything or anyone who comes near her at any time. Sorry it's a touchy subject."

"Okay, well breathe easy then because no one is having anyone's love child. However," Cyn paused and cleared her throat, "Thalion is sort of involved."

Peri's head snapped up as she looked at Cyn.

"The Elf Prince is here?" Peri's eyes widened.

Cyn nodded. "We sort of needed something he had."

"Yeah, I bet you did," Peri muttered.

"Perizada, we are not going down that road so just forget it." Cyn nearly sounded like a jaded teenager.

"It was bound to happen one day. You two have been swooning over one another for centuries now. Just go ahead and get you a taste so you can be done with it."

Cyn shook her head in exasperation. "This isn't about me or Thalion or us together. Cypher needed more information about opening the veil to the underworld. He had planned to get it from his brother. As I told you, that plan sort of got crushed by a Draheim, so we had to resort to plan B."

"Otherwise known as, Plan *Hot Freaking Elf Prince Come Light My Fire*," Peri laughed, when Cyn crossed her arms and began tapping her foot.

"You done yet?" Cyn asked, with a scowl.

Peri laughed, but finally raised her hand. "Yeah, yeah okay I'm done." She leaned her head back, stretching her neck and feeling the slight strain in it relax just a little. "So, is Thalion able to help?"

"Turns out he has the book called *Nushtonia*." Cyn waited for the reaction that she knew was coming.

Peri started laughing. Cyn's brow furrowed as she watched the high Fae. This had not been the reaction she had been expecting.

"Are you freaking kidding me?" Peri yelled. "Could this get any worse? So, now the book inspired by a demon that was in hiding is out in the open where Mona could get her grubby, dirty, filthy, blood covered hands on it?"

"Yes, but Cypher needs it. Before he was mated, he understood the risk of opening the veil. Now, he has Lilly, and it's a game changer. Not only has he decided not to help Mona, but he has promised not to let anything happen to Lilly's daughter. He had to open the veil, because he'd made a blood oath, but he needed to be able to close it immediately, before anything could get through."

Peri listened intently as her mind ran through the millions of nightmarish possibilities that were bound to happen, and by the way, things were going, they would all happen at the same freaking time.

"So, what I hear you telling me is that our Warlock King needs to accomplish the impossible."

Cyn nodded. "Essentially."

"Excellent."

"Exactly."

"Any more E words we could add to this little chit chat?" Peri asked dryly.

"Effing perfect?" Cyn grinned at Peri.

"You took the words right out of my mouth."

Peri motioned for Cyn to follow her. "So, your people want to come rendezvous with my people. We need to let Vasile and the other males know so that they don't feel like they have been snuck up upon. Have you prepped the Warlock and Prince on how to behave around possessive, butthead werewolves?"

"Not exactly."

"Then I will meet with them before they meet the wolves. This is a frickin' nightmare," Peri muttered, as she led Cyn to Vasile and Alina's room.

Peri stepped up to knock on the Alpha's door, but paused, her hand in midair. She heard multiple deep voices conversing and couldn't stifle the exasperated groan that slipped out.

"Come in, Perizada," she heard, Vasile tell her. He must have heard the groan. She grasped the handle and pushed on the latch.

Decebel, Fane, Costin, Adam, Sorin, Gavril, Alina, and Vasile's eyes landed on her and then shifted to Cyn who was standing behind her.

"Glad to see the gang's all here. That will keep me from having to repeat myself, which as you all know, I loathe to do." Peri walked farther into the room. Cyn moved to stand next to her and Vasile, Decebel, and the males who had been sitting moved to stand in front of Alina.

Alina growled behind them. "Move."

"Peri, who have you brought to visit us without announcement?" Vasile asked, coolly.

"Vasile meet Cyn. Cyn meet Vasile," Peri motioned between the two of them. "Cyn is one of the Fae Guardians. She has been with the Warlock King and Lilly while they've been on their little adventure."

Vasile met Cyn's gaze and waited. Cyn knew that it was a dominance thing with wolves so she dropped her eyes.

Peri raised a brow at the Alpha. "You done now?"

Vasile lifted a lip at her, flashing long canines, before he told her to proceed.

"The Warlock King, Lilly, the Elf Prince, and their warriors are about thirty miles from here in the forest."

"What?" Decebel growled as he took a step towards her.

"Peace wolf," Peri snapped. "They aren't coming to attack you. They are coming to help." Peri explained everything that Cyn had told her, trying to keep it as short and exact as possible.

"So he still plans to open the veil?" Vasile asked, unnecessarily.

"He made a blood oath. It's not like he really has a choice," Cyn pointed out.

"They point is," Peri interrupted, "that they want to help. They are bringing more warm bodies to assist us in fighting Desdemona."

"They are unknown males around our females," Costin snarled.

"Speaking of said females," she met Costin's stare. "Where are your oh so precious mates?"

Costin looked away. Obviously, unhappy about the question.

"They're in the kitchen drinking hot chocolate," Fane shot back.

Peri laughed. "So, let me guess, you're upset, because they wanted a break from the rooms you have no doubt kept them locked up in for the past twenty four hours, or," she laughed even harder, "you're just jealous of the mugs they are sipping the beverage from."

All of the males had the sense, to act somewhat guilty at their overbearing behavior, but none of them contradicted her.

"Are you quite finished, Peri," Adam spoke up for the first time.

"Oh I could go on for hours; you males just make it to easy. But alas, the blasted men who have come to take your women's virtue, if there is any left after the interesting night I'm sure you all had, are waiting for Vasile's approval before they arrive."

"Who said it was the males taking the virtue?" A familiar voice chirped from behind Peri. Jen and the entourage of females filed into the room. The faces of the males changed instantly from irritated to worshipful. Peri shook her head at them. She would never understand the bond between mates, unless the Great Luna had her way. Peri cringed at that thought.

"Jennifer, I thought I told you that I wanted you to go back to our room," Decebel said, as he crossed the room to her.

"You did," Jen waved to Peri with a wicked grin.

"Then why are you here?" He asked.

"Because you told me to go back to our room, duh." The girls all snickered at her while the men scowled. Jen ignored them and turned to face Peri and Cyn as Decebel wrapped his arms around her from behind and pulled her against his chest. Each of the mated pairs was in similar poses across the room.

"So Peri fairy," Jacque smiled. "What's the news that has our men so riled up about?"

"The Warlock King and the Elf Prince are waiting for permission to approach the mansion," Peri explained.

Jacque tried to push away from Fane as she took a step towards the Fae, "Cypher is out there? That means my mom is out there too, right?"

Peri nodded.

Jacque whipped around, slapping Fane in the face with her wild hair to face Vasile. "Why have you not said they could come? That's my mom out there, Vasile."

"I know that," Vasile told her patiently. "But, I cannot act rashly, I always must weigh the danger a situation poses to the pack."

"Give me a break, Vasile. There are like sixty or so dominant males in this mansion at this very moment, they must be much more dangerous than the men my mom are with."

"And, you know this, how?" He asked.

"Vasile," Alina's warning came from where she still sat shielded from view. "She is your daughter-in-law first, pack second."

Vasile stepped aside so that Alina could be seen. She stood next to Vasile and relaxed into his touch when he tucked her under his arm.

"Peri," Vasile turned to her. "You can bring them here. They are to go to the gathering room and stay there. No wandering about."

Cyn was gone before Peri could answer.

"Where'd she go?" Sally asked.

"To tell them," Peri shrugged.

~

Peri flashed next to Cyn only moments after Cyn arrived, standing before Cypher and Thalion.

"Well hello, handsomes," Peri smiled at the two males.

Lilly stepped from around Cypher who had pulled her protectively behind him when Peri had arrived.

"You must be Lilly," Peri stepped forward and held out her hand.

Lilly reached forward to shake it and Cypher snaked an arm around her waist attempting to pull her back.

"Cypher," Lilly said his name in a clipped fashion and he backed off only slightly.

"You have one of those too, I see," Peri motioned to Cypher.

"Too?" Lilly frowned.

"Your daughter has, what she and her friends call, OBBHMs."

Lilly laughed. "And pray tell, what does that acronym stand for."

"Overbearing butt head mates."

"Then yes, I have one of those too," Lilly laughed as Cypher narrowed his eyes at her.

Peri stepped back so that she could address both men. "Vasile has agreed to let you come to the mansion. But, before we go, I need to fill you in on pack etiquette."

"We already know some of it," Cypher told her.

"Not with these males you don't," Peri countered. "These males take protective to a whole new solar system, so listen up and maybe we will all live until Mona kills us."

Lilly grinned. "I like you. You are a breath of fresh air."

"You haven't known her long enough yet to declare that. Just give it time," Cyn smirked.

Peri snapped her fingers closed in front of Cyn's face, making it clear that she wanted Cyn to shut her trap. Cyn laughed and stepped back.

"The most important thing with this group of males is do not, under any circumstances, for any reason, touch any of their mates. On a good day they are touchy when it comes to other men being present around them, but they've been through some tough stuff the past several days so they are really on edge right now."

"Is my daughter okay?" Lilly asked, suddenly alarmed.

"She's fine, and I'm sure she will gladly fill you in on their adventures," Peri assured. "Next, don't hold their stare. It's all right to meet their eyes for about five seconds. After that, avert your gaze. You don't have to drop it and indicate submission, just look over their shoulder or off to the side to show that you aren't going to challenge them. Even if the man in them knows that you aren't there for a challenge, the wolf will see it differently and right now their wolves are winning the control battle more often than not."

"These men sound very unstable," Thalion pointed out.

"They are unstable. They're werewolves, what about that would make you think they are stable?" Peri shook her head at the Prince. "Oh and please, for the love of little furry things everywhere, do not point out to them that they are unstable." She stared at Thalion for a second more. "Actually it's probably better if you don't speak at all."

Thalion looked taken aback. "Why?" He asked, genuinely confused.

"Because you have not been around the Canis lupus and so your questions might sound like you think them to be barbaric animals."

"Aren't they?"

Peri's jaw clenched. "See, that is why it would be better if you kept your royal trap shut."

Cypher stepped in before Thalion could argue further.

"Is there anything else we should know? So far everything you have said, I understand because I myself, am that way with Lilly."

"Don't be offended if they growl at you. They basically growl at anything that isn't their mate, and even at them sometimes. Oh," Peri clapped her hands, "I almost forgot the most important rule of all. Steer clear of the tall, leggy, blonde. She is trouble with a capital PITA. Her mate is Decebel; he is the Alpha of the Serbian pack, and he's deadly when it comes to her. She likes to get him all riled up so if you see her coming, turn and run the other way. Oh, and she's pregnant, so, that basically means if you look at her Decebel will kill you."

"This just sounds like it's going to be so much fun," Lilly said, cheerily.

"Oh, they are a real barrel of laughs, and by laughs I mean make you want to set your hair on fire while pulling your own teeth out."

"That good, huh?" Cypher smiled. "I think I'm going to like these wolves."

"Let's just get this over with," Peri huffed as she headed in the direction of the mansion.

Chapter 19

"When you are young, life seems so big and full of possibilities. Those possibilities seem endless and limitless and you are fearless. As I look into the faces of my mate, my son, and my pack, I see possibilities, all of them endless and limitless, but for the first time in my life, I am fearful of those possibilities." ~ Vasile.

"Costin, please come here," Sally asked him for the eighth time. He had been pacing since they had returned to their room, after Peri had told them the Warlock King and the Elf Prince were coming. All of the males were restless, and upon Peri's departure, had snapped their mates up, despite their protests and hauled them off to their respective rooms. Sally, Jen, and Jacque had been texting each other, updating one another on the status of their mates and Sally tried to keep from laughing when they had all said the exact same thing.

Sally txt: ur men pacing, growling, snarling?
Jen txt: all of the above
Jacque txt: all of the above
Sally txt: Suggestions?
Jen txt: tried get n naked, no go, so I'm out of ideas
Jacque txt: lol, haven't tried that one, hold on...
Sally txt: Way TMI Jac
Jen txt: U know u want 2 try it
Sally txt: who says I havn't?
Jen txt: Hells bells! Did he take the bait?
Sally txt: I was being sarcastic Jen. U know better.
Jen txt: good point
Jacque txt: holy crap, he didn't even blink
Sally/Jen/Jac all txt: we're so screwed
Jen txt: Unfortunately not n a good way
Sally/Jac txt: ROFLMBO

The texting had gone on for nearly forty five minutes when Costin had finally acknowledged her.

"What are you laughing about?" He asked as he sat down beside her. She could tell he was still keyed up, but he was trying to get it under control for her.

"Nothing," Sally told him attempting to look innocent, and failing miserably.

Costin held out his hand. "Let me see your phone, Sally mine."

Sally shook her head.

"Sally," Costin growled.

"I was texting with Jen and Jacque," she tried to sound nonchalant.

"Then why can't I see it?"

Sally tried to think of something that would keep Costin from really being interested in reading the text. "We were talking about Jen giving birth, you know with all the fluids and blood and how her girly bits will look afterward," Sally cringed at her own words because truthfully it was not something that she would have discussed with anyone let alone her mate.

Costin's face never changed. He continued to hold his hand out waiting for her to hand over her phone.

"Doesn't that gross you out even a little?" She asked, perplexed by his non-reaction.

"It's a baby, what's gross about that? I won't be grossed out when you are giving birth to our baby."

"Uh, yeah, but that will be me, I'm talking about Jen."

Costin shrugged. "I don't know. All I can think about is what a miracle it is that she is pregnant and how exciting it is for them."

Sally slapped the phone in his hand with a groan. She threw her body back on his bead and dropped her arm over her eye. "Of all the men in the world, I would get the one who is not bothered in the slightest by female fluids or girly bits."

Costin laughed. "One day, I'll explain it to you."

"Please don't," Sally squeaked.

Costin was quiet and she knew that he was reading the texts. She wanted to crawl into a hole, but nothing could be done about it now.

"You got naked and I missed it?" He asked, as he turned back to look at her.

Sally didn't respond, but could feel her face getting warmer by the second as the blood rushed up. She felt the bed shift as he lay down beside her. He took her arm and gently removed it from her face so that he could look at her, but she kept eyes were closed. Costin laughed.

"Look at me Sally."

Sally shook her head again, squeezing her eyes shut even tighter.

Costin leaned forward and she felt his body press against her side. She felt his lips against her ear and the warmth of his breath against her neck as he spoke.

"If I had known that all I had to do to get you naked was pace around the room like a rabid dog I would have done it a long time ago," he teased.

Sally tried to push him away as she attempted to roll away from him at the same time.

"No, you don't," he teased her as he wrapped an arm around her middle and pulled her to him.

Stupid werewolf strength, she thought.

"I'm sorry I ignored you," he finally told her. "I wasn't trying to do it purposefully. I'm just trying to figure out the most efficient ways to protect you if the need arises. My wolf is extremely unhappy about males we don't know coming here where you are and I'm not much better than he is."

Sally finally opened her eyes and turned her head to look at him. She reached up and brushed his hair out of his eyes. Costin leaned into her touch and she smiled.

"No one is going to hurt me, or anyone else. You worry needlessly."

"You can't know that," he argued.

"And, you can't know that something will happen, so why stress over it? Don't we have enough to stress over?"

Costin stared into her big, brown eyes and wished that he could put her in a bubble away from all danger, but she was a healer, and it was in her blood to be with those who needed her. And, with an imminent battle on the horizon, there were going to be many who would need her. His job as her mate was to make sure she could do what the Great Luna intended her to. He had to trust that she knew what she was doing when he put Sally in his care.

"What are you thinking about?" Sally asked, him as his silence grew.

"How proud and blessed I am to get to be your mate."

Sally grinned and it was one of those smiles that made his heart dance.

"Funny, that's exactly how I feel about you," she turned on her side so she could face him and his hand slipped under her shirt. His fingers trailed softly along her back and he smiled at her as he watched her eyes glaze over.

"Sally."

"Hmm," she responded huskily.

"I need to ask you something." Costin had not planned on doing this now. He had planned on waiting until the time was right, when the atmosphere was romantic and sexy. He had wanted to show her just how much she meant to him and how he wanted to shout from the mountains that she was his. But, sometimes life did not give us the perfect moments that we've longed for and so we had to turn a small part of the messed up moments into cherished ones.

"Stop touching me if you want me to think clearly," she teased him as her lips turned up in a sultry smile.

"Maybe I don't want you to think clearly when I ask you this."

Sally's eyes snapped open as she heard the worry in his voice.

"What's wrong Costin? Are you okay, is everything okay?" Sally didn't like it when she felt the confidence he carried, so casually slip, it made her feel inadequate as a mate when he felt unsure about her.

"Nothing is wrong, beautiful. I just wasn't planning this, but I feel like it's the right time."

"Okay," Sally said cautiously. She started to sit up but Costin stopped her with his hand on her hip.

"Stay here with me," he told her, softly. He moved closer to her and raised himself up on one elbow so he could look down at her. She rolled to her back and placed her right hand on his chest, over his heart. She felt his heart beat quicken and frowned when she realized how hard it was beating.

"Costin?" She asked, nervously.

"I love you," he told her. He released her hip and brushed the wispy hairs from her face. "I never imagined anyone as amazing as you, could ever be mine. But, now that you are, I will never let go. You are mine Sally and I am every bit as much yours. I will forsake all others for you. I will die for you, kill for you, and live for you. You've accepted me as your mate, you've let me claim you through the Blood Rites, you have my markings, and you bear my bite on your incredibly sexy neck. Now, I would ask that you accept me as your husband and wear my ring."

Sally's mouth dropped open when, seemingly from nowhere, Costin produce a small ring. A solitaire diamond, princess cut set in platinum. It was beautiful. She looked more closely and realized that there was an inscription etched into the band. She couldn't read it though.

"What does it say?"

Costin smiled. "You're going to make me sweat aren't you?"

Sally let out an airy laugh, and then blushed when she realized that she hadn't answered him. "Oh, shi–," she slapped her hand over her mouth before the word slipped out and stared wide eyed at Costin who was grinning like an idiot, obviously enjoying her embarrassment.

"Sally," he pulled her hand away, "for goodness sake, love, end my torment."

"Yes," she told him.

"Yes, you will end my torment or yes, you will be my wife?"

"Yes," she answered again.

Costin grinned and then leaned down and kissed her gently. He nipped at her lips when she refused to part them.

"Sally," he growled.

"Not until you tell me what the inscription says."

Costin held the ring over her face so she could see it. He smiled roguishly. "You want to know what the inscription on *this* ring says."

"I just said that," she growled and he laughed as it made him think of an angry kitten.

"Calm down brown eyes. I have a proposition for you."

Sally's eyes widened. "You can't be serious. You aren't going to tell me what *my* engagement ring says without making a deal with me?"

"You're a sharp one," he joked and whipped his head away just in time to miss her teeth from biting his chin. "Play nice Sally," he warned, though his eyes glowed with a different kind of warning. Sally quivered under his hungry gaze.

"I will tell you what the inscription says if you allow me to kiss you."

Sally thought it sounded too easy, but she brushed aside the apprehensive thoughts and nodded.

"Okay." She licked her lips in anticipation for what she knew would be a smoldering kiss. Costin's grin grew impossibly wider.

"Roll over," he told her.

"What!" Sally tried to scurry away, but Costin caught her ankle.

"Ahh, ah, ah," he chided, "you made a contract with me love."

Sally shook her head. "I didn't sign anything."

"You agreed verbally, you are bound babe, pack magic."

Sally balked at him. "You can't be serious; it was just a playful bargain."

"Not to me it wasn't," his face grew serious and his eyes began to glow. "I want to kiss you."

"I know that, I was waiting for you to."

Costin licked his lips and Sally tried hard not to follow the slow motion of his tongue. Her heart dropped to her stomach when she looked up from his lips to his eyes and he winked at her. That damn wink, it was a weapon he wielded shamelessly against her.

"You didn't clarify the location of the kiss my succulent, shy mate," Costin's voice dropped to a growl as he crawled towards her on the bed. Sally had reached the headboard and there was nowhere else for her to go. For that moment in time, she understood what those poor little bunnies must have felt like when the wolves were hunting them.

"Worried I'm going to eat you?" Costin asked her as he picked up on her thoughts. Sally's face discovered a new shade of red in the rainbow as she watched her mate stalk her. She couldn't believe that she had missed that loop hole. She never missed loop holes when Jen was bargaining, but then Costin's hands, lips, and eyes weren't involved when she was bargaining with Jen.

"Where exactly do you want to put this kiss?" She asked, when she finally found her voice.

"I want to see my markings," he rumbled.

"Then go take your shirt off and look in the mirror," she retorted.

His smile made her shiver as goose bumps dotted her skin. "When I say *my* markings Sally, I mean the ones on your body, the ones that are identical to those on my body." Sally didn't know how anyone could make the word *body* sound so sexy, but Costin had found a way.

"So, please, roll over and allow me to look at them."

"So, you just want to kiss the marks on my back?"

Costin growled.

Sally blew out a breath, causing her cheeks to puff out. She knew how relentless the males of his race were once they were on the hunt, and Costin was definitely on the hunt. She threw her hands up in the air. "Fine, fine, crap. Back up so I can roll over, your crowding me." She pushed at him, but Costin didn't move. When she realized that he wasn't going to, she wiggled until she had finagled herself onto her stomach. She nearly jumped out of her skin when she felt him pull at the hem of her shirt.

"Shh, Sally, I will never do anything you aren't comfortable with and I will always honor your wishes, trust me," he whispered, against her neck.

"I do," she told him, breathlessly. She had to bite her lip to keep from moaning when she felt his fingers trace the markings from the nape of her neck down until he couldn't go any farther because of her jeans.

Costin leaned down next to her ear again and tugged it gently with his teeth. "How far does it go?" He asked her and she could hear the desire in his deep voice.

Sally knew that if she opened her mouth she would say something very stupid and Jen like. The possibilities ranged from *why don't you find out*, to *good grief, would you touch me already*, and her personal favorite, *I want to have your babies*. Since those really didn't seem like the wisest choices, she did what seemed to be her trademark response to him and shook her head.

Costin chuckled. "Not going to play nice are we? Okay, two can play at that game."

Sally tried to prepare herself for whatever ridiculously sexy thing he had planned, but there was nothing on earth that could have prepared her for him. He started at the nape of her neck as he kissed her skin softly. She could feel his warm breath on her back and the firm pressure of his lips made her toes curl. Sally was biting the pillow by the time he reached the small of her back. Her hands clenched so tightly that her nails dug grooves into her palms. He kissed her one last time and she started to breathe easier. He pulled her shirt back down and attempted to roll her back over, but Sally couldn't move.

"Sally?" Costin's voice in her mind, sounded every bit as seductive as the stunt he had just pulled.

"Shh," She tried to silence him.

"Why?"

"I can't concentrate on breathing if you're talking to me, so stop talking, and don't you dare touch me again."

Costin chuckled at his mate who was currently as rigid as a post. He waited patiently as he watched her body slowly begin to relax. When she rolled over, he saw the indentions in her palms from her nails. He couldn't help the smugness he felt inside at knowing that he made her desire him with such ferocity.

"Wipe that look off your face, you big fat liar," Sally frowned at him.

"What?" Costin laughed, and tried to tug her to him.

She slapped his hand away. "You said a kiss, as in a single kiss. What was that?" She pointed to her back wildly, her cheeks still flushed.

"You didn't like it?" He asked, as he attempted to look hurt.

Sally rolled her eyes. "Throw me a freaking bone. I would have to be in a coma to not have enjoyed that. Mother of pearl, even then I probably would have enjoyed it. I mean seriously, Costin, who wouldn't ENJOY THAT!" Sally's voice had risen into screechy octaves by the time she was finished speaking and she was breathing heavily.

"Did I scare you?" Costin asked, suddenly worried that maybe she was responding this way because of what had happened. "I'm not rushing you Sally."

"Costin," Sally's eyes softened, "no baby, you didn't scare me. I didn't even think about it, there was only you and your lips." She smiled at him hoping he would see the sincerity there.

"You will tell me if I ever scare you or hurt you," he demanded, as only a male dominant could.

Sally rolled her eyes. "Bossy much?"

"Do you want to know what the inscription says now?" Costin asked, calmly.

"Yes," Sally grumbled, like a sulky child.

Costin tugged her to him by her hand and this time she didn't resist. He took her left hand and as he slid the ring on, he whispered in her ear.

"It says, Mate, wife, healer, my one, my only, Sally mine." Costin pulled the hair that had fallen like a curtain in front of Sally's face, over her shoulder so that he could see her. Her brown eyes shimmered with tears as she stared at the ring on her hand.

"Are those happy tears?" Costin asked, wearily.

Sally nodded.

"You are a woman of few words tonight love."

"That's because all too often, you render me speechless," Sally told him, as she looked up into his eyes. He saw her heart in those eyes, a heart that she had fully given to him.

"I love you, and I can't wait to be your wife."

Costin smiled, flashing his dimple at her. "Oh brown eyes, I can't wait either."

Sally could see the wheels turning in his, too handsome for his own good, head. She started shaking her head. "Oh, uh uh, no way, that," she pointed to where, moments ago she had been lying frozen with need and want, "will never happen again."

Costin laughed so loudly, Sally was sure the entire mansion heard.

"You are one funny gypsy, my love, I'll give you that."

"I'm serious Costin, that, that was," she tripped over her words, as she stared into his hazel eyes.

Costin leaned forward so that his lips were brushing against hers as he spoke. "That was only the beginning love. I hadn't even gotten to the good part."

~

"I'm going, so you can stop your slamming crap and muttering under your breath. Besides, we have company so quit acting like a total butthead." Jen sat next to Jacque on her bed, while Fane stood in a very Decebel like pose, leaning against the wall. Jen noticed that something in Fane was different, something in him had hardened, and the once gentle soul was gone. He watched Jacque constantly, attuned to the smallest movement, or even the change in her heart beat. Jen should have noticed it in Decebel as well, except Decebel had always been that way. She had never seen Decebel as young and un-jaded. By the time Decebel had found her, he was cold and thoroughly warped.

Decebel stopped in mid-stride and turned slowly to face his mate.

Jacque's jaw tensed and she shivered internally as she watched her best friend bare the intensity Decebel's stare. Fane noticed his mate's reaction and pushed away from the wall to stand next to her.

Jen held Decebel's stare and though part of her really wanted to crawl in a dark hole to hide from his anger, she knew it wasn't really her he was angry at.

"How many different ways do I have to tell you no? How many languages would it take to make you understand that you will not be going anywhere near males that I do not know and do not trust?" Decebel's eyes were glowing, though that was sort of a normal thing for him now, so Jen didn't take that to mean he was at his breaking point just yet.

"Do I really have to pull out the, *but everyone is doing it* card? All the other mates will be there, backing their men up. How am I supposed to feel if you leave me here? What kind of Alpha female does that make me look like?"

"A PREGNANT ONE!" Decebel snarled. "There isn't a male wolf there who wouldn't be doing the exact thing that I am Jennifer. You are precious to me, our child is a miracle, and I will not put either of you at risk."

Jen met his eyes as she stood and walked towards him. She didn't notice Fane and Jacque slip out. Her attention was for her mate only.

"Don't you get it?" She asked. *"Did you ever stop to think that maybe I don't want to be away from you, that I can't be away from you?"*

Decebel's eyes widened and she saw that he really had never considered why she was so adamant about going, other than not wanting to miss out, which admittedly was usually a reason Jen wanted to participate. But, this was something else altogether and it made her sick to admit it.

He took a step towards her and cupped her face in his large hands. Her eyes were tearless, but he had been a fool to miss the terror that hid behind her ever present strength. Decebel forgot that it usually took an act of despair to get Jennifer to admit to anything that she would view as a weakness and because of that, he often didn't treat her with the care she needed.

"I'm not fragile, Decebel," she told him, having seen his thoughts. "I'm just struggling with everything. I don't know what's wrong with me." She was frustrated, because she felt so out of control. She felt weak, because when she closed her eyes she saw their faces, felt their hands. Mona's curse still reverberated through her mind. She knew it was gone, but it still held power over her and that, above everything, angered her. But, if Decebel was with her, if she could see him, touch him, feel his touch, and then she was okay.

"Okay," he told her, as he pulled her into his arms, "okay baby, you come with me, but you don't step a foot away from my side."

Jen nodded against his shirt as she buried her face in his chest. She was slightly disgusted with herself for needing him the way she did, but she was giving herself a pass because she was pregnant, and she was going to play that card anytime she began to feel crazy, weak, or desperate.

"I need you the same way. Are you disgusted with me?" Decebel asked her.

She looked up at him and, as usual, his good looks were nearly painful to look at. His amber eyes glowed possessively at her as his hand stroked up and down her back.

"You're a dude, you're supposed to need me," she reasoned.

Decebel chuckled. "If we're going to go with that logic then I think you would win in the needs category."

"Why, because I'm a nympho?" She narrowed her eyes at him. "Are you complaining?"

Decebel leaned down and kissed her gently, enjoying the privileges that came with being a mate and husband. "I would be happy to show you how *not* complaining I currently am."

Jen laughed. "I think we're supposed to be meeting in the gathering room remember? Just a second ago you were all ready to go ape shniz on some dudes."

"Ape shniz?" Decebel smirked.

"I'm trying to curb the tongue since we're going to have a rugrat running around repeating everything I say."

Decebel smiled wickedly at her. "I'm sure I can find a way to keep your tongue busy so there is no chance of slipups."

"I totally walked into that one," she laughed.

"Totally," he agreed, as he pulled her to their bed.

"Dec, really we're supposed to go, like, now." Jen struggled, uselessly against his hold.

"I told you when I took you as my mate that you would always come before the pack, before all others. Look at me and tell me you don't need me." Decebel watched her closely.

Jen looked down at her feet in a very uncharacteristically submissive act. Decebel tugged again and this time Jen went without a fight.

"I totally did not admit anything," she told him as he kissed her.

"I know baby. I'm glad to take one for the team until you're ready to admit that you need me with the same desperation that I need you."

Jen laughed. "Take one for the team, that's classic."

"Jennifer," Decebel growled as he tugged at her shirt.

"What?"

"Shut up."

Jen started to speak but snapped her mouth shut when Decebel's hands did what they did best.

"What do they do best beautiful?"

"I forgot, I think you should remind me."

Decebel soaked up his mate's laughter like a plant soaks up the rain after a long drought. For that sound alone, he would be late to any meeting no matter the importance.

~

"Fane, are you alright?" Jacque watched her mate as they stood in the gathering room. It was slowly filling up with more and more males and Fane's posture grew more tense with every minute.

"I'm fine Luna."

His face, his voice, his whole everything, told Jacque he was lying. He was anything but fine.

"Why won't you talk to me?"

Fane turned and looked at her, glowing blue eyes bore into hers.

"This is not the time for words. Stay near me please."

Jacque knew that look and that clipped tone. Fane's wolf had taken over. She took a step closer to him and placed her hand on his back. He subtly leaned into it and that gave her a small amount of peace. He had grown exceedingly distant as the day had worn on and, to her surprise, hadn't even tried to keep her from coming with him. She had tried several times to engage him in conversation, but each time he had simply grunted at her or given her one word answers. He hadn't been mean to her, and he had been just as touchy as normal, if not more so, but Jacque and her wolf could feel that something was off in their mate and it was rubbing them the wrong way.

She continued to stand close to him, reassuring him of her presence as the room filled. She caught Sally's eye when she and Costin walked in. Jen and Decebel were just behind them. Both males looked ready to rip some one's head off with their bare hands. And, as curious as the other packs were about the females, one glance from Costin or Decebel and they dropped their eyes. Jacque hadn't noticed until then that not a single person was facing her direction. Fane was obviously giving the males the same challenging look and it was working rather well.

Jacque gave a small wave to Crina and Elle who were standing across from her with Sorin and Adam. She hadn't gotten to spend much time with them and hoped that they were recovering all right. They had both kept to themselves since they had returned and she figured that it was to have a chance to spend with the mates they had barely had time to get to know. Rachel and Gavril moved in beside the two couples and she saw Gavril give Fane a slight nod.

"How are things?" Jacque asked Jen as the two mated pairs came and stood next to she and Fane.

Jen glanced up at Decebel and then back at Jacque. "I've promised to be on my best behavior."

Jacque smiled. "For once, I actually believe you."

Sally laughed. "I guess there is a first time for everything."

Sally's laughter brought the rumbling room to complete silence. Everyone froze and their heads turned as a collective whole to where the three girls stood. Low growls rumbled in Costin, Decebel, and Fane's chest, but the fascination with a gypsy healer was too great to be dissuaded by growling mates.

A flash of light and thunderous boom at the front of the room snapped the attention to the front where Peri stood, smiling at her grand entrance.

"Saved by the fairy," Jen muttered, under her breath.

"Word," Jacque and Sally whispered back.

Their attention was drawn to the front along with everyone else's at the sound of Peri's voice.

"FOR THE PACK!"

Chapter 20

"Do you ever have that feeling where the hairs on the back of your neck rise, goose bumps suddenly appear all over your arms and your stomach feels like hornets are buzzing around to the tune of the Battle Hymn of the Republic? Take that feeling and magnify it a thousand times, then you will have a small idea of what it's like to walk into a room full of dominant wolves." ~ Lilly

"For the pack!" The entire room repeated Peri's declaration. They stood as one, united in purpose, and joined by a common goal.

Peri let the light around her fade until she finally looked like the Peri they all knew. It was apparent to everyone in the room that, though she now looked less majestic, she still wore power equal to the strongest of Alphas.

"I know it has been a very long time since any of you have seen a healer, if you ever have. That does not excuse rude behavior. You who are Alphas and dominants know better than any, how protective your males are of their mates. So, show the respect they deserve. Show the healer just how precious she is by not acting like rampant idiots." Peri met each Alphas eyes and held them, letting them see that she was not going to play dominance games with them. She was here as their equal and they would either accept that or not. It would be much wiser of them to just let it be.

Peri saw Vasile and Alina as they approached the entry. She motioned for the wolves to look behind them.

Vasile and his mate walked through the wolves as they parted, each of them dropping their eyes and the Alphas bowing their head slightly to Alina in respect. When they reached the front of the room, Vasile turned to face them.

"We all know why we are here," he told them. "Our creator, the Great Luna, has seen the evil that threatens our species, as well as all of the others, and she has called us to stand against it. She created us for such a time as this." Vasile's voice carried throughout the room, strong and clear. "She made us stronger, more resilient, and more cunning than other species. She made us wolves, because a pack protects its own. Pack protects the weak. Pack protects when all others choose to look away. Thankfully, we are not alone in our stand against the evil that has grown. We have friends who have agreed to help and we will welcome them into our pack and hear what they have to say."

Vasile motioned towards the back of the room where Cypher, Lilly, Thalion, and Cyn stood with a slew of warriors behind them.

Cypher turned and said something to the others and the warriors stayed behind as the four proceeded forward. The room was quiet as they walked. Cypher and Thalion kept their head straight forward not making eye contact with any of the wolves. Lilly looked everywhere, searching for Jacque, Jen, and Sally. When Lilly's eyes finally landed on Jacque and her friends her face broke into a huge smile.

Jacque was out from behind Fane and running towards her mother faster than Fane could react. She was barreling through the males not caring who she ran into or how it might affect Fane to watch his mate sprint through a room full of males that he did not know. Sally and Jen were right behind her and all three males tore after them.

Jacque knew what she had done was foolish, but all she had seen was her mother and all she could think about was making sure she was safe. She should have known that Sally and Jen would be right behind her, because they loved her mom every bit as much as she did.

Jacque reached her mom and ran straight into her arms, and for a brief moment, she thought that her little stunt might not be a disaster. She should have considered that a pregnant chick was running full speed behind her in a room jam packed with bodies.

Jen stumbled and Tyler reached out to catch her, but Decebel was there before he could touch her. Decebel glared at the Alpha and Tyler held his hands up and took a few steps back. The room was still as they waited to see how Decebel would respond.

"Hey B," Jen elbowed him. "Help a pregnant chick out and carry me through the masses?"

Decebel looked down at his mate and shook his head as he swung her up into his arms.

"You are a pain in my a…"

"Tsk, tsk, Dec, no cursing remember?" Jen admonished, as she patted her stomach. Decebel growled, but held his tongue.

Lilly wrapped her arms around all three of the girls as the huddled close. She hadn't realized just how badly she had needed to see that they were okay. She wiped tears away as she stepped back to look at each of them.

"Look at you three," she swooned. "You're beautiful. Romania agrees with you."

Jen laughed. "That's about the only thing." Decebel raised a brow at her when she looked back at him and winked.

Decebel, Fane, and Costin had formed a protective circle around the women and Adam, Sorin, and Gavril had stepped forward as well. The ladies were completely oblivious to their surroundings as they fired questions at one another, barely giving themselves time to answer. A loud throat clearing finally tore their attention from one another.

"I realize that you all want to catch up, and I assure you there will be time for that," Vasile told them, not unkindly, "but there are other matters that need to be dealt with."

"We are going to talk as soon as this pow-wow is over," Jacque told her mom as Fane tugged her by the hand back to where they had been standing. Decebel, Jen, Costin, and Sally followed close behind them. Everyone seemed to gather themselves back together and the four newcomers commenced the progress towards the front of the room.

Cypher pulled Lilly close to him as they reached the front of the room. He didn't feel threatened by any of the wolves, but he still didn't want Lilly away from his side. He shook Vasile's hand and nodded to his mate.

"Vasile, it's been a very long time," Cypher told him.

Vasile nodded. "That it has. I see that the Fates have blessed you," he nodded toward Lilly.

"Hi Vasile," Lilly smiled. "Good to see you again, though I wish it were under different circumstances."

"Likewise."

Alina stepped forward and gave Lilly a hug. "How are you holding up?" She asked her.

Lilly gave Alina a small squeeze as she answered, "I'm good."

Alina looked at her face as she stepped back from the hug and she could see in Lilly's eyes that, despite all that was going on, she was happy at Cypher's side.

Thalion stepped forward and bowed slightly to Vasile and Alina. "I am Thalion, Prince of the Elves."

The room erupted into murmurs at Thalion's introduction. Vasile silenced them with a look, and then turned back to Thalion.

"I've heard of you, though in all my time we have never met," Vasile bowed in return.

"We have kept to ourselves for far too long, and for that I am sorry. I have come to hopefully right some of that wrong."

Vasile reached for the Elf Prince's hand and grasped it tightly. "We welcome you, friend of the pack." He looked at Cypher and Lilly and added. "We welcome all of you."

The rest of the meeting was spent with Cypher telling them of everything they had been through since Mona showed up in his forest with her proposition. Several times Vasile had needed to remind the group of dominants to pull themselves together, when they growled at something Cypher said and they disliked. But, by then end, everyone seemed to be on the same page.

Vasile addressed the room a last time before dismissing everyone.

"I need each Alpha to stay, the rest are free to go eat and relax as much as possible because the time for that is quickly coming to an end. Do not be foolish with dominance games or I will save your Alphas the trouble and kill you myself."

The room began to empty until all that remained were the Alphas and Vasile's core group.

~

With all the Alphas present, Vasile and Decebel's wolves, the Fae and Cypher, Lilly, and Thalion, there were fifty seven total sitting in a large circle in the gathering room.

Vasile made quick introductions and immediately got down to business.

"Skender has filled me in on most of what has been taking place here while I was away. You have come up with a battle plan, correct?" He asked. The Alphas nodded and Dillon spoke up, as he had become the unofficial go between for the packs. "We've been practicing battle tactics with each other, learning how we each fight and we think we've come up with some strategies that will work to our advantage."

Vasile turned to Cypher and motioned for him to take the floor.

"I am to meet with Desdemona tomorrow. I imagine she will not want to wait any longer to open the veil. I have explained to Perizada of the Fae where the veil to the underworld lies and she will be the one to lead you to it when the time is right. It is very important that any demons that escape be killed, quickly. Thalion and the elves will be the ones who take out the demons. They are the only one with the weapons that will kill them."

"So, what are the rest of us supposed to do?" Victor asked.

"Desdemona will know that we are coming. There is no way for us to prevent that knowledge. Peri and the Fae council will be able to cloak our numbers, but she will still know we are coming. As she has done in the past, she will use any form of evil she can bend to her will. There will likely be multiple foes to contend with and it will be our job to take them out before they get to any of Thalion's people," Dillon explained.

"Once the veil is open, it will also be the wolves' job to keep Mona occupied while I close it back." Cypher rubbed his forehead as he let out a deep breath. He appeared nearly human for a brief moment in time when the pressure and strain of all that he had endured and would endure, settled on his shoulders. "I honestly don't have a clue if any of this is going to work," he admitted to the group. Lilly took his hand in hers and squeezed it for support. "But, I'm going to do my best to keep from releasing the whole of hell into our realm."

"That's all we can ask of anyone," Vasile told him, "that we each do our best. This is not a fight to glorify one man. This is a fight to save many species. All each of us can do, is give everything we have to win this fight."

"For the pack." Decebel's voice rumbled through the room.

"For the pack," they all responded in unison.

"Get some rest," Vasile told them, as they all stood, "tomorrow we fight."

~

Peri, Cynthia, and the mated females sat in a circle on the floor of the study. Jen had sweet talked Decebel into building a fire for them in the large fire place and Sally, Crina, and Elle had managed to convince their mates to make hot chocolate for the lot of them. The males had refused to leave them, so they had taken up residence across the room, each looking equally broody and put out. Even Cypher had refused to leave and sat next to Vasile with the same fierce scowl.

They were all just settling in when Jen jumped up and squealed.

"Holy freaking cow on a stick!"

Decebel lunged across the room, standing beside her in an instant.

"Jennifer, are you okay?" He was trying to check her over and she kept slapping his hands away and pointing across from her. Sally sat with a shy smile as everyone turned to look at her.

Jacque's eyes widened as she saw Sally's hand.

"You bit—,"

"Jacque, *language*," Jen snapped and then turned back to Sally. "You bitch!"

Jacque looked over at Jen. "Why do you get to cuss?"

"Because, I'm pregnant and, like old people, pregnant people get to do a whole bunch of crazy crap and blame it on their bodies."

"Huh," Jacque shrugged. "I guess that makes sense." They both turned their attention back to Sally and she squirmed under their glares.

"Would someone please fill me in as to why we are giving Sally the death stare?" Crina asked.

"Look at her hand," Jen growled out.

There was a collective gasp as all eyes landed on the diamond.

"Please tell me that all he did was ask," Jen warned. "Please tell me that you two did not secretly get married because tomorrow we might all die and you didn't want to go to your grave with the big V hanging over you."

Sally's mouth dropped open.

"Why didn't I think of that?" Costin called across the room.

"Do not give her more ammunition," Sally snarled at him.

Costin winked at her from his casual stance against the wall that gave him a perfect view of her.

"We didn't get married Jen," Sally huffed. "He just asked me, but I haven't exactly had a chance to tell you all."

Decebel finally picked up on the fact that his mate was in no imminent danger, or having any pregnancy complications, and backed out of the estrogen filled circle.

"You've had plenty of chances," Jacque told her. "All you had to do was hold up your bloody hand while you were walking into the gathering hall. I would have been like 'hey Jen look, Sally is engaged.'"

"And, I would have been like, 'hey Jacque, she better not have gotten married just so she could jump in the sack with sexy dimple wolf.'" Jen finished.

"What is with you and your fascination of my virginity?" Sally stood up, tired of having her friends loom over her.

"I'm not fascinated by it," Jen argued.

"Then why are you assuming that I would marry Costin behind your back just so I could have sex with him!" Sally's hands were on her hips as she bore down on her friends.

Jen paused for a second as she considered Sally's question.

"Because, it's what I would do," she finally answered. The room erupted into laughter. Jen looked around at the flailing bodies, then over to her mate who was shaking his head at her. "What?" She asked, feigning confusion as to what was funny.

"No worries, Jen," Costin called out again. "I'm totally with you on this one."

Decebel growled at him and Costin laughed.

"Nobody asked you, Costin," Sally told, him through gritted teeth.

Costin blew her a kiss and she bit the inside of her cheek to keep from grinning like an idiot. And, he knew it too.

"Are you thinking about what I'm thinking about?" He taunted.

"If you're thinking about me kicking you out of my room, then yes."

She heard Costin's chuckle in her mind and felt his breath on her neck.

"Be honest with your mate, Sally. I think you're thinking about a certain bargain, a certain kiss, a certain…"

"STOP IT." Sally could feel her face blushing and knew the minute everyone realized she hadn't heard a word they had said. She hadn't even realized they'd been fawning over her ring.

Jen looked from Costin to Sally and grinned. "Are you two getting your kicks through your mate bond, right here in front of all of us?" Jen tapped Sally on the nose affectionately. "I didn't realize that he would turn you into a freak so quickly. Nice work Costin."

"The pleasure is all mine," he quipped back.

"Oh, I'm sure it is," Jacque laughed.

If Sally hadn't wanted to seep into the ground before, she was definitely seeking out a crevice now.

"As much as I love hearing all the sex jokes from the girls I raised," Lilly finally interrupted. "I would really like to see Sally's ring, then I'd like someone to tell me how Jen is pregnant, and I didn't know."

"The how is really not in question mom," Jacque laughed.

"I'm willing to explain exactly how it happened in incredible detail if Ms. P really needs to know," said Jen.

"NO!" The entire room erupted.

"Man you guys are a buzz kill." Jen rolled her eyes as she took her seat back on the floor.

"So, Sally," Lilly smiled, "how did he propose?"

Sally narrowed her eyes over at Costin.

"Your move brown eyes." He told her as he blew her a kiss.

"You're right my love, it most definitely is my move," Sally grinned wickedly, and nearly stood up and danced when she saw his eyes widen with what looked suspiciously like worry.

"Well," Sally began, "We were laying on my bed, just talking, and then things sort of got heated, you know?"

"No, we most definitely do not know," Jen interrupted. "We need painstakingly clear details, Sally, details."

"Jennifer, behave," Decebel's voice, rumbled.

"Bah," she waved him off, "you can punish me later."

Lilly coughed on the hot chocolate that she had been trying to swallow. Jen patted her on the back as she stared at Sally waiting for her to continue.

"So, as I was saying, things were getting pretty hot and heavy…"

"Third base heavy or did he go for a grand slam?" Jacque broke in.

"Good questions, Jac," Jen nodded in approval, "definitely good questions."

"Oh, he tried for the grand slam," Sally tried not to blush as she said the words, "but he struck out."

"Ouch," they heard Decebel mutter. Then a crashing sound that they all ignored. Sally glanced over the girls to see if Costin was all right. One of the chairs next to him had obviously been shoved or kicked over, he was glaring at her, and it warmed her to the bones.

"So, I sort of felt sorry for him when he finally got the nerve to ask me to marry him. I had already shut the ballpark down for any rides, so I wanted to make up for it when he was brave enough to ask me."

Jen rolled on the floor grasping her stomach as she laughed. "Shut the ballpark! Rides!" She laughed harder when she looked at Decebel, who couldn't decide if he should risk walking through the estrogen bomb to see if she was all right or make a run for it, in the opposite direction.

Lilly tried to cover her laughter as she watched the gleam in Sally's eyes, but the rest of the room had given up any pretense of trying to be cool.

Sally's eyes widened as Costin came striding across the room. He stood just on the outside of the circle and the hazel eyes that met hers smoldered.

"Oh my," Jen murmured, when she finally gathered herself. "I know that look, Jacque don't you know that look?"

Jacque looked up at Costin. "Mm hmm, girl, I most definitely know that look."

Alina smirked. "I even know that look."

Sally's eyes danced back and forth between Costin and her friends. "Well, somebody help a sista out because I *don't* know that look."

"You're about to find out," Crina muttered.

Costin smiled at her and the entire circle of mostly mated women swooned. He had one of those smiles. The dimple, the eyes, the wink, it was lethal to anyone watching.

"Shall I tell them what really happened, Sally mine?" He asked in a voice that should only be reserved for the bedroom or if you happen to work for one of those nine hundred number things.

Sally stood up slowly. She decided that it was time to fight fire with fire. She let her body unfold like a lazy cat and she smiled sweetly at him, biting her lip shyly.

"We could show them, you know, reenact it for them." Sally tried for a sultry voice and thought maybe she had achieved it when Costin growled.

Jen laughed. "I think she's got your number, dimple boy."

Sally quirked an eye brow at her mate. "I'll show them mine, if you show them yours."

Costin knew he'd been beaten at his own game and snarled when Sally's hands went to the hem of her shirt. He turned and stalked back to the side of the room where the other males were giving him sincere looks of sympathy.

"Welcome to my world," Decebel told him, as he came to stand beside him.

Costin's eyes honed in on his mate who was smiling and laughing with her friends. She was proud of herself, and to be honest, he was proud of her too. But, that didn't change the fact that he didn't like to lose and he had most definitely lost.

"Check mate," he heard her giggle in his mind.

"How do you survive," he asked Decebel.

"Killing things and lots and lots of s—,"

Costin choked before Decebel could finish. Decebel frowned at his Beta.

"I was going to say sleep you perv," he laughed at Costin's wide eyes. "I'm actually going to agree with my mate on this one, you two just need to get hitched and take care of business. The tension is so tight between you two, one of you is liable to snap and attack the other one in plain daylight."

Costin laughed, "She would break before I would."

Decebel shook his head. He looked over at Sally and then back at Costin. "No Beta, I don't think she would."

The girls talked late into the night, and when Jen dozed off, the males finally stepped in. One by one, they gathered their mates.

Lilly gave Jacque a hug before Fane picked her up. "I'm so glad you're happy Jac."

"Thanks mom, me too. Tell the Warlock King I'll kick his posterior if he hurts you."

Lilly laughed. "I'll pass it along." Cypher stepped behind her and wrapped an arm around her waist. "She's going to kick my what?"

Lilly shook her head with a smile. "She's all bark." Lilly took his hand and let him lead her out of the study.

Decebel gently picked up Jen and she curled up in his arms. He kissed her forehead and nodded to Costin as he left the room.

Costin and Sally were the last ones in the study. The fire crackled and the light from the flames danced on Sally's face. She had dozed off along with Jen quite a while ago, but he hadn't wanted to disturb her. He knelt down next to her and ran a finger across her cheek. She nuzzled it and he smiled. Even in sleep, she knew who he was.

"Mine," she mumbled.

Costin picked her up and held her close to his chest. "Always," he whispered in her ear, as he carried her to their room.

Chapter 21

"In my long life there have been none who I would say had been a worthy opponent, someone who was worth the effort it took to kill. Not until now. Finally, a worthy opponent has come forward. He is the strongest of his kind, of pure heart and soul. Yes, he is a worthy opponent, and it was almost a shame that I had to kill him…almost." ~ Desdemona

"I've been waiting, Warlock King," Desdemona walked leisurely through the trees, and though she might have sounded irritated, she looked as if she were taking a relaxing stroll through the forest.

Cypher stepped into the small clearing and met the witch's gaze.

"I have a question before we do this," he told her.

"If you must," she said tiredly, as if he were a child who had hounded her all day for a morsel of attention.

"What is it you hope to accomplish?" Cypher tilted his head and scratched his chin. "You're going to let out a hoard of demons whose only desire is destroy everything in their path, to what end?"

When Cypher had dropped Lilly off at her room last night, he had gone back to his own room and studied the *Nushtonia* with Perizada. She had known the language, though she was very hesitant to speak it out loud. When she finally decided to say the words, she said them out of order so that she didn't inadvertently invoke some unknown spell. Through their study, Cypher had learned that Mona was misinformed on her knowledge of the underworld. She believed that if she released the demons that she would be able to control them, but like any lies construed by evil, shreds of truth were woven within a web of deceit. The only control that she would have would be one request of the demon who wrote the *Nushtonia* and that was all. Desdemona did not realize that she was going to unleash not only her enemy's destruction, but her own as well.

"I don't need to justify myself to you," Mona told him, smoothly. "You are but a tool to be used in my plan. You do what I ask and then you may leave."

"You really think that it is going to be that easy? Is anything ever that easy Mona?"

"Are you attempting an intervention? Is that what this is?" Mona motioned with her finger between them. "Let me save you the trouble King, there is no saving me."

Cypher laughed. "Oh, believe me, I am well aware of just how un-savable you are, but you don't have to take us all to hell with you."

"Too late."

Cypher watched as she closed her eyes and waved her hands in front of a group of trees. The wind picked up and the sky grew darker as black clouds rolled in. A shimmer in the air between the trees formed and Cypher could feel the evil trapped behind the veil.

"You've been hiding it?" He asked her.

"I didn't want just any old idiot coming across it and I didn't want the demons using another to write a book on how to open it."

Cypher's brow rose. "You know about the book that was written?" He didn't name the book for fear that she would realize that he had it, and because he didn't want to draw attention to himself from those beyond the veil in front of him.

Mona laughed, dryly. "You do remember who you are talking to, right?"

Cypher glared at her, but held his tongue. He and Peri had decided that he needed to appear as cooperative as possible for as long as possible.

"Enough chit chat," she motioned for him to move closer. "I'm assuming that since you are here then you know what you are doing?"

Cypher moved towards the veil and pulled a knife from his leg sheath.

"You know what they say about assuming right?" He asked her as he ran the knife across his arm.

Desdemona rolled her eyes. "We all know that I'm an ass Cypher, that's not news to anyone."

Cypher cut another slash across his arm, and another.

"You aren't going to bleed out before you've opened it right?"

"Do you want me to do this or not?" Cypher growled.

"Touchy, touchy," Mona muttered, as she leaned back against a tree. She watched as Cypher slashed his other arm the same number of times as the first. Rivers of blood snaked down his arms dripping to the ground around his feet. Mona watched in fascination as the blood, almost as if it had a life of its own, began to join and flow as one towards the shimmering covering of the veil.

Cypher closed his eyes and began to murmur the words that Peri had taught him. His mind was drawn back to the look on Peri's face as she explained the requirement of the magic. She explained that dark magic could never be accomplished without paying some form of price and it was usually a life or blood. Peri's face has taken on an ashen hue as she read the words of the book. She had looked up at him and he could see the answer to his unasked question.

"It will take your blood," she told him.

"Come now Peri, we are both too old to skirt around the truth," he had teased.

Peri's eyes had shimmered with unshed tears.

"It will take all of your blood," she finally told him.

Cypher nodded. He knew that a life was the requirement to open the veil. He had hoped that there would be a loop hole.

"You've only just found her," Peri had whispered to him. "She has finally, after so long, found the one who can fill the void in her only to lose him." She had looked up at him and Cypher had felt his heart breaking as he watched one as ancient as Perizada hurt for Lilly, who she had claimed as one of her own.

"You need to tell her," Peri had growled at him.

"No," his answer had been final. He refused to leave Lilly with the knowledge that he would not be coming back to her. When he had left that morning, she had hugged him and kissed him and the smile that radiated on her face gave him the courage to do what was necessary. If it had been her tears, he didn't know if he would have been able to walk away.

So now he stood before an ancient evil that longed to be unleashed into the world and he longed for the life that he knew he didn't deserve. His blood would slowly weaken the opening to the veil and the words from the *Nushtonia* would give the demons strength.

He and Peri had gone to Vasile and explained their strategy and it was simple. He would bleed as slowly as he could, giving the wolves time to travel the twenty miles to his location. Desdemona did not know what it took, nor how long it would take to open the veil so he could use that to his advantage.

He felt the warm, wet blood flowing down his arms and fought the urge to try and kill Mona himself. He had argued for that, but Peri had told him that he alone would not be able to defeat Mona, not at this point. She had spent too many centuries amassing power.

So, he stood there, bleeding like the sacrificial lamb waiting for death to take him, and wishing for one more day with the human who had stolen his heart.

~

Ainsel stood just beyond the trees, watching as the Warlock King bled freely. He had given his blood without force or coercion. He stood of his own free will as his lifeblood created a puddle at his feet and flowed towards the veil.

"Ainsel, please join us," Mona's voice crawled over his skin like prickly insects making him want to recoil. But, she knew he was here, he had no choice but to step forward.

"Desdemona." The King of the Pixies bowed his head slightly to the witch.

"I see you have come to uphold your end of the bargain," she told him, with a toothy smile.

"I am here," was his only response.

"Good," she folded her arms across her chest as she turned back to the bleeding Warlock King, "because things are about to get interesting."

~

Vasile stood, flanked by Alina and Decebel, gazing at the warriors arrayed before him. Each of the packs, along with the Fae, Warlocks, and the Elves were assembled on the practice field in tight formations. Vasile wondered how many of them, if any, would return from this battle. He hoped they would all return. For the first time in his memory, he felt as if there was a real chance for his race to be united.

"Today will not be a day of mourning, or a day of loss," his deep voice filled the empty space reaching into the hearts of his brothers, reminding them of why they were created, and why they stood where they did today. "Today will not be a day of defeat. Today is the day that we finally take a stand against evil. Today, though we are separate species, though we come from different places, and have served different purposes, today we are one pack. Today we combine our strengths and use them for the greater good, when others cannot fight for themselves, today we will. I will not tell you to be fearless, for a lack of fear will make you reckless. I will tell you to be courageous. Stand your ground in the face of adversity, set your feet, and brace your body for impact, because today you will fight for your right to simply exist. You fight for the existence of your friends, your brothers and sisters, and your mates. Today I am proud to fight beside each of you. FOR THE PACK!"

Shoulders that had been slumped were now pulled back. Chins rose and jaws set as those who were not the same, those who did not agree on everything, did not always understand one another, and did not always like each other yelled as one. "FOR THE PACK!"

Vasile turned to Decebel and shook his hand before pulling him into a tight hug.

"You stay alive," he told his former Beta.

Decebel gave him a small smile. "I would tell you the same, but you're too bullheaded to die."

Vasile chuckled. "Too true." His voice sobered. "We run as one and as soon as we pick up the King's scent, we break off."

The other Alphas walked over and joined Decebel and Vasile.

"Victor, Dragomir, Angus, Artur, Gustavo, and Ciro, you will bank left, circle around, and fan out Dillon, Drayden, Tyler, Jeff, Decebel, and myself will bank right so that we form a complete circle. You will stagger your wolves' one facing in, one facing out, every other wolf. This will protect our flanks as we move forward. Desdemona is not a witch of simple mind. She will use anything in her power to achieve her goal. Adam, Alston, Dain, Disir, Gwem, Lorelle, and Nissa of the Fae will spread out amongst us to fight along with us. They will shield our presence for as long as possible. Jacque, Alina, Cynthia, and Crina will be fighting amongst us. They are the only females fighting with us. I do not say that I allowed this, but if you have met them, you have figured out that these are women that you don't really allow anything.

"So, as much as it is in your power, protect our females. They are precious to us. Rachel and Sally, our two healers, along with Jen, the Serbian pack Alpha female, Elle, Sorin's mate and Perizada will be a short distance away, hopefully with the stones of the Fae, if they make themselves available. They will help fight any of the forces of nature that Desdemona will attempt use in her favor.

"Our total numbers are thus: ten Fae, seven of which belong to the High Council, twenty Warlock warriors, twenty Elves, led by their Prince, two Gypsy Healers and fifty-one dominant Canis lupus, twelve of which are Alphas. This could be the largest united effort of supernatural races in our long history. It is my sincerest hope that we all come back, that we end this madness together. If we do not, I want to personally thank each of you for your help, for hearing our cry and the cry of the Great Luna and coming to our aide." Vasile stepped back and to everyone's surprise, he knelt, bowed his head, and placed his hand over his heart. Every movement stopped. Every noise ceased as they all turned to see the greatest of them on his knees, humbled.

One by one, they took a knee and bowed their heads, joining Vasile.

"My children," warmth spread across them as they all looked up at the sound of the powerful voice—the Great Luna stood before them in all her glory. "Today, I am pleased with the leader who has risen among you, who sees himself not as the greatest, but as a servant. Today, I am pleased with you all, those who belong to me and those who do not. Today, you have exercised your free will and chosen the harder path. For it is easier to give in to the darkness that dwells in each of your hearts, but much more difficult to go against your nature and take the path of righteousness. Listen to Vasile. His heart is pure and he desires nothing more than to see each of the races prosper and flourish. Go with my blessing. Know that I am and will give you strength; all you need is to ask." And, as quietly as she had appeared, she was gone.

Across the field, surrounded by the guards that Vasile and Decebel had assigned to them, the females all stood up together and Jen stepped forward. "You heard the woman people, let's bring the rain!"

Chuckles rippled across the group as they all stood and began to join with their packs.

"That is your mate, no?" Gustavo, Alpha to the pack of Spain, asked Decebel.

Decebel looked across the field to his mate who was giving him thumbs up.

"Yes, yes she is," Decebel, said with a small laugh.

"She is strange," Gustavo admitted.

"Yes, she is definitely that as well."

"But hot," Costin piped in as he came up behind Decebel.

"I'll tell your mate you said that," Decebel threatened, as the other Alphas watched Decebel warily, having seen firsthand how protective he was of his mate.

"I'll just point out that she's hotter, she'll forgive me."

Decebel rolled his eyes. "You are the only wolf whose mate wouldn't castrate you for calling another woman hot."

"Oooh, who are we castrating?" Jen asked as she wrapped her arms around Decebel who had seen her coming and held them open for her.

"Costin," Decebel told her.

"Sally won't be happy with you B," Jen looked up at her mate, grinning.

"It doesn't appear that he ever plans to need them, as slow as those two are moving, so I honestly don't think she'll mind."

Jen laughed and gave her mate a high five. "Good one babe."

Costin frowned at the pair. "Jen that was so not cool."

Jen laughed. She stood on her tip toes and kissed Decebel. The others left the couple, giving them a semblance of privacy.

"You stay safe," Decebel told her.

"I will only be as safe as you are B," Jen told him, honestly.

"I know," Decebel's voice was soft and she heard the regret in it.

"Hey," she nudged him. "Would you want to exist in a world where I was not?"

"You know I wouldn't," Decebel frowned.

"Then do not be sad that we fall together, because I would not want to exist without you."

"We have a child to think of now Jennifer."

"All the more reason for you to prove that you are the badass you claim to be and come back to me."

"Language," he growled.

"Babe, it's the end of the world as we know it. As such, I reserve the right to indulge in the pottying of the mouth." Jen smiled.

Decebel shook his head and rolled his eyes as he leaned down and kissed his mate passionately. His lips parted and Jen boldly explored his mouth. He smiled against her lips.

"What?" she asked him, breathlessly.

"I have always loved that you are not shy with me." He tucked her long, blonde hair behind her ear.

"Why would I need to be shy? Have you seen all this?" She motioned up and down her body with her hands.

Decebel grinned as his eyes began to glow. "Why, yes mate, yes I have."

Jen laughed. She took his face in her hands and all humor fled.

"You live so that we can live, do you hear me?"

Decebel nodded, and fell to his knees before her. He pressed his lips to her stomach, and then looked up at her.

"I love you."

She ran her fingers through his thick hair. "And, I'm one lucky woman because of it."

She backed up from him and blew him a kiss. As she turned to go, she looked back over his shoulder and grinned at her still kneeling mate. "Oh by the way, I love you too."

Decebel winked at her as he stood up.

"And, I am the luckiest man because of it," he whispered to himself as he watched her walk back to the group of females.

"When we get back, we are getting married," Costin told Sally, as he held her close.

Sally smiled. "You've been around Decebel too much, you're getting bossy."

Costin laughed, "No, I'm getting desperate."

Sally pulled him down to kiss her. She pressed her body tight to his and drew strength from his confident hold.

"I am yours, every square inch of me."

Costin raised a brow at her. "I'll hold you to those words Sally mine."

"I love you, I want you, and I need you," She told him, as her lips brushed against his.

Costin closed his eyes and used the intimacy of their bond.

"The time I've had with you has been the best in my sixty years. And, I want many more. You are precious to me. Please be careful out there." Costin kissed her forehead and held his lips against her. *"I love you. I want you more than you could possibly understand and I need you even more than that."*

Sally let out a shaky breath as they stared into each other's eyes. Finally, he pushed her back with a small grin. "Go do your thing gypsy lady."

Sally waved as she backed away. "See you soon lover boy."

Costin winked at her and she blushed.

Fane pulled Jacque close to him as he pressed his lips to her neck where he had left his mark. She shivered under his touch. She was still worried about him as he continued to keep himself closed off.

"I love you, Jacquelyn," he told her, solemnly.

Jacque looked up into his blue eyes. "Do you?" She asked, for the first time in their marriage and mating.

Fane's eyes filled with pain, as he felt the doubt inside her. He knew that it was his fault and he didn't know how to fix it. He didn't know how to show her just how broken and tormented he was over what she had been through while under Mona's spell. He had tried to just rejoice in the fact that she was alive and healthy now, but he just kept seeing the things she had endured and because of that he had not let her into his mind, even when he had made love to her. Even then, he had felt her pain.

"More than anything," he told her.

"Then what have I done that you keep yourself from me? Are you mad, because of what I did in the forest? Because I wouldn't let you touch me, are you punishing me?" Her voice grew distressed as she tried to understand.

Fane scowled. "I would never punish you for anything Luna. How could you think that?"

"You won't open the bond; you won't share all of yourself with me. What am I supposed to think?"

Fane kissed her fiercely as he ran his hands up her back to her hair. He released her and stepped back. "All you need to know right now, is that you are mine and I love you. We will talk after this is over. We will go into this battle safe in the knowledge that no matter what, we will always belong to each other, please believe that."

Jacque's mouth dropped open, shocked that her Fane was acting like this. "I'm pissed at you Fane Lupei."

"I can live with that, as long as you don't doubt that I love you, and I will never give you up."

Jacque stomped her foot as he turned and walked away from her.

"Being a butthead?" Jen asked, as she came to stand next to her best friend.

Jacque growled. "He doesn't know it yet, but I'm going to kick his ass when this is over."

Jen snorted. "Decebel would be so turned on if I said that."

That brought a grin to Jacque's face as Jen nudged her shoulder. "Come on Red, we have a witch's britches to kick before you can start your foreplay with your wolf man."

"Did you just say witch's britches?" Jacque asked, as they joined the group of females that Peri was currently talking to.

Jen grinned. "There's more where that came from."

"Of that, I have no doubt," Jacque agreed.

Peri pointed to Jen as she and Jacque walked up. "And, if you give me any jacked up act of heroics I will tan your pregnant hide."

"Dude, I just got here. How can you possibly be chastising me when I haven't even opened my mouth?"

"I have no doubt that you have said something, or fifty somethings, already this morning that deserve more than just chastising," Peri pointed out.

"Were you listening in at my bedroom door this morning Perizada?" Jen's smirk told the group of females more than they wanted to know and they all groaned.

"Listen up," Peri snapped. "I've already told each of you exactly what your roles are as we go into this crap shoot. Do not deviate from the plan or I will zap your ass. Be aware of your position and your enemy's position at all times. Mona will try to disorient you. Wolves use the superior senses the Great Luna gave you. Rachel and Sally follow my lead. Elle do your thing."

"What do I do?" Jen asked.

"You are going guard the healers in your wolf form."

"I thought you just said no heroics."

"Since when do you do anything that anyone tells you?"

"Good point," Jen nodded.

Peri looked over the women and saw that the males were shedding their clothes and phasing.

"Okay, it's go time. Sally, you will ride your male," Peri paused as all their heads swung to look at Jen.

"What?"

Peri tilted her head at her. "Nothing?"

"Okay, if you insist. Sally, if you need any pointers on how to hold on just let me know."

Sally's face turned bright red as she heard Costin add in her mind. *"No more waiting brown eyes, you have been ordered to ride me."*

Sally choked as she tried to swallow and Jen had to slap her on the back.

"Your man just gave you a line didn't he?"

Sally nodded.

"I knew I was gonna like him the moment I laid eyes on his lickable, dimpled, face."

Decebel walked by the group of women to meet up with his pack and slapped his mate on the butt. "Behave," he growled.

The group of females laughed.

Lilly came hurrying over and wrapped Jen, Jacque, and Sally in a hug. "You three be safe. Peri won't let me come. She threatened to hogtie me. Since when does a Fae know anything about hogtying?" Lilly frowned at the smirking Fae.

"Peri knows all forms of torture; it's her thing," Jen quipped.

"Well, I guess everyone has something," Lilly scoffed.

Jacque hugged her mom again. "Please stay here. We'll be back, I promise."

Lilly, met Jacque's eyes. "I'm so proud of you."

Jacque smiled. "I am what I am because of you."

Lilly shook her head. "No sweets, this is all you."

Lilly backed away until she was nearly at the door of the mansion. She bit her lip to keep the tears back and prayed that not only her daughter, but all those she had come to care for would return victoriously and safely.

Jen, Jacque, Crina, Rachel, and Alina undressed quickly and phased. They shook out their fur and stretched out in their wolf form and then the mated females trotted over to stand next to their mates. Each male nuzzled their faces and pressed against their smaller frames. When Crina reached Adam's side he knelt down and gave her a quick tap on the nose. "You watch yourself out there okay?" She nodded her big head once and leaned in to press her face against his chest.

"Peri has requested that I and Elle use our power in conjunction with the other Fae so try and stay as close to me as you can, but we will be spreading out," he explained and gave her one last loving tap on the muzzle.

Peri motioned for Elle, Adam, and the Fae council to spread out amongst the wolves. Peri began to speak softly as her hands moved smoothly in the air, arcing over the group as the other Fae joined in. The warlocks and elves took up the rear.

Vasile stood proudly at the head of the pack, his mate at his side. He threw his head back and howled. The pack joined in and the trees shook from the sound. He sniffed the air and found Cypher's trail. Like a bolt of lightning, he shot off with the largest supernatural army in history, at his back.

~

Sorin's legs stretch as he ran and his fur blew as the air rushed through it. He glanced up briefly at his mate, who ran beside him. She was breathtaking in all her warrior glory. The memory of the night the curse was broken came crashing down on him and he nearly stumbled under the weight of it. When he had finally been able to hold her, it had not been enough. He had not been able to get close enough. He had helped her shower and dress and then held her in his arms as she wept. When she had finally calmed down, she had opened up to him and shared all she had endured and it had enraged him. He had watched in awe as she had calmed him as only a true mate could. She had given freely her love, comfort, and touch. In his very long life he had never had felt such passion, such need as he found in her arms. Over and over, he had whispered to her all the emotion in his heart and tried to show her through his touch just how precious she was to him. She had asked him to do the Blood Rites with her because she did not want to go into this battle with the chance that they would not be together one way or the other. His wolf had howled in victory, but the man had hesitated. He did not want to seal her fate in case anything went wrong. But, she was his mate, his equal, and it was as much her choice as it was his. So, he had given her what she wanted and what he so desperately needed.

~

"I love you," Crina whispered to Adam. She felt his smile through their bond. *"I think you know just how much I love you,"* he teased her, with his never ending good nature.

She treasured the playfulness in him and knew that it was a blessing to her. But, the night all the females had been saved from the curse by Peri and the Fae, she had seen another side to Adam, a side that broke her heart. She had known that he loved her. But that night, she realized the depth of that love. To her surprise, he had wept as much as she had. His possessiveness was no less than the Canis lupus males and his ferocious protectiveness called to her wolf. She knew that the human females had waited to complete their mating until they were married, but she was not human, and marriage was not a part of her heritage. The Blood Rites was essentially the equivalent of a wedding for their race and when Adam had told her they were going to finish their mating that night, she had reveled in the dominance and her wolf had gladly submitted. It had been the best night of her life, which she was sure, was what every woman said during that time, but she couldn't imagine anyone experiencing what she had in the arms of her mate. He had worked magic that no other could.

"I am Fae you know, so I have a slight advantage in the whole magic working." Crina laughed as they ran. Here they were, running into a battle they might not survive, discussing their love life.

"What better time to think about the magic we made together? I mean seriously, I can die a happy man now that I've had the privilege of being with you. And, I totally mean that in any perverted way you would like to take it." Adam's voice brought chills to her skin as he reminded her of all they had experienced.

"I would tell you to behave, but it would be a waste of words."

"Too true, my sexy wolf lady, too true. Don't wear yourself out here today, I got plans for you."

Crina cut a glance over to him as her wolf perked up at their mate's teasing. She wanted to chase him. It was the wolf's form of foreplay, and by the grin on his face, he knew it.

Chapter 22

"With every step we draw closer, with every breath we close in on our prey. Do you feel us coming? We move silently as one, a pack united in purpose, driven by the belief that evil will not prevail. Your end is eminent; your time in this life draws to a close. We are coming. You may have never feared the hounds of hell, but you should fear us. Fear the wolves that live in us, fear the ones who join us and know that you will answer for the crimes that you have committed. You will answer and you will pay." ~ Fane

Mona felt them, Vasile, and his wolves. She knew that she would not hear them. They were hunters and, as such, would come silently, seeking the killing blow. They were too late. Cypher had fallen to his knees long ago and his pale flesh testified to his pending doom. The opening to the veil grew more and more solid as Cypher's blood fed it.

"Turns out I won't need you after all," she turned to Ainsel. "The King has killed himself. You need not worry about capturing him."

Ainsel backed away, slowly allowing the forest to swallow him up. He had felt the wolves, had felt their intent and he wanted to be as far as he could be by the time the battle started.

Mona raised her hands and looked up into the sky.

"Water, earth, wind, and fire,

Hear me now, fulfill my desire."

She called on the rain, thunder, and lightning, and the skies opened. Thunder shook the ground and lightning lit up the dark sky, shooting down into the forest.

Her hands moved wildly as she manipulated the wind, pulling and pushing the currents. The gusts were strong enough to uproot trees and send them crashing into the ground.

She watched as all nature bent to her will. It would not be enough. She called on the birds that did her bidding. The blood of the many beasts that she would summon was painted on her clothes, as the presence of blood was often required to control the minds of such creatures. She sent out her will, demanding the trolls leave their hiding places. She called upon the pixies, and though she knew Ainsel would not come, there were those among his kind with black hearts that would gladly answer her call.

Suddenly there was a blinding flash. When Mona's vision cleared, a woman stood before her.

"You are the Fae who has betrayed her people," Mona smiled.

"Peri and the healers will be moving in behind the warriors," Lorrelle told her.

"Warriors?" Mona frowned. "What warriors?"

"Didn't I mention those?" Lorrelle looked smug. "The warlocks and the elves have come to join the party."

"Is this all the help you are providing?"

Lorrelle pulled three stones from her pocket. "I have weakened my sister significantly. She doesn't have all the stones of the Fae. If that is not enough to give you a slight advantage then you are not as powerful as you claim."

Before Mona could answer, the Fae was gone.

"Coward," Mona growled.

Mona felt the power of the pack surrounding her as they moved closer. She closed her eyes and held her hands out. She spoke quietly, calling on her power. She smiled when she felt the heat of the fire that blazed. It wasn't real, but the wolves would hesitate and sometimes that was all she needed to have the upper hand.

Vasile watched as the packs broke off and moved stealthily through the trees. They fanned out and around, creating a large circle. Almost as if choreographed, every other wolf turned to face outward, taking up guard for the outward attack that was already headed in their direction. They could feel the rumbling ground beneath their paws.

Peri and the other Fae had managed to minimize the effect of Mona's influence over the storm. They had slowed the wind when wolves had started being drug back as if the wind had hands and had latched onto their legs. The rain had been blurring their vision, Peri's voice had risen above it, and as she'd slowed the downpour. Vasile had anticipated the attack of Mona's minions and so he and the other Alphas had decided that every fifth wolf would continue to move towards Mona along with three of the Fae and ten elves. The rest would stay back and hold the perimeter. If the demons were released, then none of them would likely survive. Their only hope was that they could take out Mona before Cypher completed his task. If they did not, he would have to open it or suffer the consequences of the blood oath.

Costin moved forward, pulling away from the wolves that would stay back and defend the border of their pack. He made eye contact with each wolf that he could see, who moved forward with him. As he drew closer, he could feel the witch's power pushing on him, urging him to turn and run. They picked up their pace as they fought the spell and came up short when the felt the heat of the fire and then saw the wall of flames that separated them from their prey. He paced restlessly, looking for a way through. The wolves around him let out low growls and barks, frustrated at being thwarted.

"It's an illusion!" Costin turned to see Alston, the head of the Fae council running towards them. Dain and Gwen were right behind him. Dain ran right and Gwen went left to join in the circle of wolves that stood before the fire. The Fae stepped closer to the fire until their hands were touching it. Their lips moved, but Costin was unable to hear their words. The flames started to dissipate and just when it appeared that they would disappear altogether, the flames jumped back even higher. Then, as if a snake was moving the fire, it began to weave through the forest, wrapping around each wolf. The wolves howled and danced from paw to paw as the flames closed in on them.

"IT'S NOT REAL!" The collective voice of the Fae reached through the crackling of the flames. Costin's wolf did not want to believe them because the flames looked too real. But, then he remembered when they had been running in the forest with their mates on their backs. Mona had tried to use the flames then as well. His mind made up, he lunged through the fire and emerged on the other side. Alston nodded to him and began moving forward again. Costin sent out a call and push of power to draw the wolves through and they soared from the fire, landing whole and angry on the inside of the flames. Rage boiled in their blood and surged them onward.

Fane watched as the trolls came rushing through the forest, some large enough that they knocked down small trees, as if they were toothpicks. His lips pulled back in a snarl as he decided the most effective way to take them down.

"Clip their heels, they won't be able to stand," he told Jacque.

"Got it," she answered as she lowered herself into a crouch, ready to leap as soon as they were close enough.

Fane saw his father lunge forward and took that as his signal. He rushed forward, diving under the first troll he reached, and whipping around to tear at the troll's heel, ripping out the tendon. The troll went down on one leg. Jacque, who had circled around behind the troll, now dove forward to rip out the tendon of the other heel. The troll hit the ground with a mighty boom. Fane ran swiftly and flew at his throat, ripping it open at the artery. Blood spurted, splashing onto Fane's dark fur. His wolf howled at the first kill and the others answered. He turned to see Jacque battling with a smaller troll that had already put a gash across her flank. Jacque tried to jump aside, but the troll's huge fist still caught her. She was flung backwards and smacked against a tree. Fane soared through the air, landing on the back of the troll. He dug his claws into the troll's thick skin shredding at the flesh. Jacque jumped back to her feet and maneuvered around to the side of the troll who was focused on getting Fane of his back. She made for the heels just as Fane had told her and in two swift moves, she had torn the tendons. Fane jumped from the trolls back as it slammed to the ground. Jacque moved to take out the neck, but Fane pushed her aside and did it himself. He nudged her towards another group of wolves that were battling several trolls at one time and they joined in the fight.

Peri looked around the battle field as more trolls came. Wondering why the trolls weren't filled with arrows, she looked around at the elves. Each elf was focus skyward, firing shaft after shaft into the air. Scattered among the clouds and rain were large swooping birds of prey. The elves were taking them down as fast as they could. The warlocks joined the wolves against the trolls. Everywhere men, monsters, and beasts hacked and slashed furiously at each other. Despite their teamwork, both wolves and warlocks were injured in the fighting.

"Rachel, you and Sally are going to have to go tend to the injured." Peri yelled, handing Rachel some clothes that she had carried in anticipation of Rachel's run to the battlefield in her wolf form. "There! She pointed to a wolf lying on its side. I've got your back." She turned to a wide eyed Sally. "You head that direction; Jen will protect you. Remember; only heal what is necessary for them to get back on their feet. Reserve your strength. Don't waste any time on those that aren't savable"

Shaking, Sally took off, searching the ground for injured wolves. She wasn't sure what she could do for any fallen warlocks, but she had decided that she would attempt to heal them as well if she could. Jen stayed alongside, her making sure no trolls got too close. Sally found the first one lying on his side, a nasty gash too deep to heal quickly on its own. She stepped forward and tried to radiate peace so that she would not startle the wolf.

"I'm going to touch you. If you lie still, this will go rather quickly," she told the wolf.

He looked at her with glowing eyes, and then laid his head down. She took that as the okay to begin. She laid her hands on him and closed her eyes. She sent her spirit into his body, seeking out the wound and healing it from the inside out. When she pulled her hands back, the wound was completely healed. She stood up slightly wobbly and Jen pressed her large body against Sally to steady her. The wolf stood and crouched experimentally, then turned to her and bowed his head. She bowed hers in return, and then watched as he flung himself back into the fray.

Sally yelped when Jen suddenly pushed her forward and dove beside her. Sally slammed to her knees and winced as she felt her jeans rip. A crashing sound echoed in her ears as a large tree landed where she had just been standing. She turned and looked at her friend. "You rock," she gasped.

Jen gave a small yip and a wolf smile, to which Sally shook her head at. "Not cool Jen."

Looking out over the forest, they began moving toward more injured wolves.

Decebel was moving swiftly, bounding over bushes and around trees as he chased the pixies that the others hadn't realized had joined in the mix. His wolf was relishing the hunt, enjoying the sport of chasing something so quick and cunning. He almost hated to end the chase by killing them. He rounded a large tree, just on the heels of a particularly fast pixie and slid to a stop when he saw his mate running through the middle of the battlefield following a very worn out looking Sally.

"What the hell are you doing?" He snarled at her.

"B, this isn't the time to be an asshat over me being here. I'm protecting Sally while she heals injured wolves."

"You're in no shape to fight."

"Sure I am. I'm in my wolf shape. I'm a fighting machine." She tried to joke, to lighten the moment.

"You are pregnant." Decebel's anger and fear was climbing as he ran towards her, dodging around trolls and fallen trees.

"Am I? Damn, I almost forgot. It won't matter what I am if you die, so at least let me help."

"Well, it's obvious I can't stop you so I guess I have no choice." The hurt in his voice made Jen feel like crap. She knew she had made him feel helpless to protect her and she hadn't meant to.

"I'll be okay babe," she tried to reassure him.

He kept coming towards her and when he reached her, he nipped her muzzle and growled. She lowered her head, but he nuzzled her before she could drop to the ground in submission.

"Stay beside me," he told her. She took a stance next to him in front of Sally and together they followed Sally from one wounded warrior to the next. Everything seemed to be going rather smoothly, Decebel having taken out several smaller trolls by himself and he and Jen together taking out a large one. Jen should have known things were going way too well.

Their heads whipped around as they heard Sally scream.

"COSTIN!" She was off in a dead sprint before they could take a step.

"GO!" Decebel yelled at her. Jen obeyed, immediately running after the healer. Decebel was on her heels.

Peri saw the three take off running. "Rachel, come on!" She yelled at the healer and headed after Decebel and Jen.

Costin, Skender, Sorin, Gavril, and Drake were the only wolves from his pack that he recognized as they closed in on Mona. They could finally see her. She stood behind Cypher, the Warlock King who was on his knees in a pool of his own blood. Costin could see that a river of it had formed and was flowing to a black seam that was ripping into the air of the human realm. Costin could see writhing forms through the opening, grotesque arms and legs, red eyes and sharp teeth. He shook off the feeling of oily hands rubbing over his body and growled when Mona turned and faced them.

"Welcome! So glad you could make it. Please, come have front row seats. That will make your death quicker at least." Mona smiled as if she were inviting old friends into her home. The wolves continued forward while the elves stayed just beyond her vision, bows at the ready. Their weapons were the only ones capable of killing demons, so they would be ready when the veil finally opened.

Costin's ears lowered and his lips pulled back from his wicked sharp teeth. He crouched low as he moved forward. Gavril, Sorin, and the other wolves moved along with him. Mona attempted to keep them all in her line of sight, but she had been cocky, or so the wolves crouching behind her thought.

Gavril lunged first, but his teeth only reached the bottom of her cloak before her hand flew out and sent him crashing into a tree. Costin had begun his lunge before Gavril had reached Mona and managed to sink his teeth into her leg. Each wolf lunged immediately after the other one, not giving her a chance to regroup. She pressed her hand against Costin's side and he felt a pulse of electricity enter his body. He yelped and fell flat, unable to retain his hold. He felt his heart stutter from the shock and he had to focus to keep from blacking out. He didn't realize that he had pulled on the healing power of his mate to steady his shocked heart, until he heard her scream.

He shook his head and regained his bearings. He looked up and saw that the wolves were continuing their assault, one after another lunging, some making their mark, others being thrown back before they could reach her. Costin swung around when he felt a surge of power come barreling past him.

Decebel's huge form ran straight for the witch. Her attention was focused elsewhere and so she didn't realize that she had a new enemy until Decebel's huge head was in her stomach, knocking her to the ground. He tried for her throat, but she blasted him off with a blast of wild force. Decebel landed on his back several feet away. He jumped to his feet, settling into a crouch, snarling, and circling her.

Sally came bursting through the trees with Jen, Peri, and Rachel just behind her. She ran straight to Costin and ran her hands over him.

"I'm fine brown eyes," he reassured her.

"I felt your heart stop." Her hands trembled as they ran through his fur.

"You saved me. Now, get back so that the witch doesn't decide to notice you."

Sally started to step back but her eyes landed on Cypher. She turned to Rachel, whose eyes were on the King as well. Sally knew that Rachel felt the same pull she did to go to him, to help him. It's what they were, they healed, and something in them could not stand to see someone in pain. They both started to slowly move towards him, trying not to draw Mona's attention. Gavril and Costin inched in front of the two healers trying to block any attack.

Peri's hand shot up just as Mona turned and threw a spell at her. She blocked it and redirected it back at the witch. Peri reached into her pocket and pulled out two stones. She looked down in shock. She'd had all of them, how did she now only have two?

Mona's laugh broke through her confusion and she looked up. "Your, sister, my dear, really hates you," Mona sneered. "What did you do to her Perizada?"

Peri's mouth dropped open and her head turned as Elle and Adam came rushing into the gathering circle. "Lorrelle?" Peri's eyes filled with betrayal. Elle's hand came up to cover her mouth and Adam looked just as confused and angry as Peri.

"Yes, Lorrelle. She has been somewhat helpful to me in my endeavors, if not extremely annoying with all the boo-hooing about how you thought you were so much better than her. The truth is that you are better than her, Peri. You are much more powerful and she couldn't stand it. So, if you are wondering where your precious stones are, you have your sister to thank."

Peri's face morphed into anger as her form grew and her light surrounded her. Elle and Adam's forms changed as well as they stepped forward and drew upon their own power. Alston came roaring through in his own Fae glory, throwing magic wildly at Mona.

The other Fae joined in and Mona laughed as she danced out of the way and blocked shot after shot. The wolves began to regroup and circle the witch, trying to get a get chance to move in without getting hit by one of the flying magical bolts.

Skender nudged Sorin, motioning with his muzzle toward the bulging opening. The veil was nearly open. Sorin raised his head and howled, calling out to Vasile. Mona whipped around and saw that Cypher was falling to the ground and as his body crumbled, the veil burst open. The air filled with a scream that had the wolves' eyes watering, as their ears nearly burst from the pain. A dark form flew from the veil. Before they could even get a good look at the figure, it exploded, a shiny arrow whistling through its midsection.

Mona roared as she watched the first demon be destroyed. Her head whipped around to where the arrow had originated. She started moving in that direction, but was brought up short when the Fae formed a wall between her and the elves on that side of the circle. Another dark form burst forth and another, and then another.

The demons were enormous. They began screaming, as wings sprouted from their backs. Misshapen heads attached to insect like bodies stared down with beady eyes at the fighting forms below them. Their mouths opened, revealing rows of razor sharp teeth and, as they started to scream again, arrows flew through the air. The scene erupted in a shower of green ichor, as not a demon remained standing. Mona's face grew red with unrestrained fury as she shot spell after spell, trying to reach the elves through the wall of Fae. The elves continued to shoot down demons, as quickly as they burst forth from the opening.

Sally and Rachel had fallen at Cypher's side and immediately laid their hands on him. With the exception of one enormous gash, Rachel began healing the wounds on his arms while Sally used the light in her to call to his blood. She was literally pulling it back away from the veil, reversing the flow and pushing it back into his body, forcing it through the one cut that Rachel had left open. She didn't know if it would work, but as she called the blood back, she willed his heart to pump.

"Do not give up Cypher, your time isn't over," Sally whispered to his spirit, calling him back from the brink of death. *"Your people need you, and your mate needs you. Do not leave at such a time as this."* She continued

to call his blood and she felt Rachel add to her power, now that the wounds on his arms were healed, save one. Sally could feel herself growing weak and she felt Costin at her side helping to hold her up. She felt the pull of the evil reaching for the blood, needing all of it to keep the veil open, but Sally refused to give up.

"YOU CAN NOT HAVE HIM!" She roared. She reached her hand out toward the blood still running in a river to the veil and she pulled, imaging herself grabbing the blood like a rope and yanking it back as hard as she could. She pulled with everything she had in her and pushed it into Cypher's body. She watched as the blood moved towards her, faster and faster it flowed back into the King's body. As soon as the last drop was gone the veil snapped closed, but not before, like a cannon, ten demons shot out.

She collapsed onto Costin as she watched the evil soar above her like a swarm of massive hornets. The demons' wings beat and their screams made her nauseated. She tried to keep her hand on Cypher to make sure his heart kept beating, but her energy was gone and the evil bearing down on her from the demons was too much. Darkness enveloped her.

Thalion notched another arrow as he yelled. "Faster, they're about to be on the move." Just as he said it, three demons shot off like bullets. Thalion bolted after them. Two of his fastest warriors matched his speed as they chased down the demons. The elves knew that the demons would wreak havoc on the world should they escape. They drew closer and Thalion pushed his legs faster, feeling his muscles resist at the speed. But he would not give up; he would not let Cyn, nor his people, down.

"Ready your bow," he yelled as they closed in on them. "Steady," he cautioned them. The demons began to fan out, searching for those they might devour. "Release!" The arrows appeared to move in slow motion as they flew towards their targets. The elves didn't hesitate. Each whipped another arrow onto the string, readying for another shot. It wasn't necessary. Thalion's breaths stopped as he watched all three of the original arrows find their home. Blood and guts, which both looked and smelled about like raw sewage, rained down upon the forest.

"YEAH!" All three elves shot their hands up in victory.

"That was a close one," Revion muttered, as he leaned over, trying to catch his breath and wiping a bit of ichor from his clothes.

"Too true," Thalion agreed. "Come, we must get back." He told them as he turned and once again took off in a sprint.

Mona ground her teeth, drawing in her power, ready to make her escape. Once again, she realized that she had been defeated.

"OH, NO YOU DON'T," Peri yelled and she pushed even harder, attempting to wrap her power around the witch to hold her in place.

Just then, Vasile burst through the trees, his power nearly knocking everyone to the ground. He never paused as he took one step and leapt across the thirty or so feet to where Mona fought the Fae. He landed on her chest as his massive jaws wrapped around her throat. He sunk his teeth until he felt them hit her spine. He pulled with all his might, swinging his head violently until he ripped her head from her body.

The raging storm immediately stopped and the silence froze everyone in place. Vasile's body heaved as he victoriously held the witch's head in his mouth. He dropped it on the ground and howled a long, deep bellow into the still, dark sky.

No sooner had the howl ceased than they all heard a loud slow clapping. Their heads turned towards a very tall, very large, unfamiliar man, who came striding through a billow of black smoke rolling out of the forest. His eyes were a brilliant yellow and his face was pale. His jaw was sharp and his lips thin and tight across his face. He strode casually into the opening where they had battled Mona.

"Well done," he drew out in a deep voice, as he continued to clap. Vasile's eyes narrowed on the new comer and his lips curled back. The wolves around him gathered and followed the Alpha's lead.

"You have done what no one else could have, and honestly, I have to say thank you." The man bowed his head slightly at Vasile, but they weren't fooled by the false sincerity. "With that witch out of the way, my plans can proceed. However, since you have defeated such a powerful foe, you might think yourself capable of stopping me as well. Therefore, I feel it necessary to demonstrate that I shall not be so easily thwarted. So, you should think twice before getting in my way." His words had barely registered when his hand flew outwards and a black bolt shot forth and slammed into Vasile's chest. He was thrown back into a heap and Alina, who had already, began to run for her mate, dropped in mid-stride. One by one the members of Vasile's pack felt the pain of their Alpha's death, even those who were no longer in his pack sensed the loss and agony.

Peri screamed and turned, firing her own power at the man, but he was already cloaked in the black smoke and then gone.

"Alston, get the healers," Peri yelled as she ran to Vasile's still form. She ignored the howls of the wolves and focused on the fallen Alpha.

Alston ran over to Rachel and Sally who lay exhausted on the ground, their mates hovering over them. "MOVE!" He yelled at the two snarling males. "If you want your Alpha to live then move."

Costin and Gavril phased back into human form, heedless of their nudity. Each male picked up their fatigued mates. They carried them over to where Peri crouched over Vasile. Peri handed Alston a stone and he took it and pressed it to Sally's head. Peri did the same to Rachel.

"DECEBEL," Peri yelled. "Get over here and give your healer strength."

Decebel ran over, still in his wolf form. He laid his head on Sally's lap and drew on his power as an Alpha. One by one the Alpha's all walked over and laid a hand on the healers, using the power bestowed on them by the Great Luna. They gave freely in hopes of pushing life back into the Alpha who had united them as one and defeated an evil that none of them, on their own, could have beaten.

Jacque, Jen, Crina, Elle, and Cynthia formed a circle around Alina protecting the Alpha female, waiting, and hoping to see her chest move.

Sally felt the darkness receding, she tried to open her eyes, but stopped as soon as she felt the faint trail of a spirit she knew very well, a spirit she had brought back once before at a time when Vasile's life had been hanging in the balance due to a deadly poison.

"Vasile?" She called out. *"Have you fallen? Vasile answer me!"*

There was no answer, nothing.

She felt power pouring into her and her gypsy blood knew instinctively what to do. She sought out the source of the injury, what had brought down so great an Alpha. It wasn't a spell it was damage. Vasile's heart looked charred, almost like it had been cooked. Her heart fell, she didn't know if she could heal this. She felt Rachel and could tell that the healer was moving Vasile's blood through his body and willing his lungs to take in air. She was keeping him alive. Sally felt it was hopeless. Regardless, she pushed forward, determined to save the Alpha whom she had come to love as a father, who had given her a family and a home.

She touched his heart with her healing light, and as she felt tears on her face, she called out. *"Please, you said if we called on you, you would answer, you would help. Don't take him from us just yet. He is still needed. Surely you are aware of this."* Sally continued to try and heal the damage done to his heart, but knew that she could not do it alone.

"Sally, chosen of your blood line," she heard the Great Luna's melodic voice in her mind, *"mate of Costin, and healer to the Serbian pack. I have heard you, you who are pure of heart, and give of yourself so freely without regard to your own safety. I will grant you this. Do not give up Sally the battle is not over. You have been tested and found faithful; my children have proven that goodness can prevail. So take heart now, your Alpha, my beloved, will live, and you may rest for a short time. But, where one foe falls, another arises. You must continue to stand firm, you must continue to be what I have called you to be, to follow the path set before you and if you stumble I will be here to help you regain your footing."*

Sally felt renewed strength flow out of her and watched in awe, as a heart that was beyond repair, was healed, strong, and healthy once again. It pounded in the Alpha's chest and pushed blood through his veins. His lungs drew in fresh air and filled the blood with oxygen. With every beat, life returned to Vasile.

"He's breathing," Sally heard Peri say. She kept her eyes closed and felt strong arms pick her up.

She was so tired. She just wanted to sleep, for a very long time.

"Not too long Sally mine, you have a wedding to attend." She heard the precious sound of her mate's voice in her mind and took comfort in knowing he had her.

"Always," he whispered, against her ear.

Chapter 23

"Every little girl dreams of her wedding day. She picks out her wedding dress and the flowers. She imagines the music playing as she walks down the aisle to a faceless groom she has yet to meet. She pours her hopes and dreams into a day that may or may not come. My day has come. It is nothing like I dreamed. There is no music or flowers. There is no elaborate dress adorned in rows of beads. There is only me and my groom, who has an amazing face. No, it's nothing like I dreamed; it's better."
~ Sally Miklos, Mate of Costin Miklos

"What gifts have you brought to give your mate," Vasile asked Costin as he and Sally stood before him. The only other people in the room were Decebel, Jen, Jacque, Fane, Peri, and Alina.

It had been two weeks since Mona had been killed and the strange man had attempted to murder Vasile. Though Rachel and Sally had healed many of the wolves, there had still been casualties. The Alphas of the fallen wanted to bury their dead in their homelands. Vasile had declared a night of mourning and they all had shown their respects to the Alphas and the wolves that had given their lives.

Dillon had stayed for two days after his pack had traveled back to the states. He spent this time with Jacque. He had even gone to Lilly and Cypher, wishing them a happy life together. Cypher had frowned the entire time while Jacque and her mom had tried to keep from laughing.

Lilly was with Cypher, who had a very long recovery ahead of him. Vasile had granted him protection if he wished to stay and recuperate in the mansion.

So, now they stood in the small indoor garden in the mansion, bathed in moonlight. Sally wore a simple white dress with lace sleeves that showed her skin beneath. The back was low, but her hair covered it completely, much to Costin's relief. Costin was in his customary jeans, but he was wearing a white dress shirt at least, though it was un-tucked. Neither of them wore shoes, because of the customary washing of feet during the ceremony. Much to Sally's embarrassment, Costin had washed not only her feet, but her calves all the way to the tops of her knees and probably only stopped there because she had swatted him with the towel. He had kissed down her legs to her feet and Sally was giggling like a school girl by, the time he was done.

Decebel had rolled his eyes and said loud enough for everyone to hear "We'll be lucky if they make it to their bedroom." This only caused Sally to blush even more.

"The three gifts I have brought for my beloved," Costin smiled as he held out a box wrapped in shimmering silver paper. Sally took it and unwrapped it slowly. Costin took a step closer to her and watched as she opened the box. Inside were three items. The first was an ancient looking book bearing no title.

"Peri and I did some digging into the history of the gypsies and, with Wadim's help, we found your lineage. That book," he motioned to it, "is the story of your ancestors." Sally's mouth dropped open as she stared at the book. So many questions of how she came to be a gypsy healer, and the answers might lie right before her, because of him. "Thank you," she told him, but knew that she could never express her gratitude in a way that was worthy.

"Oh, yes you can brown eyes," He winked at her. Sally laughed as she looked back in the box.

There were two other items. The second was another book. This one was leather bound and when she flipped it, open she saw that the pages were blank. She looked up at him. "It's blank."

"It will be our story, our history. You and I together, will fill the pages with the legacy that we bring to our people. One day our children will read it and see what amazing things we experienced, trials we overcame, and most importantly, the love their parents had for one another, a love that nothing and no one can come between."

Tears streamed down Sally's face as she held the book to her chest. It was the most touching, thoughtful gift anyone had ever given her.

"And, the third gift," Costin said as he reached into the box and pulled out a much smaller box. He opened it and held it out for Sally. She gasped and nearly dropped the journal. In the box lay a locket. A locket that she knew had been in her family for generations. She'd seen her mom wearing it before. Now, that she stared at it, the piece of jewelry took on a whole new meaning. Strange symbols adorned the outside of the locket, symbols that she had often wondered about in the past. Sally, now understood, that the markings were gypsy runes. She pulled it out and opened it and there inside was a picture of Costin and Sally. She looked up at him. "How did you get this?"

Costin grinned and that wicked dimple flashed. "Your mother likes me."

Sally's eyes widened. "You told my mom we were getting married?"

Costin's smile widened, "Sure. I just didn't say when."

Sally made a sound that was half groan, half sigh of relief. Costin took the locket and walked around her. She started to move her hair, but the growl from Costin made her freeze. He positioned her so that her back wasn't visible to any one and then moved her hair over her shoulder. He wrapped the locket around her neck and clasped the ends. Before he pulled her hair back over her shoulder he ran his finger lightly down her spine and chuckled when she shivered.

Vasile cleared his throat and brought their attention back to him.

"Costin has informed me that he wishes to say his vows in private," he said to the audience.

Costin nodded.

"Okay, then I will simply ask, do you take Sally to be your wife."

Costin smiled. "Definitely."

"Sally, do you take Costin to be your husband?"

Sally shook her head, and then laughed at Costin's frown.

"Yes," she finally said, "yes, definitely."

"I pronounce you man and wife; you may kiss your bride." Vasile smiled at the couple.

Costin cupped Sally's face and pulled her to him. She stood on her tippy toes as he kissed her deeply. She wrapped her arms around him and sighed into his strong hold.

A throat clearing had them pulling a part. Costin grinned at her. "Wanted to make sure it sticks."

Sally shook her head. "The kiss isn't what makes us married."

Costin's eyebrows rose. "Oh, what does make us married?"

Decebel groaned. "Get a room already!"

Costin swept Sally up in his arms and she squealed. He strode quickly past the others while Jen yelled at his back. "Details Sally, I want details! Take notes if you have to!"

"Are you needing pointers?" Jacque asked her.

"Psht, girl, please. You think I got like this," Jen pointed to the small hump in her belly, "if I needed pointers?"

Jacque raised a brow at her friend, as she stared at her stomach. "Too true, you have got the whole mating thing down to an art."

"Oh and what a beautiful art form it is," Jen grinned at her mate.

Decebel growled, he grabbed her hand, and waved to Fane and Jacque. "My female and I have art to make." He tugged a giggling Jen after him.

Jacque looked over at Fane who had an amused look on his face. She smiled up at him and he wrapped an arm around her waist and pulled her close.

"I suppose you want to talk," he told her.

"I always knew you were a bright one," Jacque took his hand and pulled him forward. "Night, Vasile and Alina," she hollered over her shoulder.

"Do we at least get to make art first?" Fane asked. He turned those glowing eyes on her and it made it very difficult to hold her ground.

But she did. "Nope. You've been holding out on me."

Fane groaned. "That means what I think it does, doesn't it?"

"Like I said, I always knew you were a bright one."

~

Costin led Sally from the bathroom, into the bedroom, and then over to their bed. He couldn't take his eyes off her. She wore a black nightgown that barely came to the top of her thighs. It was cut low in the front and nearly non-existent in the back, which allowed him to see the marks on her soft skin that matched his own. He turned her to look at him and smiled when she blushed. She reached up and started unbuttoning his shirt with shaking fingers.

"Shh," he murmured, as he slowed her hands down. "We have all night love and, personally, I plan to make the most of every minute."

"You're not helping calm me, if that was your plan," she teased.

He leaned down and pressed a kiss to her forehead, breathing in her scent at the same time. Costin groaned as the desire of his mate hit his nose. His head fell back as he fought his own desire to keep from rushing her or worse, scaring her. He opened his eyes and pulled his head back down to look at her. She stared up at him with such love that it nearly drove him to his knees.

"Are you nervous?" Sally asked him.

Costin smiled at his mate, his wife. He took in her long, brown locks, her large expressive eyes, and her beautiful smile. She was amazing, and she was his.

"Of course, I think that's normal," he admitted.

"Why?" She asked.

"What do you mean?"

"I mean, why are *you* nervous? I mean look at you, Costin. You have the physique of a freaking Calvin Klein model, you're more handsome than any man I have ever seen and you have a dimple that could give most girls ammunition for years of fantasies."

Costin laughed and shook his head at her. "I'm nervous, because I have the most amazing woman as my mate and she deserves the best, the best of everything, even the best first experience making love. Can't you see how that would make me nervous? If you wake up tomorrow and you regret tonight it will be because I didn't give you what you need, and that is one of the scariest things for any man to face. The idea that he can't be what his female wants and needs."

Sally started to speak, but Costin stopped her with a finger to her lips. "This is important, I need you to hear." She nodded and he took his finger away, but rested his hand on her neck. "There are so many things that are important in a mating, a marriage; communication, respect, love, and even the physical aspect of it. I need to know that I am doing everything I can in each of those areas to make you feel loved, cherished, and adored. You need to know that you are the only woman I want. You're the only woman I desire, the only woman who makes me feel like the man I want to be. I'm nervous, because tonight is the first time of many that we will share in something so important and precious. I need you to feel all of these things by the way I love you tonight."

Sally blushed. She didn't know what to say to him. Her mind was reeling at all the things he had said and she just wanted to throw herself in his arms and scream do it already. She nearly laughed out loud at herself. She wondered what he would say if she did just that. She looked into his eyes and could see the earnest need for approval there. He truly wanted to please her, wanted her to know just how precious she was to him.

"If you aren't ready, Sally, we can wait. I won't rush you." Sally knew that he meant every word. He would wait for her forever if she asked.

"Costin," Sally huffed, "we did the Blood Rites. I wear your markings and your bite and now I'm your wife, what else am I waiting for?"

Costin grinned. "Those things are all true, but you are still young, and I am still the first guy you have ever been intimate with. I will completely understand if you want to move slowly."

Sally tapped her lips with her finger and Costin could see the mischief dancing in her eyes. "Slow is good I'm sure, but according to Jen sometimes a little rough is just as necessary."

Costin coughed, trying to swallow. Sally's face turned bright red and she laughed. She couldn't believe she had just said that. Well, that wasn't entirely true, it didn't totally surprise her. She had lived through a hellish evil spell, helped kill a witch, and fought an evil hoard of demons, saved a Warlock King, and brought a powerful Alpha back to life, so joking about sex with her mate and husband really was a piece of cake at this point.

"Sally mine," Costin's voice dropped low and caressed her skin. She shivered as she felt his fingers begin to skim across her calf and up to her thigh. He tapped her hip playfully as he grinned wickedly, "rough you say?" She squealed as he flipped her on her back. One second his hand was on her hip, teasing, and the next he was over her. Sally's breathing increased, as she stared up into glowing, hazel eyes. Costin's unique scent wrapped around her drawing, her closer to him. She growled at him and nipped his shoulder. He chuckled at the surprise and longing he saw on her face.

He kissed her deeply pulling her tight against him and when she shuddered, he tugged her bottom lip with his teeth. "Rough it is," he whispered, hoarsely against her lips.

Epilogue

"Every man makes mistakes. Every man faces times in their life when they would give anything for a do-over. Unfortunately, life doesn't work that way. Once the mistake is made, the only thing left to do is deal with the consequences. That is when the measure of a man is made, when his character is revealed." ~ Cypher

Vasile sat in his office facing a group of solemn faces. He had called this meeting of his closest men and of Decebel and his top four to discuss the new enemy that had risen, just as Mona had fallen.

"Has anyone ever heard of this man cloaked in smoke with yellow eyes?" Decebel looked over at Wadim.

"I know you might think that I know it all, because I'm the historian, but I got nothing on this one." He threw his hands up in the air and let them fall to his thighs.

Vasile let out an exasperated breath. He had been wracking his brain, trying to remember where he had seen those yellow eyes. It had been a very long time, but he was sure that he had met the man at one point in his long life.

"Whoever he is, he is deadly," Costin said, from where he leaned against the wall, his bartending towel tossed casually over his shoulder. He had been at the bar working when Vasile had called and hadn't bothered to set it down.

"He is deadlier and more dangerous than you can possibly know." A deep voice rumbled from behind them. They all turned to see Cypher standing in the door. He still looked weak. He was, however, finally walking on his own strength.

"Please, come in Cypher," Vasile motioned for him to take a seat among them.

"You know him?" Sorin spoke up.

Cypher nodded. "He is Reyaz, my brother."

~

Decebel lay next to his mate, watching her sleep. Her face was relaxed and peaceful, no lines of worry, no pain danced in her eyes. He gently rubbed her stomach where their baby was nestled safe and growing. Every day was one day closer to her birth, one day closer to the promise the Fates had made to take her from them. In all the chaos of the past weeks, they had not had much time to think about the impending birth. In the few quiet moments they'd had, they spent them talking of a future that might never come, but they refused to acknowledge that possibility.

Decebel had a made a decision that he knew Jennifer would not like, but he did not know what other options he had. He kissed her gently on the forehead and then quietly rose from their bed.

Once in the quiet garden he closed his eyes and knelt to the ground.

"I request an audience with you Great Luna. It is of great importance and I beg of your help."

"*You need not beg child,*" her voice spread warmth into the cool room and Decebel felt a hand urge him to stand. "*I have told you that all you need do is ask and I will answer.*"

Decebel met her eyes and he clenched his jaw, determined to get the words out without breaking down. "My mate is with child and the Fates have determined that her life is the debt that will be paid for Jennifer's life being spared."

He watched as she took his words in. She had known what the Fates had decreed and she had chosen to wait to see how Decebel and Jennifer would respond.

"*What is it you ask of me?*"

"I want to take her place. She is an innocent, her life is not supposed to end. I have lived a very long time. I have been blessed to have found my true mate and it is only right that I should die before my child."

The Great Luna's eyes softened, "*And, what would your mate say about this?*"

"Jennifer will survive losing me if you will break the bond between us. I do not believe she could survive losing our child." Decebel told her, honestly.

"*Don't you think it should be her choice?*"

"I cannot ask her to choose between me and our child; that isn't fair. I have always told her I would protect her from anything, even herself."

"*This is truly what you want?*" She stepped towards him and placed a hand over his heart.

"Yes, if it is the only way to save her life, it is what I want."

The Great Luna nodded. "*So be it.*"

And, then she was gone.

Decebel fell to his knees as he felt his heart tear in two. His body shook with his grief and his wolf cried out for their mate. He kept the bond closed, not wanting to wake her. And, in the quiet of the garden he reached for the darkness that had tormented him for so long, for it was only in the darkness that he would be able to hide his shattered soul. He cried out for his love, for the woman who had saved him and brought meaning to his life once again. He prayed that she would be able to forgive him and that one day they might be united once again. He vowed that until the moment that the Fates sucked the life from his body, he would treasure every second he had with her.

He stood and shook off as much of the pain as he could. And, with final resolve, he turned and went back to his love, enveloped her in his arms and whispered three words in her ear.

"Please forgive me."

~

Sally lay contentedly in Costin's arms hours later. She could hear his heart beating where her head was pressed against his chest and she found comfort in the steady rhythm. After so many dangers they had faced, so many ugly things that had been thrown at them, now she lay in the arms of her mate and it was beautiful.

"You are beautiful," he whispered.

"Are you listening to my thoughts?" She asked with a grin.

"Always," Costin squeezed are affectionately. "Are you alright?" His words were soft and she heard the apprehension in his voice.

She pushed herself up on her arm so she could look him in the eyes.

"I'm better than alright, Costin."

"I love you," he told her as he reached up his hand and caressed her face.

"Thank you." Sally's head tilted to the side as she looked down at him, her eyes narrowed thoughtfully. "Hey, we never said our vows."

Costin grinned mischievously, he kissed her neck and then looked back up at her.

"Do you remember me whispering in your ear tonight or the words I sent you through our bond?" He asked her.

Sally nodded.

"You are the air I breathe, the food I eat, the water that quenches my thirst, Sally mine. You are what I have waited for, what I have so desperately needed and what I could never deserve. Every whispered promise, every confession, every longing, hope and dream I have shared with you this night, those are my vows to you my love. All you need know is that I am yours, unequivocally and you are mine."

Sally stared into the eyes of the man she loved, the man who was more than a man and more than anything she ever imagined she could have. She saw every thought that coincided with his words, felt every emotion as intensely as he did and she found joy in the love that he held for her. She was his, no matter what new evil they would face, no matter the trials, the triumphs or the fury that would come knocking at their door. She was his and he was hers, fate had destined them and loved had bonded them.

More books by Quinn Loftis

The Grey Wolves Series:
Prince of Wolves
Blood Rites
Just One Drop
Out of the Dark
Beyond the Veil

Elfin Series:
Elfin
Rapture

Visit www.quinnloftisbooks.com to keep up to date with the latest information on characters, release dates and fun give aways.

Thank you so much for taking time to read Fate and Fury. It is my sincerest hope that you enjoyed it.

Printed in Great Britain
by Amazon